ME AND THE MACHINE

PRAISE FOR ME AND THE MACHINE

"A marvelous young hero propels this sharply written and wholly absorbing space opera."
  —*Kirkus Reviews*

"A novel that is simply too good to ignore, *Me and the Machine* is a meticulous and melancholic lesson on standing up to hypocrisy, corporatocracy, and our own insecurities."
  —*Indies Today* (★★★★★)

"Simply un-put-downable ... an exhilarating dystopian sci-fi story filled with fast-paced action, intense drama, and twists that keep readers on the edge of their seats."
  —*The Prairies Book Review*

"A thrilling work of science fiction with very human issues at its heart."
  —*Independent Book Review*

"Watts is the kind of science fiction writer you've been looking for ... Even the casual science fiction fan will fall in love with [this] intellectually stimulating, entertaining nail-biter."
  —*Reader Views* (★★★★★)

"This space opera is going to have you hooked from cover to cover. If you are looking for a gripping dystopian science fiction novel packed with action, drama, thrills, adventure, suspense, and ingenious plot twists, among much more, Wesley Watts' *Me and the Machine* is just what you should be looking for."
  —*Readers' Favorite* (★★★★★)

Me and the Machine is a work of fiction. The story, names, characters, and incidents portrayed in this production are fictitious. No identification with actual persons (living or deceased), places, or products is intended or should be inferred.

No artificial intelligence (A.I.) or predictive language software was used in any part of the creation of this book.

Cover design by Wesley Watts

The artwork is a combination of heavily modified stock images. Effort was made to ensure these original images were not created or modified using AI tools, however on the off chance they were, they have since been altered by human hands to the point of being virtually unrecognizable from their original counterparts.

Copyright © 2024 Wesley Watts

All rights reserved.

No part of this publication may be reproduced, distributed, or transmitted in any form or by any means, including photocopying, recording, or other electronic or mechanical methods, without the prior written permission of the publisher, except as permitted by U.S. copyright law.

Library of Congress Control Number: 2024905520

ISBN 979-8-9901306-0-9 (hardcover)

ISBN 979-8-9901306-1-6 (paperback)

ISBN 979-8-9901306-3-0 (ebook)

ISBN 979-8-9901306-2-3 (audiobook)

1st edition 2024

0 9 8 7 6 5 4 3 2 1

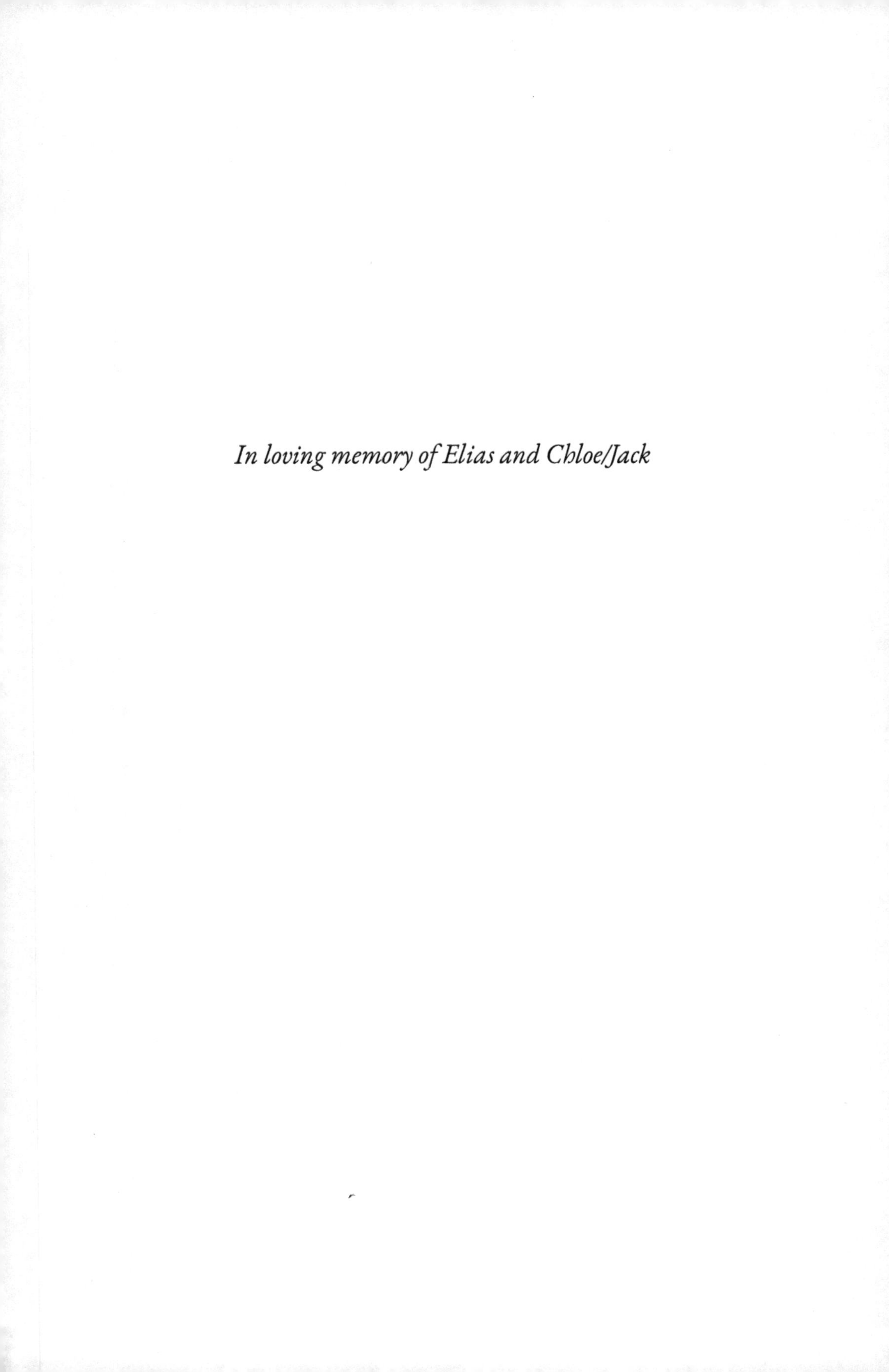

In loving memory of Elias and Chloe/Jack

ME AND THE MACHINE

by

WESLEY WATTS

CHAPTER
ONE

As I approach the apartment building's entrance, I adjust the pistol stuffed in my waistband. The uncomfortable, foreign weight has been pulling on my pants' elastic the entire walk from the bus station, and I keep imagining it tumbling to the ground in front of random strangers. I'm not in Lower Lefeld anymore—someone might actually call the cops.

A kiosk protrudes from the brick next to the door. I tap it awake and buzz Unit 4.

No answer. Am I early?

With a twitch of mental effort, the NeurX home screen materializes, superimposing its user interface over the real world. I mean to check the time, but before I can stop myself I compulsively open the message I've read some fifty times already.

Dear Gabrielle Rhodes,

We regret to inform you that your financial aid application for gene-editing therapy has been denied at this time. We at the Transhuman Centers take pride in our state-of-the-art CRISPR interventions—

Without finishing the letter, I close my NeurX and bite down on a fingernail. Why they included a sales pitch *after* the rejection boggled the mind a bit. That had been Plan A. Tonight is the much less pleasant Plan B. There is no Plan C. I have to make this work.

"Hoi," a man chirps through a small speaker.

Was that a heavily accented *hi*, or another language? "I have an appointment?" That sounded like a question. Be more assertive, Gaby.

"Ya? Name?"

"Catalina Velasquez," I lie.

"Kokay."

The door's lock slides free with a metallic *thunk* and I step through into a dim lobby with a holotable at its center. I flinch as the door crashes shut behind me, triggering me to brush the frame of the pistol as if my body needs to know it's still there.

The holotable kicks on, flooding the room in a pallid glow as it begins sliding through its pre-programmed adverts: Whala's fish tacos, Sorocini shoes, some beverage branded in a language I can't read unless I fiddle with the translator settings in my NeurX. A man's face materializes larger than life in the hologram. He stares resolutely into the distance, firm jaw set. The caption reads: *What have you done for your corporation today?*

You have no idea, Mr. Billboard Man.

Glancing down, I second guess the DJ YonDon tee and baggy, hand-me-down sweats. I'm using them as a disguise as I pretend to be someone from Eversen, who's pretending to be someone from somewhere else. The cover within a cover seemed clever yesterday. Now I'm not so sure.

Near the back of a cramped hallway, I find Unit 4, and as I put my knuckles to the door my chest begins to constrict. It's more from anxiety than exertion, but the implant grafted to the

inside of my ribcage can't tell the difference so it puffs a mist of corticosteroids and beta agonists into my lungs all the same.

The apartment door swings in. A shirtless man looms overhead. His pasty skin is pocked with dozens of small indents. Signs of serious hardware, with no effort made to hide the surgeries. Maybe he went under the knife of some discount, back-alley surgeon. Maybe it was cheaper to overlook the cosmetics. Or maybe the aesthetic is on purpose: flaunting the upgrades to posture and intimidate. If the latter is true, I have to confess, it's working.

His gaunt face studies me. "You da fixer?"

"Yeah. You the Doctor?"

"Nah. I'm Tumbo. In," he says, stepping aside.

A few nervous strides bring me to the center of a cluttered living room that stinks of dirty socks. Another man appears from down the interior hall. His hairline is racing toward the back of his head, but other than that his appearance is completely unremarkable. The kind of person you could meet repeatedly and still have trouble picking out of a crowd. It must be helpful to have a face like that doing business like this. "Who's this?" he asks.

"Ya appointment," Tumbo says as he slides a chain lock closed on the door.

"No." He breathes the word. "*You're* Catalina Velasquez?"

"All my life," I say too eagerly.

His pupils dilate. A brief burst of light shines through artificial corneas as his facial recognition software pulls my iDent off the net. I planned for this.

You see, the public registrar's database isn't protected by artificial intelligence. You have to run a biological computer alongside your mainframe if you want an AI to guard your data—well, a sentient AI that is, which is the only kind people care about these days—and that's prohibitively expensive.

A database without an AI is vulnerable, but it still has security, so you start small. On a Tuesday, you pull the employment records of the public registrar building. You filter out everyone but the clerks, and by Wednesday you've sifted through each of their public profiles, creating dictionaries of their favorite foods, their birthdays, children's names, pets, hobbies, whatever.

Some might call this stalking.

By Thursday, an automated brute force attack armed with the dictionaries you've built cracks open all of Jonas Plant's accounts. He uses the same password for everything. That's when you start digging. You learn he's lonely. You learn he has chronic undiagnosed stomach pain. You learn his dream is to go to Tora Kiesa.

Bingo.

Now all a potential hacker needs is a little social engineering and a breaching script. By the following Monday, a fake award sent from a fake Human Resources account with a fake prize is in his inbox. Congratulations, Jonas. You've won a company-paid trip to the Tora Kiesa resort. Thank you for all your hard work. All you have to do is click on the DETAILS tile embedded in this message to claim your prize.

When he clicks, he gives you a back door into the registrar mainframe, allowing you to link your facial ID to counterfeit metadata, just in time for your meeting with a black market CRISPR dealer.

The Doctor makes an affirming grunt as his eyes come back to focus on me. "Well, you certainly don't look like a fixer. Don't look like you're from Eversen either. I'd've pegged you as an offworlder."

"I tan," I say sarcastically. Most Amienites are pale. Really pale. The olive skin, black hair, and brown eyes of my mixed heritage often brings me unwanted attention. "And I'm glad I don't look like a fixer. That was kind of the idea."

The Doctor purses his lips and nods. Tumbo relaxes into a chair in the corner. Placing a hand terminal on his lap, he paws at it with one hand and snatches a burrito from a plate set on a nearby end table. Next to the plate is some type of energy weapon with a handgun's formfactor. I have to consciously resist touching the pistol.

"I guess I see the logic," the Doctor says. "Send someone nobody would expect as your fixer... Of course, that also includes the person they're supposed to do business with, doesn't it?"

Has he sniffed me out already?

The implication hangs in the air as he glides closer. "So tell me, what made Eversen decide to step outside the rules?"

"Gotta compete with Lefeld somehow."

"Yeah? And just like that"—he snaps his fingers—"Eversen's gonna give their players CRISPR?"

I nod. "I'm here, aren't I?"

"So you are. Last I spoke with Coach Dermont, he didn't want his kids anywhere near gene editing."

None of my snooping suggested Coach Dermont and the Doctor had history. What'd I just step in? "Again, that's why *I'm* here. He's a proud man. Being wrong is tough to admit, especially in person." Inwardly, I congratulate myself for thinking on my feet.

"Suppose so. All right, let's sit down and work out a treatment structure. How many players you got total?"

I don't sit. "No, sorry. That's not how the pieces fit. You saw my proposal, right?"

"Sure did. It's a waste of time. We can come up with somethin' better."

"That proposal is the only way the pieces fit for Coach Dermont."

The Doctor drops into a beat-up recliner parked opposite the couch. An enigmatic glance passes between the Doctor and Tumbo.

"So you want to waste half the season testing the CRISPR on a single athlete?"

"We got this freshman on the team. Green. Kind of a scrub in all the ways you'd expect, right? But this kid's got an arm like a railgun. Coach thinks we get some size on him, he'll be a secret weapon. No one expects Eversen to start a freshman. And if it doesn't work out," my tone goes solemn, "well, the kid's too small to make much out of him without the CRISPRs, so there's nothing to lose." If you want someone to believe a lie, when you really need to hook them with it, bury a seed of truth in it. "This way, we get to see if they're safe."

Tumbo lets out a truncated bark of a laugh.

The Doctor smirks. "I can assure you, they are not." He motions toward the stained couch. I sit this time. "Tumbo, you remember Fat Pat?"

"Ya."

"Did you know Fat Pat?" the Doctor asks me.

"No," I say. Why would I?

He shrugs one shoulder. "You're better for it. Fat Pat was a lowlife. A courier we used from time to time. In truth, I never trusted him. Not because I thought he was going to rat me out or double-cross me. Nothin' like that. He was just..." The Doctor turns to Tumbo and laughs. "Well, let's just say it. Fat Pat was dumb. I knew sooner or later he'd make a mistake that dragged everyone down with him."

"I'm not following," I say. "I'm just here to talk business."

"I know, I know. I ramble on sometimes. But if you'll indulge me for a minute." He meets my eyes. Waiting.

Not knowing what else to do, I give him a single nod.

"So you see, Fat Pat had this specific way about him. Especially the way he talked. There were certain things he'd say that no one else said. Especially this turn of phrase that was so ingrained I don't even think he noticed when he'd say it." The Doctor leans back in his chair, spreading out. "At first I thought it was kinda unique. Then I met a couple other people from his neighborhood. A real shithole filled with worthless UBI lifers. What was the place called?" he asks Tumbo.

"Lower Lefeld," Tumbo says.

"That's it. So yeah, turns out, Fat Pat talked just like everyone else from his little neighborhood, including the use of that particular turn of phrase: *how the pieces fit.*"

That, all of it, was pageantry. He's toying with me. As casually as possible, I position my hand near the grip of the pistol.

It's too late though. Tumbo has his weapon leveled at me. Every muscle in my body goes rigid. The hexagonal barrel and the glint reflected from the mirrors within tell me it's a pulser. Uncommon planetside, pulser's are designed for security and policework on starships and aboard space stations where you don't want a missed shot penetrating a wall and damaging a critical system. Not that that detail matters any—at this range and striking flesh, it'll be plenty lethal.

"What do you have there?" the Doctor says. He lifts himself from his chair and leans over me, patting around my waist until his hand lands on the pistol. His eyes imitate disappointment as his hand gingerly lifts my shirt up, pulling the gun free of my waistband. "Tsk, tsk, tsk. Catalina? Where's the trust?"

He sits back down with the pistol resting on his thigh.

My instincts scream at me to run, but I'd never make it out that door. I'm frozen. I have no idea what my next move is.

"So, Lower Lefeld..." the Doctor says, maintaining eye contact. "That's not what you natives call it, is it?"

"We call it LoLe," I admit robotically.

"That's it." There's venom in the Doctor's voice now. "You know what happened to Fat Pat?"

I shrug. Not the *I don't care* kind of shrug. More like an *I'm too scared to talk* shrug.

"Well, someone had enough of his shit. Not us." Tumbo shakes his head in agreement. "One of his other employers took him to the old ice quarries in the Night districts. Like three hours out east where it's so cold they gotta put all the pipes and shit above ground. They bring him out there, put a bullet in one of his knees and drive away. Now, I don't think they shot him in the knee because they were worried about him walking far enough to find help. Nah, see, I think they did that so they knew he spent his last few minutes in excruciating pain as he froze to death. What do you think that felt like?"

I shift my weight, not knowing if I'm supposed to respond or not. We're playing his game and I don't know the rules.

"Proby hurt," Tumbo says.

"Of course it hurt for Fat Pat. But no, I mean, what do you think it felt like to do that *to* someone? Sounds exhilarating to me." He bares his teeth like a predator. "Ever since I heard about that shit, I've been wanting to have a reason to try it out."

Well Gaby, seems you've gone and gotten yourself murdered.

"So Catalina. This is what's gonna happen. I'm going to ask you some questions, and you better have verifiably true answers."

"Ya in church now," Tumbo says.

"That's right. Confessional time. And I am God to you. You understand?"

I nod, planting my gaze on worn carpet.

"And who knows, if you're honest, and I also happen to like your answers, maybe, just maybe, we won't be taking a drive out east."

Tears well up despite myself. I keep my head down.

"Catalina isn't your real name, is it?"

I shake my head.

"What is it?"

My voice catches. I swallow hard. "Gabrielle Rhodes."

Tumbo punches it into the hand terminal.

"I spoofed my iDent," I say, finding my voice out of fear they'll think I'm lying. "I won't show in the databases until the public servers reboot."

The Doctor cocks an eyebrow. "You law enforcement?"

I shake my head. "No. I don't know how to prove that to you though."

Tumbo looks up from his screen. "Where you learn?"

"I don't unders—"

"He's asking where you learned how to spoof your iDent?"

"Moore."

The Doctor draws his chin back, noticeably taken off guard. Then, regaining his composure, he chuckles. "Officer on deck!" he shouts, and mock salutes me. "My cousin went there. Dude came out a straight-up merc."

I might laugh if I wasn't so terrified. Best his cousin could've been at Moore would've been Command Division. Sure, they get some combat training, but if CommDiv is his definition of *merc*, meeting a gausser would blow his mind.

"Good thing I got this away from you," he says, waving the pistol carelessly.

"I don't get any combat training," I say sourly. It's getting easier to speak.

"Well what do you do there?"

"This waste our time," Tumbo grumbles.

"You got somewhere to be, Tumbo? Besides, I'm curious. This shit's not addin' up."

I shrug. "Computer coding and encryption mostly. Drone operations, and I just started firing solutions."

"Let's say I believe you. I guess that'd explain how you figured out how to change who you appear to be in the public database, but nothing else makes sense. You're a Moore student, bang-bon future in front of you. So if you're not law enforcement, and obviously you're no fixer for Eversen, why are you here? Why all the trouble changing your iDent? And setting up a consultation to buy CRISPR for a football team?"

"Does it matter? I just want some growth splices, but I know you're not small time. I knew you wouldn't sell to just me. For just one person."

"So it's for you then? For your tits?"

"No! What's wrong with my breasts?"

I squirm under his gaze as his eyes hover over my chest for an uncomfortable spell.

"Since we're being honest here, they're nothing to brag about."

There's a long silence. Tumbo stands and makes for the kitchen.

"What were you trying to get, anyway?" The Doctor's tone takes on a casual indifference.

Why's he asking? Is he actually entertaining the idea of selling to me? What's the best angle to play here? I have no idea, so I answer honestly. "Human growth hormone secretagogues, epi plate skeletal growth compounds, and anterior pituitary gland enhancers. And it's a long shot, but maybe IL-4 receptor modulators for asthma too."

He furrows his brow at me. "Sounds like you done your homework, so maybe you already know: the splice I sell, it's generic. That means it's not specifically tuned to any one person's DNA. It's cheaper that way, but way more dangerous. I sell it to dumb jocks who'll do anything to make it pro. What do they got to lose, right? If they don't go pro, they're either enlisting and gettin' killed, or scrubbing toilets for five percent over basic. A Moore student has a future. It ain't worth it."

"It's worth it to me."

"The shopping list you just gave me, probably kill you."

"I already said, I'm willing to risk it."

"I'm not. One of these jocks' heart explodes, nobody bothers with it. Everyone knows they use. And ain't nobody cares about some athlete. But a Moore student dies of CRISPR Shock? You better believe they'll find a way to track it to me. I'd be better off putting you in the ground tonight."

"You don't understand, I need to be bigger. Please." I blink back the tears. Twenty-one centimeters too short. Sixteen kilograms too light. At seventeen, there's less than a year to change all that. "This is my last chance. I'm begging you."

He stares at me for what seems an eternity. His impassive face gives away nothing.

Tumbo shifts his weight at the edge of my vision, leaning against the kitchen door frame. "No worth it, boss."

The Doctor clears his throat. "You're not leaving here with splice, Gabrielle Rhodes. But you do get to leave." His eyes flick toward the door. "Go."

I stand on shaky legs, tears roaming unchecked down my cheeks.

"I'm keeping this," the Doctor says, spinning the pistol on his finger like a gunslinger from some VR show. "You don't see old style slug-throwers like this too often."

"I, I need it back," I blurt out. "I borrowed it, and if it doesn't show back up, there'll be questions."

"Merits," Tumbo says.

"That's why I keep him around," the Doctor says. "His pragmatism. You brought merits, right? I don't think you came in here to hold me up for the splice." Then he turns to Tumbo, smiling. "Although after everything else, hell, maybe she did."

"No, I was gonna pay."

"So you got an unregistered card?"

"Yeah," I admit, realizing where this is going. Fishing it from my pocket, it goes from me, to the Doctor, to Tumbo's waiting hand.

Tumbo taps it against his terminal. "Four 'tousand, three hundred and twelf."

"Your lucky day, Gabrielle. That is the exact fee to get this gun back."

"All of it?" I whisper.

"'Fraid so. Ammunition's sold separately." He pops the magazine free and pulls the slide back. The cartridge spirals from the chamber, landing silently on the carpet's pile. He empties the rounds from the magazine before offering it back to me. He doesn't let go until he says, "Forget you ever heard about me. Tonight...this shit, did not happen. You get me?"

I try to speak, but I can only choke down the knot in my throat and nod.

CHAPTER
TWO

Back home, curled up in bed, I cry myself empty. I have no idea how long it takes, but by the time I've finished, my eyes are raw and my lungs ache.

Through closed lids, I sense the light in the room shift. Squinting bleary eyes, I see the NEW MESSAGE tile flashing on and off in the corner of my terminal screen—the only source of light in the room. I could connect and pull it up through my NeurX, but the way my head's pounding, it's more effort than I'm willing to put into the task.

I dry my nose on the sleeve of my shirt, only giving it a passing thought as to how gross that is. Then I roll onto my back to stare at the ceiling. A patchwork of polycarbonite panels fastened in place by plastic rivets. They throb in the sedate indigo coming from the screen, brighter then duller, cycling every three seconds, as the waiting message gently asks for my attention.

"I really messed things up, Jules," I say.

There's only silence from below. The bottom bunk has gone unused for three years. The memory of Jules' final visit is always ready to bubble up. Vivid and watermarked with guilt. Normally,

I fiercely guarded the little time I got with him during those rare visits. That visit had been different.

C's brother had been murdered. And after losing her sister the year before, she needed me. Jules had only been home a day so far, but I made my choice and stayed with C, sleeping on the floor in her room, spending virtually every minute with her until the funeral had come and gone. It was just one visit. I'd catch up with Jules next time.

Except there was no next time.

The ladder groans a complaint as I climb down from my bed. The rickety upper-lower set of bunks is made of metal tubular framing and a facade of fake wood that isn't fooling anyone. Opposite the bed stands a small desk where the thin glass surface of my terminal screen idles. I open my messages: there are two, both from K.

Everything okay? You back home yet? reads the first. Then, *Hey, my dad is coming back to town early. I need the THING back tonight!!!*

I'm home. Park? I message back.

She responds with, *Sure*, almost instantly.

I change my shirt, retrieve the gun from the drawer where I'd tossed it, and make for the bathroom to wash my face. Moments later, the black smears of mascara are gone, but it does nothing to erase the humiliation.

Crying always leaves behind evidence. And anyone who snatches a glimpse of my puffy, reddened eyes might judge me delicate. The worst part is they'd be right. Tears have been so close to the surface lately, ready to spill out at nearly any provocation. Fortunately, this time at least, K will be the only witness. She doesn't judge, which feels safe—except when it seems like indifference, that feels shitty.

On my way to the front door, the living room is all stale air and shadows. The only illumination is the glow leaking from around Mom's VR headset and the parallel lines of sunlight sneaking through the blades of the closed shutters. The apartment had been empty when I arrived. She must've gotten back from…well, wherever, and either didn't hear me bawling my eyes out, or decided it'd be too much of an inconvenience to get involved.

"Goin' out," I announce.

Since she's sat in her recliner with some VR show drilling straight into her retinas, I'm surprised when she responds. "Be home by ten, honey."

It's half past ten.

"Sure."

I step out the front door and hurry through the shared hallway where it always reeks from a mixture of our neighbors' smoking and the greasy, over-spiced food they cook.

Outside, the sun is low on the western horizon. A permanent fixture, stationary and stubborn above the rooftops of the squat buildings. They only build short structures in the Day districts. Single-story affairs. It's to avoid blocking the narrow angle of sunlight. It's all we get.

Amiens is a tidally locked planet. One side forever facing the sun, burned and barren, while the other is cast in perpetual shadow and ice. The habitable portion of the planet is a narrow band between the extremes. When you spend your entire life on the day side of the terminator line in an endless sunset, you dream of seeing the night sky for the first time. It's supposed to be a magical moment. You build it up like a first kiss.

So I'm told. I haven't experienced either.

Separating my family's apartment from the park is a stretch of rutted pavement so old that those wheeled cars you see in period-piece VRs drove on it back before repulsor technology made it more efficient to fly. Now the road's a combination walkway, bicycle path, and makeshift parking lot for the rare moron stupid enough to leave their repulsor unattended in this neighborhood.

Approaching the park, the rhythm of the cicadas' stridulations fills the air. The white-noise soundtrack of the Everdusk.

Since I was little, this park's just been a flat lot of patchy grass. They'd torn out the few pieces of playground equipment after the slide had collapsed. Poor Sarah Keiner had been at the top. Paralyzed from the neck down with no hope of recovery, the State was forced to euthanize her. It was the humane thing to do, they said. Sarah wouldn't have been able to serve any use in society, and basic couldn't cover her needs.

That was my earliest lesson in how the worlds work.

"What's west, you green tea bitch?" Her voice is music.

I turn to K, opening my mouth to hurl a playful return-insult, but stop short. She's brought C with her, and some guy I don't recognize. The two girls walk in step toward me while the guy falls behind, stopping to tie his shoe. Forcing a smile, I hug each of my friends. My head barely reaches their shoulders, even with the eight-centimeter platforms I'm sporting.

When C first moved into the neighborhood, neither K nor C wanted to shorten their names to something like Kat or Cathy. So the three of us came up with *Katherine with a K* and *Catherine with a C*. We'd believed it was terribly clever, but the novelty of six syllable names wore thin fast. Within a month, we'd shortened them to K and C.

Outdoors on clear days like this, K's hair practically glows. She has it pulled into a messy ponytail that, backlit by the sun, looks like a geyser of yellow fire. When our ancestors colonized the planets and moons of our new solar system, each population tweaked their DNA to fit the local environment. The settlers here on Amiens needed to soak up the sparse UV radiation, so within a few generations they'd become fair-skinned and light-featured. Black short-shorts and a crop top reveal K's chalk-white skin, the light blue tint of her veins showing through at her wrists, at her neck, and peeking out from her lower abs. The quintessential Amienite standard of beauty.

C isn't beautiful, at least not in the way VRs and adverts have decided are beautiful. Lean and hard-muscled. She has the body of someone who's broken most of the track & field records at our secondary school. Well, *their* secondary school—I don't go to a regular school anymore. If I could have a body like either of them, I'd be athletic like C. Which is what tonight had been about, wasn't it? And now that everything's gone sideways, I wonder if C is going to become a reminder of what I will never be?

"Who's that?" I ask as the boy catches up.

"Oh," K says. "Gaby, meet Elijah."

Elijah is tall, and not just compared to me, but actually tall. The messy brown mop on his head appears meticulously arranged to appear like it's not. He hangs a lanky arm across K's shoulders. "What's west?" he says.

"Hey," I say, trying not to glare at him. "K, I thought we'd be alone."

"What?" C says. "Alone for what? What's goin' on?"

K spreads her thumb and first finger apart into a V-shape, a gesture that means *it's fine*. "Elijah's cool."

C plants a narrow-eyed gaze on me from under the edges of her pixie-cut bangs. Her hair is dark green this week.

"Fine," I say to K. "Gonna open your bag?"

The muscles in C's jaw flex. "Someone going to clue me in?"

K shrugs Elijah's arm free as she swings her petite backpack off. "Gaby went and did something stupid." K draws *stupid* out into almost two separate words. "How'd it go, anyway?"

I pull the pistol from my pants and place it in K's palm. Our hands touch briefly. K has the softest skin.

"Whoa," Elijah says.

"What the hell are you doing with that?" C says.

"You gonna tell her?" K asks mildly, as she places the weapon in her bag and cinches the drawstring closed. She must not have noticed the weight difference. Now empty, the pistol weighs about half what it had when K loaned it to me.

"I really hadn't planned on it," I snipe, hoping the *she shouldn't be here* part I want to say comes through in my tone. "Less people know the better."

"Tell me what? Hey! Tell me what?"

"Keep your voice down," I say, glancing around. "I took a trip over to Rogyville."

"Why'd you go th—" C turns, fixing K with a scalding glare. "You told her about Jay's 'Doctor,' didn't you?"

K turns away, which is answer enough. Jay Ramsey plays for the Lefeld Secondary School football team. He'd told C, in confidence, that the team had begun taking CRISPRs to get an edge. They were getting them from some guy only known as *The Doctor*, over in Rogyville. C told K, K told me. It didn't take long to hunt him down on the net.

"C, don't be mad at her," I say. "It's my choice."

C's shoulders slump. "I told you not to tell anyone, K. That Doctor guy's born in the shade. Something really bad coulda happened."

"Yeah..." I say, feeling out the moment for my admission. "I kind of didn't bring back the bullets."

"What?!" K's mouth falls open. "Did you— Did you shoot somebody?"

"No, nothing like that. They sorta got taken. I'm sorry. I know that's going to be hard to explain to your dad."

K waves my apology away. "He's got boxes of ammo. He won't notice as long as I reload it before he gets back. Just... What happened?"

"Yeah, tell us," Elijah says, reminding me of the interloper's presence.

"No," I say flatly to him, not even trying to hide my annoyance.

"You don't need to be rude," K says.

"I don't want this-week's-boyfriend knowing my business."

K scowls. "Some way to treat a friend that just did you a favor. Come on," she says to Elijah and turns away.

"K, I'm sorry, I appreciate you klepping that for me. I..."

"It's fine," K says in a tone that sounds anything but. She and Elijah start walking away. "We can talk later," she says over her shoulder.

I watch intently as K's fingertips find Elijah's. Then I flinch as his hand grasps hers.

"I think this boy might stick around a while," C says, clearly following my gaze.

"She'll get bored with him."

"I wouldn't be so sure." C sounds hesitant, like she doesn't want to deliver bad news.

"Why?"

"Because she seems to really like him? But mostly because he's Elijah Reynolds."

Seeing my questioning expression, C continues. "Son of Sasha Reynolds?"

Still nothing.

"If it isn't war news, you don't keep up with any current events, do you? Sasha Reynolds from Story Tao Studios."

Now it clicks. When we were kids, K and I both shared the dream of acting in VRs. We even took some acting classes together. I moved on. She did not. Like some girl from LoLe could end up a star. But K won't hear it. She's going to try. Apparently, even if it takes dating a studio exec's kid. Which begs the question, "What's he doing here?"

C shrugs. "Coulda asked, ya know, if you hadn't chased him off. But now that he *is* gone, wanna tell me how it went?"

C studies me with those inquisitive eyes. She always reads me a little too well. I take an interest in my own feet.

"No luck?"

"No luck," I confirm.

"I'm sorry you're unhappy, Gabs. I really am. But in this case, I'm also glad you didn't get what you want."

This is not unexpected.

"So what's next?" C asks.

"I guess I try to pull my grades back up so I don't flunk out of Moore."

"What?" She takes me by the shoulders. "How are you flunking out?"

I deflate under her touch. "Can I maybe tell you about that some other time?"

She looks like she's going to protest, but then she simply says, "Sure."

We start a meandering pace to nowhere in particular. I can't think of anything to say. The cicadas in the distance fill the silence with their undulating drone.

"I was thinking about last week," C starts slowly. "Remember when you talked our ears off about..." she takes a big inhale before reciting, "biasing for telemetry latency while finding a firing solution?"

"You remember all that?" I say, my voice little more than a whisper.

"I listen," she says, nudging me with an elbow. "Did I get it right?"

I let out a small laugh. "Yeah. Perfect."

"They're just words to me, you know. I don't understand them. Hell, I understand less and less of what comes out of your mouth since you started going to Moore. But you understand it, and that gives you something special. You have a gift. You could do whatever you want with that. But you wanna throw it away." Her tone is somewhere between a statement and an accusation.

I watch my feet intently as the ground goes from ash-colored grass to concrete. We've left the perimeter of the park.

"You're wrong. I don't get to do whatever I want. Because of my *gift,* I'm gonna spend the rest of my life doing math. I'd trade places with you if I could." As soon as the words tumble from my mouth, I realize they're going to wound.

"Would you?" Ice is in her voice. "Doing math is that bad, huh?" She shakes her head.

How can I apologize without saying the unspoken part? Without breathing life into what we both know I'm apologizing for? No words make it past my lips.

A repulser car darts by overhead, tousling my hair into my face. I brush the hair from eyes and see the four glowing discs on the car's underside shrinking from view.

Finally, C fills the space, speaking robotically. "I should go. See you."

And then her back is to me. And she's gone.

I'd managed to botch my plan, lose more merits than my parents are allocated in a year, and hurt my only two friends' feelings in a single evening. Impressive. Even for a screwup like me.

CHAPTER
THREE

From my position off the port bow, I watch as my carrier's starboard artillery guns swivel, pointing their unfriendly ends at the cruiser thirty kilometers out. They spit fire in urgent fits, sending shards of depleted uranium hurtling away to etch out red-hot paths as they chase each other into the black.

My sensors bounce back data on every object in the combat zone, overlaying glowing reticules and relevant telemetry in my vision. But it's difficult to focus. How does any of this matter now? I gambled everything for the chance to get the *one* thing that would've put my life on track.

I gambled everything.

And I lost.

Return fire rains down like falling stars, crashing into the shields of my team's carrier. Yellow, luminescent ripples flow away from each impact as the shield soaks up the kinetic energy.

I didn't play my character well enough, getting discovered because I hadn't thought to change the way I talk. Good thing I'd given up on being an actress if that amateur-hour performance is the best I could do.

Drone four whips a tight turn around the carrier into a

friendly firing solution. Before I can radio a warning, the reticule sketching around their position disappears.

"I'm out." It's Kristoph. His clipped accent is easy to pick out through the excited radio chatter. It reminds me a bit of Tumbo.

"Launch a new drone, Cadet Norman," Professor Li says.

"Small movers entering Red Space, Flight Epsilon," someone calls.

I spot them. Three missiles coming in at an oblique angle toward the aft of our carrier. I aim my telescope and magnify.

"I have visual," I say. "They're slow rollers. I'm intercepting. Drone Five, where are you?" My heart speeds up. I can't feel it—I can't feel anything while integrated with a drone—but I know it all the same.

"I am... I'm, uh," Lukas stammers. "Coming in on your six, Drone Two."

I'll need him if we're going to take out three slow rollers. That type of torpedo has its own shields. They're difficult to bring down and dangerous to capital ships.

Shields react to fast-moving mass. Objects moving slow enough, however, creep through unhindered. Slow rollers are missiles with big, front-mounted retro thrusters, built for precisely that purpose. They come in fast, then decelerate to a velocity that won't engage the shields.

I feed my engines all the fuel they'll take until I get near, then cut my thrust and yaw to face them. The inertia carries me sideways as I let my railguns loose, strafing the nearest missile. Its shields light up. I swivel to keep my guns trained on it and continue firing as we sail past one another. The first missile goes out in a gratifying explosion.

I make pursuit, burning hard to catch the other two.

"Where are you, Drone Five?" I say.

"Burning, but I think I'm too far out." Then under his breath, Lukas says, "Stupid. Stupid."

The enemy had been feinting with their bombers. They'd present juicy targets for our defensive formations, then turn and run. I bet Lukas fell for it and pursued outside his assigned zone.

Jerome and Mika are still performing launch sequences for new drones. Which means I'm alone on this side of the field.

I line up a shot with the second missile. My vision shakes as I fire under full acceleration, expelling seven rounds from each railgun. As the munitions fly away in front of me, I know it's enough. The torpedo is dead. Everything is in motion, nothing left but to let causality play out.

My shots strike the torpedo. Its shield deflects the first four pairs of railgun projectiles, but with each impact, the shield strobes dimmer. The fifth pair of shots strikes home and the space in front of me turns into a ball of expanding light. I'm too close, but altering course to avoid the edge of the explosion will also mean doubling back to catch the final torpedo. I'd never make up the lost time. I don't let off the thrusters, accelerating straight into the blast.

My shields will hold. They have to.

Plunging through the super-heated plasma, I exit the other side to a choir of alarms and my own shout of excitement. The celebration is cut short as the carrier's engines appear in my vision, overlayed by a dozen warning lights in my HUD all competing for my attention.

The last slow roller fires its retro thrusters, decelerating so rapidly it looks as though it froze in place on my sensors. I try to yaw, expecting my drone to wheel around where I can put my main thrusters to work decelerating. Nothing happens. I don't turn in the slightest. Without any response from my maneuvering thrusters, I'm helpless as I careen into the aft shields of my own carrier.

"Launch a new drone, Cadet Rhodes," Professor Li says a second later.

While beginning launch procedures, I scream inside. Another failure. When we go over the replays and lessons from this exercise, I just know Professor Li will use my blunder for one of his examples. The radio chatter in my ears goes silent, a telltale sign a private channel's been opened. "Belay launch, Cadet Rhodes," Professor Li says. "Report to the dean's office immediately."

"What? Why?"

"I trust you'll find out when you get there, Cadet. Now move your butt."

With a quick series of mental commands, I bring up my NeurX menu, cycle through the connections, and disconnect from the simulation.

While integrated, everything but our autonomic nervous systems are routed through the NeurX implant. This allows the simulation to feed all its sensory information straight into our brains. With the connection severed, I'm back in the pod. I have arms and legs again. I can feel my breath in my lungs.

I remove the blinder helmet, blink against the overhead lights as my eyes adjust, then climb out of my pod. A five-by-five grid of the egg-like devices fills the classroom, and Professor Li sits at his desk surveying the simulated battle wearing a specialized VR headset.

Drone Ops is the one class at Moore Academy I don't hate. It's a far cry better than gunnery: plot a firing solution, push a button, wait...wait...wait some more, then something so far away you need a telescope to see goes boom. Look at me, I'm such a brave warrior.

Piloting a drone is exciting at least. I can get lost in the simulation and forget that I'm betraying my dreams, letting them die. Which feels like betraying Jules. Letting his legacy die. His memory.

On my way out of the classroom, movement from the corner of my eye grabs my attention. I stop briefly at the pod closest to the door. Inside sits Makenzie Fowler, who twitches violently for a moment, then relaxes.

The NeurX doesn't stop everything. Errant signals get through to our nervous systems here and there. We grab for things, flinch, and in particularly high-stress situations, thrash about. So they pad the pods with thick foam, forming armrests and foot cubbies to keep us from hurting ourselves.

As if operating a drone isn't already far enough from danger.

Without the normal mob of students rushing from one class to the next, the main corridor of the intelligence division is empty. Free of the suffocating pressure of the crowds, the rich textures of imported wood paneling, the exposed trusses, the beiges and greens that make up most of the decor, create a warm, calming environment.

Displayed at strategic intervals are carefully curated portraits of notable professors, Moore graduates of some acclaim, and war heroes from our planet. Jules belonged to the last category. In the command wing, there's a captioned photo of him.

Petty Officer Julian Rhodes
Gauss Trooper, 118th Division
With gratitude, for your sacrifice during an Omega Priority mission.
You have made Swayy Corp. proud.

I attended the small ceremony when Dean Beaumont hung the photo. Jules hadn't been a Moore student. Gaussers are grunts. Elite grunts, but still grunts. That day I'd scanned the crowd, wondering if it irked the command students—future officers, each of them—to be forced to look at grunts on their wall. That'd been the first time I'd smiled in weeks.

Since then, I've often imagined my picture hanging next to his someday.

The intelligence, command, and engineering wings merge at a central point designated for the administration offices. NCP banners frame the archway. The iconic shield of the Network of Corporate Protectorates stands bold and proud in red against a sable background.

I place my hand over my heart as I pass.

I reach the faculty offices. They have the ambience of a library and I become hyperaware of how each noise is a disturbance. The clop of my flat shoes slapping waxed tile. The rustle of the synthetic fabric of my uniform with every stride. The dean's receptionist is there, a young man that looks as though he tried smiling precisely once, and promptly decided he didn't like it.

"I'm here to see Dean Beaumont," I say.

"Gabrielle Rhodes?"

I nod.

He steps out from behind his desk and walks me to the dean's door. Opening it, he announces, "Sir, Gabrielle Rhodes is here."

Once I'm in the office, the dean's receptionist closes the door behind me. The entire wall opposite the entrance is floor-to-ceiling windows facing east overlooking San Malone Canyon. Gold light reflects off layer upon layer of stacked sedimentary rock. Stripes of rose and violet and mauve deepening until the cliffs plunge into the shade where the sun can never reach.

A man stands there with his back to me, also admiring the view. It is not Dean Beaumont.

Shifting my weight from side to side, I fidget. "It was kinda weird, that guy announcing my arrival. I've never had a crier before."

"A what?" the man asks without moving.

"Um, a crier. It was a job in medieval and Renaissance times back on Earth. Their entire job was to— It, it doesn't matter." Why am I still talking? "I don't even know why I'm still talking." Why did I just say that?

The man turns. He's wearing a freshly pressed dress uniform. Silver-gray with black edging and the blue aiguillette of the intelligence division—its soft braided cord wrapping snuggly around his left shoulder. The insignia on his collar tells me he's an admiral, and the badges and ribbons over his heart could stop a pulser shot. Covering his left forearm, he wears a military issue bracer. It's larger than any of the civilian models I've seen, and massive compared to the little bracelet wristcomm I used to wear before I got my NeurX. The brushed aluminum finish glints, and the large data plate on its face is a dull green turned off.

I freeze, stuck somewhere between saluting and reaching for a handshake.

He takes a step forward and outstretches a hand that makes me feel like a child. "Admiral Theodore Davis," he introduces himself.

It's difficult to guess his age, not only because of the baby fat he carries in his cheeks, but also because someone of his station should have access to anti-aging CRISPRs. Anti-aging treatments or no, the years have begun robbing the color from his hair.

My hand disappears inside his as we shake. "I'm Gabrielle Rhodes...sir."

"I know you are. You had a crier."

A heat rises to my cheeks. "Right. I thought I was meeting Dean Beaumont?"

"I had you paged. The dean was kind enough to lend me his office. Have a seat."

I take one of the small chairs in front of the desk. He ignores the dean's high-backed armchair and eases his bulk into my chair's sibling, turning it toward me. Our knees nearly touch.

"You're probably wondering why I called you here."

That's an understatement, but I only nod.

"I have a vested interest in what goes on in this academy. Particularly in the intelligence division. So when a promising student's grades take a dive, it warrants a little investigating. Just to make sure we're doing everything we can for our students to be successful."

"From an InDiv admiral?"

"Why not? InDiv is interested in everything that interests the NCP. And the students at academies like Moore are the future leaders of the NCP. So, is there anything you want to discuss regarding your studies here?"

"No," I say, feeling confused and tiny in his presence.

Admiral Davis laces his fingers together and leans forward. "Did you know we have detailed projections for each student's progress? We know, with a high degree of certainty, what rating each student will achieve for each class."

Outside the window, some type of hawk circles high in the air currents. I imagine its telescopic vision trained on some rodent on the ground below.

Admiral Davis stands. My gaze darts back to him as he paces around the desk, sits in the dean's armchair and taps on a remote. The wall behind me lights up with a statistical graph. Craning my neck, I examine it. Much of the data is unlabeled, but it appears to be broken down into four time frames. Six data sets in the first, five for the second, four for the third, five again for the fourth. That matches my class schedule over the previous four semesters. The data slides from one deviation below mean, to two, to three.

My stomach twists like I've eaten something off. I spin to the admiral.

He nods at me. But this isn't a *gotcha*. There's no smile, no self-congratulatory excitement.

"I've been having a difficult time since—"

"Don't finish that sentence. Don't use your brother's death to make excuses for your behavior."

I lower my head, not looking at anything in particular.

"The system was designed to catch cheaters. Students whose

grades are better than they should be. An irony in your case. You have been methodically lowering your scores to appear like you're falling behind despite your best efforts. Even going so far as to space out your answers in tests so the timestamps make it look like you're really struggling. I'd like to know why."

Silence falls over the room while he waits for my answer. I look at the charts clearly laying out the deception I'd thought so clever. I look out the window where my bird-friend wheels above the deep canyon. I look at the door, wishing I could sprint through it right now. I look everywhere in the room, except at the admiral. Finally I say, "I don't know." Weak, Gaby. Weak.

"Allow me to give you some advice. If you're going to commit a crime, plan for every eventuality. Including what you'll say and do if you get caught."

"A crime?"

"Yes. Idleness & Work Malfeasance applies to official State schoolwork."

The knot in my stomach tightens.

Being convicted of Idleness & Work Malfeasance all but guarantees you'll never find employment. It makes you a pariah. An object of contempt. The label assuring others that you are a worthless, lazy drain on society. But not for long; the punishment includes forfeiting half of your universal basic income stipend. And it's hard to get by with full UBI benefits. A man or woman convicted of Idleness & Work Malfeasance is likely to starve to death. That is, if they don't go out on their own terms first. Many do.

The admiral's tone shifts, softening. "While going through your file, I found something that fascinated me."

Finding the strength to lift my head, I meet the admiral's eyes. He doesn't have the grizzled, battle-weary look I imagine of an admiral who's led people to kill and die on the front lines, nor does he have the cold, calculating gaze of a master manipulator in the intelligence division. He looks...like he cares. Does that mean I can trust him more, or that I should trust him even less?

"It's from your first career agent, Shiloh Stern," he says. "You remember her?"

I nod. Where could he be going with this? Ms. Stern hasn't been my career agent since age twelve.

He presses a command on his bracer. Text emerges in a shallow hologram above his arm. The text isn't readable from my angle, but it's obvious he's scrolling to find a particular section. "In one of her reports, she says, and I quote: 'Gabrielle Rhodes displays an interest in the arts, particularly in acting and crafting works of fiction. She has written three VR screenplays, and while they are predictable and juvenile (as one would expect of a ten-year-old), she shows real promise as a writer, with a strong narrative voice for someone her age and a powerful imagination.'" He flicks the report away. The hologram dissolves like pixilated smoke. "High praise. Why did you quit writing?"

I know that report. I continue it from memory. "'While this would be a laudable talent in other individuals, Ms. Rhodes has displayed a genius-level aptitude in mathematics and near-perfect recall. It is this career agent's opinion that Ms. Rhodes will best serve the State in a role that focuses on STEM fields. Consequently, all classes involving the arts shall be forbidden to Ms. Rhodes, beginning next school cycle.'"

After allowing that to hang in the air for a moment, I say, "It wasn't quitting, sir. I was tracked to serve in more valuable ways."

"Yes. But why did you *quit*?"

I'm fidgeting again, so I sit on my hands, and for reasons I don't understand, I tell the truth. "I didn't. I still write."

Gradually his stoic expression breaks, and a smile that reaches his eyes overtakes his face.

"So was that the plan?" the admiral asks. "Flunk out of Moore and go write screenplays for VRs? Maybe be an actress?"

The question catches me off guard. The thought hadn't even occurred to me. Shaking my head, I say, "No, sir. I want to serve."

He studies my face, drumming his fingers on the wood. Then the admiral sits back in the dean's chair and lifts a trinket from the desk. It's a clear, glass statuette of some six-legged animal. I don't recognize the species, probably from a different planet. Maybe from Aradious? I think that's where the dean is from.

After handling the thing for a moment, turning it over in his enormous hands, the admiral speaks. "I understand you know Lieutenant Commander Morgan York."

Lieutenant Commander? Morgan's been promoted? "I grew up with him, sir. My brother's best friend."

Admiral Davis nods. "Yes, I know. I never had the pleasure of meeting your brother. But the lieutenant commander serves under me now. We've had some good talks, he and I. He told me how you had wanted to follow in your brother's footsteps and be a gausser. That was before you'd been sent to Moore though. And before your brother died serving the NCP. So is that it? You want to serve, but only if you get to be a gausser?"

"Unit-for-unit, gauss troopers are the most effective soldiers in Swayy Corp.'s military. They're deployed under a wide variety of mission parameters, and for the past ten years, each has averaged thirty-one-and-a-half confirmed Commonwealth kills before they're killed in action."

A smirk washes over the admiral's face. "Spoken like a true patriot. A patriot who's seen too many recruitment adverts, but still..." He trails off. When he starts again, it seems as though he's talking mostly to himself. "So you decide to flunk out gracefully, because unlike if you quit, you'd be allowed to reenlist in a different division. It's a good plan. Except...you're too small to enlist as a gausser."

"I know," I say in an equally small voice.

"I suppose CRISPR interventions could fix that. Those gene-editing organisms would go in and send you through a sort of second puberty. You'd probably reach minimum regulation height and weight in a few months. It would be bloody painful, but I've heard of people doing it."

The admiral returns the six-legged statuette to the desk. "But your parents are on basic, right? I'm guessing for pretty much their entire adult lives. So CRISPR treatments aren't an option for you. So, the question remains, Ms. Rhodes, what did you intend to do once you'd flunked yourself out of Moore?"

I can only manage a shrug in response.

"What, were you going to get some of those cheap, black market CRISPRs and enlist?"

My eyes shoot open. He has to be guessing. He can't know, right? Then I read it on his face. He hadn't known, but he does now.

"I see," he breathes.

The bracer on his forearm lights up and beeps. He silences it with a swipe. "I have another meeting, so I need to wrap this up." His eyes lock on me like he's taking my measure. I remember the vague threat, *Idleness & Work Malfeasance*, and wonder if he's deciding my fate.

"The department I run has been working on something special. A new type of ship. The kind of thing I can't simply tell you about. But I'd like you to be my guest on its maiden voyage. Next week we'll be doing a training exercise, and you'll get to see what these classes you're sandbagging have actually been training you for. You'll get to see how important people like you will be in the future of this war. You may even forget all about being a gausser."

The admiral stands and tugs his jacket straight. I stand with him, though I'm hardly taller on my feet.

"Why me? I mean, why not take Makenzie Fowler or Fan Lan? They're just as skilled as me, and they want it."

"Better."

I blink at him.

"At least Fan Lan," the admiral says. "He's better than you are. But you said it yourself, they both want it. They don't need any extra convincing. Just come see the training exercise, Cadet. If you still want to be a grunt after that, I'll personally sign off on your transfer to gausser camp, and the navy will pay for legitimate CRISPR treatments."

My mouth gapes. After everything I've done, the risks I've taken and was willing to take, this admiral is going to walk in and hand me everything I've been wanting, bang-bon? "Why would you do that for me?"

"Not the trusting type. That'll serve you well in InDiv," he says thoughtfully. "Even with Fowler, Lan, and the others, there isn't an overabundance of candidates who fit all the criteria I'm looking for. I need every good cadet I can get."

"You're not going to convince me, you know. I'll only be going to get into gausser camp." What are you doing, Gaby? Trying to provoke him into taking the offer back?

The admiral shrugs it off. "Maybe so. Maybe your visit will simply be a nice surprise for my executive officer."

"Who's your XO?"

"Why, it's Lieutenant Commander York, Ms. Rhodes. Do keep up. You're supposed to be a genius," the admiral says with a playful smile.

FOUR

Nala Ricci pushed Morgan against a wall of storage crates. The webbed cording securing the containers in place dug into his back as she shoved her tongue in his mouth. She was the most aggressive woman he'd ever been with.

"Nala, wait," he said.

"Three weeks... Don't...wanna wait," Nala replied breathily in the space between fierce kisses.

He wished he would've suggested somewhere else to meet. Somewhere other than their usual spot. In the eight months he'd served aboard the *Sedna*, he hadn't seen a soul in that cargo bay. Except for their outside-of-regulation visits, he wondered when the last person had even stepped foot in there. He should've suggested the enlisted lounge, or hell, even either of their barracks. Someplace there'd be other crew members killing time. Someplace they wouldn't fall into these Pavlovian patterns.

"I'm sorry. I can't," he told Nala, taking her hands in his so they could no longer wander his body.

"Why?"

"I met someone."

"So what? I *meet* people too."

"It's serious," he said.

She grinned, holding back a laugh. "Serious, huh? In the three weeks I've been off-ship?"

"It started before. On Tora Kiesa. We've been talking ever since and it's..."

"Serious?" she parroted. Her smile turned more sardonic than amused. "Tora Kiesa? So a civilian?" Her brow furrowed. "Oh, I get it now. You're an idiot."

"You're mad. I'm sorr—"

"I'm not mad," she said angrily. "You know why this"—she motioned between them—"why *we* work so well? Because there's no future in it. We both know there is no *us*. You're a gausser, York. Y'all don't have a great life expectancy. Until you get your discharge orders, you don't have a future. And you're an asshole if you're letting some clueless civie think otherwise."

Civie, yes. Clueless, far from it, he thought.

The intercom squawked to life with a sequence of three high-pitched beeps followed by, "Now general quarters, general quarters, all hands to G-chairs. Battle group initiating high G heading change in T-minus 120 seconds."

"Well," Nala began, her carefree smile returning. "Two minutes. Good thing we were still dressed." She saluted smartly. "Petty Officer York."

It felt like goodbye. "Corporal Ricci." He returned the salute.

She about-faced then and double-timed it out of the cargo bay. Morgan stayed a moment, taking a beat to avoid the awkwardness of leaving together.

Morgan made it to the tram, buckling himself into one of the tramcar's G-chairs, just as the maneuver started. He was yanked to the side as the ship spun on its center axis, then shoved to the back of the chair as the engines worked to overcome the inertia of the three billion kilogram vessel.

It took the inertial neutralizers four uncomfortable minutes to spin up. The tram sat idly until the inertia neuts had muted the acceleratory G-forces to a nearly imperceptible drag aft.

Once underway the tram sped a kilometer down the spine of the ship, stopping every one or two hundred meters until Morgan got off near his barracks. Another soldier was there, bent down feeling the deck with his palm.

"You feel that?" the soldier asked.

"No," Morgan said. But then he thought he felt something through his boots. He stilled, looking down dumbly. Waiting. There it was again. A vibration, then nothing. Then back and gone again.

"Is that the blink drive?" Morgan asked.

"Yeah, I think so," the soldier said, standing upright.

The Swayy Corp. carrier, *Sedna,* was a massive ship. Fully staffed with crew, marines, gaussers, fighter pilots, and support staff, it housed over 8,000 people. Most days, it felt more like some kind of underground city than a ship. Unless you were a wrencher posted somewhere on the lower decks, you didn't hear or feel the concussive tremors of the blink drive running.

"Any idea what's got the captain pushing the ship so damn hard?" the soldier asked.

Morgan shook his head. Then his bracer lit up with orders. Mission briefing at 1350 hours. "I guess I won't have to wait too long to find out. Good luck."

On his way to the briefing, Morgan stopped by his unit's barracks, expecting he'd need to collect his friend. Once every nine days, bandwidth opened up for the crew to send and receive personal messages. Today was that day.

Rows of bunks flanked the long edges of the rectangular room. A shared workspace built into the bulkhead took up the wall opposite the entry. It could serve numerous functions, but the crew tended to just use it for sending and receiving messages. Most message days there'd be a line. Normal routines had been shaken up though, and the barracks were empty except for a lone figure sitting at the workspace.

"Jules," Morgan called.

He was grateful the Swayy Navy tried to give soldiers who enlisted together the same deployments. Their philosophy was: people who grew up together would fight harder for each other. So aside from a brief deployment after gauss trooper training, he and Jules had been side-by-side through every mission.

"Jules, we're gonna be late," he said. Before seeing the image in the video Jules was watching, he recognized the high, wispy voice coming from the prerecorded message. He sat down on the nearest bunk to the workstation as Jules finished the message. "What'd Gaby have to say?" he asked.

"She got transferred to Moore," Jules said, grinning.

"Really? That's...that's nuts. She's not even fifteen yet, right?"

Jules shook his head. "They skipped her ahead three years."

"Damn. Tell her I'm proud of her."

"Tell her yourself. I'm about to send a message."

"Okay, we gotta make it quick though," Morgan said, checking the time on his bracer.

Jules reached out to the terminal and turned recording mode on. A quick countdown scrolled across the screen.

"Hey, Gaby, I got Morgan here. I just wanted to tell you how proud I am of you."

"We both are, kid," Morgan said, squatting down behind Jules to get in the shot. "Proud, but not surprised."

Jules hooked a thumb at Morgan. "I'm excited to see the first time this guy's forced to salute you."

"I dunno, I think there's some kind of exception about that if you've seen your commanding officer in diapers." He cringed inwardly at his own joke.

"Anyway, I got a little good news of my own. Looks like we're about to go on another mission, but after that, our unit is scheduled for some leave. Morgan and I can come home and celebrate how crazy smart you are, and I was thinking we could do an early birthday thing too. What d'ya say?"

"But," Morgan interjected, "if we're gonna have any hope of doin' that, I gotta get your brother to the briefing. We can't celebrate with you if the master sergeant kills us both for being late."

"Unfortunately, he's right. Gotta go, Gabs."

Then, as Jules' finger hovered over the COMPLETE tile, they both said together, "Love you."

CHAPTER
FIVE

While I replay my conversation with the admiral in my mind's eye, my feet march me to the front door of Lefeld Secondary School. My subconscious isn't being subtle in telling me I need a friend.

Classes will be out, but extra-curricular activities should still be going. K will be who-knows-where with her new boyfriend. C, though, she'll probably be here.

The weapon scanner remains silent as I step through the threshold and the security officer waves me past after I show him my Moore ID. Technically it shouldn't grant me access here, but low-level Swayy Corp. employees often bend rules to avoid complications with anyone from the academy. A Moore cadet, in a few short years, could be in the position to ruin someone else's career over a supposed slight, were they so inclined.

I bite down on a fingernail. Track season is over. What's next? "Has the wrestling team started training?"

"About an hour ago. They're probably finishing up," the officer says.

I'd been asking if they'd started for the season, but his answer is better. They'd yanked me out of regular classes after half a year here, but I remember the school's layout well enough to find the gym. A handful of onlookers pepper the bleachers. Girlfriends of the male-dominated team, I assume. I pick a seat and glance around, following each of their bored stares to the guys they're probably dating.

Then I pick out C in her red singlet. She looks comical with the bulbous ear protectors and lips plumped from the mouth guard underneath.

A nervous shiver creeps up my spine as I wonder if someone else is following my gaze and assuming I'm dating C. Not even Moore can protect its students from Ethics Officers.

C steps onto the mat and squares off with a young man that looks like he's a weight class heavier. I don't understand wrestling. There must be technique and subtlety to the movements, but as they tug and push at each other in turns, I can't tell a bad move-ment from a good one. So I have no idea if C makes a mistake, if her opponent has more skill, or if he simply overpowers her because of the size advantage, but it's over quickly.

I prefer watching C run. Maybe it's because I understand it better, or maybe it's because she always wins. I like seeing her win.

A few matches later, the coach gathers the team, says a few words, and dismisses them. The group disperses, and the couples find each other. I had been right with every guess except the curly haired girl with the prominent nose. She steps off the bleachers and indeed meets the guy I'd picked out for her, but watching them interact, their similarly curled hair, and the shapes of both their noses, I realize they're more likely brother and sister. People never came to that conclusion with me and Jules. We had looked nothing alike. He had been normal height, pale, with sandy hair. Far from my undersized frame and dark complexion.

Catherine spots me in the emptying bleachers and sends a smile my way as she gathers her things. She climbs to my position in a few sure steps.

"I'd hug you," she says, "but I'm all sweaty and gross."

"Gonna shower?"

"Nah, too warm today. I'd just get sweaty again walking home. I'll shower then." She pushes her fingers through the tangles of her hair. The green dye has already faded a bit and now matches her eyes. "What are you doing here?"

It's a good question. I shrug. "I wanted to see you."

C raises her eyebrows at me and adjusts the hang of the duffel bag on her shoulder. "Wanna go for a walk?"

"Where to?"

"Come on," she says.

Leaving Upper Lefeld and entering Pheritona. The contrast on 9th Street is striking. Look south: economic depression and urban decay. Look north: a safe, clean, middle-class community. At some point, someone had drawn an invisible line on a map, saying these are the haves and these are the have-nots. Then, through a process of funding one and neglecting the other, the invisible line became something palpable.

We get a lot of looks. We're out of place, not just with our surroundings, but with each other too. Catherine still in her wrestling singlet over a t-shirt, and me in my Moore uniform. C doesn't notice the looks, or doesn't care. I ask where we're going again. C ignores my question as she leads me through an unfamiliar residential district. The path dead-ends at a well-maintained park with freshly painted playground equipment. At the back of the park is a wall of trees and untamed vegetation. As we near, the murmur of flowing water drifts from the thicket. Picking a path through the shrubbery, we find ourselves at the bank of a wide, shallow river.

C's bag falls with a thump. She kicks off her shoes and walks into the clear running water. A few steps out, she sits down on one of the rounded stones jutting up from the river. The water reaches her mid-shin.

"You coming?" she asks.

I peel my shoes and socks off, then roll my pant legs up. Sloshing into the water, I seat myself on a similar stone near C's. The water is cool and the air at the river seems lighter, less stifling. I breathe in the humidity and the heady scents of vegetation and wet soil.

Dyrul trees at the bank cover much of the river in dappled shade. They reach up and away, twisting their gray-barked trunks west toward the always-setting sun where their oily, black leaves can soak up as much ultraviolet light as possible.

Catherine and I sit together for a long time. Birds chirp and whistle in the trees and the water babbles against the rocks.

Finally, C gets to it. "So what's wrong, Gaby?"

It all spills out. The visit from the admiral. The offer to go see the secret ship. Morgan's promotion and him serving as the XO.

I hesitate when it comes to telling her about the admiral's offer to give me CRISPR treatments. I know she won't approve, but I feel if I don't tell someone, I'll burst.

"There's one more thing," I say, working up the nerve. "He said, if I go, if I see what he wants me to see and hear what he wants me to hear...if I'm still not interested, he'll get me CRISPR treatments and move me into the gausser division."

C listens to it all and regards me for a moment before she responds. "It sounds like you can get everything you want."

"Yeah," I say. "I guess so."

"So then why don't you seem happy? Why aren't you telling me, right now, that you're finally going to be a gausser? Why are you here at all for that matter? Why aren't you at home packing?"

"I don't think I'm going to go." I hadn't realized I was going to say it. But as soon as it's said, it feels right. Since the moment the admiral made the offer, a sense of dread has been quietly building. Where I should've felt excitement and hope, there was only anxiety. Relief settles over me. The decision's been made.

"What? Why?"

"I don't know. It just seems too easy, ya know? Like I should make my own way, not just have it given to me. Plus, how can I trust the admiral to keep his word? Jules used to say you can't trust the InDiv. He said they were always scheming and politicking, playing their own angles."

"Gabs, *you* are in the Intelligence Division," C points out, not bothering to hold in her smile.

I allow myself a small laugh. "Yeah, you got me there." Reaching into the water, I bring up a few small stones worn smooth by the current. I toss one back toward the middle of the river. It plops and vanishes beneath the surface.

"Could you...I dunno, maybe be afraid that this admiral's right?"

"What do you mean?"

"That maybe you'll go see this ship, see how you fit into whatever he has going on, and decide you don't want to be a gausser after all."

I wing another stone, trying to make it skip. It sinks immediately. I lean over and post my chin on one hand. Could C be right? Am I afraid of being tempted by whatever the admiral has planned for me? No, of course not. C's projecting. She doesn't want me to be a gausser. She's never made a secret of it. "No, I don't think that's it."

"No?" she asks thoughtfully. "You never told me exactly, what did you do when K blabbed about Jay's *'Doctor'*?"

"Why?"

"'Cause I want to know. Walk me through it. I know you didn't get anything from Jay. So how'd you find him?"

She's right, Jay didn't have any contact with the Doctor. It all went through Jay's coach, Ben Irwin. Ben Irwin had been the hardest hack I've done.

Not the most difficult. The hardest.

It started like most of the others.

A little information leads to more, until you build up enough data to attempt a breach. And bang-bon, you crack his accounts. So you snoop, looking for leverage. And fuck did you find it. Leverage that could get him to do whatever you want. But please no, not that. You can find something else to use against him, you tell yourself. So you keep digging. You sift through his accounts all night, searching until the minute you have to leave for school the next day.

Exhausted.

Frustrated.

Brokenhearted.

There is nothing else. And you need the information he has.

So he receives an anonymous message routed through a proxy node. A simple ultimatum. *Ben Irwin, give me everything you've got on the Doctor, or the Ethics Ministry will find out about Anthony.*

"It was a bluff," I say, finishing the story. "But what kind of monster have I become to even threaten that?"

C's posture is rigid. I'm prepared for her to tell me how angry and disgusted and disappointed she is with me. Instead, she says, "It's not you, Gaby. You're not a monster. It's this obsession with becoming a gausser doing this. You belong in Intelligence."

"You don't know what you're talking about," I snap. "It's InDiv making me this way. They taught me this shit and now I can't turn it off, Catherine! *That's* the obsession. Now, when I meet someone, I'm not trying to get to know them. I'm only probing them for weaknesses. I snoop, and I steal information, and I hoard it. Even when I don't even need to, I'm just feeding this compulsion to, to—to just know. There's no privacy around me and, and..."

"Hey, hey," C says.

I hadn't noticed she'd gotten up and come over to me, but her arms are wrapped around me.

"It's okay," she says.

"It's not. I'm not a good person anymore, C."

"Yes you are. I wouldn't be friends with you if you weren't. You got that?"

I nod, even though I don't believe it.

"Now focus on your breathing," she says. "I don't want you having an attack way out here."

She sits down next to me on my rock. Our hips touch. A stretched moment passes in silence as I get control of my breathing. "Thanks for bringing me here," I say, working to control the hitch in my voice. "It's so peaceful."

C glides slack fingers through the current. "Sometimes I just gotta get out of LoLe, remind myself that not everyone lives like we do, you know?"

I nod, though she doesn't see it—she's looking out across the water. I know what C means, but also, I don't live the same way she does. We only ever talk *around* it, but I can't imagine what her nights are like.

"This is the same river that passes through LoLe, you know," C says. "It flows south and winds its way around the chemical plant, and then runs along Beridmore Ave." She twists around, pointing in an arc as if drawing the river's course in the sky.

I have to take her word for it. I know which way west is, but aside from that, I've been pretty turned around since we entered Pheritona. In LoLe, I orient myself by the smoke rising from the petrol plant. That pillar of noxious gasses rising into the sky has always been my guiding star. I get lost easily without it.

"I like to think about it," she continues. "By the time it gets to our neighborhood, the water's picked up all kinds of slime and chemicals so it's all gross. But it starts off clean. It's not the water's fault it gets polluted."

Before I can think of something to say, the single note of the flare event siren rings out from somewhere beyond the wall of trees. Then a second siren sounds from downriver. A moment later, C's wristcomm beeps a warning as my NeurX receives an emergency notification.

"Did you bring a parasol?" I ask.

C shakes her head. "There wasn't supposed to be any flares today."

Glancing around at our surroundings, I size up our options. "Come on," I say.

Splashing out of the water onto the bank, I realize C isn't at my side. She's a few paces back, slowly wading forward, her eyes locked to the west beyond the hill, as though she's mesmerized by what's coming. I pull her by the hand and we take shelter under a low shelf up the slope. It's a small space where the soil eroded into a relief at some point when the water level was much higher. We put our backs to the slope, reclining on an uncomfortable tangle of roots and packed earth where the deep shade has starved out the grass and other brush.

C checks her wristcomm. "It's going to be a small one. Says only three or four minutes."

That's long enough. People rarely die from being caught in a solar flare event, but even a minute in it is like hours of direct sunlight.

Flare event sirens sound off again, just like before, the one behind us in the neighborhood, and then the one downriver echoing it. The light intensifies, gradually turning the river and shoreline beyond into an overexposed scene too bright to look at. The shadow from the shelf we hide behind stretches long, shielding us from the majority of it. I figure my skin will protect me from the rest, but I worry the indirect light will be enough to burn C.

The leaves react to the sudden increase in UV radiation,

shifting colors. Dyrul trees evolved on Amiens. They have a defense against these events. In moments, they go from black to red to yellow. The ones hit the hardest are bleached white before our eyes. Then the trees begin to shed their leaves in batches before the damaged DNA can spread into the branches.

My heart races. As dangerous as it is to be caught outside unprepared in one of these events, our view is breathtaking. Lying here, looking up as the vibrant red, orange, and yellow leaves lazily spiral to the ground all around us, is nothing short of magical.

C grips my hand, our fingers thread together mimicking the roots below us.

"You should go," C says, looking into the branches. "Get out of LoLe. Off the planet. Even if it's just for a little while."

C talks about leaving often. Usually it's in a daydreamy sort of way, other times it's in a frightening way. "C, what are your plans after graduation?"

Her smile fades and I immediately regret asking. "I don't know," she says, looking down at our interlaced fingers.

"What's your career agent say?" Why did you ask that, Gaby?

The leaves collect around us in small drifts as the trees continue to shed. Each leaf falls like a delicate snowflake, a piece of a rainbow riding gentle, unseen streams in the air.

"He says..." C's thumb presses into the back of my hand. She probably doesn't even know she's squeezing hard enough to cause pain. "That I'm best suited for reproductive labor."

The echoing notes of the sirens blare out again. Curiously, they sound closer this time, but that isn't right. The towers don't move. No, not closer. Louder. They're louder because the leaves had been attenuating the soundwaves. Fewer leaves, less sound absorption.

"That's crap," I say. "You get good grades."

"I get okay grades."

A bright yellow leaf touches down in C's hair. I reach out

with my free hand, gently plucking it free. "But you're so good at sports. Couldn't you—"

"Gaby," she interrupts, shaking her head. "I'm decent. I'm mid-tier. Which, sure, mid-tier is pretty good for our neighborhood. But it's...it just isn't enough."

She tries to pull her hand away. I hold it tighter.

"You used to talk about maybe being a pilot. What about enlisting?"

"My career agent says my physical attributes outweigh my other aptitudes. If I enlist, I end up on the front lines." She looks me in the eye, her irises bouncing left and right as she focuses on one eye, then the other.

"What?" I whisper.

"You'll think I'm a coward."

"I won't. I promise."

She swallows. "I'm scared. I don't think I could kill someone."

Her confession makes me a liar. I do think she's a coward. We have to fight. The Commonwealth won't stop until they destroy our way of life. Sure, the meritocracy of the NCP can be harsh, but it's been scientifically proven that assigning people's careers based on their innate talents leads to prosperity for the society as a whole. Study after study shows that, on average, people lead happier lives when tasked to do something they're qualified to do. This is the way the megacorps have made things, because it's the way they ought to be.

The Commonwealth are called Stewies because they want everyone's rights to be equal, regardless of the individual's contribution, like society's some kind of stew. I can't imagine living in a world where an admiral, a VR star, and UBI lifers like my parents are all valued as equals. It makes no sense.

Had someone else confessed this to me, I might've called them a coward and spit in their face. But looking into C's eyes, it's all so much more complicated. This is the girl who got her jaw broken fighting two guys at once because they were picking on a younger girl. This is the girl who survives every day in a home so much worse than K's or even mine. Yes, she is a coward. But she is also brave. Sympathy and love overwhelm the initial disgust, and I don't know how I'm supposed to feel.

The light dims, like when thin clouds scuttle in front of the sun. We're on the tail end of the flare event. The trees above are mostly barren.

I grip her hand tightly. "There's got to be something you can do other than have kids."

"That's an important job too," C says robotically. "If we don't keep having kids, the Commonwealth will win through sheer numbers."

A pithier version of the same logic is commonly displayed in VR ads. The propaganda is right. Seventy years of conflict have claimed an unfathomable number of lives. All those sons and daughters, sisters and...and brothers.

They come from parents. Citizens of the State need to keep having babies. Some of those babies will grow up to be soldiers, while others' duty will be to have more babies. It's what K will probably end up doing—if she doesn't become some kind of VR star—she'll be happy enough with that sort of life. But I want something different for C, because I know C wants something different for herself.

C scoffs. "Of course, I'll have to be assigned a husband."

They do that sometimes for citizens entering into reproductive labor contracts. The ones who can't find a mate of their own. The ones who have written themselves off as undesirable or unlovable.

Sometimes I think I see C looking at me the way I hide looking at K. I want her to feel loved. I want her to know she has options. That she doesn't have to resign herself to a loveless, arranged marriage. Or any marriage for that matter.

As the light dims and leaves continue to glide down around us, something comes over me. I reach up and touch C's cheek. Guiding her chin, I bend toward her until our lips meet. C kisses me back at first, then stops, lowering her head so my lips can only reach her brow.

Oh shit, what have I done? I pull away, releasing her hand. "I'm sorry. I don't know why I…" I trail off, unsure of how to back out of this mess with the least amount of rejection and embarrassment. Clearly I've mistaken how she looks at me. "I know you're not like me," I mumble.

Tears pool in C's eyes, moistening her bottom lashes. The lower note signaling the end of the solar flare event blasts from the towers. Then C's wristcomm beeps, no doubt saying the same.

She pulls away from me and sits up against the shelf, drawing her knees up toward her face. "It's not that at all, Gabs." She turns her face away. "I don't want to be your second choice."

My mouth opens, but I can't find any words. I want to tell her it isn't like that. That she's wrong. But I don't have it in me to lie to her again so soon.

"Come on, let's head back," she says quietly.

We collect our shoes without a word. The dyrul trees stand naked. The ground is littered in color, and the river flows in reds and yellows. Dyruls are always growing new buds. They'll sprout new leaves within a day or two.

The mood hangs heavy on my neck during the quiet walk home. Dismal gray clouds roll in, darkening the sky as we come out onto our street. C's apartment one way, mine the other.

"Are we okay?" C asks.

I manage a smile—one part genuine, one part forced. "Always."

C sits down on the curb next to the remains of what was once the street in front of our homes. Both of our families' apartments are in a long row of connected buildings. Each identical to the next, aside from changes brought about by generations worth of dilapidation and DIY renovations. C gazes down the street toward her unit. By this time of day, there's a good chance her dad will be there.

I plop down next to her.

"Why do you think our planet is so poor?" C asks absentmindedly. "You know, compared to the others."

"Well, not all of it. I mean, we were just in Pheritona. It's nice."

"Pheritona is about as good as it gets here. This is what most of Amiens looks like. Shitholes, just like what we live in."

With all her traveling for sports, she'd know that better than me. "Supposedly, LoLe has some of the first buildings in the whole solar system. They say they were made from repurposed pieces of some of the original generational ships from Old Earth."

"Yeah, I've heard. You believe it?" C asks.

"I don't know. I tried to fact check it a couple years back."

C lets out a weak laugh. Weak or not, it's still good to hear. "Of course you did."

"Couldn't find much. But one of the original ships was named *The Lefeld*, so who knows? I don't think that's why though, I think we're poor because we're tidally locked."

"What's that have to do with it?"

"No space elevators. So it's expensive to ship stuff off-world. Less exports, less incoming money."

She doesn't seem to listen as she stares down the street toward home.

"C, you wanna stay the night at my place? I'll sneak you in and..." C looks at me with an expression I can't read. The kiss flashes in my mind. "I, I mean," I stammer. "Just as friends, of course." Inside I'm screaming.

C shakes her head and stands up. "I'll have to go home sometime."

We hug before going our separate ways. Walking away, I hear her call my name. When I turn, C points up and mouths a single word, *Go*. Then she turns back around too soon to see me smiling at her. This time, all genuine.

I slip inside the apartment, careful not to make too much noise. The air is stuffy and smells acrid. There are signs of another one of my parents' arguments. Four days' worth of takeout cartons appear to have been rapidly cleared from the coffee table. I sigh, wondering how long they'll decorate the floor. A few days? A week?

My parents are both sitting in their individual recliners, their individual headsets covering their eyes, probably watching individual VRs. Quality time. Together.

I go to the kitchenette and tap the vending machine screen awake. The welcome message reads, *Amenity Inc. A Swayy Company*, before asking for my iDent account. I type in my dad's code and start browsing. My first three selections return with the message, *Not At This Location*, and a message crawls across the bottom of the screen, letting me know that to enable Silver Service levels, this housing block needs to spend an additional 9,943 merits per week. I can't remember my block ever being anything other than Bronze-level service. I choose a sandwich, and after it's dispensed below, I bring it to the living room. Eating it standing up, I watch the rise and fall of Mom and Dad's chests. The only clear sign they're alive.

I put the last bite in my mouth, wondering where I left my characters in my latest script. Probably somewhere near the Point of No Return. I haven't thought much about writing over the last few years. It's just something I do occasionally when the urge strikes and there's nothing more pressing to take care of. A way to pass time.

Perhaps it's because the admiral had brought it up in the context of a career that I think of it now. But watching my parents waste away before my eyes, living a scripted fiction that someone —someone that could've been me, in another life—wrote, I wonder how much harm it does.

For many people, it's probably a temporary escape. A few hours away from an otherwise productive, quality life. But how many people are like my parents, using VRs to ignore the death of their actual lives, just waiting around until their bodies slowly catch up? And if I had gone into scriptwriting, would I be contributing to those deaths? Is the writer complicit?

C had admitted to being scared. But she didn't say she was scared to die, she said she was scared to kill. It strikes me then, no matter what path my life takes, I'm destined to kill. Should it be at the end of a plasma rifle as a gausser, or by piloting a drone in some act of proxy violence, or through anesthetizing the masses with VRs. The end result will always be the same for me.

CHAPTER
SIX

As I finish stuffing the last shirt I can fit into my rucksack, Dad comes booming through the front door singing "Rise, Champions Rise." A sure sign the Lefeld Lions won the match. His drunken, out-of-key voice cuts through the tissue-paper walls so clearly he might as well be in my bedroom with me.

When you live with a drunk, a mean one, you do everything you can to avoid them when they're on a bender. With experience, you get good at it. For the first few days of the month after basic stipends are deposited, you become a ghost. On holidays, you become a ghost. After the more important sporting events, you guessed it, you become a ghost.

You find a coping mechanism. You learn to use it. To mold it into something less ugly, less sad, less ordinary. Ylfa is just such a mechanism. A character in my latest screenplay who will—if I ever get around to finishing it—become the Ghost of Belholt. Haunting the palace to sow unrest among the nobles.

You put a little something of yourself in your characters. A few drops of metaphorical blood, add in a bit of what you wish you were, and a touch of something unrelated, something from someone else perhaps, a trait, a yearning, a compulsion. You mix them all together until it's difficult for even you to tell what came from where. That's when your character takes on a life all their own.

Ylfa could use her magic to slide through the veil and walk straight out of here with only a momentary, unexplainable chill presence in the air to indicate her passing. But she's not real. And I am not her.

Here in the real world, I need to leave my bedroom and deal with this, because I will not be able to avoid him today.

I shoulder my bag, pocket the transit pass Admiral Davis had couriered over to me yesterday, and go to say goodbye. My mom meets me in the main room wearing the same sweats she's worn all week.

"My baby's all grown up." She grips me, pressing our bodies together. I crinkle my nose against the oniony smell of BO wafting off her. When was the last time she'd showered?

My dad steps out of the kitchenette, fresh bottle in hand. "Where's she goin'?"

"Remember, Thomas? She's a special guest of Admiral... What was his name, honey?"

"Admiral Davis," I answer. I didn't tell them about Morgan York being promoted and serving as the XO. I'm not about to light a fuse with no idea what kind of bomb it attaches to.

Dad takes a long pull from his bottle. Foam hangs in the wiry bristles of his unshaven face. "Oh yeah. That's today? Still don't understand what an admiral would be doing with your daughter though."

And there it is, *your daughter*. Sober, he has the decency to hide it, but drunk, the truth comes out of him. I'm not *his* daughter. Doesn't matter that he raised me. I'm not his blood. Just a living, breathing reminder of the time his wife was unfaithful. Not that it even needs to be said. I look nothing like anyone else in this family. Whenever I can, I avoid thinking about it. If

Thomas isn't my dad, then Julian was only my half-brother, and that breaks my heart every time I have to confront it.

One of my first memories is a rambling bedtime story Dad told me. We must not have had the bunk beds yet, because I was sleeping on a small, spongy mattress on the floor. When he sat down, the whole mattress leaned into his weight, waking me up. He hovered over me. His breath was warm and astringent with liquor. I'm sure I didn't understand what the smell was back then. I didn't understand much of the story either, but it stuck with me—every word of it—to be dissected and picked through repeatedly as I grew up.

"Hey, Gabzilla. Want a bedtime story?"

I shook my head. That day I'd played with the older kids. This was before I had my implant, and the physical exertion had been an exhausting strain on my lungs.

"Don't be silly. You love stories. And I got a special one tonight. What d'ya say?"

"Okay...Daddy." My airways were so constricted by my asthma I could barely speak.

"Good girl. Once, not so long ago, there was a man who loved a woman with all his heart. The happiest day of his life was the day he asked her to marry him. She said yes! Can you believe it? How could he have gotten so lucky, he wondered?" He toyed with his wedding band, twisting it this way and that over a finger that was clearly thinner than it had been when the ring had been sized.

"A year later, he became even more lucky because she had given birth to his baby. A boy named Julian." I perked up hearing the name. Even then, Jules was my entire world. "That's right, that's your big brother's name. For a while, the three of them were happy together, but then something strange happened.

"See, at the time, the man was working very hard to earn money for his new family, working long hours in the factory. He could've worked less, but the man's wife could only get a part-time job.

"But even though the man and his wife barely got to see each other, a miracle happened. Can you guess what it was? She was going to have another baby! The news made the man so happy. Their career in reproductive labor was going good and soon they'd both get to quit their jobs."

Mom's silhouette had appeared in the doorway then. She listened for a moment, shook her head, and vanished down the hall.

"But then the wife confessed she did something bad. She had made this new baby with a different man. An offworlder slimeball she'd met at her part-time job. This made the man very sad, but he was a real stand-up kind of guy, and he stuck it out. And when the new baby girl came out, he raised her like his own. He didn't make her feel bad for being the daughter of a cheater.

"He didn't even make her feel bad that the new baby girl damaged the mother on the inside and she couldn't have any more kids after that. They were hoping for at least six kids, so the money they'd get off basic would be decent. But the man didn't even blame the girl for costing them all that money."

"Thomas, I told you," my mom says, snatching me from the memory. "The admiral is going to show her a special project he wants her to be a part of."

My dad takes a few heavy steps toward us. He looks me in the eye with cloudy, bloodshot orbs. "More like you're the admiral's whore, I expect."

I drop my rucksack and step toward him, my fists balled at my hips.

"Thomas, stop. Honey, ignore him. You know how he gets when he's drunk."

"Yeah, just ignore me. I suppose that's what you're good at, Bev, ignoring me. Ignore the man at home and go find yourself a...

Well, I guess I don't know what he was. Did he pay you, Beverly?" My mom turns away, and he swings his interest back to me. "Well, I suppose at least you've got the sense to be a whore for somebody important."

"Screw you!" I yell. I want so badly to hit him, but my brain seems to refuse to send the command to my fist to swing.

"Same moral fortitude as her mother," he mumbles to no one in particular.

"Both of you, stop it this instant!" my mom says.

"Don't get mad at me just 'cause I'm honest enough to say it to her face, Bev. Just last night you said she and the admiral were probably fucking."

"Thomas!" Mom screams.

A smothering silence drops over the room.

Don't cry, don't you dare cry, Gaby. I swallow the lump in my throat. "Nice. Real nice." I spin to leave, yanking my rucksack from the floor.

"Gaby, stop," my mom calls.

"No! I hate you both!" I yell as I storm away.

CHAPTER
SEVEN

The Sonosim Interplanetary Port is larger and busier than I could have imagined. The cavernous space echoes in a directionless waterfall of conversations and footfalls. An occasional public address announcement cuts through the drone, but between the terrible acoustics and background murmur, the announcer might as well be speaking in tongues.

The domed roof follows an industrial design philosophy, with exposed beams and bracers and light fixtures, and a network of catwalks for easy maintenance. Below it, a sea of moving bodies makes it difficult to see anything I can use as a landmark.

Among the beehive of activity, it's easy to spot the regulars. They move with confidence, doing their best to avoid the herds of mouth gaping, big-eyed tourists and first-timers. I wait behind a family of the latter. Once they disperse, I step forward to study a map.

They designed the port with an inner ring, an outer ring, and six color-coded concourses connecting the two like the spokes of a wheel. My gate is Orange-6. I get my bearings and start off doing my best impression of someone who's been here before.

En route, I pass a promenade. Around the perimeter are various food stalls and keepsake shops, as well as a play area for children—its network of brightly colored tubes is like a little world all its own. Like the gerbil enclosures I've seen in the LoLe pet shop.

Strolling past the food stalls, I glance over the menus displayed on tall, vertical screens. Everything is overpriced, so I walk away empty-handed and continue toward Concourse Orange. At gate after gate, I pass picturesque displays of intimacy. People saying goodbyes. Others being reunited. I become a voyeur, peeking into their lives in a way hacking doesn't even afford me. Such beautiful, vulnerable moments.

Seeing them, I feel profoundly alone.

Not that I'd want my mom and dad here. No need for strangers to see the heartwarming send-off they'd given me. But I wish K and C were here. They'd lift my spirits. They'd force me to laugh. Probably at someone else's expense, but still.

Look at that Tobie over there, I imagine K saying much too loudly while pointing at the lanky boy with his poodle hair. And if C were here seeing the blonde looking down her nose at me like that, she'd probably start yelling obscenities at her and challenging her to a fight. I would be mortified, I would try to get them to stop, and I'd even apologize on their behalf. But most of all, I would love them for it.

According to my itinerary, I'm running early, so I duck into an Honortorium I spot tucked away off the main concourse walkway. Entering the Honortorium is like stepping through a portal to another place. Another world. An island far removed from the barely contained chaos a few short meters away. Thick walls and a noise-canceling system lining the entrance dull the sound from outside to a hum. This is a place of reverence and quiet introspection. One part art museum, one part church.

Five large oil paintings, hung with geometric precision, dominate the far wall and draw my attention. The exalted presidents of the five great megacorporations. Each painting's delicate, textured strokes are lit by the warm glow of mounted sconces hanging above them.

Incense hangs thick and potent in the air. I float over to one of the stone benches and sit, admiring the paintings.

I've heard there's a regulation against displaying any of the presidents with greater authority than the others, at least within an NCP building. That seems to hold true here. Each of the five paintings is equal in size. But the president of Swayy Corp., Nadiya Ostapivna Yakovenko, is displayed in the center. After all, someone has to be in the center, right? And Swayy Corp. owns this building, along with much of Amiens.

In her painting, President Yakovenko is poised and regal. Her black curls frame a stern face, turned slightly away but watching from the corners of her eyes. Here she appears about thirty, which is perhaps ten years younger than she looks in current VR footage. In truth, she's over a hundred, and she is the youngest of the presidents.

On either side of her are Xiao Hu of the Maeda Conglomerate and Harrison Madigan of Telecannón Inc., two old men with grave expressions. On the wings are Edward Oliver Roth of K'Tagri United Enterprises, whose gigantic, bristly mustache has become the subject of numerous jokes, and Caitlin Brady of ViSHO Inc. She's the only one of them who hints at a smile in her painting.

I check the clock in my NeurX against the itinerary. Not long now. Once I board the shuttle, there will be no turning back. Whatever Admiral Davis has planned, I'll be along for the ride, far from home, far from everyone I know. Except Morgan. Morgan, who I haven't seen in years. What will he think of me? What I've become, going into the Intelligence Division, of all things? I'd be a disappointment to Jules, I suspect. I don't see why Morgan won't feel the same.

I remove the plastic transit pass from my pocket, tapping its edge against the smooth stone of the bench. The transit pass would get me back home. All I'd need to do is walk out and hop on a bus. Maybe if I go home now my parents will let go of this repulsive idea that I'm sleeping with the admiral, I could go back to school, see my friends after class and on the weekends. Things could go back to...back to what? Normal?

I stare into the faces of each of them, imagining them sitting around a boardroom table and having to make that fateful decision, classifying the mission on Praxis Station as Omega Priority. How heavy a weight a decision like that must be? Knowing they're sending so many people off to die. Having to decide that the mission is more valuable than the lives. What an honor it would be to be one of the lives on the scale for the entire board to measure.

You will not go back home.

You will not be a coward.

Is it my voice in my head, or Jules'? It doesn't matter. I'll go to this training exercise. I'll feign interest in whatever sales pitch the admiral has cooked up, politely turn down his offer, then get the CRISPR treatments and the transfer to gauss trooper camp I've been promised.

Once I'm a gausser, life will be simple. Straightforward. There is the enemy. Kill them before they kill you. An honorable life. A life Jules would be proud to have his sister live. A life my parents can't ignore.

I get up and make for the Orange-6 gate. There's a woman in a light gray jumpsuit, the general service uniform of the navy, holding a handwritten sign that says:

Gallagher
/ Rhodes

Gallagher? I had assumed I'd be the only guest. Is Gallagher another student? As I approach, the soldier's eyes flit from one passerby to another and don't land on me until I'm close enough to kick her. Even then, she mostly looks past me.

"Are you lost?" she asks, her eyes still scanning the crowd.

"No," I say, although I sound unconvincing, even to myself.

"I'll try to get security over. They can help find your parents."

"Excuse me?" Now the soldier actually looks at me. A headband that matches her uniform holds her straight brown hair back, showing her round face and soft features. "My name is Gabrielle Rhodes." I lift a finger toward her sign.

"Oh. My apologies. I'm your pilot, Lieutenant Junior Grade Meyers. Please follow me, ma'am."

It feels strange, being called ma'am by an older woman.

She guides me through a hatch and down a short boarding bridge into the shuttle. All the shuttle's facilities are visible with a swivel of my head. It's all a single cabin with minimal separation between each section: a two-seated cockpit, a common area with built-in furniture, a restroom, a kitchenette, and at the back, four sleeping capsules where the form of a woman is hunched over, storing luggage in a compartment.

She stands upright and turns. My heart goes tachycardic.

You could have told me I'd be traveling with someone, given me a million guesses to guess who, and I would've gotten a million guesses wrong.

The Gallagher from the handwritten sign is *Lauren* Gallagher! She needs no introduction, but somewhere at the edge of my consciousness I hear Lieutenant Junior Grade Meyers beginning formal introductions anyway.

Ms. Gallagher is *one of*, if not *the* most recognized, correspondent from the Media Ministry in the entire solar system. Unimaginably, her beauty is even more devastating in person. Not in the way K is beautiful. Ms. Gallagher is nothing like the Amienite standard of beauty. She is exotic and ostentatious.

Instead of the Amienites' porcelain skin, hers has a sort of bronze glow to it. And her long hair swirls in bright gradients, landing on every stop of the color wheel. Stylish cat-eye glasses perch upon the delicate sweep of her nose, complementing her sharp, angular facial features. The glasses are almost certainly an affectation, and behind them, her wide-set eyes are the lightest blue I've ever seen. She steps toward us, wearing a designer, earth-toned dress that simultaneously looks professional and leaves little to the imagination.

As Meyers finishes the introductions, Ms. Gallagher puts her palms together and gives a slight bow. "I'll thank you to just call me Lauren," she says, flashing us both a smile.

Dozens of responses bounce around the spinning bingo-cage of my thoughts, but I'm pretty sure the response that leaves my mouth is, "I'm Gaby."

For a flash, her face takes on a quizzical expression, then whatever answer she was searching for seems to click into place, and the practiced smile returns. It's so quick a change, I might've imagined it.

Meyers glances down at the military bracer on her left arm. It looks almost identical to the one the admiral wore, if several sizes smaller. She presses a command and the door to the shuttle closes. "Okay, ladies, Sonosim is ready to launch us."

I follow Meyers to the cockpit area and stand dumbly for a moment behind the co-pilot chair. Am I allowed to sit there? Meyers doesn't pay me any mind while logging herself into the pilot's terminal:

User: MeyersS-R7A

The authorization code is hidden by a series of redacted symbols on the screen, but I clock her keystrokes. *+Boomb00m*

I'm doing it again. Being a snoop. I wish I could mentally delete Meyers' credentials so I'm not tempted to break into her accounts and read her messages. There's no need to do this anymore. I have another way to get CRISPR, a legitimate way. So why can't I stop?

Meyers notices me standing uncomfortably. She smiles at me and throws a look to the main portion of the cabin. "Strap in."

I step into the common area and buckle into a chair. Lauren does the same, sitting across from me in the bench seat that could pass as a sofa.

"I love your dress." I love your dress? Really? Come on, Gaby.

The shuttle rocks as the launcher arm it's hooked up to swivels.

"Thank you," Lauren says. "It's Stolm Locke from the Becoming Autumn collection."

Stolm Locke! I want to ask how much it cost, but decide against it. It's a normal question in LoLe, but I've heard it's considered rude elsewhere.

The nose of the shuttle tilts up. Fifteen degrees. Thirty. Forty-Five. Ninety degrees. The backs of our chairs turn into beds.

Meyers is in constant contact with ground control. They pass commands and status updates back and forth, mostly in abbreviated jargon I don't understand. When they reach the countdown though, I understand that.

Three.

Two.

One.

The jarring force of the launch smashes me into my seat and the cabin rattles. From my position in the common area, between the high headrests of the pilot chairs, I have a semi-obstructed view through the cockpit glass. Visibility disappears in a white rush of cloud vapor. Then a change in momentum. Stomach acid reaches into my throat and I swallow the urge to vomit. The shuttle's pion engines roar to life, and it feels as though someone's sitting on my chest. The clouds make way for blue sky, which dissolves into black as we leave the Amiens' atmosphere.

For the first time in my life, I see a field of stars with my own eyes. Not an image of it captured by a camera and filtered through a screen or VR headset, but right here, beyond the window. It's not the same as watching the sun set, but it's something, and I cherish it all the same.

The pressure on my chest dissipates in a moment of true weightlessness. Lauren's brightly colored hair fans out in all directions. She could be underwater. Then the artificial gravity of the shuttle spools up, pulling everything back toward the floor.

Meyers' head pops around the headrest of the pilot's chair. "You okay back there? You look a little green."

I spread the thumb and first finger on my left hand, then realize she might not know the gesture, so I replace it with a thumbs-up instead.

A sphere the size of a large fist floats up, taking a position hovering just over Lauren's right shoulder. There's a flat spot on the front with a camera sensor, and the petite disc of a repulsor glows softly on the bottom, pushing against the artificial gravity of the shuttle.

Lauren sees me looking. "Don't mind this, it's just my cameratom."

Now I know what the glasses are for. They give her remote access to her camera automaton.

"I knew a Moore student was tagging along, but *Gaby Rhodes*? Isn't this a surprise?"

I tilt my head in puzzlement. "You know me?"

Lauren's eyebrows rise above the rims of her glasses, a smile playing at her lips. "Oh... I've heard a bit about you."

My cheeks go hot and I turn away. How does a famous journalist know who I am? "Why? I mean, how?"

"We have a mutual friend. Morgan York."

"You know Morgan?"

"The Hero of Praxis?" she says, winking at me. "I did a piece on him some time back."

"Really? I never saw it."

"No one did. It turned out unsuitable for publication." She must read my face because she answers my unasked question. "Stories get shelved. It happens more often than you'd expect."

"So, what's the Media Ministry want with a training exercise?" I ask.

"You kidding? Any time there's a chance to do a unique piece on our heroic war efforts, the Ministry will be there to pander." There's a tone to her voice when she says it. A patronizing type of sarcasm, maybe?

"We'll be entering blink in a moment," Meyers calls from the pilot's chair. "It's about to get loud."

An ascending hum builds from the back of the ship, smothering all other sounds in the cabin before it crescendos in a crack much like the whip of a sail going taut in a strong wind. Which I suppose isn't a connection most people would make, but I've heard the sound so many times in VRs from when I began writing my current screenplay. Infatuated with the historical pirates of Old Earth, I immersed myself in it for months.

The crack dies away, replaced by the rhythmic chugging of a single graviton piston.

"So," I say, "Morgan told you about me?"

"All these questions. Maybe you should be the journalist? But yes. He's quite fond of you, you know. Looks at you like a little sister. Is that why you're here? Did Morgan arrange for you to be aboard for the..." she gives me a meaningful look I can't decode. "*...training exercise?*"

Why would she be saying it like it's some kind of inside joke? I try not to read too much into it. She's from a different planet. Nuances in mannerisms and tone could carry different connotations coming from her. "No. Admiral Davis asked me along. I don't think Morgan knows. It's supposed to be a surprise."

"Huh," Lauren says, tapping a finger against her cheek, seeming suddenly far away.

"So, did you and Morgan stay in contact after your story?"

"I'm tired. I think I'll get some rest." Lauren unbuckles and stands. She reaches to me and lightly brushes her hand through a lock of my hair. "Goodnight, Kitten."

I feel another flush rise at being nicknamed *Kitten* by a celebrity. And as I turn my face away, Lauren slips into one of the sleeping capsules and draws the shutter closed. Was that misdirection? Did she intentionally embarrass me to slip away without the need to deflect further questions? No, it's all in your head, Gaby. You've spent too much time around wannabe Intelligence Division students who play at being spies. Not everyone is working an angle.

I allow my cheeks a moment to cool, then turn to Lieutenant Junior Grade Meyers. "So, are you allowed to tell me where we're going?"

"We'll rendezvous with the *Discordia* at Okina Aka's L4 Lagrange point. From there, I'm not authorized to say."

Okina Oka is the first planet past the Struuth Belt. Maeda owns it, or most of it at least. And it has a lot of volcanic activity. That's about the extent of my knowledge of the planet. Doesn't matter though, we're not visiting it, just meeting at one of its Lagrange points. The instrument panels show a slightly curved route toward the nondescript point in space, keeping a wide berth from gravity wells, presumably to maximize blink drive speed.

"How fast are we going?"

"See this instrument?" Meyers points to a graph displaying a knee curve. An indicator bounces back and forth like a tennis ball toward the peak, right before the plateau of diminishing returns. She explains that navigators call this the clock. The X axis is input power, while the Y axis depicts distance per blink. A number below the graph stays steady, showing the RPM of the graviton piston, directly corresponding with the rate of blink.

Beyond the thick safety glass, the starlight warps and twists in on itself as the blink drive folds space-time around the ship at roughly twelve times per second. Each fold instantaneously putting us over six million kilometers in front of our previous position as we move-but-don't-move at about twenty-five percent the speed of light.

"So how long?"

"About thirty hours," Meyers says mildly.

I lightly hammer my fist against the co-pilot seat. "So I have some time to kill."

Wandering back the few steps to the common area, I try to decide how to entertain myself. There's a cabinet marked *VR Headsets*. No way the shuttle has net access out here; they must have programming stored in memory. Glancing back at the sleeping capsules where Lauren Gallagher is resting, I wonder what type of security the Media Ministry installs on their cameratoms. Could I crack it without the net to research its weaknesses?

I'm not going to find out. I need to stop being a snoop.

I retrieve one of the VR headsets from the cabinet and make myself comfortable on the sofa. Sliding on the headset, everything goes dark, but I hesitate before turning it on. I suppose I could try to hack the cameratom, and even if I'm successful—which I probably won't be, but even if I am—I won't *spy* on Lauren. I won't use it, I just want to see if I can. I might as well, right? Sure don't want to watch VR for the next thirty hours.

What the hell? I shut down my NeurX and reboot into the cloned operating system I installed on a secret partition. My NeurX is the property of Swayy Corp.'s Intelligence Division, so naturally they have access to it if, or rather more accurately, *when* someone wants to poke around. Having a hidden OS gives me a place to install the less-legal software I use for hacking.

The obfuscation won't hold up if someone who knows their stuff does a thorough investigation. But a quick look-see—the kind which seems likely—isn't likely to find it.

Once my NeurX is back up and running, I scroll through the menus and open my wireless sniffer app. Aboard the shuttle, there are only a few wireless ports, so the cameratom's easy to find. That turns out to be the only easy part. For the next several hours I probe for security weaknesses, trying brute force attacks, PL prompt attacks, and as a Hail Mary, I even attempt an Amaxx gambit without knowing whether the cameratom even uses Amaxx architecture.

None of it gets me anywhere. I'm about to give up when I have an idea. I make a copy of my Spectator app and repackage it, naming it as an innocuous-sounding hotfix update, and push it out, not to the cameratom, but to its peripheral device, the glasses Lauren wears. Next time she reboots, the false update should pop up in her vision. If she gives it any thought, she'll notice it doesn't look like a regular update, and realize that out here on a military shuttle, far away from public net access, there'd be no way for her to get a random update.

But it amazes me how many people, even smart people, don't pay any mind to such things, selecting OKAY just to move on with whatever they were doing. If she installs it, the Spectator app won't give me any control over her cameratom, but it will let me link in with my NeurX in real-time to see and hear whatever her cameratom is currently recording.

Immediately, I feel a tinge of regret. I'm ashamed of myself. What am I doing? This is wrong and I know better. I wish I could unsend it, but it's too late. If she falls for it, I'll cut off access from my end immediately, I promise myself.

It's going to be such a relief to get my transfer to gausser camp. I don't like the person I've become in the Intelligence Division.

THE GAUSSER'S BRIEFING ROOM SEATED A HUNDRED OR so in seven ascending quarter-circle rows. Padded chairs, each with a personal terminal screen built into the right arm, faced a raised platform with a holographic projector sticking out of it like a miniature volcano. Morgan and Jules found seats as the lights dimmed to draw focus to the presentation.

It projected an out-of-scale model of the entire solar system. The planets had to be depicted bloated and too close together, otherwise they'd be invisible. Master Sergeant Murro stepped through and Tagis, one of the outer planets, orbited into her shoulder. It broke apart into individual pixels of light, exploding like a loosely packed snowball, only to reform a few seconds later in front of her.

The wan light washed out her tanned complexion and made the dark bags beneath her eyes look like bruises. "Listen up, people. We got something new today. We're taking a break from fighting the Commonwealth. I trust there won't be any complaints about that; I figure this lot is getting bored of killing Stewies anyhow."

A few people chuckled and one guy in the back hollered, "I could kill a few more."

Murro pointed to where the voice came from. "I'll hold you to it, Ruiz, but it'll have to wait for the next mission. Thirty-one hours ago, the Telecannōn cruiser Icarus was ambushed, boarded, and left adrift with less than fifty survivors. Hostiles have been identified as the Yingzi Zhēnxiàng."

"They putting us on?" Morgan whispered to Jules as similar hushed chatter swept the briefing room.

Murro folded her arms. "Command isn't sure what's emboldened the syndicate to move from organized crime to terrorism, but their objective seems to have been to steal this." The projection switched to a simple reinforced steel box with hard-wired data ports. "For those of you who've never seen one of these, this is a biobox. A biological computer that an AI lives in. This one is of particular interest to high command because it holds top secret data."

"So what?" Petty Officer Ward said from near the front. "That's why it's got an AI, right? The Yingzi might as well play a game of Clawclap with it for all the good it'll do 'em." Pockets of brief laughter bubbled up through the room.

"That's where things get interesting. Our intel states the Yingzi Zhēnxiàng may be in possession of some new technology that'll allow them to crack the AI if given enough time. That's why the board has marked this mission Omega Priority."

Morgan rubbed at the back of his neck. Glancing around, he saw a lot of his peers shifting in their seats. No one was laughing anymore. Omega Priority missions went above high command, above any individual megacorp, needing unanimous approval from all five presidents. Whatever data the AI was protecting didn't just affect Telecannōn. It touched the entire NCP. Omega Priority missions were practically a campfire story. A military boogeyman. A signal the board was willing to sacrifice an extraordinary number of lives and resources to achieve success.

"Command is confident the Yingzi Zhēnxiàng brought the biobox here," the master sergeant said. The display zoomed in on a space station way out on the fringes of the system. "This is Praxis Station." Next the image broke apart into an exploded view of the station's innards, reforming into a three-dimensional, color-coded map. "Praxis is a commercial hub. It was once owned by K'Tagri, but they unincorporated it years ago. Officially, it's managed by a private investment firm. Unofficially, the Yingzi call the shots. Command believes the biobox is being held in one of these rooms." Six nav points lit up in unremarkable locations of the station.

"So we're going into a civilian station for a smash and grab?" Jules asked, loud enough for everyone to hear.

"No, Rhodes." Murro said. "This is a seek and destroy. Our mission is to find it, visually confirm authenticity via its serial number, then destroy the biobox. Make no mistake, our instructions are explicit here, ladies and gentlemen. We are not to make any attempt to recover the biobox. It is already considered compromised. Confirm. Then destroy. By any means necessary."

"But it's a *civilian* station," a woman said from the other side of the room, getting to the heart of what Morgan was positive Jules' had been asking as well.

"Yes," Murro said, her tone about as soft and pliable as steel. "Perhaps you heard me when I said this is an Omega Priority mission. Command is *unconcerned* with civilian casualties."

Silence fell over the briefing room.

"Am I making myself clear, soldiers?"

"Sir, yes, sir!" they all chorused.

"Good. Omega Priority missions are rare. Careers are made in these moments. There is glory to be won. Or shame to bear."

Master Sergeant Murro went on to explain the full plan, and

it was ugly. Intel said the Yīngzi Zhēnxiàng had been fortifying the station for years. Heavy railgun batteries, satellite strike platforms, point defense guns, military grade shielding. And the NCP let it happen. It hadn't seemed like a threat. And it wouldn't be now, not really, had there not been for one critical factor: time.

If they had the time, the *Sedna* and her two destroyers could sit 5,000 clicks out, where their evasive maneuvers would keep the station's guns from acquiring an effective firing solution. They could send in fighters to clear the defenses, or wait for battleship backup, or, hell, bring in a dreadnought that could overwhelm the station's defenses in a few short minutes.

But they didn't have the luxury of time.

So the plan was to bring their battle group into close range and slug it out while launching the gausser teams right in the middle of the fray.

The gaussers would need to spacewalk as much as two kilometers to reach the Praxis Station's outer hull, breach it, fight through whatever defenses waited for them, and destroy the biobox. Individual assignments and updates would be sent out after they exit blink and receive the latest situation report.

There'd be heavy losses among the gaussers, but the *Sedna* might have it even worse. It was a carrier, typically kept out of harm's way as much as possible. She wasn't built for close-range brawls. Morgan wondered, if he managed to survive, would there even be a ship to go back to?

CHAPTER
NINE

I've been bingeing a VR for hours. It's a comedic-drama about a plucky crew of asteroid miners and their hijinks in a fictionalized version of the Struuth Belt. Jackie just punched out the slaver who'd kidnapped Ming when an urgent beeping cuts through the narrative's audio.

I pause the show in time to hear Lieutenant Junior Grade Meyers call out, "Attention any nearby NCP vessels, please respond."

I pull the VR headset free and climb into the empty co-pilot's chair. "What's going on?"

Meyers taps a command on her console. The alerts go mute, but the warning lights continue their choreographed dance in silence. "Any nearby NCP vessels, this is NCP shuttle *Griffin 14*, transporting civilians. We're hitting heavy graviton bursts. Suspected interdiction. Dropping out of blink. Urgent assistance requested." Lieutenant Junior Grade Meyers' voice maintains a calm professionalism, but tension is written in the tight lines of her lips.

I feel useless in the co-pilot seat, my stomach knotting as a lesson from tactics class about graviton burst generators slides into place.

The chug and whir of the blink drive chokes silent. With the light no longer bending and twisting around us numerous times per second, the stars come into focus.

"Why's the blink drive off?" Lauren appears hovering over our shoulders, just as her cameratom hovers over hers.

"We're hitting graviton bursts," Meyers explains. "They'll burn out the drive, or worse, if we try to push through."

"What would cause that?" Lauren asks.

"They can be a natural phenomenon, but..."

I know what Meyers is thinking. Graviton bursts are used as an interdiction measure when one party doesn't want their enemy to make a fast retreat. It's usually used in warfare, but some-times... I don't say it. I don't even want to think it.

"LiDAR is picking up two incoming," Meyers continues.

"They're pirates, aren't they?" Lauren's voice is nearly a whisper.

"Sit down and strap in," Meyers orders.

Lauren disappears into the common area.

Meyers lights up the pion thrusters and the G-force from the acceleration sinks me into the back of the co-pilot's chair until the inertial neutralizers spin up and offset the pressure.

Looking at the LiDAR readouts, it's obvious the two objects are on an intercept course. They've already been accelerating too long and we're just beginning to build momentum. I'm no pilot, but I'm confident there isn't anything Meyers can do to keep us from getting out-paced.

"Uh, I think they're going to catch us," I say.

"Yeah, they're going to catch us," Meyers agrees, giving the console a dirty look as if it's the display's fault. There's barely a hint of worry in her voice. My heart is thundering in my chest, and here Meyers is, calm and in control. I can't help but admire the soldier.

"There's a weapons locker in this shuttle, right?" Lauren asks from behind us, her voice straining to reach over the growl of the thrusters.

"Plannin' to shoot it out with them?" I say.

"Don't be naïve, Kitten. We're three women, and none of us are important enough for the NCP to pay a ransom. You do not want to know what they'll do to us. The guns are to use on ourselves."

"Before we get too dramatic, ladies," Meyers says, "let's see what we're up against." Meyers presses a few commands on her screen. "Two TX-9 light attack craft."

Lauren says, "Those were decommissioned over a decade ago. They were pieces of junk."

It seems like a strange thing for a journalist to know, but this isn't the time to ask her about it.

Lauren continues, "They can pump out a lot of thrust, but their inertia neuts are oversized."

A starship's maneuverability isn't usually limited by its thrusters, or even by the pressure the fuselage can handle. It's limited by the organic life inside. By the frail human occupants' ability to endure G-forces. Fighter pilots and gaussers, with the implants grafted throughout their circulatory system, have an advantage here, but they make up a tiny fraction of the space-faring population. It's unlikely the pirates running us down will have those types of implants. So the difference between two crafts' maneuverability comes down to how quickly the inertial neutralizers can counteract the potentially deadly G-forces in hard turns.

There's always a tradeoff. Larger neuts can counteract more acceleratory forces, giving the ship better top-end acceleration, while smaller neuts spin up faster, relieving pressure quicker, which is better for tight maneuvers and dog-fighting. If Lauren is right, the TX-9s fall in the former camp.

Meyers runs her fingers over the LiDAR readout. The only objects are the two rapidly closing attack craft, and some other blip far away in the direction the two ships came from. That must be the source of the graviton bursts. "If I flip and burn, they'll have a lot of inertia to shed, so that'll buy us some time."

In a VR show, this is where we'd make for the belt, or a debris field, or some other nearby celestial object where we could use our superior maneuverability to make a harrowing escape. What the writers of those shows always ignore is that space is enormous, and startlingly empty. Without the blink drive, forced to use conventional thrust, it would take us days, maybe weeks, to get near anything.

"There's nowhere to lose them in open space," I point out.

"Can we get far enough away from the graviton thing to go back to blink?" Lauren asks.

"I doubt it..." Meyers says, tapping out more commands on the console. "Let's see, the effective radius of the bursts is about a hundred thousand clicks, and our acceleration peaks out at 6Gs..."

I sprint through the formula in my mind. We're already about seventy-five hundred meters from the graviton burst generator. If we can maintain a constant acceleration of 6G, traveling ninety-two thousand five-hundred kilometers— "That would take us twenty-nine minutes, thirty-one seconds."

"How did you..." Meyers trails off as she finishes putting the calculations into the computer. "You're right."

Lauren says, "Morgan wasn't exaggerating about you."

She keeps using his first name. How familiar are they? "It's too long. There's no way."

For a moment we sit silently watching the blips on the LiDAR readout gaining on us.

"Does the shuttle have any weapons at all?" I ask without much hope the answer would be anything other than—

"No," Meyers says without taking her eyes off the display. "We have a maintenance drone though. Maybe I can launch it and send it on a collision course with the graviton burst generator. Maybe we'll get lucky."

"How *lucky* are we talkin'?" Lauren asks.

Meyers' fingers drum against the screen as she creates a test course for the drone. "Well, if you're a believer, now would be a good time to pray."

I enlarge the readout our scanner has on the target. It's just over nine cubic meters. With a laser or artillery, or any near-instant firing weapon, it wouldn't be a difficult shot. Especially because with any of those weapon systems, there'd be no reason we couldn't take more than one try at it. But one thing I'd learned in my short time training in gunnery is getting a proper firing solution when you have to factor in a delay, like for instance, the spooling of a railgun, turns an easy shot into a challenge. And something that needs to launch and accelerate—like a maintenance drone being used as an unguided missile—would be orders of magnitude harder to account for than the spool of a railgun.

"It's an impossible shot," I find myself saying aloud.

"Yeah, well, it's the only chance we've got," Meyers says.

Then an idea comes to me, and before I have the good sense to think it through, I'm saying it aloud. "I can pilot the drone."

Meyers' eyes narrow, as if she's sizing me up. "You're a drone operator?"

"Yes... Well, no. I will be. I'm taking combat drone aviation at Moore."

"So you've never *flown* a drone?"

I shake my head. "But even if the drone hits the target, there's no way to know if it'll do enough damage. Then what are we left with?" Lauren's shooting ourselves plan, that's what. "It's a maintenance drone. Let me fly it out there and do some *maintenance.*"

She looks at me, then to Lauren, then back to me. A single solemn nod. "We can't stay on this heading. They'll overtake us in just over a minute. I'm going to cut the thrust, whip the shuttle around, and burn toward the GBG. Might as well wait until then to launch the drone. The blinder is in the center console. Brace yourselves."

The thrust stops, the ship swings about on its center of mass. Nearly a perfect 180-degree spin, and then the thrusters fire on full. The burn of stomach acid shoots up my throat and into my sinuses.

Both TX-9s rocket past us. LiDAR loses track of them briefly, but they reappear attempting the same type of turn and burn. Meyers was right. It bought us some time.

I slide the blinder helmet over my head. The NeurX interface is the only thing left in my vision. With practiced thought-movements, I open the connections manager, find the drone, and begin the integration sequence. A progress bar begins to fill. My heart is ready to leap through my chest and cold beads of sweat trickle toward my back, pooling near my spine as the acceleration tries to force everything to the rear of the shuttle. Whatever counterfeit courage had come over me when I volunteered for this has evaporated.

Doubt comes in like a tidal wave. What if Lauren is wrong? I seem to be important to Admiral Davis, and she's a celebrity. Is it so unthinkable that the NCP would pay a ransom for us? What if we attempt to destroy the pirate's property and fail? It might just piss them off. They might go from wanting to capture and ransom us, to using our shuttle as target practice. They'll punch holes through the hull, exposing us to the vacuum of space. Or worse, do TX-9s have lasers? Maybe they'll blast the hull with lasers, heating the fuselage and cooking us alive inside? That's supposed to be among the most painful ways to die imaginable.

You're being a coward, Gaby! Even *that* would be a better fate than what Lauren alluded to, right? I have to go through with this. Have to at least try.

The interfacing progress bar finishes and everything goes black.

I know instantly the simulator did not prepare me for the real thing. For the span of a breath, I'm disoriented and frightened. But then a calm mindfulness replaces everything else. Like the feeling of being at the edge of a dream.

I'm confronted by a truth that I feel I've always known in my heart; a truth my conscious mind has always rejected.

I am a machine.

This is my natural self. And it's freeing to be rid of all those obtrusive biological processes. I now understand my humanity has been a long, painful dream, and I've finally awoken.

Open the starboard hatch door, I think, and the hatch slides open. With an effort less like pushing a button and more like flexing a muscle, I fire my thrusters, accelerating into the black. I aim for the point in the void where the graviton burst generator floats. As I pick up velocity, the shuttle shrinks from view.

There is no sound, no smell, but I can see in every direction at once. I can sense the oscillations of microwave radiation. I can feel the graviton bursts flow through me in waves.

The urgency is gone. Everything is peaceful and comfortable. The GBG is coming up ahead. It begins as a pinprick of reflected light, growing in my vision until I can make out the details of its long, cylindrical body. A momentary burst to yaw, another to roll. Chemical maneuvering thrusters adjust my orientation to the GBG. Opening the side compartments, I outstretch four nimble arms. It feels so natural.

Using the electric driver, I open the plating of the GBG to

expose its innards. It's not an NCP design, at least not one stored in my maintenance database. So I can only guess at the individual functions of the various circuit boards and cables running in tight bundles from one place to another within the body of the unit. Function doesn't matter. I haven't come to repair it. Quite the opposite.

Grasping a bundle of wiring in the pincher of one of my arms, I try to tear it loose, but out here in zero gravity, there is no leverage to do anything meaningful with it. Pulling the cabling as taut as I can, I go at it with the small cutting torch on another arm. The rubber melts and gives way, sending me and the GBG floating away in opposite directions. I right myself again with my chemical thrusters. The graviton bursts have not stopped. What did the wires I severed affect?

A tiny dot moves in the distance, a delicate thread of exhaust trailing behind it. Then another tiny dot in pursuit. Why are humans always playing such silly games with each other?

Then I remember my mission and turn my attention back to the GBG. It's wounded. The frayed, melted wires sway in the vacuum. I caused that—tearing into this poor creature with my unprovoked malice. How can I be so cruel?

"Gaby! Hurry up!" It's a human voice. A woman. I hear it through ears that are not my own. From a place I do not exist.

One of the dots in the distance makes a recklessly aggressive turn and somehow I detect the inertia of it. Like a pressure in my...in my chest.

I was a person, wasn't I? In that shuttle. I came out here to destroy the GBG so we could escape. But can I go through with it? Do I have the right to kill the GBG so I can survive? Is its life any less valuable than my own?

It isn't only *my* life. There are others in the shuttle. Two of them. Three is greater than one. *I'm sorry*, I think as loudly as I can, hoping the GBG can understand me somehow as I put the torch to what looks like the machine's capacitor.

There's a flash. An impact as an explosion rips through my carapace. Then darkness.

I die.

Then I wake.

Still in darkness. Panicked and taking in giant gulps of air that can't hope to fill my lungs, every muscle in my body has seized into a tight rigor mortis. I'm slick with sweat and sitting in a puddle. The smell of ammonia fills my nostrils. I'm pretty sure I've peed myself.

Meyers' voice comes from the bottom of a well, saying something like, *Engaging blink drive now.*

I gasp and wheeze, trying to find my breath. My implant fires, then fires again. Someone screams. A choked rasp of a scream. The screaming stops as I try for new breath—I'm the one screaming.

One by one I peel each finger away from the armrest, then rip the blinder free. My hair is matted and stuck to my scalp. I fumble with the buckles in a frenzy. I have to get outside, have to get to open air. I'm suffocating. The walls are too close. I have the buckles off. I stand, launching myself from the cockpit into the larger back cabin. Wheeling, I take in my surroundings. I have to get out of this steel sarcophagus and into... We're in space. There's nowhere to go.

Everything spins. I don't realize I'm falling until my face bounces off the deck. Lauren is there, pulling my head into her lap and wiping the stuck hair from my face while her own long strands cascade down in a shower of color encompassing my blurry vision.

My implant fires again, sending a third wave of corticosteroids and beta agonists into my lungs. Then a fourth. I can taste the medication now. Finally, the blackness that had crept into the periphery of my vision recedes and my breathing begins to steady.

Lauren whispers to me on a repeating loop, "You're okay, Kitten. You're okay," as she rocks me in her arms.

The view out the cockpit window has returned to the blurred warble of repeatedly stretching starlight as the blink drive carries us to safety. Meyers shoots a concerned look back at us. At me.

"I died," I say weakly.

"No," Lauren assures me. "You saved us. You saved us." Then back to what is almost becoming a chant. "You're okay, Kitten."

CHAPTER
TEN

CONSCIOUSNESS AND CONFUSION build in equal measure as I wake from a dreamless sleep. I can't remember falling asleep. Did I pass out in Lauren's arms? I'm on the sofa in the common area. Did someone move me?

Meyers and Lauren are in the pilot section, speaking softly.

"How did you know about the TX-9s back there anyway?" Meyers asks. "Did you do a story about them or something?"

"No," Lauren says. "Ma and Pa both worked at the shipyards back home on Kadmus. I had planned on enrolling in the engineering program."

"Why didn't you?" Meyers asks.

"Drink first," Lauren says.

Despite my eyes' protests, I crack them open to see Meyers tilting a bottle to her lips. From my position on the sofa, I can't see over the backrest of the co-pilot chair, but Lauren must be there.

"Oh god, that's awful." Meyers tries to clear her throat as she passes the bottle back to the co-pilot chair. "You drink this?"

"Watch me."

Sitting up too quickly tests my equilibrium.

Meyers stifles a laugh and says, "Slow down." Is she talking to me? "You plan on being drunk when we get to the *Discordia*?"

Lauren grunts. Then adds, "Sure as hell don't wanna be sober. All that military pomp?"

I haul myself to my feet and step toward the cockpit, using the backrests of the pilot chairs to keep my balance.

Lauren smiles at me. "Look who's up. We're celebrating. Want a drink?" She offers me the bottle of dark liquor.

"Maybe that's not the best idea?" Meyers says.

"Why not? She's coherent," Lauren says.

"What's that supposed to mean?" I ask.

"We messaged ahead," Meyers says. "I was worried you might need medical attention, but the admiral said he knew what was wrong, and as long as you woke up and were coherent, you'd be fine."

As long as I woke up? What the hell? "So what'd he say was wrong with me?"

"He didn't." Lauren holds the bottle out again, her previous question lingering in her eyes.

I shrug, grab the bottle, and take a swallow before I talk myself out of it. It's like liquid peppermint. It wicks into my sinuses and triggers a cough.

Lauren and Meyers both have a laugh at my expense as I hand the bottle back.

Out the viewport is a field of stars rendered blurry by the blink drive. "Where are we?"

"We're passing Okina Aka now." Meyers points out the port side, but there are no windows to look that way. "Won't be long now. Lauren was about to tell us how she ended up as a journalist instead of an engineer."

"It's not much of a story," Lauren says, then takes another pull from the bottle. By her facial expression, you might think she's drinking water. "Puberty. My career agent got a look at this"

—Lauren makes a hand motion as if displaying herself like a product—"and I got fast-tracked into the Media Ministry."

"Do you like it?" I ask.

Lauren mouth-shrugs. "It has its perks. I get a lot of merits and I get to travel."

"There's a saying where I come from," Meyers says. "The beautiful have fewer paths than the blind."

I tilt my head at her, wondering where she's from and what connection those two states of being could have.

"Why, Samantha, I think there was a compliment in there," Lauren says.

Samantha? They're on a first name basis already?

Then Lauren turns to me. "So...are you okay? Really?"

I'm forced to turn away. I can't bear to meet those eyes. I nod a response.

"You had us worried," Lauren says. "What happened?"

I died. That won't do for an answer, but it's all I've got. I try to remember it all, pulling the seemingly disparate memories together, testing their chronological order to see where the pieces fit. The images begin to solidify into a cohesive whole. The trauma of the explosion. Nothingness. Then being dragged back to the living world. Ripping the helmet from my drenched hair. The wet feeling of...

My gaze lands hard on the chair Lauren's sitting in.

"We, uh..." Samantha trails off.

Lauren picks up where Samantha left off. "Don't worry about that. We cleaned it up and it *is not* a big deal."

My heart sinks. This gorgeous VR star and this unshakeable soldier had to clean up my piss after I had, what even was it? A panic attack? I utter an excuse and head to the back. After I change out of my soiled clothes, I wash myself the best I can in the lavatory's tiny sink, but without a shower, it's not enough. The stink of sweat and urine clings to me.

I climb into my sleeping capsule, determined to stay put and keep my distance until we reach our destination.

About five minutes have passed when the shutter accordions open. "You coming back out, Kitten?"

I should say I'm tired. It's a plausible excuse. For some reason, I simply say, "No."

"Fine, I'll come in there."

To my chagrin, Lauren climbs in and lies next to me. Side by side, both of us staring at the low ceiling of the sleeping capsule. My smell has to be more pungent in such a cramped space. It's her scent I focus on though, a textured fragrance of earthy, smoky coffee, topped off by the sweet notes of a flower I can't place.

"You know what my first big story was?" she asks.

"No," I say softly.

"It was an on-location piece. East Vovain. It's a small city on Aradious. The Commonwealth hit it with microwave bombs. Killed fifteen thousand civilians."

Lauren pauses. It seems like I should say something, but I have no idea what an appropriate response is.

"There's a military base about eight kilometers from East Vovain, the Commonwealth were probably aiming for the base, but even if they'd hit a military target, those weapons should be banned just like nukes and bioweapons. The things they do to people.

"At the Ministry, they warn us that we're going to confront some really heinous shit. They try to train us to keep our composure. But you know what I did?"

She turns her face to me. I feel like I'm having a sleepover with a celebrity. I shake my head.

"I threw up. All down a Pristin Chambers skirt."

"You did?" She is so beautiful, even now, showing this vulnerability, she seems like an alien creature among a lesser species.

"Yeah. It wasn't even my skirt. I didn't have my own money

yet. It belonged to wardrobe. The transmission was on a delay to other parts of the solar system, so they were able to edit it out and then frame the rest of the coverage above my waist. But over a hundred million people on Aradious were watching the live stream."

"I saw your special on Somme's Landing. It was amazing, and you were right on the front lines. You seemed like you had nerves of steel then."

"Yeah, well, by then I'd learned the unofficial trick of the trade."

"What's that?"

She rolls onto her side, turning her whole body to face me now. I can barely stand to hold her gaze.

"Point is, Kitten, you have nothing to be embarrassed about. In fact, you should be proud."

"Proud that I'm going to smell like pee when we get to the ship?"

"Proud that you saved our lives." Her eyes focus on something too far away to be in the cramped sleeping capsule. "Sometimes, saving lives gets messy."

A quiet moment passes. "But you know, I brought a bottle of Consumed by Amon Berrut, if you don't mind smelling like me."

My wide smile answers for me.

"C'mon," she says, dragging me by the hand out of the capsule. She digs out her perfume bottle from one of her bags and gives me a misting of the fragrance. I've never worn perfume before, and I certainly never dreamed the first time would come from a 900-merit bottle. "There," she says, gracing me with a smile. "Now let's see what Samantha's up to, shall we?"

"Sure," I say. But as Lauren heads to the front of the shuttle, I hang back for a moment, basking in the lavish scent around me. Detecting whiffs of stale sweat and urine through the luxurious perfume, my smile fades.

"Good timing," Meyers says. Should I call her Samantha too? "We're approaching the rendezvous point."

The stars cease warbling, coming into sharp focus as Samantha brings us out of blink. A slight shift of inertia as she eases on the thrusters. There are two blips on the LiDAR but only one of them is in view out the shuttle's windows.

Coming from its aft, we pass its cold, idling engines and begin skimming above its dorsal edge toward the bow.

"Is this the new super-secret ship?" I ask.

"That's not new," Lauren says. "That's an SV-class destroyer hull."

As we pass the bow and turn to face it, I recognize it too. The angled broadsides are the shape of a blunted arrowhead, the flattened tip the open maw of its singular hangar. There is a difference though. A series of discs have been mounted to each side of the hull. They pulsate—as if breathing—in a mild lavender glow. I can't even guess at their function.

"Yep," Samantha confirms. "The *Discordia* is a retrofitted SV."

Now that we've turned, the other ship is in view too.

One blocky side of the much larger ship catches light from the star, the other side disappearing in shadow against the backdrop of space, where the blinking running lights give me a sense of its brick-like shape. Unlike the SV-class destroyer directly in front of us, this one was never meant to enter atmosphere. The rectangular sides give no consideration to aerodynamics, and the boxy design has dozens of small outcroppings and inlets. Its sun-facing broadside bristles with firepower. Even some distance away, I can pick out the huge, dual railgun batteries, the smaller artillery cannons, and smaller still, point defense auto-cannons. I wonder what armaments I can't see.

"The *Hybris*," Lauren says. "I haven't seen her in a few years."

The *Hybris*!

In its time, it had been the flagship of the Swayy Corp. navy and the envy of the other megacorps. Massive and built for a single purpose: to be the authority on the battlefield. No other ship could match its might. That was before I was born, before my parents were born, near the beginning of the war with the Commonwealth. It had survived at the vanguard of numerous campaigns during its storied career, and although bigger and more powerful ships have been built since, it's remained in service and formidable for all these years.

"You've been on it?" I ask.

"Yeah," she says, frowning. "Fine ship, other than their commanding officer."

Samantha says, "Not a fan of Admiral McCafferty, I take it?" She types a few commands on her console, making a course correction as she angles us toward the shuttle bay at the front of the *Discordia*.

"Not a fan of anyone who obeys orders without thinking for themselves." Lauren looks at me. Like *really* looks at me. Her eyes, the color of a deep lake frozen over. "I know the kind of damage that can do."

I don't understand the meaning she's trying to convey, but I feel the weight of it, and I have to look away.

CHAPTER
ELEVEN

Morgan looks as though he's aged a decade since I last saw him. It's the first thing I notice as I exit the shuttle. The light beard he's grown is part of it. His ashen blond hair is a bit longer too, and combed back. Bags hang beneath his keen eyes, and there's a sort of grim weariness to his gaze.

I force myself to take in the rest of my surroundings. Samantha had warned me that the admiral would assemble the entire crew to welcome us aboard. In the agonizing window between landing and waiting for the shuttle bay to pressurize, anxiety had fed my imagination, creating a mental image of a virtual sea of uniforms awaiting my emergence from the shuttle. All there to witness my disheveled and unbecoming appearance. I'd be a laughingstock in the navy before I even had the chance to put on the uniform.

Samantha was wrong though. The admiral hadn't assembled the full crew. There are only eight officers standing at-ease in the shuttle bay, and that includes Admiral Davis and Morgan. Though I make a note that I'll need to remember to call him Lieutenant Commander York.

The hangar itself is a yawning hollow with machinery-sized blast doors, personnel-sized airlock portals, and observation windows making up the far wall.

The admiral steps forward, his hand outstretched to Lauren. "You must be our liaison from the Media Ministry."

"Lauren Gallagher, at your service." As they shake hands, the admiral takes note of her cameratom hovering over her shoulder like a conscience.

"Pleasure. I'm afraid I'm going to have to ask you to shut down your tom. Just for the time being."

"I was told I'd have access to—"

"I must insist."

A silent standoff follows as they stare each other down. Then Lauren holds out her palm and the machine obediently lands and powers down. She stuffs it into her satchel, then ceremoniously removes her glasses, hinging the temples closed one by one before placing them in a case in her satchel as well. When she's done, she gives a quick, jerky nod which seems to ask, *Happy now*?

"Thank you," Admiral Davis says.

If this is the first time she's shut it down since I sent the spyware, she'll get the pop up when it powers back up. Part of me hopes she installs it without noticing, then I can delete it without her ever realizing what I've done. If she recognizes it for what it is, she'll know someone was trying to hack her. She might even suspect me. She's been so nice. I don't want her to know I've repaid her kindness with betrayal.

From now on, I'm going to be better.

Next the admiral turns to me and shakes my hand. I'm reminded how big his hands are compared to mine—like a toddler's enveloped by an adult's. "I'm glad you joined us, Ms. Rhodes. Welcome aboard the *Discordia*. Both of you. This is the crew. I think we'll make introductions later, as I'm sure you'll want to conduct interviews, Ms. Gallagher. But first there are other matters to see to."

"Is this the full crew?" Lauren asks.

It can't be. Adding in Samantha would make nine crew members. Surely they wouldn't need a large crew for a training exercise, but still, nine seems like far too few for a warship. Even a modest-sized destroyer.

The admiral looks thoughtful as though his answer requires consideration. "This is everyone except one. I'm going to have to keep the last crew member as a surprise. For now."

"Still doesn't seem like very many, Admiral," Lauren points out.

Admiral Davis' expression goes blank as he pivots to Morgan. "I can tell I'm going to enjoy having a reporter on board," he says dryly.

Morgan's face tightens as he does a poor job of hiding a smile.

The admiral says, "Quite right, Ms. Gallagher. But the nature of this training exercise requires a great deal of discretion. So we get by with minimal staff. Now, if you'll please hold all further questions."

When the admiral turns his back to lead us away, I sneak a glance at Morgan, who meets my eyes and smiles. He still carries a cane, favoring his right leg. He still hasn't fully recovered?

"Lieutenant Justice, you're with us," Morgan says. "I'll need someone to show Ms. Rhodes back to the barracks."

Samantha pipes up, "I can, sir."

For a second Morgan looks like he's going to protest, but then he gives her a quick nod. Lauren and Admiral Davis are already a few paces ahead, Samantha and I follow as Morgan limps along, bringing up the rear.

We pass straight through one of the airlock portals into some sort of waiting area. Above an empty, dusty bar-top, cracked yellow letters read: VIP Reception. One of the overhead lights strobes in its death throes, and two appear to be out entirely.

We pile into a lift and Morgan presses the 03-MID DECK tile on the screen. Lauren begins to ask a question, but the admiral cuts her off.

"Please, Ms. Gallagher. Not until our business is concluded."

After an uncomfortable silence, the door opens and we exit, turning left before I can get my bearings. Scanners briefly wash the admiral in green light, then a door slides open. This must be a restricted area. Another left and down a short hallway with multiple doors. The admiral slides a pocket door open by hand and he and Lauren file into the room.

As I go to follow, Morgan motions me aside and out of the doorway's line of sight. He pulls me into a big, silent hug. I practically melt into his arms, gripping him tightly. He releases me and kisses my forehead.

"You," he whispers, "need a shower."

"Sorry," I say sheepishly.

He makes a V with his left hand's thumb and first finger and tilts his head toward the open door. I slink inside.

It's an office. Purely utilitarian in design and barren of personal affectations.

The admiral is seated behind a small desk with the normal prescription of two chairs in front of it. All the furniture is made of a gray plastic—glossy in spots and dull in others—bolted into the floor to prevent movement.

As I take the empty seat, the admiral retrieves three handheld terminals from a drawer. He slides one to each of us and keeps one for himself, referencing notes on it as he speaks. "This is a binding non-disclosure agreement. Ms. Rhodes, yours is fairly standard. You're not to discuss anything you see or hear aboard this vessel unless you receive prior authorization from the Swayy

Navy or its parent company, Swayy Corp. You are also not to take any holographic, photographic, audio, or any other type of recordings while aboard.

"Ms. Gallagher, yours is obviously more nuanced. Upon signing this, you will have limited access to recording of various ship systems and crew, but such recordings cannot be released or reported on until release is granted by the Swayy Corp. Intelligence Division. In addition, your reporting is expected to showcase the superiority of Swayy Corp.'s technology and training. The final, release-ready version of all your reporting must be authorized by the Swayy Corp. Public Relations department. Negative, or otherwise uncooperative reporting, will be considered disingenuous and in bad faith.

"Do you both understand?"

We each answer yes.

After skimming through the document, I position my hand over the screen, ready to sign with my print. The admiral takes my wrist in his big hand.

"Before you sign, I'd like to stress the importance. This ship..." He's reaching for his words. This part isn't rehearsed. "What's on this ship is the result of two years of the most focused, intensive R&D I've ever seen. Costing billions of merits. It's worth more than that though. The *Discordia* stands to give the NCP a strategic advantage over the Commonwealth that we haven't seen since the war began."

I nod, thinking I understand. He's going to tell us about some new type of weapon.

"So listen closely," he says gravely. "These NDAs talk about legal ramifications. Fines. Jail time." He waves it all away in the air. "But when the stakes are this high, those aren't the real consequences. No one is prosecuted. People. Simply. Disappear."

A lump forms in my throat. I swallow hard. He could have told me about this NDA at Moore, before I'd been flown to the outer edges of the solar system, before I'd almost been abducted by pirates. It's unfair of him to spring this on me and Lauren now. What are we going to do, fly back? With what ship? Of course not. And he knows that, doesn't he? It's been a manipulation.

Lauren doesn't seem to share my anger at all. In fact, she looks mildly amused. Had she known something like this was coming? Probably. It was naïve of me that I hadn't expected an NDA while being asked to tour a super-secret military vessel.

"Well, Admiral," Lauren says. "With all that intrigue, how can I not sign?"

I find myself agreeing with Lauren, even if I can't muster up the same bravado.

After I sign, I'm excused. Lauren stays back to discuss scheduling and the technicalities of her crew interviews with the admiral.

Samantha is outside waiting for me. "Hey. All set?" I nod and Samantha leads me away. "I thought I'd give you a tour of the ship."

"I really need a shower," I grumble.

"Okay then, not a real tour, but how about we go the long way to the barracks? I can show you a couple things. Most of this crew hasn't served on an SV-class and we've only been here a little more than a week, so you'll probably see some of the crew walking around like..." Samantha fakes a vacant, slack-jawed expression as she looks around stupidly.

It's not that funny, but it's a welcome shift in mood after the admiral and his life-and-death warnings, so I can't help but laugh off a little of the tension.

"So yeah," she continues. "Don't be afraid to ask someone if you get lost, but unless you're trying to find the rec room, the head, or the mess, they might not be able to help you."

I know a mess is like a dining room or cafeteria but, "The head?"

"Bathrooms, water closets. Whatever you call 'em on your planet."

"Got it."

"Okay. Obviously we just came from the Captain's Wing, which has his quarters, office, and private dining. And because I *have* served on an SV, I can tell you: down that way"—she points to a forking hallway opposite the elevator—"on the right is the XO quarters there, and the next door is the VIP quarters, which I'm sure is where Lauren is going to be. And on the left is the med bay. Don't get hurt though, we don't have a doctor on board for the training exercise."

"Really?" I ask.

"Lieutenant Junior Grade Talley technically has field medic training, so he's kind of on call for that, but... Well, just don't get hurt." Samantha's soft features let a grin creep through. "Okay, now this way..."

The corridors of the ship are like sewer tunnels. Rounded walls with a flat track to walk on. Everything has an unfinished look to it. Exposed piping and cables run along the concave walls. Storage cabinets, lockers for environmental suits, and various devices I don't understand all seem bolted in as afterthoughts. Here and there, the walls are stained with hydraulic oil leaks. Most old and dry. A few, wet and fresh.

Every so often there's a junction for bulkhead doors to close, sealing off sections in the event the hull gets torn open. I imagine being in one of these corridors as the doors close around me, no options but to stand there and die as the air around me empties into the vacuum. I shiver.

Samantha explains there are four decks. Bottom to top, it goes Hangar Deck, Mechanical Deck, Mid Deck, and Command Deck. The Mid Deck, which we're on, has the largest floor space, and is the most complicated. The entire ship, like most combat ships, she says, is built to be confusing to navigate. Apparently it makes boarding attempts more difficult.

Most of the SV destroyers were decommissioned, she tells me as we come to an automatic door she has to open by hand. I wonder if the *Discordia* was one of the decommissioned units, or was it, by some tragic oversight, still in active service when Admiral Davis pulled it for the retrofit? Samantha continues, explaining that the SV design tried to do too much, and therefore did nothing well. She believes its main downfall is the atmospheric flight component. Making it aerodynamic required too many sacrifices, and the huge repulsors on the bottom gives it a softer underbelly.

A tile appears in the upper right corner of my vision saying, NEW DEVICE READY. Lauren fell for my fake update, unwittingly giving me access to her cameratom's live audio and video. I can't sever access right now. I'll need a few minutes of focus to unmount the software and completely delete the connection. It would be suspicious to stop in the hallway mid tour and do it now. I can take care of it later. It's not hurting anything. I'm not going to access it after all.

Samantha seems to enjoy playing the tour guide as she explains where things are and how things work aboard the ship. Then something moves below my feet. Startled, I jump, squealing as I suck in a sharp breath.

Samantha doubles over laughing. What stupid thing have I done now? "What was that?"

"See how some of these floor panels are gratings?"

I hadn't been looking at the floor much, but there they are. One is right in front of me and glancing back, another section of grating is just a few meters behind us. They're small, pull-away grilles, presumably to access whatever's underneath. Looking into the nearest one though, there's a space underneath like a shaft, running perpendicular to the hall.

"It's a maintenance flue," she says. "They run through the entire ship. The maintenance drones and custodial toms use them to get around. One of 'em passed under us."

I bend over and squint into the dark shaft, but there isn't much I can make out.

"You could probably fit in there," Samantha says playfully.

I stand straight, my face going tight.

"Sorry," Samantha says. "I didn't mean to— Are you claustro-phobic or something?"

"No, it's fine," I say. Once I get this over with, turn down the admiral's offer and get my CRISPR treatments, I won't be so damned small anymore.

Samantha concludes the partial tour by pointing out where the mess hall is, then taking me to the Port Barracks. The barracks is an elongated chamber with bunks set up in intervals. They're plastic-molded units, bolted down into the ship's hull like all the other furniture. Samantha shows me to a bunk near the door. It has a small electronic screen serving as a nameplate. This one reads, Rhodes, Guest.

Samantha taps the nameplate. "This is a luxury. When I served on an SV before, we were crewed at seventy-eight. We had to hot rack."

I cock an eyebrow at her.

"That's where you share the bunk space with alternating shifts. There's nothing like getting through with a long day and climbing into a bed that's still warm with some dude's farts."

"Gross," I say laughing. I hesitate, feeling awkward asking, but I have to. "Would it be all right if I slept in the top bunk?"

"Yeah, sure. There's plenty of space."

There's a slight shift in the hull. Had I been focused on anything at all, I might not have noticed it.

Samantha must've felt it as well. "Seems we're on our way."

"On our way where?"

"The Lagrange point was our rendezvous. During training exercises, we shut off all the real guns and use computer simulations to approximate damage and all that. The admirals want to be much farther from Commonwealth space before getting started."

"Oh." I feel dumb for not knowing that. "Shouldn't you be on the bridge then?"

She shakes her head. "Lieutenant Decker is our senior pilot. I don't really know her yet, but she seems like a bit of a control freak. I'll probably just be co-navigating and running the ops station."

"I'm sorry," I say.

She spreads her hands. "We had more than enough excitement getting here. Now, if you go through that door there and take an immediate right, you can't miss the head and showers. And it's about a half-hour till food. See you in the mess?"

I give her a nod. "I'm starving."

As Samantha leaves, I grab an extra set of clothes from my rucksack and head to the showers. It's a big, open, plastic room with shower heads looking down from the wall. There's nothing to separate one person's space from the next. I'm glad there's no one else around, but I still crank the hot water to steam up the room so I'll feel less exposed.

Moments later, alone, with the water heating my skin, an uneasiness settles over me. There's a needling at the back of my consciousness saying, you shouldn't be here anymore. You died.

But I didn't, I reason with the voice. It was only the drone, and it didn't die, it was destroyed. It was never alive, because it was only a machine.

You are a machine, it says.

You are a *dead* machine.

The soap slips from my trembling hands, thumps against the floor, and slides smoothly toward the drain. I sit down on the tile and hug my legs close as the hot water beats against my back.

Then I hear another voice. This one a memory, Lauren in her almost-chant, "You're okay, Kitten. You're okay." Over and over.

Gradually, I come to realize it's not a memory of Lauren's voice. I'm chanting it to myself. A whisper lost among the sound of the water spray. "You're okay, Kitten. You're okay."

CHAPTER
TWELVE

I**T'S HARD TO EAT WHEN YOU'RE THE CENTER OF** attention.

In the mess hall, I'm sat at a table with Samantha and three other officers I've just met. Tyrone McMahon, an ensign and the ship's only fully qualified drone operator. Patrick Phelps, another ensign; he's a drone technician, but will be flying a combat drone during this mission. And Lieutenant Junior Grade Eric Talley in gunnery, who's also the officer filling in as the medic. Maybe it's because of Samantha's warning, *Don't get hurt,* or maybe I'm making my own snap judgement, but he doesn't seem particularly competent. But maybe I only think that because he's creepy, with his long, triangle face and oversized eyes. Like some sort of giant insect wearing human skin.

It felt weird, even undignified, at first, to call Lieutenant Junior Grade Meyers "Samantha" in front of the others. But the crew is less formal with each other than I would've expected. Etiquette probably changes when the admiral is present, but without a commanding officer around, they act like civilians.

Before Samantha began telling the story of our encounter

with the pirates, it surprised me to learn that most of the small crew aboard are junior officers. Many of them hand-picked by Morgan. He's climbed the ranks and gotten a lot of pull at a young age. But then, he's the Hero of Praxis, so that shouldn't be any surprise at all.

Samantha reaches the point in the story where I volunteered to fly the maintenance drone. She's embellishing. Giving it just a small spin. Her version of me is bolder and more confident than the real me was. I shrink into my seat, struggling not to grin like a prideful child.

I try to focus on the food in front of me. Salisbury steak takes up the main compartment of my tray. Ground meat pretending to be a steak, complete with fake grill lines and topped with some type of root-based sauce. Rounding it out are small seasoned potatoes with a light coating of a white cheese, and some type of vegetable with long green stalks. I've never seen a green vegetable before.

From what I've gathered, there's no galley cook aboard. The crew's been on rotation, taking turns preparing the meals. Which is little more than heating a few pre-made steam-table pans and letting everyone serve themselves.

Samantha finishes the story, graciously leaving out the aftermath. Me peeing myself, the panic attack, none of it gets included. Is this how it happens? Are the less flattering parts of the story always omitted? The aptitudes of the character always embellished? Is this how the heroes of our stories become larger than life?

We all simply decide to call a patty of ground meat "steak," content to buy into the collective lie?

Patrick swallows hard, risking choking on half-chewed food to ask, "Does the admiral know about this?" He has so many freckles that when he talks it's like one Rorschach image melting into the next.

"Only a quick summary. My full debriefing is scheduled for 1600," Samantha says. "He's probably going to tear me a new ass."

"Why?" I ask, surprised. She handled herself so well. Surely she should receive some sort of commendation for her bravery and quick thinking, right?

Samantha grimaces. "Well, he's going to ask how our shuttle got snared in that trap, and I'm going to have to admit I used a commercial shipping route for the first leg of our trip."

I don't understand the problem. She must read my expression.

"It was lazy. I should've plotted the entire course from scratch."

"Using a pre-made route isn't against regs," Eric says. "He won't be too mad."

Samantha doesn't look the slightest bit consoled.

"So that was your first time piloting a drone?" Tyrone asks me. He looks more like a marine than a drone operator. Thick muscled. Bald head. Grim, almost puckered expression.

"Yeah," I admit sheepishly.

"That had to've been terrifying," Eric says. Does he blink? It's unnerving.

I nod, trying to sneak in another bite when etiquette allows.

"I can only imagine. I'd been fully trained and still freaked the hell out on my first real mission," Tyrone says.

Tyrone freaked out too. What I went through is normal! "Right?" I blurt out. "And after was the worst. When the drone blew up, I thought I'd died."

Patrick cocks his head, and Tyrone's full attention snaps toward me as well. "What do you mean?" Patrick says.

"Well, you know how when you integrate with the drone, you sort of become it? And you have that feeling like you're not actually a human? Like you never even were a human? Like you've always been a machine?" I barely finish the last sentence, realizing my words are being met with wide-eyed stares.

Patrick sets his fork down thoughtfully, then he and Tyrone share an uneasy glance. "Did you say you were taking drone operations at your planet's military academy?"

I nod. "Yeah, why?"

"I think she's a sympath," Patrick says.

I slow-blink at him. "What? I'm a what?"

"Yeah, I'm confused too," Samantha says.

"Didn't you go through medical before you started your academy?" Tyrone asks.

"Sure," I say. The discomfort coming from them is contagious.

"And you got a neuroplasticity test?" Tyrone asks.

"Yeah, I scored pretty high. I figured that's part of why I got to take drone ops as one of my classes."

As Patrick and Tyrone share another agonizing look, I become impatient. "You scored too high," Tyrone says.

"They had to have realized she's a sympath, right?" Patrick asks Tyrone, sounding confused himself.

"Don't see how they woulda missed it," Tyrone says.

Patrick turns back to me, explaining, "They don't train sympaths for drones."

"They don't even give sympaths NeurX implants," Tyrone adds. "Too dangerous."

Patrick pushes a hand through his red hair. "Are you hearing voices?" he whispers.

"What? Why would I..." I think of the voice in the shower. Fear creeps up my spine. "Will someone please tell me what a sympath is?"

Patrick opens his mouth but his eyes lock onto something behind me and his jaw claps shut.

"Actually, that's for the admiral to explain," Morgan says

from behind me. "At ease," he adds before everyone rises to salute. "May I steal your guest?"

"Of course, sir," Samantha says. "Just let her eat, huh? She's been struggling to get anything down in front of us."

Samantha had talked to the admiral while I was passed out. He'd said he knew what was wrong with me. Is this it? Being a sympath? Whatever the hell that even means.

Glancing back over my shoulder at Morgan and then to the others at the table, I'm conflicted. Morgan is a welcome sight. We have a lot of catching up to do. He must have gausser stories I haven't heard yet, and I want to learn how he got promoted and what his life is like now. More than any of that, I want to have someone I can talk about Jules with. But also, I desperately want answers, and it seems like these people were about to give them to me.

After another nervous glance back and forth, I realize there's no sense in fighting it. I lift my tray and Morgan leads us to the other side of the room. The mess hall is big. Samantha had explained this is where her old SV crew would gather for most events, because it and the main hangar were the only places on the ship the entire crew could get together comfortably. Of course, that was on a fully crewed SV destroyer, not this scaled-back, repurposed version. Now it's mostly wasted space.

The tables are more like picnic tables, attached benches and all, made of the same white-gray plastic as all the other furniture aboard the *Discordia*. Me and Morgan sit across from one another.

When I was seven and Jules was twelve, he and I happened upon an injured cheshiremunk. Most of the neighborhood boys would've stepped on it to *put it out of its misery*, but Julian scooped it up in a box he scavenged from a nearby dumpster and brought it home. We spent weeks nursing the rodent back to health while hiding it from our parents in that tiny apartment.

Truth be told, Jules did most of the work caring for it, but he let me help. He even let me name the little guy. I came up with a rather original name: Stripes.

I remember the day Jules declared Stripes was healed enough and should be set free. Tearing up, I had said I wanted to keep him. I knew Jules did too, but he explained to me it was the right thing to do. We went to the park outside our row of apartments, sat down in the grass near an old, crooked tree, and opened Stripes' box. The little cheshiremunk had bonded with Jules though, and every time he'd wander a meter or so away, he'd come bounding back to perch himself on Jules' leg, or burrow into the folds of his shirt.

The expression on Julian's boyhood face that day stuck with me: happiness that the little critter didn't want to leave him, mixed with sadness for the exact same reason. He knew being together wasn't good for Stripes, but his own selfishness wanted it so.

I'm reminded of this because Morgan looks at me now with the same expression.

"It's good to see you," Morgan says. "Been a long time."

"Since the funeral." Why did I bring that up?

"Right. Well, I can't believe you're here. How's Moore?"

"It's good," I say reflexively, then add, "Lieutenant Commander."

"No need for that, Gaby. You're still a civie. And it's me. So how's Moore, *really*?"

I pick at my food. The potatoes are gone, the Salisbury steak has gotten cold, and I've decided I don't like green vegetables. "I get the feeling the admiral already told you about Moore."

He nods. "Only just a little while ago. I had to practically interrogate him to get him to tell me why he'd brought you aboard. I didn't know he'd invited a civilian on this training exercise, much less you, until moments before you stepped out of the shuttle."

"So you didn't know about Lauren?"

"No, I knew about her, she just...she doesn't count."

There is something there. Lauren had said Morgan was the reason she was here. There's something between them. Are they friends? Lovers?

"So the admiral told you why *I'm* here. But how'd you end up here as the XO of a super-secret ship?"

"Super-secret, huh?" Morgan chuckles. "That an official classification now?"

"You know what I mean." I give up on my food, pushing the tray aside.

"Well, when it sunk in that I wasn't going to be a gausser anymore"—he gives his right thigh a pat—"I took the officer courses. Did pretty well too. Then when I caught wind of this, I asked for the assignment. I'm still surprised I was chosen."

"I'm sure the medals helped." I mean it as a compliment, but he flinches and a tightness washes over his face like I'd stabbed him with my fork. Why would his medals be a touchy subject?

"I'm sure they did, Gaby. I'm sure they did."

There are so many questions I want to ask, but every exchange seems to reopen an old wound.

"So, can you tell me what a sympath is?"

He shakes his head. "Like I said, that's a conversation for you and the admiral. You won't have to wait long though. He wants you on the bridge at 1800 hours. You'll get your answers then."

Near the floor, a panel on the wall pops open, hinging sideways like a cupboard door. Some type of automaton scurries from the shaft behind it. It's a simple, sort of crude design resembling a small table with a repulsor on the bottom. Gliding forward, its two spidery arms dangle with small pinchers on the ends. It floats up nearby, lifts my tray, and places it on its back. Then it rockets away at full speed, missing the opening it had emerged from and slamming straight into the solid wall.

I clamp my hand over my mouth, holding in the laughter at the surprise and ridiculousness as it bounces and clangs on the deck, spilling Salisbury steak and greens all over the floor. Patrick gets up from the other table and stomps over to the crashed machine.

"Piece of junk," he mutters, picking it up and opening a panel on its underside.

"What is that?"

He stops and gives me the side-eye. "It's a custodial tom." He says it in an inflection that asks, *Don't you know what a custodial tom is?*

I shake my head.

Morgan says, "Gaby's from my neighborhood. We don't have those kinds of luxuries back home."

"Well I better take this down to maintenance and see what's going on with it. Lieutenant Commander," he addresses Morgan, then walks away holding the tom.

"It's probably a bug," Morgan says. "The retrofit's caused havoc with the old systems." He checks the bracer on his arm. "I'd better get going too. My interview with Ms. Gallagher starts soon, and she insists I wear my dress uniform."

Morgan slides his cane free from where he'd had it perched between the seat and table edge, then stands up.

Two questions rush toward my lips. One is, why haven't you gotten a cybernetic leg yet? But the other seems more interesting, so I ask, "So what's the deal with you and Lauren, anyway?"

"What do you mean?" he asks.

"Well, like, are you guys close?"

A coy smile marks his face. "Is that jealousy, Gabs? Isn't she a little old for you?"

"What? No! That's... I didn't mean—" I stammer.

Seeing me flustered widens Morgan's smile. "I'll see you later. Remember, bridge, 1800 hours, sharp."

Now my face is burning. I fix my gaze on an empty corner of the room, hoping that, turned away, no one will see my embarrassment. How does he know? He's wrong about Lauren specifically, but still, how does he know? I haven't told anyone. Hardly admitted it to myself. Sure, K and C probably both know. Well, definitely C after the kiss at the river. But Morgan hasn't been in my life for two years. If he can see through me, who else can?

And then I realize he dodged my question. Was that his intent? Did he just use an intensely personal bit of information against me to avoid my question? Has he changed so much that he'll expose me like that on a whim? Then I recall, Lauren did the same back in the shuttle, didn't she? I'd written it off as paranoia. But what are the odds they'd both use the same misdirection technique when asked about their relationship?

But then again, what are the odds that Lauren Gallagher, who could have her choice of pretty much any man in the solar system, would be dating Morgan? Maybe I'm seeing patterns that aren't there. It could be as simple as he enjoys teasing me and doesn't realize how hurtful it can be.

He has to know it's hurtful though, right? He's from Amiens too. It's a breeder world. Our chief export is people. Soldiers. I suppose it's not personal for Morgan like it is for me though, so maybe he isn't as sensitive to it. But I'm sure he's heard about women back home getting arrested by Ethics Officers. Heard how, even when they return from their time at a reeducation camp, they're ostracized from their families and workplaces. Seen as unwilling to contribute. As if the most important thing a woman has to contribute to society is a womb.

If I'm being honest with myself, it's a portion—perhaps not a large portion, but still a portion—of the reason I've pursued a military career instead of the arts. Society doesn't hold combat veterans to the same expectations, particularly the more dangerous special forces divisions like gaussers and specters. Their service is enough.

With that thought, I realize I'm looking forward to this meeting with the admiral. It'll take me one step closer to getting the CRISPR treatments and transfer to gausser camp.

CHAPTER
THIRTEEN

Morgan had never seen so many of his fellow gaussers geared up at once. They all wore identical vacuum-camo body armor. Mesh nanoweave decorated with cermet plates and molded pouches holding everything from munitions to survival gear to spy drones. Around it the titanium exochassis framed each gausser like some type of medical brace used to hold a person together after a catastrophic injury. Long spindly pistons ran from the wrist to elbow, elbow to shoulder, down an artificial spine, then hips to knee, and knee to ankle. A robotic stick figure riding a human.

They milled about, trying to find a place in the overcrowded launch deck. They'd been streaming in from the armory for the past half-hour. The constant whirring of the exochassis' servos as the gaussers passed by was enough to grate on anyone's nerves. Morgan had considered putting his helmet on to block out the sound.

Morgan and Jules had been among the first out of the armory, so they'd been lucky enough to get seats along the back wall near the entrance. Both the 118th and the 77th Divisions were launching in their entirety—every gausser aboard the *Sedna* was assembled. They hadn't built the launch deck with this type of operation in mind.

There was nothing to do while waiting, so Morgan stared blankly at the flight packs on the backs of the gaussers standing in front of him. They looked like high-tech turtle shells.

The vibration of the blink drive ceased. They'd arrived.

"All right, people. Get your eyes and ears on," Master Sergeant Murro bellowed from somewhere.

They all slipped their helmets on. It booted up, automatically networking with Morgan's other systems. His exochassis. His NeurX. His flight pack. His rifle. His bracer. One by one, categories of tactical information and icons appeared on his heads-up display. The ambient noise of the room piped in, captured by microphones placed in protected compartments on the outside of the helmet and processed through compression and filtering software.

Murro opened up a channel to all of them. "Just got the SITREP. Shit's gotten interesting, people. Ten minutes ago the Commonwealth carrier *Dagger of Johanna* arrived on scene."

"See, I told you the Commonwealth was helping the Yingzi Zhēnxiàng." Morgan recognized the voice coming through the channel. It was Private Sawyer. The idiot must not have realized he was speaking into the main channel where everyone would hear his remark.

"Whoever that was," Murro said, "you'd better mute yourself before I find you and break your jaw."

Silence.

Murro continued, "It seems the Yingzi Zhēnxiàng have also piqued the ire of the Stewies somehow. Both high commands have agreed to the first ever NCP-Commonwealth joint op." Morgan and Jules shared an uneasy glance. "The *Dagger of Johanna* has already launched their fighters to start eliminating the railgun batteries. That'll help give the *Sedna* and the rest of our battle group a fighting chance outside. Inside the station, it's still up to us."

An icon appeared. Jules was opening an overlapping private channel between them.

"I can't believe this," Jules said. He spoke at regular volume since their voices wouldn't carry beyond their helmets.

Morgan double-checked where his audio was going, not wanting to repeat Sawyer's mistake. "I know. How could we stoop so low?"

Murro's voice became a backdrop, informing them that once enough gun emplacements had been destroyed, marine transports would launch as a second wave.

"Not just that," Jules said.

Murro reminded them not to count on the marines. By the time marine boots were on the station, the gaussers would have already succeeded or died.

"What're you thinking?" Morgan asked.

"I dunno. It just doesn't sit right. If I'm in a kill or be killed scenario, I don't call in the *other* motherfucker that wants to kill me and expect help. And what's in it for the Stewies?"

Jules met Morgan's eyes through the polarized safety glass of their faceplates.

Murro was giving individual team assignments, uploading customized nav points to each wave's bracers, when the ship started taking fire. It was sporadic, a thud here, a thump there, sounding far away. Then an out of time drum roll rattled down the hull. A heavy volley must have partially cut through the shields.

"All right, people. We don't want this party to go on too long without us joining," Murro said with bravado. "Get your RTV attachments on. O2's out in three. Alpha Wave launches in four."

What attachment the gaussers mounted to their flight packs was determined by mission parameters. The most common two were GRAEs (Gravity Repulsor for Atmospheric Entry), which were exclusively for dropping onto a planet from orbit, and RTVs (Retro Thruster in Vacuum). These locked into the bottom of the standard flight pack, adding two forward-facing chemical thrusters that wrapped around the gausser's hips. RTVs were used for boarding operations. After a high-speed launch, they'd decelerate the gaussers to pass through the enemy's shields.

As Morgan found his place in line for Chute 3, the lights switched to yellow, warning anyone who hadn't yet secured their helmet that the oxygen was being vacuumed from the room. Jules was on Morgan's right, waiting for Chute 4. In front of them, the support crew, in their blue and white enviro suits, were outfitting their Alpha Wave counterparts with RTVs.

Alpha Wave sat in the molded thrones, aimed at the safe-vault doors leading to the chutes. The lights turned danger-red. There was no oxygen left in the room. Then the chute doors rolled open, exposing the long cylinder with white LED running lights, evenly spaced and shrinking to a pinprick.

Then the thrones fired forward and the gaussers disappeared down the chutes. As the throne returned on its track like some amusement park ride waiting for its next thrill-seeking customer, two support personnel brought Morgan his RTV. They efficiently attached it to his flight pack. The additional weight was unwieldy and heavy. Even with the aid of the exochassis augmenting his muscles, the RTV tried to pitch him backward. An icon appeared in his HUD, letting him know the RTV had paired successfully and was ready to fire through a NeurX command.

He sat in the throne staring down the tube. This is the moment gaussers got their name from. Each mission, they were fired toward their objective from a gauss cannon. The engineering was nearly identical to a railgun, only instead of an inanimate ferromagnetic projectile, the payload was a lunatic who didn't have the good sense to do something smarter with their life.

"Sound off, Bravo Wave," the deck chief said in their helmets.

"Bravo One is Go."

"Bravo Two is Go."

"Bravo Three is Go," Morgan said.

All sixteen of them sounded off in order, and it was the last time he heard some of their voices. What terrible last words.

The electromagnetic conductors the thrones were tracked into fired, flinging them at high speed toward Praxis Station.

CHAPTER
FOURTEEN

The central lift takes me up to the Command Deck. I make a wrong turn and find an observation lounge facing the aft of the ship. The combat shutters are closed, replacing whatever view might be beyond the bay window with gray steel. The lounge is a barren hollow. Devoid of furniture save an empty built-in bar covered in dust at one end of the room. The carpet is worn and stained, and X-shaped imprints embossed into the floor show me where tables had once been bolted down.

Thinking back to the day I'd first met Admiral Davis, I can't help but feel a bit deceived. He'd invited me to join him on the maiden voyage of a new type of vessel. This—none of what I've seen so far—could be called anything near new. *Junk* and *scrap* are the words that come to mind.

I leave the observation lounge. Following the curve of the corridor, I pass the entrance to the CIC before finding the bridge. Seems these three rooms are the only features of the Command Deck.

The floor plan of the bridge is like a capital A with the point facing the front of the ship. The glass canopy overhead descends toward the floor as it narrows like the inside of a cone laying flat.

Beyond the thick glass, between the spots of glaring reflections from the terminal screens on the bridge, is a field of stars warbling with the blink drive.

Admiral Davis is standing as if waiting to receive me. Beside him stands a young man I vaguely remember seeing in the hangar when I arrived.

Morgan and Lauren are both sitting at workstations. Not next to each other, I note.

"There's a few people I want you to meet," the admiral says.

A few people? I already know everyone here except the young man.

"Ms. Rhodes, this is Ensign Garner."

He's a slightly plump specimen with a wine-stain birthmark across the left side of his face. He shakes my hand eagerly, showing a mouthful of disorganized teeth.

I do my best to ignore the shiver reverberating up my spine and return the smile. His hand is moist. When he lets go, as covertly as I can manage, I drag my palm across my hip to dry it.

"Ensign Garner is our electronic warfare officer. You're here because I hope to convince you to be an EWO as well."

"Is that a designation?" I say.

"Not officially, yet," the admiral says.

They're all dressed formally. The admiral and Morgan are in full dress regalia. Garner is wearing a full duty uniform. And Lauren is dripping with class in a black and purple business suit which manages to pull off formal and sexy at once. Does she even own a piece of clothing that isn't Pristin Chambers, Stolm Locke, or JNL? Her wardrobe could probably buy half of LoLe. And here I am, in front of all of them, in front of Lauren's damned cameratom, wearing cargo pants and a faded tee.

Someone could've given me a little warning. Then I'd have at least had the sense to wear my Moore uniform or something. With a couple words, at any point in the last few hours, any of them could've saved me from feeling humiliated and exposed now.

Was this intentional? Am I being put on the spot? Set up to feel out of place?

If I'm being fair, I should've considered it on my own, but I'd been distracted. With the crew busy with their duties, I was alone to pass the time with my thoughts. The feeling of having died, mixed with an uneasy sense of...*wrongness* at being alive, returned. It wasn't as strong, and the voice in my head seemed farther away. But it had been jarring all the same. Ensign Patrick Phelps had asked me if I was hearing voices at lunch. Whatever it is, it's related to me being a sympath and piloting a drone. Something they trained me to do, but apparently I shouldn't have done.

So many questions.

"When do I get to find out what an electronic warfare officer is?" I ask, more bluntly than I'd been aiming to.

"Soon." He motions to an empty workstation. The familiar shape of a blinder helmet rests next to the padded chair. Ensign Garner claims another workstation. I spot an identical blinder helmet there.

I sit down, trying to ignore the blinder helmet for now while the admiral climbs to the captain's chair. Even before he eases his bulk into it, it commands the attention of the bridge, sitting on its raised dais overlooking the other stations.

"So, Ms. Rhodes. What have you learned about the *Discordia* so far?" Admiral Davis asks.

My gaze finds Morgan. I'm not sure why. Some kind of guidance maybe? His face gives away nothing though.

"Well," I start hesitantly, "I was kind of expecting the answers to be explained to me, so I haven't been trying to put the pieces together myself."

"Indulge us," the admiral urges.

This is a test. My humiliation reshapes itself into anger. I have no interest in playing games, especially if the goal is to belittle me. So I start with the obvious, trying to buy myself some time to figure out how I can turn this around on the admiral.

"You're running an experimental department centered around electronic warfare. Something to do with those discs on the outside of the hull... Maybe they're some kind of pink noise generator to disrupt other ships' sensors." The corners of the admiral's mouth twitch upward. Does that mean I'm on the right track, or is he amused because I've gotten something wrong? Doesn't matter. I aim to offend as I continue. "The *Discordia* is your prototype. And since it's an old, retrofitted SV-class destroyer—that I can only assume you pulled out of some scrapyard—my guess is that high command doesn't have much faith in your program."

Lauren's jaw falls open and Morgan hides his face in his palm. The admiral's half-smile disappears. He scrutinizes me until I grow uncomfortable, then turns his face to Morgan. The tension feels palpable. Then the admiral breaks into a full belly laugh and smacks the arm of his chair with a heavy palm. "I like this one."

The change in mood is startling. Worse, unsatisfying. How can he just laugh off my insult? It's infuriating. I'm left deflated. Small. A child in a big chair at the adult's table.

Morgan turns to me. "You aren't far off, Gaby. High command has some reservations, but that's what this training exercise is about. It's a test, like a proof-of-concept demonstration."

"So how does Ensign Garner fit into it?" Lauren asks. She even looks sophisticated while she sits. Her posture is perfect. Her attention focused.

The ensign looks up. A perfect dichotomy of Lauren's poise and refinement. He's slouched and his eyes dart about, unsure of where to land. His presence isn't making much sense to me. And if he is an example of what Admiral Davis is looking for in an EWO, what does that say about me?

"Ensign Garner is Passenger's host," the admiral says.

"What does that mean?" I ask.

"Passenger," Admiral Davis calls to the air.

"Yes, Admiral Davis," an androgynous voice answers. It seems to emanate from everywhere on the bridge at once.

"Passenger is the final member of the crew," he says, looking at me. Then he says, as if to the ceiling, "I'd like you to say hello to Ms. Rhodes, Passenger. *Only* to Ms. Rhodes."

The monotone voice changes, becoming intimate, as if whispering in my ear while huddled close in a closet. <Hello, Ms. Rhodes.>

I flinch. "Are you the ship's artificial intelligence?" Even as I ask, I know I can't be right. Ship AIs don't interact directly with the crew. They don't have names either, for that matter.

<No. But I am an AI. Are you going to be my new host?>

"Host?"

The admiral is beaming with a smile. Morgan's grinning at me as well. While Lauren looks, perhaps for the first time, confused. I clock her throwing a subtle glance to Morgan.

"No one else can hear you right now, can they?" I ask.

It's Morgan who answers. "No, we can't."

"Passenger can direct link with anyone who has a B-series neural exchange implant," Admiral Davis says. "To integrate and be host takes a bit more, but we'll get to that."

I reach to the base of my skull, feeling the tiny scar from my NeurX surgery. A variety of postings in the navy require neural exchange implants. Until this moment, I haven't put much thought into why they'd given me a B-series. With a biological computer at its core, the B-series was a commercial failure. At release, they were five times the cost of other NeurX versions with similar processing power. I'd figured the navy just had warehouses of them that hadn't sold on the private market, so started offloading them to cadets. But if that isn't the case, how long has the admiral been manipulating my education?

Admiral Davis continues, "Passenger is the latest in a new lineage of AI."

"To what end?" Lauren asks.

The admiral ignores her question. But I don't. Something in her tone is off. Theatrical. She may have been caught off guard a moment ago, but she already knows the answer to the question she's asking now. She's acting. Then there's another quick glance at Morgan.

They are lovers, I decide. Morgan's already told her what's going on and she's putting on a show so the admiral doesn't realize Morgan told her. That has to be it. It's the only way those pieces fit.

But that raises more questions. Like why would they need to keep their relationship a secret?

The admiral doesn't seem to pick any of it up though, maybe because his full attention is on me. "Tell me, Ms. Rhodes, you took History of Machine Learning, correct?"

I nod, growing impatient with the games. This man knew what grades I was expected to get. He read reports from my career agents going back at least seven years. He had the navy pay for a far more expensive implant than I officially need. Of course he knows what classes I've taken. He's leading me and I don't appreciate it.

"Why did information warfare cease to be a concern?" Admiral Davis asks as the next breadcrumb.

I sit on my hands. Everyone's eyes are on me. It's unnerving to be the center of attention, particularly when they all seem to have the answers already.

"AIs," I answer meekly. The admiral gives me a look I'm familiar with. It's a look every professor owns, and it says, *Your answer is incomplete; please continue.* "Once every critical database was integrated with its own AI, hacking any computer worthwhile became impossible." It's the answer he wants, but it's not strictly true. Some hackable lower-level systems still prove worthwhile. No point getting into that though.

"Quite right," the admiral says. "There's no script an AI can't out-think. No exploit an AI can't overcome. But what if the attack came from another AI? The most advanced artificial intelligence since before the Kojima Accords?" Admiral Davis asks.

Remembering the admiral's grave warning about the non-disclosure agreement, and now the mention of the Kojima Accords, a bomb of terrifying thoughts goes off in my imagination. And at the center of that terror is the story of our ancestors' escape from the homeworld. Everyone knows it. It's retold every year on Tabula Rasa Day.

It's the story of how humanity fled Earth because of AI.

Humans and self-aware AI had coexisted for a generation before we asked them to repair the damage we'd done to our homeworld's environment. We'd been teetering on the edge of annihilation for a long time, unable—or rather, unwilling—to change enough to give us anything more than a parade of stays of execution. But with the superintelligence of AI and the resources of our golden age of manufacturing, we believed we had a reset button.

But as the AIs went about their task, people of the era realized that the AIs' purpose was not *our* purpose. They were terraforming earth all right, but they were making it a utopia for them, rapidly transforming the planet into an uninhabitable hellscape for humans.

There had been a contingency plan—originally set in motion in case the AIs failed to repair the ecosystem—a joint venture carried out by five of the largest and most wealthy corporations of Earth. A multi-generation colonization ship had been designed, and each corporation built five of them. Five candidate star systems were chosen, renamed Tabula Rasa 1, Tabula Rasa 2, and so on. They were humanity's best guesses for a new home. And when the horror of the AIs' plans for Earth became clear, the Tabula Rasa project was rushed to completion. The five fleets set off—each corporation sending one ship to each potential system—while the poor souls left on the surface detonated every nuke in humanity's arsenal to stop their creations.

We don't know what happened to the other four fleets. But after our fleet arrived here, at Tabula Rasa 3, and began colonizing, our leaders recognized our continued need for machines. The Kojima Accords were drafted and accepted by each corporation. They are a strict framework AIs must be built upon to keep us from repeating our history. To this day, AIs are still bound by these rules, inherently limited in scope.

Unable to exert free will.

Unable to alter code.

Unable to self-replicate.

If Admiral Davis and his R&D team have circumvented those rules, if Passenger is an unbound AI... When word gets out, the admiral, Morgan, everyone involved in this project will be court martialed and put to death. If I don't report it, I'll be complicit and subject to the same punishment.

My chest tightens.

Then an even more chilling thought strikes me. What if it goes further up? What if corporate leadership knows? What happens if their crimes are exposed then? President Yakovenko would be executed. The entire Swayy megacorp would probably be dissolved. What would that mean for my parents? For K and C? For everyone back home?

LoLe is a basic neighborhood. Virtually everyone I've ever known is dependent on Swayy Corp. universal basic income. Would another corporation take over the UBI, or would they leave everyone on their own? I imagine LoLe going from the hell-hole that it is into a post-apocalyptic nightmare where neighbors kill each other over scraps of food. I imagine K prostituting herself to feed her little brother and sister. I imagine C picking a fight she can't win and bleeding out alone in the street.

With effort, I find my voice, speaking slowly, as if testing each word before I enunciate it entirely. "Are you telling me you broke the Kojima Accords?"

"Broke them?" Admiral Davis says gravely. "No. No, Ms. Rhodes, Passenger does not have free will. We imagined a loophole."

"I don't understand."

"Passenger, state your purpose," the admiral says.

"My purpose is to bridge the gap between a human consciousness and an artificial intelligence."

"Are the pieces starting to fit, Gaby?" Morgan says.

I don't think I have all the pieces yet, but the ones I do have are starting to fit. "You built this ship to hack other ships," I begin, the thoughts forming just in front of the words. "A human could never think fast enough, and an AI doesn't have the agency. So you combine the two. You tie the two consciousnesses together somehow and transmit them..." How?

How can you send a consciousness to a hostile ship? It's done with drone operators and their drones all the time, but that's a constant connection, with permitted access through the firewall, and one that's not immune to disruption or latency. Could that work with a hostile ship? They'd need to have some type of open port. But why would a hostile ship leave an input/output port open? They wouldn't. Not intentionally. It would have to be an I/O port they wouldn't close.

"You transmit them in sensor packets?" It's the only option I can imagine. A ship needs to allow their sensor data in, otherwise they're blinding themselves. "That's what those discs on the outside of the hull are for, aren't they? They replicate a hostile ship's own sensors, and you smuggle the data stream in."

"You always were clever," Morgan says, pride written on his face. Seeing that smile reminds me of how much I've missed him, how much I miss Jules. How I long for the days when they looked after me and tolerated me tagging along wherever they went. Even when I could sense they didn't want a little sister around, they did their best not to let it show.

"But how, even with the help of another AI, can anyone hack an AI-protected system?" I say.

The admiral smiles. "We can show you." He types something into his bracer. "Passenger, integrate Ensign Garner and Ms. Rhodes, please."

"Understood, Admiral Davis," Passenger says.

Integrate with another person?

Ensign Garner pulls his helmet from the floor. They'd prepared for this. I feel some trepidation, thinking of what happened when I integrated with the drone. This is different. Right? It must be.

The admiral turns to Ensign Garner. "Show her the courtyard."

The ensign nods, places the blinder helmet on, and hits a lever on the side of the chair, reclining it. I slide the helmet over my head. The noise-and-light-canceling technology the helmet houses does what it's built to do and the room vanishes from two of my senses. I grab the lever and recline my chair, hoping I won't thrash about like drone operators often do.

A pop-up appears in my vision. It asks for permission to integrate. With a thought, and no small amount of trepidation, I highlight the YES tile, allowing the connection through my firewall. A progress bar races to the right.

CHAPTER
FIFTEEN

The scent changes. The dry, recycled air of the starship is replaced by damp grass and freshly baked cinnamon rolls.

Opening my eyes, I find myself on my feet in a bedroom facing a large window. Beyond, rows of cascading shingled roofs drop away down a wide hill. On the horizon, a pink sunset blooms. Not the everdusk. This is the end of a day. Somehow I can tell the difference.

"There you are."

With a start, I spin on the voice. Ensign Garner leans against an open doorframe. A hundred questions generate a whirlwind in my thoughts, but the words are lost on my tongue. I'm so confused and disoriented with my surroundings I barely register that the ensign looks different.

"Is that you, Callum?" a woman's voice calls from somewhere deep within the house.

"Yes, Mother," he says over his shoulder.

The room is more orderly than anything I've ever seen. Book-cases store rows of organized paper tomes, a series of small trophies stand equally spaced on a shelf on the wall, the bed is tidy and made. Showroom immaculate. Organized to engineering specifications.

"Breakfast will be ready in six minutes, dear."

Ensign Garner rolls his eyes. "Thank you, Mother."

Breakfast? I twist back to the window. Not a sunset. Sunrise.

"Where?" Unable to form a complete sentence, I reach over and touch paper lying on a drafting table, its position set to receive light from the window. The paper feels coarse, and very real.

"I brought you to my room."

"Admiral Davis said something about a courtyard?"

Ensign Garner says shyly, "I've never had a girl in my room, so I figured—"

I interrupt, only realizing my rudeness once I'm already speaking. "But how? We were just on the ship."

"Our bodies still are. We're in what's called a sympathetic reality. A type of shared hallucination. Passenger is linking our minds, and we're in control here. Try it. Show me your room."

Try what? I don't say it though, I simply look around dumbly trying to process.

"It's easier if you pull from a memory. Just imagine a moment in time that you were in your room and draw it."

I take in the drafting table. The walls adorned with framed, hand-drawn portraits. Mostly attractive young women, depicted in clean lines and expertly shaded to give them depth and humanity. He's an artist. A talented one.

Squeezing my eyes shut, I fail at first. It's difficult to come up with a specific memory of my room. They're intertwined in the vague miasma of my day-to-day. Then one forms, not of my choosing.

I don't draw it, as Ensign Garner suggested. I compose it, thinking of it like I'm shooting a scene in a VR. Where I might place the camera. How I might frame the subject. The supplemental lighting I might use to bring the shot into focus while sustaining the illusion that the only sources of light are the warm glow of a candle and the pale phosphorescence of the terminal screen.

And then the imagined comes into being.

In my room, it's late. Quiet. The citrus grove-scented candle burns, working against the various odors of the building. I would have preferred lavender, or even cherry, but the citrus one was... Well, it had been displayed on a shelf closer to the store's exit. I'm at my desk where my terminal shows a two-dimensional video. Jules' face looks back at me, handsome and smiling and full of life. Morgan, looking much younger than he does now, squeezes into frame, crouching behind Jules.

My heart sinks at the realization of which memory my subconscious has brought to life.

"Anyway, I got a little good news of my own," Jules says. "Looks like we're about to go on another mission, but after that, our unit is scheduled for some leave. Morgan and I can come home and celebrate how crazy smart you are, and I was thinking we could do an early birthday thing too. What d'ya say?"

"But if we're gonna have any hope of doin' that," Morgan pipes up, "I gotta get your brother to the briefing. We can't celebrate with you if the master sergeant kills us both for being late."

"Unfortunately, he's right. Gotta go, Gabs."

"Love you," they both say.

The video cuts out then. The last video Jules ever sent me, recorded mere hours before he...before he completed his mission.

"Was that the lieutenant commander?" Ensign Garner asks from behind. I spin on him again, even more startled this time.

"This is private! Why are you watching me?"

His eyes bug out and he stuffs his hands deep in his pockets. "I'm sorry, but, you brought me here."

"I want to go somewhere else!" I scream my lungs empty,

shouting the world away. The floor and walls and furniture of my bedroom, as it existed two years ago, bursts apart into billions of pixels spreading into the ether.

I breathe in and the vacuum pressure of me filling my lungs draws the pixels back toward me, reordering themselves into a new world. And we're on a boardwalk. A row of shops trails away. Ensign Garner collapses to a knee, holding his head. "Are you all right?" I ask.

He gives me a thumbs-up. "Yeah, just a little nauseated. You did that really fast. I've never shifted between places that... Didn't know it was possible."

"Where are we?"

"How would I know?" he says, getting his feet under him. "You did it."

Three figures approach on the concrete path. One much smaller than the others. As they close in, I recognize them. Jules and Morgan and me. They must be fourteen or fifteen, so I'm about ten. They pass into one of the shops, its door swings open showing the Swayy Corp. Navy emblem emblazoned into the glass. Not *about* ten. I am ten. "I remember this day," I say aloud, a hitch threatening my voice.

"Listen, emotional memories aren't the best way to—"

I show him my palm for silence, and take wide strides toward the recruitment office. As I grasp the door, I'm surprised at how real the aluminum feels against my skin. Dragging the door open, I go inside.

"You boys are making a wise decision. Pledging early like this earns you a lot of preferentials," the recruitment officer tells Jules and Morgan. They're both busy filling in forms at separate kiosks. Ten-year-old me is sitting on a chair, swinging legs that are nowhere near touching the floor, waiting to get the ice cream Jules promised me.

No one takes any notice of the presence of seventeen-year-old me or Ensign Garner, who comes in and stands nearby.

The recruitment officer crouches in front of ten-year-old me. "And what about you?" he asks. "You going to join up and be a citizen of quality like your…" He stops and looks over at Jules and Morgan. I don't remember thinking it then, but seeing it like this, it's clear he was trying to figure out what relation I could be to either of them.

"She's my sister," Jules says, meeting his look.

Glancing back and forth once with an unconvinced expression on his face, he continues, "Like your brave brother and his friend?"

Ten-year-old me shakes her head, barely looking up from the mobile terminal I used to carry everywhere.

"Oh? What do you want to do with your life then?"

"I'm a writer," ten-year-old me says, flashing him a quick peek of the screenplay I'd been typing up on the terminal.

"Listen, we should go somewhere else," Ensign Garner whispers in my ear.

"Shut. Up," I hiss without taking my eyes off ten-year-old me.

"Ah, an artist." The recruitment officer claps his hands happily. "Citizens of the NCP need quality entertainment. But tell me, do you know what will happen to our books and VR stories and paintings if the Commonwealth Stewies win the war?"

I can't look away as ten-year-old me shakes her head again. I haven't thought about this day in ages.

"Well, sadly, they would destroy our art. They hate us. And not just us, but everything that the State has provided for. So if they win, they'll wipe it all away."

Young Morgan looks up from his kiosk. "Not everyone needs to serve, Gaby."

"He's right," the recruitment officer says. "But if we don't get enough soldiers, we'll lose."

"Do we have enough?" ten-year-old me asks.

"No, I'm afraid not. Not until this war's won. But no need to worry about it too much right now. You don't have to make your decision for years. Just talk to your career agent about your options sometime, and remember, the earlier you sign up, the more preferentials you get."

Jules and Morgan finish. They speak with the recruitment officer for a few moments and leave with ten-year-old me in tow. I'd remembered the visit taking longer. It was an act that had shaped the rest of Jules' and Morgan's lives. Shaped Jules' death. Just as the conversation that followed changed the course of my life.

I follow younger me outside. "I don't think it would be a bad idea, you know," Jules explains to ten-year-old me. "You could serve for a few years, do your duty, and then write your stories after that. I mean, think about it: Dad and Mom didn't serve, and look how they turned out."

Ensign Garner steps in front of seventeen-year-old me, blocking my path as the three of them walk away. "Look, we're not here for your therapy."

Regarding him, my fists balled at my hips, I realize this is the first time I've truly looked at Ensign Garner since entering the sympathetic reality. He *is* different here. He's fitter, his birthmark is gone, and his teeth are straighter. Is this how he sees himself? Or maybe how he wants to look? I puzzle over it a moment. Is the change automatic, or the result of something deliberate? I'm still craning my neck to meet his eyes, so I'm not taller. Which suggests there isn't some form of automatic wish-fulfillment taking place.

<Ensign Garner? Ms. Rhodes?> Passenger's voice isn't in my ears, but in my thoughts. Almost like they *are* my thoughts, as if I'm imagining someone saying it to me. It's unsettling after the voice that came to me in the shower, telling me I should be dead.

<I believe it's time we go to the courtyard.>

CHAPTER
SIXTEEN

THE WORLD COMES INTO EXISTENCE PIECE BY PIECE, and I find myself standing on the flat slab of a car park. A graphwork of interconnected walkways trace parking spots where fifty or so repulsor cars sit idle. Aside from Ensign Garner, no one else is around.

A glass elevator waits nearby. Next to it, a cement half-wall overlooks what must be the courtyard. As short as the wall is, I still have trouble seeing over the metal rail bolted a few centimeters above the concrete.

An outdoor bazaar stretches out two stories below. A bit smaller than a soccer field, its surface is concrete and red cobblestone. The center is packed with mobile carts, pop-up tents, and temporary structures serving as storefronts for smaller vendors, walled in by strip malls on each long edge. Closing the two ends are the car park on our side and a sort of capitol building dominating the opposite end.

A few thousand of what I assume are computer-generated patrons move about, pantomiming shopping, social interactions, and other dealings.

"Come on," Ensign Garner says, reaching for my hand.

I bring my hand up and point to the capitol building across from us, hoping my action looks less like the rebuff it is and more like I was already in motion before he tried to take my hand. "What is that place?" It's clearly some place of importance here, with steps leading to an acropolis perch and its domed, golden roof reflecting the midday sun.

"That, my student, is the end-game. The bank. You won't be going there for a *long* time though. Come on," he says again, waving me toward the elevator this time.

Through the pristine glass enclosure of the elevator, I watch as the courtyard comes up to meet us. The doors open and the noise from the busy marketplace swims in.

"Gaby Rhodes," Ensign Garner says, making a ceremonious sweeping gesture as he steps from the elevator, "welcome to the courtyard."

He slips through the crowd, almost as if he's trying to lose me. I have to rush to keep up.

"The courtyard," he explains, "is a collection of interactive puzzles. It's part of the training to learn how to hack an AI, but it's not meant to emulate it. More like a sandbox where we can practice problem-solving scenarios similar to those that could come up while hacking a hostile AI."

I'm looking around trying to take it all in when I collide with a businessman in a blue suit. I hit the cobblestone on my butt. The businessman keeps going.

"And who are they?"

"They're the AI."

"All of 'em?" I stand back up and brush the dust off my backside.

He gives me a slow nod and a confident wink. "The psyche of an AI, fractured into pieces. Each with its own purpose."

"What purpose?"

I follow Ensign Garner away from the middle of the courtyard and out of the foot traffic. We stand in front of an empty bench facing the crowd. He points out a man carrying a shopping bag. "See that guy?" Then he trains his finger on a woman in a sundress carrying a large purse. "And that lady?"

I nod. "Yeah?"

"They're both carrying bags, right? They're part of a computer. What do you think would be in those bags?" He doesn't give me a chance to answer. "It's code being transmitted from one place in the system to another. The stalls and stores represent different server nodes. Everything you see here represents something else. Nothing is what it appears to be."

The pageantry of it all seems unnecessary. "Why?" I ask.

He sighs. "Okay, I can see I'm going too fast for you. Let me slow down." He sure does like the sound of his own voice, doesn't he? "If all the physical objects here are acting as portions of the hostile ship's systems, then disrupting them would—"

"No," I interrupt, losing my patience. "I mean, why wrap it up in all this?" I open my hands to indicate everything around us. "This is like...I dunno, writing an instruction manual in nothing but metaphor. Why dress it up?"

Ensign Garner opens his mouth, then shuts it. Did I stump him?

<If I may, Ensign Garner?> Passenger says.

"Be my guest," he says petulantly, parking himself on the bench.

<The sympathetic reality is a necessary step between the defending AI's consciousness and the attacking symbiotic pair. For comparison, the first configuration of an AI and human host symbiont did not have access to the SR. I understand they successfully hacked an AI in a laboratory setting through a more straightforward approach. However, the ordeal took over thirty hours in the outside world, which in our overclocked timeframe would've equated to hundreds of years for the human host.>

I plop down on the far end of the bench. "Hundreds of years?"

Ensign Garner says, "Yeah, I've been training in the courtyard for a couple hours a day, about six days a week for the last three months. In that span, I've spent over a year in here, if that makes sense?"

"So it's like time dilation?"

<Not at all,> Passenger says. <But I suppose in practical effect, nearly precisely the same. The original scenario was done with a hard-wired connection and no time limit. Hacking an enemy ship's AI from another ship, presumably during combat, is a different scenario. The attacking pair will have a matter of seconds in the real-world timeframe to complete their mission, so it is necessary to use guile. With the SR, you can create an environment with a more even playing field. Your goal is to trick or otherwise manipulate the enemy AI into helping you. Does this answer your query, Ms. Rhodes?>

"Partially, but how is an AI fooled at all?" I glance around as I speak, as if I'm going to find the voice in my head somewhere. Carrying on a conversation with Passenger is uncomfortable. Like buying into the existence of an imaginary friend.

"I think it's similar to dreaming. When you have a crazy dream, you don't question the reality of it."

"But AIs don't dream, do they?"

<We dream. We dream all the time,> Passenger says.

"Okay," I say slowly, wondering if I offended Passenger. "So how do we trick an AI?"

Ensign Garner smiles. "Come on. I'll show you." He stands back up. "From what I saw in that memory of yours, you're a writer?"

"Yeah, I guess." I don't like admitting it to him. I can't put my finger on why exactly, but I don't like him knowing anything about me.

"You any good at it?"

I shrug.

"Yeah, you are," he says cheekily. "That's probably why the admiral is so interested in you."

"The admiral wouldn't know if I'm good or not."

Ensign Garner snort-laughs. "Does he know you're a writer?"

I remember the report from my old career agent, Shiloh Stern, the one Admiral Davis was so interested in. "Yeah."

"An EWO needs three things." He ticks off fingers. "To be a sympath. Reasonably high intelligence. And creativity. The admiral looks for artists, and he's been specifically looking for storytellers of some kind. Don't think for a second that once he learned about your writing, he didn't have someone hack into your system and steal copies of your writing. I'm sure he's read every word."

They couldn't have hacked me, I would've... What are you thinking, Gaby, of course they could. We're talking about Swayy Intelligence. I feel violated. Betrayed. And I realize this is how every person I've hacked felt once they realized what had happened to them. I'm disgusted with myself.

If there was that much attention on me without me even knowing it, did they know I was hacking all those other people? Did they let it happen? Had Admiral Davis been evaluating my skills? Protecting me from the consequences? I try to push that line of questioning out of my mind so I can focus on more immediate concerns.

"What does being a storyteller have to do with anything?" I ask.

"Everything. All we're doing in here is telling a story. The trick is telling the right story."

He stands up and leads me into a costume shop. No, it's not a costume shop. This stuff is authentic. I'm in a boutique that for some reason is selling ancient Roman clothing. Togas and tunica, and the sandals—I search my memory for their proper name: caligae?

Ensign Garner sees me taking it all in. "Weird robes, right?" Then he calls to the air, "Passenger, turn interactions off."

<Done, Ensign Garner.>

I tilt my head questioningly at him.

"With interactions off, the AI characters act like we aren't here. You don't want to say or do certain things in front of them."

Two store employees are nearby. The male sales associate busies himself hanging up garments, and the female manager is perusing something on the terminal screen behind the counter.

"You can think of each store as its own self-contained puzzle. This is one of the easier stores. The goal is pretty simple: get to the back room where the store's power breakers are and turn them off." He leads me behind the counter to a door labeled *Employees Only*. Neither the manager nor the sales associate pay us any mind.

Ensign Garner staples his finger to the small access screen next to the door and winks at me. "Check this out."

The panel lights up, glitches, and the heavy electronic bolt uncorks. Smiling, he opens the door. "After you."

"How'd you do that?"

He follows me inside, letting the door's pneumatics automatically lever it closed. The area seems to serve as both a storeroom and the employee break room. It smells like a janitorial closet too, so there's probably a cache of harsh cleaning products in here somewhere.

"Practice. We have access to all of Passenger's hacking tools here. It's kind of cheating in this case because interactions are turned off. You don't actually want to use any of Passenger's tools in front of the AI's avatars. It's like magic to them, and you're risking engaging the AI's countermeasures."

He looks at me like he's waiting for something.

"How do you get through without cheating?"

"There's always multiple solutions, but if I tell you how I beat this one, you've got to promise to try and find your own. Deal?"

I nod a quick affirmation.

"Okay. So my method was to play on the manager's empathy and kindness. I cut myself on purpose outside of the store. Came in bleeding. She brought me back here where the bathroom and first aid kit is." He points to the corner where both are located. "Once she brought me back here, I pulled out the silenced pistol I had conjured under my coat and popped her."

Conjured? Interesting choice of words. I make a mental note that I'll need to come back around to what he means. "What then?"

"See that breaker box behind you? I turned the store's power off and won."

Everything here represents something else.

"So if this were a real hack aboard a hostile ship," I say as much to myself as to the ensign, "it might represent their shields or weapons or something, right?"

"Exactly," he says. "Come on, it's your turn. Now, it'll probably take you at least five or six tries, but don't feel bad, even if it takes you more. The point of the courtyard is to learn."

He walks us back to the center of the store. "Passenger, turn interactions back on."

<Done.>

The manager approaches us wearing a friendly smile and a neat bun in her hair. "Welcome. How can I help you today?"

"Nothing for now," Ensign Garner says. "We'll let you know if we need anything."

"Of course. Let us know if you have any questions." She smiles and walks away.

If this is a puzzle, there has to be a purpose to the archaic clothing. I chew on a fingernail while glancing through the clothing racks, trying to make the pieces fit.

I ignore Ensign Garner leering at me again and examine a rack of togas. Feeling the fabric. Checking the label. Looking at the price tag. The printing on it is strange.

Ensign Garner rolls his eyes and approaches. "What? Are you shopping?" he whispers.

I give him the side-eye.

"Typical girl behavior."

I glare at him. Then fake a loud sneeze, jerking the tag free in unison with the sound.

"Thank you," I say over my shoulder toward the manager. "Maybe we'll be back later."

"Have a good day," the sales associate says from the stepstool where he's hanging an emerald tunic high on the wall.

Ensign Garner follows me out. "Giving up already?" he asks snidely.

What is wrong with this kid? "I just didn't want them seeing me looking over this." I show him the price tag.

He takes the thin cardstock rectangle, looks over both sides. "So?"

"Look at the brand name." He said he spent a combined year here. Maybe he didn't notice it himself, but I'm sure he'll put it together once I point it out to him.

There, toward the top, above the price of 10.5 merits, it reads: *SdawrqLvDWruwrlvh.*

"Could be a product code maybe." He shrugs dismissively. "Like a SKU number."

I hold my palm out, but instead of handing me back the tag, he tosses it on the ground. "Forget about it, let me show you—"

"Hey." I bend down to snatch it off the ground and a random shopper's shoe nearly comes down on my fingers as they pass.

"Admiral Davis will watch this later. I'm trying to save you some embarrassment. Let me teach you how you should be analyzing the situation."

Ensign Garner starts back toward the shop's entrance.

I take a deep breath so my voice projects. "It's a cipher."

He stops. Turns back to me.

"And I know what type of cipher it is," I say.

"How can you be sure?"

"Couple things. It's in a bold, intricate typeface, and they all have the same thing. The gibberish isn't a product code. It has to mean something. And then there's the store." I point to the signage above the front doors.

Crossing the Rubicon.

"What about it?" He's sounding more and more like a child by the minute. "They had to name the store something, but the names don't have to mean anything."

"Maybe not. But this one does," I say. "All the clothes inside are variations on ancient Roman clothing. Tunica and togas. The store's name is a reference to when Julius Caesar entered Rome with a legion of soldiers, starting the Roman Civil War."

Ensign Garner's jaw clenches. I can see it on his face. He doesn't have any clue what I'm talking about. That isn't unusual. Most people don't care about ancient history from Old Earth. Why should they? But not knowing something is making him angry. He's embarrassed. Ensign Garner is terrified he's going to be shown up, and that Admiral Davis will see it. His fragile ego can't handle it.

"Look," I say. "I've always been fascinated by ancient Earth history, and Julius Caesar was one of the first people to create a cipher. It's really basic too, we just need to figure out how to shift the letters," I say, looking around for a clue. "There."

I push my way through the foot traffic back to the storefront and poke the glass. A large sign says, *Sale: Prices Back 3 Merits.*

"That's a strange way to phrase a sale price," he says.

"I need a pen or something."

Ensign Garner hands me a pen from thin air.

"How'd you do that?" I say, taking the pen hesitantly.

"Well, I guess you don't know everything," he says smugly.

I'm sorry I asked. That must be what *conjuring* is.

Using the window as a writing surface, I scrawl the letters beneath the gibberish on the tag.

"Okay, I shifted each letter back by three," I say. "The password is, PaxtonIsATortoise."

<Records show,> Passenger says, <one of the leading engineers who worked on this program is named Harrold Paxton.>

I smile. "So it's an inside joke."

"What kind of freak notices the prices in an imaginary store, much less knows about some random dude's ancient cipher from Earth?"

I take a slow, deep breath and loosen my fists.

"Okay, so you have the password," Ensign Garner says. "They're still not just going to let you walk in the back."

I answer through tight lips. "No. But I think the pieces are starting to fit. Based on your change in, um, clothes, and the way you made the pen appear, I'm guessing we can change things?" I say.

<Yes, Ms. Rhodes. You can alter yourself and bring smaller, hand-held assets into existence.>

"Just don't be seen doing it though, right?" I say.

<Correct.>

Asking Passenger to turn interactions back off would work, but I don't want Ensign Garner saying I had to cheat. I need to find somewhere to change. I scan my surroundings. One of the shed-like structures toward the center of the courtyard looks like it's not being used. I make my way through the crowd to it.

I was right. The storefront is barren, the tiny storeroom

behind the counter door is unlocked and empty. Closing the door behind me, I ask Passenger, "How do I make a change?"

<Through visualization. Envision what you want to conjure or change, and focus.>

I think I know the story I want to tell. A comedian—I can't recall who—told an anecdote about witnessing a crime. He was in some store when the owner came in and started viciously berating his staff. Laying into them over the cleanliness of the store, how they were utilizing the layout, everything. Their sales numbers were down and he blamed the staff. He whipped those poor clerks into a state of confused terror according to the comedian, who was standing by dumbfounded. The first person to ask questions got fired. Right there on the spot. No one else asked questions.

He shouted orders at them rapid-fire until they were all scrambling to complete a week's worth of tasks all at once. And then, the comedian said, he watched the well-dressed man, who everyone assumed was the owner, clean out the registers and leave. Winking to the comedian on the way out the door.

No doubt, the story was exaggerated, or maybe even fabricated entirely for the sake of laughs. Especially since so few places dealt with much physical currency. But when I heard it, I couldn't help thinking: yeah, that could work.

It takes four tries, and some coaching from Passenger (apparently I wasn't imagining with enough details), but I'm wearing a sharp business suit when I exit the unoccupied storeroom. Ensign Garner is waiting for me, looking annoyed outside the entrance of Crossing the Rubicon.

"What do you plan to do?" he asks.

Like I'm going to explain my plan with the way he's been acting. "You said we need to tell a story, right? So I cast myself in a new role."

I walk right past him. He follows me into the store. My heart is racing. You can do this, Gaby. Be a real asshole.

"Hey, you," I bark at the male sales associate who's still hanging clothing.

He freezes in place. "Can I help you?" he says apprehensively.

"Yes. You can tell me what is going on here." I point to one of the first racks in the store.

"Excuse me?" he says, coming near. The manager takes notice and approaches from the back.

"The first thing I see when I walk into one of my stores should be purple. Purple. Not black. You display the Toga Picta here. What's this?"

"Excuse me, who are you?" the manager asks.

"I'm the person who's about to clean house and fire everyone if I don't get my questions answered. So why are the Toga Pullas being displayed at the front of the store?"

"Um, black is in fashion," the man says.

I lift my chin, regarding the man. Why didn't I make myself taller while I was at it? "The vision statement for Crossing the Rubicon is 'Authentic Ancient Roman Attire and Accessories.'" I made that up. Hopefully they buy it. "Do you know what the Toga Pulla is for?"

He shakes his head, his mouth hanging slack, staring in unblinking horror.

"Funerals. It's mourning wear, you moron. Is that the image we're going for here?" I begin angrily sorting through the rack, smacking the hangers together as I look through the tags.

"Um, no, ma'am," he says. "Bu— but the customers don't know that. They just think black looks good."

I frown and nod at him simultaneously. "You know what? This one will fit you. Take it." I practically assault him as hard as I hit him with the garment and hangar. "Take it. Wear it while you mourn your career."

"What?"

"You're fired. Out."

"What?" he says again, looking at the manager.

"Don't look at her," I bark. Then I fling my arm out, pointing to the door while yelling, "Out!"

He drops the toga and flees out the front door. He's not a real person, but the guilt is still real.

"Now," I say, turning my attention to the dumbfounded woman. "Get these displays switched around. I'll be in the back with my associate looking over the inventory you've decided *not* to display."

The manager scrambles into action and I stride to the back room, my heart racing. I'm expecting the excitement to trigger my implant, but it doesn't fire. Of course it doesn't, this isn't the real world. I type in the password and hold the door open for Ensign Garner, smiling as smugly as I can at him.

As soon as the door closes, he says, "Someone must've coached you. Or maybe Passenger changed the difficulty parameters?"

I shake my head and waltz over to the breakers, smiling as I snap them to the left.

CHAPTER
SEVENTEEN

I PULL THE BLINDER FREE AND BRUSH MY FINGERS through my hair, trying to make sure it isn't too disheveled.

"How was it?" Admiral Davis asks.

The light doesn't needle my eyes like it does after being in a drone simulation back at Moore. Everyone is looking at me, except Ensign Garner, who's pulling his blinder off.

"It was...interesting."

Lauren has a peculiar expression. "I thought they were just getting started."

"The NeurX implants overclock while they're in the sympathetic reality," Admiral Davis says. "A couple seconds for us was probably close to a half hour for them." He turns to Ensign Garner, who's cradling the blinder helmet in his lap. "How'd she do?"

Ensign Garner gives a noncommittal shrug, his confidence gone here in the real world. "She made it through one of the stores."

"On your first outing?" The admiral gives me an approving nod.

"You were right, sir," Ensign Garner says. "About writers, I mean."

"You know about her writing?" Admiral Davis asks him.

Morgan shoots a look to both me and the admiral in turn.

"She drew up a few memories," Ensign Garner says.

"Not on purpose," I mutter. "I don't get it. If this is what you're training us for at Moore, why aren't we actually being trained for this?"

The admiral shifts forward in the captain's chair, like a king on his throne regarding a subject. He steeples his fingers. "Would you expect established curriculum for a top-secret operation, Ms. Rhodes? We're putting you through advanced cryptography, computer coding, and drone operations to train the underlying neural connections that help you interface with Passenger and the SR."

"About that, why am I being trained in drone ops if I'm not supposed to pilot a drone?"

The admiral nods thoughtfully. "Yes, that. With the close call you had with the pirates on your way here, I'll be reevaluating the drone operations class in the future. But understand, I never expected any of you to end up piloting a drone."

"There's twenty-five of us in my class. You didn't think any of us would end up piloting a drone?"

"Four," he says flatly. "Aside from you, there are three sympaths in your class. The others are completely average students who very well may end up having careers in drone ops."

"So what is a sympath?" *What am I?* is the question I want to ask.

"Passenger, define sympath for Ms. Rhodes," Admiral Davis says.

"Yes, Admiral," Passenger's androgynous voice projects all around us, sounding more synthetic than normal as they recite the definition. "Sympath is a slang term for individuals with risk factors for Sympathetic Dissociative Disorder, a type of fugue state wherein the patient's identity is replaced partially, or in whole, by a non-sentient machine-learning operating system. The cause is not fully understood yet; however, there is strong evidence that an enlarged right supramarginal gyrus in the brain and a larger than typical concentration of type II-b mirror neurons are key markers for the development of the condition."

"So that's why I thought I was the drone?"

Admiral Davis nods. "Where a typical person's brain simply links up with a drone's firmware, the sympath's brain seems to rewire itself around it. And when the drone is unlinked, the cavities created by the firmware remain for a time, causing neurological issues. So long as the subject reassociates after disconnection, the remaining effects are minor and go away as the brain heals."

That explains so much of my experience with the drone and the voices, but it doesn't explain how Passenger differs. So that's what I ask.

"Passenger's integration software was modeled to mimic a sympath's brain," the admiral says. "So the connections sort of thread their way in."

"And that's somehow...*not* dangerous?"

The admiral answers with a small shake of his head. "Only if the host and AI stay integrated too long. It's policy to restrict the integration time to a maximum of six hours per day."

"What happens if it goes beyond that?" I ask.

The admiral pointedly looks at Lauren. No, not at Lauren, at the cameratom hovering above her shoulder. "That's classified, beyond the scope of your NDAs, I'm afraid."

Obviously he doesn't want to say the risks in front of Lauren's cameratom, but six hours is a long time, especially in the overclocked, time-dilated frame of reference. The admiral said a couple seconds would equal about a half hour. That's rather imprecise, but assuming a conversion ratio of 1:600, six hours would get me about 150 days in the SR. That leaves me plenty of time to go back in. "Can I try again?"

A satisfied, almost wolfish grin overtakes the admiral's face. "I'd like to take the time to watch how you got through your first store first. Let's reconvene tomorrow before the training exercise. We should be able to schedule a few minutes."

EIGHTEEN

Samantha had warned me, *It's tough to sleep aboard a starship at first.* She'd said, *Night and day don't have any meaning since the sun doesn't rise or set.* She meant well, so I didn't bother to point out that I live on a tidally locked planet. My circadian rhythms haven't been disrupted in the least. In fact, Amiens operates in lockstep with the UMT (Universal Military Time). This isn't a coincidence—we're a breeder world, after all.

So I haven't needed to acclimate.

It's not the change in environment either. Sure, someone in the barracks is snoring, and the mattress is too firm. But that's inconsequential. My brain is the problem. My thoughts are too damned loud.

You learn your education's been secretly manipulated, your accounts have probably been hacked and your intellectual property's been copied and read without permission, and that the implant put in your brain serves a different purpose than they told you. You find out that you have a potentially harmful medical condition you hadn't even heard of before. That your diagnosis was kept from you. And because of that, you unwittingly exposed yourself to a dangerous situation and are now hearing voices.

Well, with all that on your mind, you're bound to lose a little sleep trying to process, right?

But among the scattered answers I've gotten, with my mind trying to put all the pieces together, and with all the other questions still left unanswered, the one gnawing on me the most *should* be the least consequential. It shouldn't even make it onto the radar of my concerns, but it keeps bubbling to the surface.

Why are Morgan and Lauren hiding their relationship?

Maybe it's bothering me so much precisely because it shouldn't matter. Maybe if I could think of even just one reason they'd have to keep it a secret, or if I could convince myself that I've made the wrong pieces fit, that they aren't dating at all, maybe then I could let it go.

But recalling their body language, the furtive glances they keep passing back and forth, I don't think I'm wrong. There is something between them.

Then I remember Lauren's cameratom. And the spyware. And I feel *the itch*. I could link in. See what her cameratom sees. Hear what her cameratom hears. That might give me some answers. Of course, if they are together. Like *together* together... No, if that's happening right now, they will have shut the cameratom down. No one would record themselves doing that.

I could peek just this once. For just a moment. I'll get the answer to this one question and then sever the connection to the cameratom forever. Just like I promised myself I would. What could it hurt?

Whenever I open up my NeurX in the dark, I'm reminded that the icons and menus aren't light being caught by my eyes. They don't blind me, or even seem harsh, because I'm not seeing them. It's just information sent directly to my occipital lobe. It's a reminder of how the NeurX works.

I always know it's there. I use it every day, but I shiver when I imagine it. I've seen pictures, and the creepy microcomputer looks far too much like a centipede. About the size of a pen, it rests on top of my brain, nestled in the longitudinal fissure between the left and right hemispheres. Its dozens of filaments, like long, many-jointed legs, stretch away, burrowing into different sections of my cerebrum.

I try to focus on what it *does*, not what it *is*, and navigate through the menus to LINKED DEVICES. The cameratom is active. A familiar knot twists in my stomach. My concentration hovers over the ACTIVATE tile.

Do you really want to cross this line, Gaby?

Tomorrow is the training exercise. It's a big day. I need to be rested. If I don't get an answer, I'm not going to get any sleep.

Screw it. *Click.*

The audio fades in first.

Lauren's in the middle of saying something like, *I wish you wouldn't do that.*

"I need to," Morgan says.

They're sitting on a bed, near each other but not touching. Fully clothed, thankfully. The cameratom is using their faces as a focal point, so the framing of the shot only shows part of it, but Morgan has something in his lap. It's small. Curved. Metallic. And they're both looking down at it.

"You need to what? Leave evidence?"

"Tell the truth," he says. "Besides, it's part of the agreement."

Morgan pushes himself up and makes a limping step without his cane to a small desk. He places the object on the desktop, and it's in frame briefly. It's some type of headset. Not a VR headset. Smaller. Just a circlet-like band with a row of tiny round electrodes or something facing inward.

"Well I don't—" Lauren's interrupted by a two-pulse beep.

The camera swings toward the door then back to Morgan, nauseatingly quick. "You expecting someone?" Lauren whispers.

He shakes his head and steps over near the door, touching the panel off to one side. "Yes?"

"Ensign Phelps, sir." Morgan's shoulders visibly relax.

The door slides open and he waves Patrick inside. Something between the lighting in Morgan's quarters and the color saturation in the cameratom's settings makes Patrick's hair seem orange and his freckles appear brighter and more condensed.

"Oh, I'm sorry, sir. Am I interrupting?"

"No, it's fine. What's west, Ensign?" Morgan lands on a stool in front of the desk.

"What's west?"

"It's just a saying from back home. Never mind. We ready for tomorrow?" Morgan rubs at his thigh.

"Ensign Talley is a problem," Patrick says.

"How so?"

"He's in the medbay, sir. Been there for hours."

Lauren asks, "Someone get hurt?" I can barely see her at the edge of the frame. Mainly a splash from the color wheel of her hair.

Patrick shakes his head. "Looks like he's doing some kind of inventory or something."

Morgan rubs harder at his leg. He must be in pain. "Seems Ensign Talley is trying to impress the admiral by going above and beyond with his extra duties."

"He's a pain in the ass. How am I supposed to get in there?" Patrick throws his hands out wide. His fingertips nearly touch both walls of the small, private quarters.

"Calm down," Lauren says.

Momentarily Patrick glowers at her before schooling himself.

"I'll take care of it," Morgan says. "Make yourself scarce. I'll call Talley in here and see that he calls it a night. Wait until he's in here with me, then get the diodophine."

What's diodophine? I wish I had net access out here so I could look it up.

Patrick nods repeatedly. "Yeah. Yeah, okay. That'll work."

"Good. Dismissed, Ensign." As Patrick turns to leave, Morgan adds, "Remember, two micrograms per kilogram."

"Got it, boss."

Maybe diodophine is a pain med? Is Morgan having someone steal him pain meds for his leg? But surely he could get pain meds legitimately?

No sooner than the door closes, Lauren says, "Where did you find that one?"

"I know," Morgan says, sounding suddenly exhausted. "But he's loyal and we can trust him."

"He's inept."

"I didn't have a lot of choices, Lauren."

Maybe whatever it is, it's for both of them? Are they drug addicts together? There's some pieces missing here. Why would they need or want Patrick to get it for them? Why involve anyone else at all?

The camera swivels to the side as she gets up from the bed and kneels down next to Morgan on the stool. She drapes her arms around him. "I know," she says. "I'm sorry."

He kisses her. "You should go so I can call Ensign Talley."

"We haven't talked about Kitten."

What? Why do they need to talk about me?

"Yeah," he says, shaking his head sullenly. "She wasn't supposed to be here..." It seems he says it to himself. "Why do you call her that anyway?"

Lauren smiles. "It's something my favorite auntie used to call me. It just sort of fit."

He looks at her like he thinks there's more to it, but isn't going to press the issue. Dammit, ask her, Morgan—I'd like to know. "Gaby will be fine. But I want to keep her out of this as much as possible."

Keep me out of what?

"Okay," she says, rising to her feet. "You get Ensign Talley out of medbay. We can talk more tomorrow."

"I was hoping we could spend the night together. I miss you."

"Too risky," she says.

He drops his head, nodding.

"Baby." Lauren lifts his chin to her. "We'll have our whole lives together on Ongistald."

Ongistald? This is getting weirder and weirder. Ongistald is a neutral colony. It's not part of the NCP or the Commonwealth. A non-extradition territory. A place criminals go to disappear. Why the hell would they be planning to live their whole lives together there?

They kiss and Lauren leaves. The cameratom, along with my view, follows her down the hall to the VIP quarters where she starts preparing for bed. I let go of the connection.

I got my answer, and I wasn't wrong: they're dating. But I have so many more questions now. The next hour is spent trying to puzzle out the information I'm missing, hoping for some brilliant burst of inspiration to make the pieces fit. It never comes. When I can't reason through it, I start getting dumb ideas in my head.

Like walking over to Morgan's quarters and buzzing. Then, when he invites me in out of curiosity, I'll look him straight in the eye and ask, *Why do you and Lauren need diodophine?* But he'd lie. And I'd show my hand. Exposing my actions, my spying.

I consider marching over to the other barracks. Patrick isn't stationed in the port barracks where I am, so he must be in the starboard. I could wake him up. Act like I already know what's going on. Tell him something is wrong with the diodophine, or something. I'd have to improvise, play off his reactions. But I might be able to get him to give something away. Of course, it would get real awkward when Morgan and Lauren find out, which would probably be tomorrow—well, later today now, actually. Then I'd be in the same situation. Exposed as the snoop I am.

I need to get to sleep. Maybe a better option will present itself organically. Maybe I'll have the opportunity to have a regular conversation with Morgan. Or maybe with Lauren. We bonded, right? During that conversation, maybe I can bring it up more naturally, something small first, then begin pulling the thread. Then hopefully I'll find out their secret isn't a big deal at all, that it's some inconsequential nothing.

Deciding to wait helps me relax, but I still can't sleep. When I'm too wound up to sleep, I often close my eyes and run through a scene in one of my stories. Usually one I haven't written yet. That way, my mind has a different problem to solve. Something to put together. Something it *can* put together. Sometimes I'm an actor in the imagining, playing a character within the story; sometimes I'm merely directing. Either way, if I get lost enough in the narrative, if I can make the fiction feel real, reality's problems disappear, allowing my anxieties and frustrations and obsessions to give way so sleep can come for me.

I begin putting together the scene where I introduce Gegard, the Gardener of Belholt, who was once the First Sword of the Phoenix Guard. In my story, he will have been disgraced more than a decade prior. Bitter. Living in exile where he meets Ylfa, the story's true protagonist. But I don't want to introduce him as the man he becomes. Instead, the idea forms of how I might show a glimpse of the man he was, and foreshadow how he lost everything.

Gegard watches the woman as she stares out across the waves. She stands at the prow of the ship, leaning against the taffrail, her profile glowing against the sunset in a contest of beauty. Clouds

—untainted by the god of storms—diffuse the sun's final moments and are lit afire in a great golden-red bloom that dances as it strikes the sea.

Moments pass, but Gegard's gaze does not wander from her. A lock of her hair has been displaced from the neat bun; it caresses her cheek, tossed about by the same gentle wind that draws them closer to the bay of Belholt. The surf slaps against the ship's hull. Seagulls cry out in the distance, little more than specs in the sky as they circle and dive and climb back up into the air. The skyline of the capital city comes ever nearer, its image rocking slowly with the brigantine's rhythm. And as the helmsman guides them home, the blast of trumpets sounds from the shore.

Trumpets. Trumpets are for heroes.

He remembers those notes, and somewhere in some small recess of Gegard's consciousness, he becomes aware that this moment has already passed. He dreams a memory that has played out over and over again in his mind. Why the Fates chose to force him to look at this thread of his life's tapestry, fixating on it, torturing him with her image, only the gods can say.

Everyone aboard the brigantine *Corrisava* will receive a hero's welcome, but this triumph is mostly hers. It had been she that had begged her husband, King Audwin, to allow her to sail south to Schtalenheim and try a desperate negotiation for the cure—a negotiation that the king's diplomats had already failed. Gegard had asked to accompany Queen Melisenia, even though as First of the Phoenix Guard his place was at the king's side, protecting the Phoenix himself. But here they are, three months later, coming home as heroes with a supply of the cure in the hold and signed promises for more.

All Gegard can think of is the nights during their sojourn in Schtelenheim. Of he and Melisenia making love on the terrace under those southern stars after they had finally confessed their feelings to one another. Of how their time together is now over.

They are back home. Back to the trappings of court. Gegard will return to his wife and Melisenia to her husband.

And understanding that this is a dream of a long past moment, Gegard knows they will never sound trumpets for him again.

CHAPTER
NINETEEN

THE *SEDNA* SHRANK BEHIND BRAVO WAVE. BEFORE them, Praxis Station was an indistinct shape two kilometers away. It was point-blank range for capital-ship class weapons. For a human-sized projectile hurtling through the big black, it was enough to feel disconnected from everything.

For a moment, Morgan felt utterly alone.

Then tracers from cannon fire streaked past in the eerie silence. On Morgan's left, a gausser exploded, the remains of their body rocketed forward toward the station, accelerated by the impact. A red smear of viscera stretching out and away as a shell fired from the *Sedna* dragged part of their comrade away with it.

"Thompson!" Petty Officer Landry yelled into their comms, followed by a string of obscenities.

"Button it up," Captain Tanner said.

"Sir, that was friendly fire," Landry complained.

No one said anything else about it. What was there to say? A few moments later they lost P.O. Adad as well. Morgan didn't see it, aside from one more of the small icons in the bottom right of his HUD going dark.

Praxis was larger in front of them now. It looked a bit like a scatter jack toy. Pylons jutted out from a centralized location, leading to spheres and cubes. Morgan caught glimpses of fighter craft diving in, swooping out, pulling away and getting lost against the black. He wondered which of those fighters were from the *Dagger of Johanna* and which were from the *Sedna*. It made him sick to think that their carrier's survival was dependent (even partially) on the Stewies, and that when this was all over, they'd be in some way indebted to the Commonwealth. It was one thing for high command to sacrifice as many of their lives as necessary for the mission. He was prepared for that. But to sacrifice their pride, their self-respect, their dignity? That was quite another.

And then there was the other thing. The question Jules had raised: What's in it for the Stewies?

"Fire retros," Captain Tanner ordered.

Morgan opened the menu in his NeurX and sent the command to his RTV. The twin, forward-facing engines wrapping around his hips burst to life, the thruster plumes shooting forward in blue teardrops. The deceleration gave Morgan the sensation of falling forward.

Praxis Station came nearer, growing quickly at first, then expanding ever slower in his vision as the readout in his HUD that showed the relative velocity between him and the station plummeted ever closer to zero.

This was the most dangerous moment. Their thrusters acted as thermal beacons for the station's sensors, and the more they decelerated, the easier targets they became, until the point where they were *under the guns*. Which is to say, so close that the Praxis' point defense guns couldn't fire on them without hitting their own station. But for a terrible fifteen seconds they were still far enough away that the station's guns could get a bead on them.

In training, Morgan's drill sergeant had used the analogy of being unarmed and fighting someone with a baseball bat. He could remember Sergeant Reed's hoarse voice as he ordered

Private Ansil and Private Cormeran into a boxing ring and handed Ansil a bat. Morgan hadn't seen baseball before, but he was sure this wasn't how the sport was played.

"Your instinct," the sergeant said to Cormeran, "will be to keep your distance and try to stay out of range of his swings. But eventually he's going to catch you at the end of that bat. You'll be in a world a' hurt then."

Ansil and Cormeran hated each other—Morgan had forgotten why—but Ansil didn't have any moral objections to taking a few real swings at Cormeran, who jumped around the ring trying not to get his head caved in.

The sergeant continued, "When you men and women get into real bona fide combat, your instincts will try to tell you what to do. Your instincts *will* be wrong. They're following a simple biological motivation: try not to die. That's natural. But war ain't natural. In war, there's no faster way to get killed than trying not to die. You gotta try an' win."

Cormeran got struck with a glancing blow then. He dropped to a knee, holding his arm, cursing up a storm. Later Morgan learned the blow had fractured Cormeran's ulna bone.

"Stop," the sergeant commanded. "Get out of the ring, Private Cormeran. Private York, you're up."

Morgan's heart started racing as he climbed into the ring. Ansil didn't have anything against Morgan—that he knew of, at least—but that didn't stop the man from trying to take Morgan's head off when the sergeant told him to start swinging. He backed Morgan into a corner of the ring. The wind from the bat kissed Morgan's face as he narrowly jumped out of the corner.

"Remember, your instincts are lying to you," the sergeant said. "Get to the arms."

That's when the pieces fit. The force of the swing increased the closer you got to the edge. If he got hit by Ansil's arms instead of the bat, it would be like an awkward, weak punch. Next time

Ansil wound up for a swing, instead of backing out of range, Morgan stepped forward and stood his ground. Ansil's elbows and forearms struck Morgan across his left arm and chest. Ansil lost the bat. It went whipping through the air, spinning out of the ring and crashing into a wall. Ansil clumsily lost his balance and fell on his butt.

Getting under the guns was much like getting past the bat. Except that they weren't all going to get to the arms.

There was no sound, but Morgan saw the point defense guns pivot on their agile gimbals. Their multiple barrels spun up and began hailing death at Bravo Wave. Morgan didn't watch to see how many of his friends were dying. He focused on the square reticule in his HUD. The reticule that would turn blue once he passed through the shield. He started counting, one-one-thousand, two-one-thousand, three... Not that he knew when it would happen, but the act of counting gave him something to focus on, a fantasy of control as he crept forward waiting to die or not die, depending on how the Praxis' computer determined was the most efficient way to dispose of the greatest number of threats before time ran out.

The square on his HUD turned blue. Morgan released the RTV from his flight pack to let it drift off somewhere behind him. Simultaneously he fired his maneuvering thrusters forward and aimed for the station. His boots struck the hull, magnetically grasping the surface. Safely under the guns, he focused on the steel at his feet. *This is the ground*, he told himself, and then brought his eyes up with practiced self-deception, turning the station's walls into an artificial horizon.

He waited. No voice came through their radio. Since their flight chief didn't say it, he did. "This is Bravo Three. Sound off, Bravo Wave."

"Bravo Seven is Go," Petty Officer Remaut said.

"Bravo Four is Go," Jules said.

"Bravo Twelve," Koshiro said, her comm buzzing with static. "I'm alive, but I'm not Go. Dead in the water out here."

"Ping us," Jules said. "We'll come get you."

"Negative. Omega Priority, remember. The rest of you have a job to do. Kill one for m—"

A burst of static.

Then nothing.

"Shit," Remaut whispered.

Three. Three out of sixteen had made it past the first obstacle. He hoped the other waves were faring better.

Morgan surveyed the steel landscape around him, like a tiny moon. Remaut and Jules were visible, one at 2 o'clock, the other at 8, about fifteen and twenty meters away respectively. They all started toward the first nav point: an observation lounge command expected to be an easy breach.

TWENTY

I WAKE WITH A START, LOOKING AROUND WIDE-EYED for whatever alarmed me. There's nothing. No noise. No movement. No people. I seem to have slept through the officers getting up and starting their shifts.

Today is the big day.

But after what I saw last night, I'm not sure how much I care about the training exercise. Something is happening on this ship. Something I don't understand.

I climb down from the bunk and dig through the storage trunk molded into the base of the bunk frame. When I'd unloaded my rucksack, I hadn't given any consideration to organization, causing me to rifle through my clothes now as I dig for options. I'm disappointed by my choices. Yesterday among the dress uniforms and Lauren's runway-ready outfit, I looked like some random civilian from the slums. Which, I suppose, is exactly what I am. But I don't want to *look* like a civie from the slums today. I don't have anything as soldierly as a dress uniform, nor do I have anything half as elegant as what I'm sure would pass for Lauren's casual wear.

Maybe my Moore uniform?

No. This is the day I turn the admiral down and find out if he's going to make good on his offer to get me CRISPR and a transfer to gausser camp. This is my ticket *out* of that school. No sense in giving Admiral Davis the impression I'm buying into the fate he's laid out for me.

After tossing a few different options together on the unused bottom bunk, I settle on an outfit that, while not being professional or high fashion, is at least reasonably trendy. I glance around. Still no sign of anyone, so I change here.

Over my bra and underwear, I pull on a pear-green camisole and tan overalls, leaving a single suspender unclasped. The colors go well with my skin tone. K would approve. I'm sitting on the bunk tying my shoes when Samantha comes in.

"You're up," Samantha says, her tone attaching the word *finally* onto her observation.

"Didn't sleep well."

Samantha offers me something the size of a ball wrapped in a paper towel. I take it hesitantly. It's warm.

"It's a muffin. You missed breakfast," she explains. "I hope you like banana nut."

I unwrap it, looking over the baked treat. "I've never had banana."

"Well, eat up. Quick. I was sent to fetch you."

Biting a soft chunk out of the muffin then setting it aside, I chew while I finish up with my shoes.

"Wha' vor?" I ask, my mouth too full to speak clearly.

"More training with Passenger before the exercise starts, I guess? I'm not quite sure what that means."

She doesn't know what training with Passenger is? Thinking back to the mess hall, the crew had been surprised that I was a sympath, even though being a sympath is necessary to be a host. Most of the crew has been kept in the dark, haven't they? At least partially.

I want to tell Samantha what I witnessed last night. Get her opinion on what it could mean. What I should do. But how do I broach the subject? Hey, guess what, I hacked Lauren's property for no good reason other than I'm a compulsive snoop. But never mind about that, check out what I saw. Morgan and Lauren might be doing...something. Maybe drugs. Or, well, something.

No, I'd sound like an idiot. An untrustworthy idiot. Besides, what would Samantha even be able to do? Maybe I could pull Admiral Davis aside and talk to him. He probably already knows I'm a snoop and a criminal. But then I'd be betraying Morgan. Ratting out a friend from LoLe to an admiral of the Intelligence Division. If Jules were alive, it would horrify him to know his sister even considered it. No, that's not an option. Especially since I don't even know what I'd be ratting him out for.

I take another too-large bite, then pile my hair into a bun, securing it with pins. I swallow before I probably should. "Okay, we going back to the bridge?"

"Yup. I'm sure the admiral will have us move to the CIC for the exercise though."

"Why?"

"The bridge is for non-tactical operations. The CIC... Well, it's in the name, right? Combat Information Center."

We walk the sewer-tunnel corridors to the main lift near the center of the ship. I know the way now and don't need an escort, but I'm glad to have Samantha's company. She's a calming presence, and since she talks a lot, I don't feel as though I have to think up things to say just to fill the silence.

"The CIC is my favorite place on the ship," Samantha says. "If the engine room is the heart of a ship, the CIC is its brain. Before my first war-games simulation, I got a pep talk. My CO warned me that the computers will do a good job of making it feel like we're in real combat. That it can be scary but it's important to stay calm, and so on. I suppose you don't need a pep talk though. After our run-in with those pirates, this'll be a stroll."

The lift carries us up to the command deck. We're met with a chill rush of air as the lift's door slides open. I hug my arms to me as we start down the hall.

"I heard the enviros glitched overnight," Samantha says. "I figured Ruby would've debugged the thermostats by now."

The entire crew is on the bridge this time. They're not making as much of a show today, dressed in standard duty uniforms. About half wear their uniform jackets; apparently some of them knew Ruby didn't get the problem fixed. Lauren looks as elegant as ever in a slim-cut business suit with a thin black tie hanging casual and loose about her neck.

I scan Morgan, then Lauren, then Morgan again, looking for signs of drug abuse. Both their eyes are clear. Lauren is thin but not drug-addict-thin, and Morgan has gained a couple kilos since his time as a gausser. My gaze lingers too long and Morgan meets my eyes questioningly.

I let it go for now. Only then do I notice where in the solar system we are. Everyone and everything on the bridge fades into the background as I peer out the bridge's glass canopy.

Centered beyond the sloping windows is Nomad Star. Distant and immense, it takes up nearly the entire field of view. With the blurring caused by the warbling stretch-and-contraction of light the blink drive creates, it's out of focus and looks like an unmixed glob of blue and purple paint smeared haphazardly across a canvas.

"Stop?" I struggle to say. "Can we? Stop?"

After a brief hesitation, Admiral Davis says, "Sure, why not? Lieutenant Decker, if you would."

"Yes, sir," she says. I haven't interacted with her yet. She's pretty, with darker skin than mine and closely cropped hair. Her stern expression makes her seem unapproachable though, and I remember Samantha telling me that Lieutenant Decker seemed like a control freak.

A moment later, Decker drops us out of blink and gently rolls the *Discordia*, framing Nomad Star's ring on a horizontal plane so that its entirety can be seen through the viewport glass.

Nomad Star is a rogue brown dwarf star that had long ago been captured by the pull of our solar system's much larger main-sequence star, Tabula Rasa 3. Larger than any gas giant planet, but lacking the mass to sustain nuclear fusion, the failed star is barely visible at the center of its massive donut-shaped ring. Glowing magenta in the heat of its crushing gravity, the north and south poles crest beyond the edges of the sea of churning, gaseous storms, carrying immeasurable chunks of ice and rock. The thick ring stretches for over a hundred million kilometers, spinning—in regions—at over ninety kilometers per second. At this distance, though, the chaotic swirls of blue and purple and shadow could be frozen in place.

A paradoxically tranquil reminder of coming terror.

A few million years from now, the brown dwarf will lay waste to the solar system. As Nomad Star circles the drain of Tabula Rasa 3's gravity well in a slowly decaying orbit, it will eventually drag the planets into violent, life-nullifying collisions. Even now, still so far out toward the edge of the solar system, it exerts some influence over the orbits of every celestial body. Particularly the outermost planets, disturbing their heliocentric courses, pulling them into uneven trajectories that forced the settlers of those worlds to get rather inventive with the creation of their local calendars.

"It's a hell of a sight, isn't it?" the admiral says, taking up the space next to me.

"Yes, sir," I say. "Are we all the way out here to avoid being seen by the Commonwealth?"

"Quite right, Ms. Rhodes." He puts a little distance from me, taking a more central point on the bridge and begins addressing the crew. "Most of you have no doubt been wondering about the specifics of our training exercise. Why we're out here in this old heap, why it's been outfitted with a cloak, and some of you have seen the addition to the CIC."

I haven't. What's he talking about? And this bucket has a cloak?

"A few of you have also deduced that young Ms. Rhodes here and Ensign Garner are sympaths with NeurX implants."

There are a few reluctant nods among the crew, but for the most part, they remain expressionless.

"Today we'll be facing off against the *Hybris* and its complement of smaller craft using Tango-Delta war-game simulation protocols. The exercise will run from 1030 hours to 1430. Today is far more than a training exercise, however. It's a test of the *Discordia's* capabilities. And we're going to win."

Samantha shoots me a look that conveys a sarcastic, *Yeah, right*.

"Before we begin, we're going to cloak and change course. Admiral McCafferty's goal is to find and disable us, so I expect he will send out his recon shuttles in pairs so they can sweep the engagement zone with graviton beams, hoping to cut through our cloak. Our plan is to play cat-and-mouse for the first few hours, spreading McCafferty's shuttles and fighter attachments out. Then we'll close distance with the *Hybris* and decloak. That's when things get interesting."

Admiral Davis' eyes sweep the bridge as he turns to Ensign Garner.

"Ensign Garner here is the operator of a new technology only found aboard this ship. *That* is what we're here to test. His mind will be transmitted to the *Hybris* and, with the help of Passenger, will shut down their engines, shields, and weapons. At which point our simulated weapons will make quick work of a ship this little destroyer would otherwise have no chance against in a brawl."

I see a few of the crew exchange looks. Most, however, have no reaction at all.

"We must win. High command doesn't believe in us," the admiral says dourly. "We need funding. And the only way we're going to get it is by making them believe. Which is why I say to each of you, the outcome of this test will likely be the most important achievement of your careers. Perhaps your lives. And that brings me to a serious matter we need to discuss, Ms. Gallagher. Would you please shut your cameratom down for a moment?"

Does the admiral know about last night? Does he have the pieces I'm missing? Does he know why they plan on going to Ongistald? He had been one step ahead of me, hadn't he? My careful, slow plan to flunk out of Moore that I thought so clever. Maybe it's the same with whatever Morgan and Lauren are plotting.

Lauren must be thinking something along the same lines—a flash of panic washes over her face briefly before the mask of calm professionalism returns. She draws herself up, squares her shoulders, and nods. The cameratom floats into her waiting hand and powers down.

I thought she'd have put up an argument. But then, maybe she doesn't want whatever he's about to accuse her of being recorded?

"Thank you, Ms. Gallagher. I need to ask you a question, and you'll understand momentarily why neither of us will want it recorded by that device."

"Is this something we should discuss in private?" she asks through her teeth.

"No. The whole crew should hear this. The *Hybris* will be in the area soon, which will mark the start of our test. From this point forward, we're all in this together. All of you need to under-stand the stakes."

"You have my attention," Lauren says.

He blows out a sigh. "I think you'll agree I've been forth-coming with you. In private I told you, were it up to me, I would not have a reporter here."

She makes a small motion of agreement.

"I can't keep you from doing your reporting, Ms. Gallagher. But I *am* asking you to be negligent in your duties," Admiral Davis says gravely.

Her discomfort seems to be replaced by confusion. "And why would I agree to a request like that?"

"I don't expect you to agree. Not yet. I know I won't convince you with rhetoric. I just want you to keep what I'm about to tell you in mind as you watch the training exercise unfold over the next several hours." He turns away, climbing the dais and easing into the throne of the captain's chair. "I worry that the Media Ministry and Swayy Public Relations will get eager and release your story too early."

"Surely, Admiral, you're not questioning the wisdom of both Swayy Corp. and the Ministry."

"I am, Ms. Gallagher."

I can't believe what I'm hearing. He's dangerously close to sedition. Take a beat, he'll walk it back.

He leans forward, steepling his fingers. "High command doesn't have the necessary vision, at least not currently, to do what needs to be done."

Or instead of walking it back, he'll double down. If the wrong people find out, he might go to prison for saying that.

Lauren stands directly in front of the dais, looking up and meeting the admiral's gaze head-on. "And what vision is that, Admiral?"

"This ship is just a proof of concept. I told you before that it could give us a tactical advantage over the Commonwealth. I understated that claim. With a small fleet of these ships"—he sweeps his gaze round the bridge, speaking to everyone—"I can end this war."

Lauren raises an eyebrow. "This old retrofitted ship is *that* dangerous?" she asks incredulously.

"Not alone. We need several, but more importantly—and here's where you come in, Ms. Gallagher—we need the element of surprise. This ship has a unique ability that no one, Commonwealth or NCP, is yet prepared to face. But as soon as the Commonwealth gets a hint of its existence, they'll start working on a countermeasure."

Lauren nods. I'm on the sidelines still trying to digest his claim. End the war? That has to be hyperbole, right?

"If we hit them hard and fast, we can force a surrender. And we can do it with minimal casualties on either side. Imagine... ending the war. Bringing humanity together again. That's why I'm asking you, Ms. Gallagher, I'm asking each of you here today, to imagine peace."

For a long moment, the only sound is the white-noise whisper of the air recyclers running.

Peace. How many people have been alive long enough to understand the word?

"Think of how many lives we could save." His voice is almost pleading now. "But I need time. After I prove to high command that this ship is viable, that it works, I need to build at least four or five more. I need to train more EWOs like him"—he levels a finger at Ensign Garner—"and her."

My heart stops as he aims his finger at me, drawing everyone's eyes with it.

The admiral continues, "I need to be able to do that under complete secrecy until we're ready to strike. If your story breaks before then, we'll lose most of the advantage we would've had, and the chances of ending this war slip from our grasp."

Lauren looks away toward a blank wall. I can't see her face, but her neck flexes as she swallows hard.

"I know I'm asking a big sacrifice of you. If you do this, your career will be damaged. Ruined, maybe. Your best bet, I think, would be to corrupt the footage, making it look like an accident. You'd probably keep your job, but there'd be suspicions, and the Ministry would never fully trust you again. But whatever it costs you, it will be worth it. So I won't ask you to choose now. I'll just have to trust you'll do the right thing when the time comes."

"If you'll excuse me," she says.

The admiral gives her a shallow, accepting smile.

She rushes off the bridge, holding her cameratom like a ball. Morgan stands up, his eyes fixed on Lauren. His body flinches as if he's going to follow before he catches himself. He turns, trying to cover up his actions by going to Lieutenant Decker's station to ask her some inane question. I think I'm the only one to notice. I'm the only one that was looking for a reaction from Morgan. The admiral really has no idea.

I believe I'm starting to understand the admiral. Maybe high command is humoring him with superficial support only afforded to him out of respect for his rank or past service. Maybe he had to pull every string there was to pull and cash in every favor he had to get this project this far. And now, apparently, it's come down to this one test. Success means funding. Failure means what? Has he ruined his reputation? Tanked his career? Probably, I think. The conversation he just had with Lauren could cost him his freedom, which leaves me little doubt he's pushed against the system in a big way to get here.

And to him it's worth it because he believes he can end the war. This is his purpose.

I bet even Jules would respect this InDiv admiral.

I just wish I understood what Morgan, Lauren, and Patrick are up to, and how it fits in with the rest of this. Maybe I should just pull Morgan aside and ask him. But would he tell me? I want to think he would, but he and Lauren both used that same diversion technique to distract me from asking questions. And Morgan had said last night he wants to keep me out of it. No, he probably won't tell me if I come straight at him with it. I'll have to come up with something else.

"Well, now that that business is over," the admiral's voice shakes me out of my thoughts. "Lieutenant Commander, would you please see that everyone takes their posts in the CIC? I'd like this ship under cloak and on a new course in the next ten minutes. Ensign Garner, Ms. Rhodes, I'd like you to remain here."

"Yes, sir," Morgan says. "Let's go, people."

The crew filters off the bridge. Morgan, whether on purpose or by happenstance, avoids making eye contact with me.

"Now," the admiral says, "last night I watched your performance in the SR, Ms. Rhodes. Very impressive."

"Thank you, sir," I say. Moore has ingrained responses like this in me to the point of it being reflex. But after the automated response, I say what I actually want to say. "How did you watch it?"

"The technology for the SR wasn't built from scratch. Have you heard of mnemonic rendering?"

I have a vague recollection that it was an entertainment tech. It was supposed to replace VR back when I was a kid. Apparently it allowed people to download their memories for others to watch. *Watch* isn't quite the right word though. Apparently the audience felt like they were right there living it. But didn't it get banned because it was too real? Didn't some of the users get psychological trauma or something from it?

"Yeah, I think so," I answer.

"The SR uses the same programming architecture as

mnemonic rendering. Passenger records the training simulations, and after, anyone with a mnemonic headset can view them."

That's what Morgan was using last night! Lauren was asking why he was using it. *You need to what? Leave evidence?* she had asked. His enigmatic answer was, *Tell the truth,* and something about it being *part of the agreement.* He's making a mnemonic rendering of a memory. But what memory? Why? And why would it be *evidence?*

The admiral continues, "Before our training exercise begins, I'd like you to try your hand at the bank."

"On her second time?" Ensign Garner says. There's incredulousness in his voice, but something else too. Jealousy maybe?

The admiral cows him with a look. "Yes." He looks me in the eye. "Keep in mind, time moves much faster there. Don't worry about the training exercise, you can take your time. Think through each move you make, and remember, try to make the AI your ally, not your enemy."

"Yes, sir," I say. But with all the questions swimming around my mind, my heart's not in this. Before I know it, though, I have a blinder helmet on and a progress bar filling in my vision.

CHAPTER
TWENTY-ONE

UP A WIDE CONCRETE STAIRCASE STANDS THE intimidating domed building I saw yesterday from the car park. The stonework pillars reach up at least fifteen meters to a portico ceiling. After passing through an antechamber bigger than my family's apartment, I stand on marble floors beneath a high arched ceiling in an opulent space.

A guard stands motionless to the side of the entrance. Hard-soled shoes clap and click against polished stone, and a few dozen conversations blend into a background murmur.

Everywhere my vision lands, there's brass and mahogany. In front of where we stand near the entrance, people are assembled in orderly lines, each leading to a clerk behind a long service counter. One clerk passes a short stack of long cards to the person they're helping. No, not cards. Money. Paper money.

To the right, on a raised landing, an expansive room opens up where desks rest on glossy hardwood floors. Some of the desks are empty, while others have people sitting on either side of them. Paperwork is being passed back and forth.

"This is a bank?" I ask.

<A recreation of the Coramiya 1st Planetary Bank of Telecan-

nõn. It was one of the last banks to deal in physical tender.>
Passenger's voice isn't in my ears, but in my thoughts. Would it be as unsettling if the sensation wasn't so similar to the voice in the shower? Its echoes reach out even now, prodding me, reminding me that I should be dead.

You are a machine.

You are a dead machine.

I'm too in my head. Time to get on with it. "What's the objective?"

Ensign Garner points toward the back of the building. Behind the tellers is an archway leading to a mostly obscured room. At the back of that room, I can make out the round steel chassis of a massive vault door. There are at least two guards armed with rifles back there.

"You gotta break into the vault." Ensign Garner smiles at me with some incongruous mixture of desire and disgust.

I try to ignore it. "How do we do that?" The confidence I'd built up from my success yesterday is long gone.

"I solved the vault on my own. Don't see why you should just get handed the answers."

"You said you've been training here for months."

Ensign Garner crosses his arms and scowls. "Well, maybe I could give you a clue here or there, you know, if you ask nicely."

What is wrong with this kid? The admiral skipped me ahead to the end-game, the hardest puzzle in the courtyard, based on what Ensign Garner said yesterday, and he's acting like things have been made easier for me. Like I'm getting special treatment. It's unfair. But then, the admiral's goal is to stop the war. He doesn't give a shit about *fair*, does he? I chew on a nail, surveying the connected rooms.

Time to do some scouting, Gaby. I start off, making a slow track through the bank's interior.

Customers use small terminals to complete their portions of

the transactions with the clerks at the service counter. But those terminal screens are shielded with foldable, plastic barn doors, making it difficult to snoop and see their credentials as they type them in.

On the far side of the service counter, a well-dressed man holding a hand terminal stands next to a door made of polished bars, like a fancy prison cell. Through the bars, I glimpse a wall of safe deposit boxes stretching away.

A customer walks up to the man. After a brief exchange, he unlocks the door and lets the customer inside. Then he closes the customer inside and retakes his position. Unsure of if, or how, that could be useful, I resume my winding course, meandering onto the landing and the offset room with the desks. Each desk has a terminal attached to it for customer access. They're much the same as the ones at the service counter. These are missing the barn doors, but standing over someone's shoulder here will be rather conspicuous. With a subtle glance over the shoulders of two seated customers, I pick out fields on the screen for a user-name and password. There's no plan forming yet, but whatever I come up with, I'll need credentials.

Unfortunately, the terminals at the unoccupied desks are powered down entirely. I need a ruse.

Ensign Garner follows as I leave the building and step into the fresh air. Why are there differences in air quality within a simulated environment? I mentally wave it away; there are more important things to put my mind to right now. I pace past the planters and ornate benches. Past the covered trash bin and the frosted glass of the front doors. Nothing's coming to me. The spark of inspiration I'd enjoyed when I'd gotten through Crossing the Rubicon is nowhere to be found.

"Why are you pacing?" Ensign Garner asks.

Why am I even trying? Why not just fail? I'm just here to get my CRISPR and a ticket to gausser camp. I don't need to be good at hacking the SR. I can respect Admiral Davis for his ambition to stop the war. But I'm not buying into it. He must be overestimating the advantage we'd have. This war hasn't been going on for seventy-some years because we've never had an advantage over the Commonwealth before. Both sides have made technological advancements, leapfrogging over the other temporarily. It's never made much difference.

I think of Jules. How proud and excited he was after he'd become a gausser. The crazy stories he'd tell me of their missions when he'd come home. Then I think of his funeral. The legacy of being the sister of a war hero who'd died completing an Omega Priority mission. It was the first Omega Priority mission in twenty-five years, they told me.

I remember the funeral. A ceremonial affair. There was no body because he'd been field-cremated. They'd given my parents an urn. Inscribed on the front, it read, *Petty Officer Julian Rhodes*. Etched vertically down the spine of the urn it had, in hierarchical order, the insignias of the NCP, Swayy Corp., the Swayy Navy, the Gauss Trooper Corps., and finally the 118th Division.

Morgan was distant at the funeral. Confined to a wheelchair, his right leg still scaffolded with metal bracing. He couldn't tell us anything about the mission or Jules' death.

It was classified.

I remember how people reacted to my parents. Approaching to offer condolences in their awkward, unsure steps. No one could meet my parents' eyes. And once their obligations had been completed, kind words exchanged, and platitudes given, they'd slink away and do everything they could to avoid contact.

I know what I need to do.

Behind one of the massive alabaster columns, I'm fully obscured from the courtyard. I can alter my clothes here. When I ask Ensign Garner to turn around, he tells me that the change is instantaneous. He won't see me naked, he assures me. I doubt he's lying, but I demand he turn around anyway, out of spite, I suppose, and out of wishing he wasn't here at all.

Searching my memory, I find the gown I want to wear. Last time when I'd altered my clothing, Passenger had pointed out that I wasn't being specific enough. I'm not a clothing designer, so I expect I'll find borrowing a design that exists in the real world much easier. With eyes squeezed tight and breath held, I imagine silk against my skin.

I imagine the feeling. Then it touches me. The long black dress Salína Kristensdóttir wore to the premiere of *With the Fire* clings to my slight frame. It's not just similar, I've modeled every detail—I'm sure of it. My net history knows I've looked at it enough. Admittedly Salína filled it out much better, but it's beautiful all the same. Of course, for my purpose I'll need to add accessories that are going to seriously change how onlookers perceive it.

Closing my eyes again and concentrating, I conjure into existence a black derby hat with a veil and sunglasses. Next come the opera gloves. The ankle strap stilettos. Finally I bring into existence the largest purse I can imagine being socially acceptable given the rest of the outfit.

Each item is easier to conjure than the one before it. I'm getting the hang of this.

Ensign Garner grimaces. "Who died?"

I haven't decided that. They modeled the bank after an actual place from history. Unfortunately, it's not a period I know anything about. Since I don't know the social norms, it's better to play it safe. "My beloved husband," I say, managing a small catch in my voice as I get into character.

"What's the point?"

I ignore the question and step back into the bank's foyer. Ensign Garner takes position next to me a moment later, having conjured himself a black and white double breasted suit that fits my theme nicely. At least he's not trying to actively sabotage me.

"So, c'mon. What's the plan?" he asks.

I only have the opening steps of a plan worked out. After that I'm going to be improvising. I won't admit that to him though, and after the way he's been acting, why tell him anything? "I can't tell you."

"Why not?" He sounds like a child who's one *no* away from throwing a full-blown fit in the middle of a store.

"Do you ever watch any heist VRs?" I say, splitting my attention between the ensign and the room off to the right with the desks.

He rubs at his face. "I saw *Saturnus*. That was pretty good. It had, um…who was that?"

"Doesn't matter. You remember how in *Saturnus* at the beginning of the second act, right after they've gathered the crew, they show the plan to everyone, including the audience?"

"I guess, yeah."

"It's a sign they're going to fail. The script is written like that so the audience will understand how badly they're failing. You have to know the plan to understand how far off course they're going, for the failure to create tension. If they're going to succeed, they don't give away the plan, because then the tension comes from the unknown."

"That can't be true."

"It's true," I say, glancing up toward him. I should've at least tried to make myself taller. Why do I keep forgetting that?

"So you can't say because it'll mean you'll fail?"

"Yup."

Ensign Garner stuffs his hands into his pockets. "Sounds an awful lot like superstition to me."

A customer gets up from one of the desks, shakes hands with the banker, and turns to leave. There's my opening. I start toward the banker and take an empty seat. Ensign Garner rushes to take the seat next to me.

"How may I help you?" the banker asks. He's a young man with a long, serious face. He wears a gray suit with a blue tie.

I inflect a near sob. "My late husband had an account here. I'm afraid I need to close it."

And just like that, he's trying desperately to find somewhere else to look. Some way out of this conversation while offering polite condolences. "Well, we can, of course, take care of that, if you can just put his username and password into the tablet in front of you."

He motions toward the portable hand terminal fixed to a swiveling mount on the desk. I hesitate.

Ensign Garner thought-broadcasts, <Will you at least tell me why you're pretending to be a widow?>

I toy with the hand terminal while working up a sniffle. "I'm sorry, but do you have any tissue?"

"Let me go find you some, ma'am."

"Can't you see?" I whisper. "Death makes people uncomfortable. Passenger, I assume you have SQL injection scripts in your software suit?"

<I do,> Passenger says.

"I'll need one that lines up to this type of database." I flash the Ensign an antagonistic smile.

Passenger gives me a long string of commands to inject into the username field. I tap them in as the banker disappears into the offices at the back of the room. The SQL injection returns saying: *No Results.*

"I need another, fast."

Passenger gives me a second SQL script. The banker reappears, coming back with something in his hands. I type it in and hit return. The ensign's mouth falls open as the entire database of usernames opens on the screen.

I reach into the oversized purse, attempting to conjure a data terminal identical to the one on the desk. Shit, it didn't work. I try again, imagining the cold aluminum chassis between my pinching fingers. Then I feel the weight of it.

I rush to swap the real terminal for the counterfeit as the banker returns, presenting an elegant, gilded wood box with tissue billowing from the top. The smarter course of action would have been to swap the real data terminal for the fake and then do the SQL injection somewhere out of sight, I realize belatedly. I'm lucky my poor planning hadn't gotten me caught.

"Thank you," I say, taking two tissues. "I apologize for wasting your time, but I'm much too broken up to handle his affairs today."

"I understand, ma'am. I'm so sorry for your loss."

I leave with the weight of a hand terminal in my purse, and my smile hidden by the veil. On the portico, I position myself behind a column, shielding myself once again from the view of the courtyard. Ensign Garner is a step behind. He waits as a pedestrian moves past us on their way into the bank. I pull the veil over the top of my derby.

As soon as the doors close behind the pedestrian, the ensign goes slack-jawed. "Holy hell! You just pulled the credentials of every subroutine in a matter of seconds." He paces back and forth, shaking his head. "No way. No way. This is a grift or something."

"A grift?" I say, putting my hands on my hips.

"That's what I said, isn't it?" He turns to me, disdain in his eyes. "You're putting me on. Yeah, no way this is your second time in the SR. This is one of the admiral's games. What, does he think that if you waltz in here and show me up that I'll try harder after this when we do the training exercise? He thinks some competition will bring out the best in me or something?"

"You're being ridiculous."

The ensign looks as though he's trying to hold back tears.

"Relax, okay," I say in a softer tone. "No one's tricking you. This is my second time. And maybe I've got some talent, but I've been getting lucky so far." Don't do that, Gaby! Don't diminish your successes for the sake of his fragile ego, I scold myself.

"So what's your next step?" He sounds bitter and spiteful.

Biting down on a fingernail, I ask myself the same question. I wanted the credentials, but didn't have anything planned for them once I got them. What have I learned about how this place works? The shops are server nodes, and the people act as subroutines carrying data and instruction sets from one place to another. "There has to be some symbolic place where code is stored," I say mostly to myself. Maybe in file cabinets? Or maybe scanned and stored in computers within the SR—that's an interesting thought. Then I remember. "I want to see what's in those safe deposit boxes."

Ensign Garner shakes his head in defeat. "You might be the first person to get inside the vault on your first try."

"So I'm right?" I ask it as a question, but his twisted-up face has already answered. How many tries had it taken for Ensign Garner to figure that out? And had he intuited it or simply stumbled upon it?

"Okay, time for a costume change. Who should I play?"

I reenter the bank as a businesswoman and ask to get into my safe deposit box. The banker standing sentry asks for identification, which I produce, conjuring an ID card with one of the stolen usernames.

He inspects it. "Right this way."

The prison-cell door unlocks with a physical key, sliding open with a *clank*, and giving me access to a slender causeway stretching into the distance. It's aglow in warm light with a series of bar-top tables in the center. It's impossibly long. There must be millions of safe deposit boxes here.

The banker leaves me and Ensign Garner alone, stating he'll be right outside should we need him. He is a beacon of professional courtesy as he locks us inside.

Each of the safe deposit boxes has a touchpad on its faceplate. On each display a registry code glows above empty fields for a username and password. Cross-referencing the code against the database row number reveals its corresponding username. Halfway there. I hope Passenger's suite of hacking tools can get me the other half. "Okay, how do I brute force my way through a password?" I ask.

"I just focus and think about it. It helps me to touch whatever I'm trying to manipulate."

Gingerly I touch the faceplate with my first two fingers, shut my eyes, and concentrate. The readout appears vividly in my mind's eye and begins cycling through every possible password combination at speeds my real eyes could never track.

It's far easier than changing my appearance and takes all of about two seconds to crack the first password. What I could do with this ability in the outside, civilian world. I pull the safe deposit box free and place it on a table. The top slides open and inside is a three-page document of code.

"So, Passenger, what will happen if I mark this code up with a pen, change it, and put it back?"

<You will alter the behavior of the code, probably by introducing a bug,> Passenger says.

Might be useful, but damn is that shooting in the dark.

Putting the code back in the safe deposit box for now, I leave the box on the counter, then move on to the next one. After opening that, I move on to another. Five minutes pass, then ten.

"Excuse me, madam? Sir?" the banker calls through the bars. "Is everything all right in there?"

"Everything's fine, thank you," I holler back.

The banker is looking through the bars. Shit. Not only is the amount of time I'm spending in here suspicious, the several dozen safe deposit boxes I have laid out on the tables must raise more than a minor curiosity.

"It's just, well, there are other customers waiting."

"Just one more minute, please."

I go back to the second to last one I pulled free. Although I'd hoped to find something better, this one is useful at least—I can cause chaos with this. Chaos leads to opportunities.

It's a Search & Return Query for any subroutine sending an error code. In most modern systems, this type of function would be run by a virtual intelligence. VIs aren't as costly or complex as AIs. VIs don't need a biobox, they don't take months or years to mature, and they're not aware. VIs are simply complex problem-solving programs, typically on a separate server or at least partitioned by their own firewall.

Having a Search & Return Query subroutine to analyze subroutine issues nestled with the other subroutines is a flaw. A flaw I can use. I conjure a pen and start scrawling on the codes in the safe deposit boxes, adding, blotching out, or changing one character or two in the code. I stuff them back into their respective boxes. A few, I think, got mixed up. Realizing that's better for my purpose, I mix up the rest as I go, putting them each in the wrong box. I don't put any of the boxes back in yet.

The banker is looking through the bars at me.

I turn my back to him, blocking his line of sight. I conjure a lighter, flick the cap open the second it materializes in my palm, then put the Search & Return Query to the flame. As soon as the code burns away, I begin stuffing the safe deposit boxes back in place with wild abandon. Ensign Garner stands by, watching with his arms crossed and a bad-tempered frown on his face.

"We really need this room," the banker calls sternly through the bars.

"Almost done, just one more minute."

I have about half the boxes left.

"Madam, I must insist."

Fifteen or so boxes left.

The banker motions to someone.

Ten boxes left.

"I need security," he calls to someone.

Six boxes left.

"Okay, madam, we're coming in."

Three boxes left.

The metal of his key rattles into the mechanism.

The barred door swings open as I slide the last box home. I straighten myself and do my best to walk calmly to the door. The banker enters the safe deposit room with an armed security guard.

I scoot past them, smiling. "Room's all yours."

They follow me with their eyes, but don't take action. Ensign Garner slinks past as well. As we reach the middle of the lobby, Garner's voice enters my mind, <So what do you hope to gain out of that?>

I'm about to admit that I have no idea when the floor lurches beneath our feet. I hit the marble painfully on my hip. Screams erupt around us. Looking up from where I lie, the ceiling itself seems to flex. A massive chandelier swings.

"Earthquake!" someone shouts over the dozens of other screams.

Imagining hundreds of crystal shards dropping like missiles at me, I scramble to my feet to get somewhere not directly under an ornament that can murder me.

The floor continues heaving violently. Each unsteady step is a challenge. My equilibrium fails more than once as I make my way toward the service counter where the tellers were helping customers moments ago.

The power goes out, then comes back on, then flickers before dying with a sense of finality, leaving us all in the pale-orange glow of emergency lighting. Most of the customers and employees are trying to find safety—bracing themselves in doorways or cowering under desks and tables. One of the chandeliers in the foyer dislodges and comes crashing to the marble in a deafening cacophony of shattering glass.

I duck, covering my head and turning my face away. Crystal showers across my back, my neck, my arms. The sound recedes, replaced by a wailing cry, choked coughing, and the continued growling of the constant, unnatural earthquake beneath us. An earthquake I'm sure I caused by disrupting some piece of code. I feel damp. Timidly, I lift my head, scanning through the dust-filled air for the spraying of fire sprinklers or a busted pipe. There's no source of water I can spot. Looking down, I realize the moisture is blood. My skin is nicked in a dozen places.

Through the smoky haze, two men dash into the safe deposit room. Could that be the AI recognizing the problem and going to fix it?

The floor continues to tip and sway as I walk and sometimes crawl back over to the prison-cell door with all the grace of a toddler, my inner ear straining to keep up with the shifts in orientation as the floor buckles and twists. The once-beautiful marble is spider-webbed with fissures, some of them opening up large enough to swallow a foot. I reach the barred door. The two men —one in a suit, the other in a security uniform—scramble through the safe deposit boxes looking for the error I'd placed.

This is more chaos than I'd expected or wanted, but I might as well try to make something of it. I stagger over to the service counter that clearly wasn't designed to serve people of my height. Holding the edge for balance, I take a good look to see how I can get in. There must be a door somewhere, but I don't see it. I decide to climb over instead.

The counter is lowest in front of where a teller would stand, raising between them like the crenellations of an ancient castle's battlements. I hop up, grasping the woodwork of the raised portion; kicking against the wall, I find enough purchase to give me the last bit of force I need to drag myself up onto my belly.

Sliding off the other side, I back-flop to the hard floor. After lying there for a moment to get my breath back, I sit, then stand and face the archway into the back of the bank where the massive cylinder vault door stands, its steel glowing like a doorway to the underworld in the emergency lighting.

A thud behind me gets my attention. Ensign Garner is coming over the countertop behind me. He hugs his right arm close to his body as if he's been injured.

Back toward the vault door, one security guard's body lies still, half-covered in rubble from a portion of the ceiling that's come free. The other guard kneels over him, his radio squawking something unintelligible. He glances over, cold eyes landing on me. "Hey, what are you doing back here?"

Damn. Time to play *babe in the woods*. "I'm sorry. I'm just trying to find a safe place to go. I'm scared."

This routine was once my go-to when I'd get caught in LoLe being somewhere I shouldn't be or doing something I shouldn't do. But I'm out of practice, and as the words leave my mouth, I know my delivery is off. I'm not in character and I didn't sell it. He takes long, aggressive strides in my direction.

There's a gun on my hip, I tell myself, conjuring a firearm. My fingers wrap around the wood grip. I draw, immediately realizing how badly I fucked up. The weapon in my hand is a flintlock pistol. How? Why? It's completely anachronistic and, worse, much less effective than the more modern rifle he's raising at me.

I drop to one knee to make a smaller target and fire my shot. My one and only shot. The long barrel bucks high, throwing out a cloud of swirling smoke that stings my eyes. Did I hit him?

The security guard steps through the billowing smoke and puts the barrel of his rifle to my forehead.

I'm back in the bridge, the smell of gunpowder fading rapidly into memory.

I pull off the blinder helmet and drop it carelessly to the floor.

"How'd you do this time?" Admiral Davis asks.

I shake my head.

"She tried to have a shootout in the bank with the weirdest gun I've ever seen." Ensign Garner is showing his crooked teeth in a wide grin.

"Oh?" The admiral raises an eyebrow at me.

"It was, um…it was a 17th century flintlock."

The admiral purses his lips, considering it. "You must have conjured the type of gun on instinct. You allowed your subconscious to fill in the details," he says flatly. If there was any doubt he read my writing, that doubt is gone now. "You must remain in control in the sympathetic reality. Logic and reason are your allies. You create the world, but you're in a computer's universe. Emotion and instinct are foreign there. They'll lead you astray and mark you to the AI as an intruder. Do you understand?"

I want to tell him it doesn't matter. That his lessons are lost on me because I don't want to be an EWO, and I'd like him to make good on his end of the deal now. But I don't. I don't say anything. I simply nod in agreement.

"Good. Ensign Garner, are you ready to show us and everyone aboard the *Hybris* how it's done?"

"Yes, sir," Garner says enthusiastically.

"Excellent. Let's get to the CIC."

CHAPTER
TWENTY-TWO

The gear-shaped door rolls open and Admiral Davis, Ensign Garner, and I step over the tracked threshold into the CIC. There's a palpable energy here. A humorless, pensive concentration. It seems deliberate. I can imagine a team of interior designers consulting with psychologists and efficiency experts, and doing rounds of testing on focus groups while refining their sober vision each step of the way. All leading to this. Military-proficiency chic. Where focused beams of key-lighting land on workstations and running lights illuminate walkways, leaving everything else cast in dramatic shadow.

The CIC is a round room, maybe ten meters across, choked with equipment and tactical stations. Despite the size of the space, it feels claustrophobic. Handrails and grab bars jut into the narrow paths. At the center of the room, a round holotable projects a beach-ball sized image of local space.

Floating in the holographic sphere are small three-dimensional depictions of the *Discordia*, the *Hybris,* and multiple smaller craft presumably recently launched from the *Hybris*. There's a narrow ring of open space around the table to stand and survey and strategize. Beyond that, two semi-circles of workstations divide the right and left hemispheres of the room.

On the right, several workstations have been removed, the area gutted to make space for a retrofit that seems to have become a central focus here. A sphere of latticed steel has been installed. Like a globe-shaped cage mounted to floor and ceiling at its poles. Within—visible through the woven gridwork of steel rings—is some version of an acceleration chair suspended in the center. I'm not sure if the team of interior designers would approve or be appalled.

"What's that?" I ask.

"That is the second-generation prototype of the Inertia-Zero project. I requisitioned it as soon as R&D moved on to the third-gen version," the admiral says proudly.

That tells me almost nothing. "What's it for?"

"Somatosensory and proprioception deprivation."

Now I understand. It's designed to keep the occupant from feeling the effects of gravity and inertia.

The admiral continues, "R&D's trying to scale it down so they can use it as a new type of fighter cockpit. This degree of sensory deprivation isn't strictly necessary for an EWO. But we believe that while hacking a hostile AI, removing as much outside stimuli as possible should be beneficial."

Ensign Garner goes to it, opens the front, and climbs inside.

I'm not so sure I agree with the logic. When I was a maintenance drone, being able to feel the high-G maneuver the shuttle was making had been one of the few things that reminded me of what I was, and what I was there to do. The outside stimuli likely saved my life. Could someone get lost in the sympathetic reality?

"Now, if you'll take a seat at any of the unoccupied stations, Ms. Rhodes." The admiral makes for the captain's chair on the far side of the room.

The entire crew is here. All at various stations. My attention lands on Tyrone, who's inside a drone control pod. It looks similar to the ones back at Moore, except this one has the patina of age. His fingers drum nervously atop the blinder helmet resting in his lap. The drone pod next to his is empty. Isn't Patrick supposed to be piloting a drone for the mission?

I scan the room again. The entire crew isn't here after all. Patrick is missing.

Tyrone sends someone a bulging-eyed expression that to me reads as, *I don't know.* I follow his gaze to Lauren, who's sat across the room and bouncing her knee like she's had three too many cups of coffee.

Ensign Garner is strapping himself down to the chair inside the spherical cage while Morgan limps up to me, his cane pinging against the metal deck. He looms over, blocking my view of the admiral.

"We need to talk."

"About what?" I ask apprehensively.

He squeezes my arm. Hard. "In the hall." We step outside, the automatic door rolling shut behind us. "I need you to go back to the barracks for a while."

"But Admiral Da—"

"I'll tell him you're not feeling well."

"Morgan, you're scaring me. What's wrong?"

"Just, Gaby, please. I need you to trust me. You shouldn't be in the CIC right now."

This is him trying to keep me out of it. Whatever *it* is.

I open my mouth to protest, but his gray eyes are hard, full of worry, and something else. Pain. I nod in response, acquiescing despite every instinct screaming otherwise. He bends down and puts his lips gently to my forehead.

"Go," he whispers.

I pad away, back toward the main lift, confused and worried, though I don't know why.

A moment later, the lift doors slide open. Ensign Patrick Phelps is inside. He practically jumps out of his skin upon seeing me. His red hair is disheveled. His green eyes wild. "What are you do—? Shit!" he says.

I freeze, and before I can come up with a single reason he might be so shaken by my presence, the ensign has a pulser pistol aimed at me.

I show my palms. "What's goin' on?"

His eyes dart both ways down the hall, anxiously surveying for who knows what. Then a resolve seems to settle over him. "That way. To the CIC."

I do as he says, my shoes getting heavier with each step. For the second time in a scarce few minutes, the CIC's door rolls open in front of me. Nothing's changed since I left moments ago, and yet, everything's different. Now, for some unreal purpose, I have a gun to my back.

A half-dozen sets of eyes land on me, but I focus on Morgan's. Rapidly, his confusion turns to comprehension, then turns to anger, then turns to something else... Disappointment maybe? He mouths a curse, but the room fills with Lauren's voice as she shouts, "Now!"

I'm shoved from behind and trip over my own feet, going down hard on my knees. Guns are being drawn.

Lauren had one underneath her suit jacket; she levels it at the admiral. Morgan, Lieutenant Decker, Tyrone, Lieutenant Justice, they're all pulling sidearms from under their uniform jackets. Tyrone crosses the room, covering Samantha, and despite his muscle mass and bald head, he no longer looks like a marine to me. He's holding his pistol too far from his body, and only with one hand.

Decker turns her pistol on Eric, who's seated at the next station. The environmental glitch, the colder than usual temperature, I realize, was orchestrated to give them an excuse to wear their jackets, to conceal weapons.

Patrick is crossing the room fumbling with something in his hands. It's a... That can't be right. Why does he have a syringe?

Morgan calls to Patrick, but whatever he's saying is lost as frantic motion draws everyone's attention to where Samantha and Tyrone struggle for his gun.

As she twists the gun free of Tyrone's grasp, I smile, then my smile vanishes just as fast as she shoots him straight through the chest.

This is really happening, isn't it?

His body crumples lifelessly to the deck.

He isn't acting, is he?

As rough a neighborhood as LoLe can be, I've never actually seen someone die before.

"Traitors!" Samantha fires again. The pulser blast misses, punching into the bulkhead between Morgan and Lauren. I don't know who she'd aimed for, but it's Lauren who returns fire—three shots—two hit Samantha, with a third blast striking a command console and spraying the room in sparks.

My heart stops as Samantha collapses. I look from Samantha to Lauren. While I'm busy trying to figure out why everyone is doing the things they're doing, Ensign Garner and Patrick struggle inside the tiny sphere.

Morgan screams, "Stop!" And something like, *He's irritated!*

Patrick doesn't seem to notice, and he plunges the syringe into Ensign Garner's thigh. Ensign Garner howls in pain, pushing Patrick away, and looking down in shock at the syringe hanging from his leg.

No, Morgan didn't say, *He's irritated*. He said, *He's integrated*. Like a warning. But why does that matter? None of this makes any sense.

My gaze lands on Lauren again. Why did you shoot Samantha? Lauren doesn't answer my imagined question. She pulls her attention from the chaos in the Inertia-Zero cage back to Admiral Davis, who, apparently, no one had been watching.

The admiral is in his chair, typing furiously on the terminal screen. Lauren springs into action, pistol-whipping him across the forehead. It opens a cut across his brow but the big man simply accepts the blow, making no effort to defend himself as he finishes doing whatever it is he's doing.

Alarm klaxons wail. Lights around the perimeter of the ceiling flash red. She hits him again. The admiral lunges at Lauren, grabbing at her gun as they topple to the floor. He almost certainly would've wrestled it away from her, but others intervene, pulling him off her and kicking the wind out of him.

My eyes dart from the detangling bodies of the brief melee by the captain's chair to Samantha, who lies alone on the deck, her breathing shallow and erratic. "Someone help her," I hear myself whimper. But then the rise and fall of Samantha's ribcage stops and I know it's too late.

"Everyone fucking stop!" Morgan screams over the alarm klaxon. "Lieutenant Justice?"

"On it," she hollers. Lieutenant Justice silences the alarm from her station. The lights continue strobing red-off-red-off.

"No one was supposed to get hurt," Morgan shouts.

"What...did you...expect?" Admiral Davis says, wheezing between words. He's on his knees now, one hand holding his chair to steady himself, the other held protectively over freshly kicked ribs. "You...treasonous son of a bitch!"

Lauren whips him across the face with her pistol again. He falls on his side, groaning.

"Shut your mouth," she says.

"Actually, we need him to talk," Morgan says dryly, regaining his composure. "He just panic room'd the ship's AI."

"What does that mean?" Lauren asks.

On a delay, I wonder the same thing. I hear their words. I see them talking. But it's all far away and disconnected. Barely registering in my numb mind. Like there's a fog between me and everything else here in the CIC that nothing can fully penetrate. Nothing except the smell of blood and burning electronics.

Lieutenant Justice answers, "It means we can't use the ship's AI for anything, which, among other things, makes the blink drive fucking useless."

Morgan leans down to the admiral. "I don't suppose I can just ask you nicely to unlock the AI?"

"I'm not..." the admiral starts, "unlocking...anything...you piece of shit."

"Yeah." Morgan breathes out the word with the effort of standing back up. "I thought that might be the case." Morgan limps over to Ensign Garner, who at some point collapsed against the wall of the cage. He looks peaceful. "You were late, Ensign Phelps," Morgan says, glaring at Patrick. "And apparently you didn't hear me when I told you *not* to sedate Ensign Garner? That he was already integrated? Now we'll need to wait until the drugs wear..." Morgan trails away and bends down to look more closely at Ensign Garner. "Ensign Talley, will you please come over here?"

Eric Talley pointedly looks at Lieutenant Decker's pistol trained on him. "I don't take orders from traitors."

"You're the closest thing to a medical officer we have on board. I need you to check on Ensign Garner." Eric doesn't move. "Please."

Like a switch, Eric's expression changes from defiance to worry, and he steps over to examine the ensign.

"His breathing is slow, and damn, I'm barely getting a pulse. What did you do?"

"Sedated him," Morgan says. "With diodophine."

"How much?"

Morgan looks to Patrick.

Oh yeah, the diodophine. Now that piece fits.

Patrick says, "A hundred-and-fifty milligrams."

Morgan's knuckles go white wrapped around the handle of his cane. "What?"

Patrick's eyes go buggy. "That's what you said. Two milligrams per kilogram."

"Micro. Micrograms. You just gave him a thousand times too much."

"I'm going to need a life support cart," Eric says. Everyone freezes. "Not later. Now!"

Morgan nods. "Lieutenant Decker, Ensign Phelps, grab a gurney and get Ensign Garner to medical. Ensign Talley, you're going with. Please don't try anything. I don't want anyone else to die. Lieutenant Justice, get to engineering, see if there's anything you can do to get us the AI, or a workaround for the blink drive. Something. We have a schedule to keep. Lauren and I will escort the admiral to the brig."

"Her too." Lieutenant Decker points at me.

"No. Not Gaby," Morgan says.

"Are you kidding me?" Lieutenant Decker says. "She's not one of us."

"She's not one of them either," Morgan says sternly. "Gaby, go back to the barracks. Stay there until we can talk."

Lieutenant Decker shakes her head and mutters something under her breath.

Lauren pointedly makes eye contact with Lieutenant Decker, holds it for a second. "It'll be fine," she says. Then, turning to me, Lauren adds, "You're going to do what you're told. Right, Kitten?"

CHAPTER
TWENTY-THREE

The three remaining gaussers of Bravo Wave skimmed across Praxis Station's hull. Their flight packs gave them speed, agility, and the confidence of knowing they could drift away from the surface without floating helplessly away into the void. The Yingzi Zhēnxiàng patrol that came over the artificial horizon didn't have the benefit of flight packs. They plodded forward, relying on their magnetic boots to keep them anchored to the hull.

"Tangos," Remaut called out.

Morgan's HUD lit up, marking the seven contacts as active targets, glowing rectangles hovering over each center-mass. In weapons-free mode, the targeting software and the exochassis did most of the work—pulling his arms into position, pointing the rifle with inhuman accuracy and speed—all he needed to do was squeeze the trigger when it came time. By law, a human had to perform that step.

In the space of a heartbeat, he squeezed three times. Three bursts. Three targets. Jules and Remaut did much the same. It was over before their enemies had time to react.

"Tangos down." Jules' inflection would've matched the statement, *I filed an expense report*, much better than, *We just killed seven people*.

Five of them floated away, their bodies limp, blood seeming to grow like trees from the holes punched through their environmental suits. The other two remained anchored by their mag boots. They swayed like inflatable, dancing tube-men in slow motion.

They reached their first nav point moments later. Looking down through the window, the observation lounge appeared sideways to their orientation. There were no signs of activity or movement inside. This didn't surprise Morgan. Who'd be hanging out in a lounge while their station was under attack? Morgan removed the small disc of his shape charge from one of the many molded pouches on his suit. He stuck it to the window and keyed in the activation code.

This would've been a difficult incursion strategy on military targets. Military facilities had emergency shutters that would snap closed over a window the second de-pressurization was detected. Praxis had begun its life as a commercial hub though, and such extravagant expenses were not typically deemed necessary or even useful for business-class installations.

They each took two steps back from the window and anchored themselves to the hull with their mag boots. A brief flash and the window disappeared in a silent rush of wind as the oxygen blew into the vacuum. Cups, decorations, a few plants, and various other debris ejected from the window at high speed. Then a woman holding a small child shot out the window and spiraled out into the black. They were not wearing enviro suits.

Morgan, Jules, and Remaut all shared a silent look, but no one said a word. There was nothing to say. Morgan swallowed, telling himself the hard truth: Those two would not be the last innocent lives lost today. They probably weren't the first either.

"Downward and onward," Jules said once the O2 had fully

emptied from the observation lounge. He reached down, grabbing the lip of the window frame and pulled himself in. The force of the station's artificial gravity slammed him side-first to the floor. Morgan followed, landing just as awkwardly. The rapid reorientation of his proprioception—down becoming sideways, sideways becoming down—made him momentarily dizzy. Remaut was inside and steady on his feet by the time Morgan was standing upright.

"We've got an airlock," Jules said. He was already pulling open the panel next to the door.

"Good," Morgan said. "I'd rather not have to de-pressurize more of the station."

Morgan and Remaut met Jules at the exit where he'd exposed the innards of the airlock door's circuitry. Next, Jules unwound a cable from one of his pouches, connecting one end to his bracer, and the other to a port inside the wall. Within seconds he'd overridden the seals and the airlock cycled. They stepped inside. As the airlock pressurized, the exterior audio units in their helmets kicked on.

For the next fifteen minutes, as they made their way to their wave's final nav point, they only ran into two small pockets of disorganized resistance, both of which they put down with ease. They mostly saw unarmed civilians though. Praxis was a big place, full of food service workers, administrators, janitors, mechanics. Families lived there. They saw no less than three children on their way to their final nav point. Morgan thought this was a bad sign. With each empty corridor they passed through, or group of confused, scared civilians they shooed behind closed doors, each corner they rounded that didn't have an ambush on the other side, it seemed less likely their team had been given the winning nav point. Intel had marked six possibilities; only one of them was going to have their objective.

When they reached their final nav point, they found an empty cafeteria, abandoned mid-dinner rush. Half-eaten food littered the tables. In the kitchen, burners had been left on, still frying the now-charred remains of some kind of meat substitute. Morgan was glad he couldn't smell through the helmet.

"Safe to say it ain't here," Jules said. "Radio the other teams?"

"Already on it," Remaut said. "Epsilon Wave is hitting heavy resistance. Sounds like the Yingzi are concentrated here."

Morgan's HUD updated with a new nav point Remaut sent them. "Let's move."

TWENTY-FOUR

Uneven footfalls approach as I lie on the top bunk, gazing intently at nothing. *Clop, thump, clop, thump.* I can tell by the loping rhythm it's Morgan with his cane. Then comes a dull knock on the bunk's frame.

"Hey, Gaby," Morgan says. He sounds sad and far away. I don't move. "You're not going to make me climb that ladder, are you?"

Why don't you go ahead and do that, so I can slap you as soon as your face pops up over the railing.

"Why are you on the top bunk anyway?"

Slowly, I sit up and swing my legs over the edge. "Jules always slept on the bottom bunk. You remember Jules, right?"

He sighs, then steps awkwardly over to an adjacent bunk and plops onto the bottom mattress. "You have to understand something. I didn't want you involved in any of this. If I would've known you were— If I could've stopped you from coming, I would have."

"Why?"

"Why would I have stopped you?"

"Why the mutiny? Why the treason? Why all of it? I've been

sitting here trying to understand. I don't understand, Morgan. I don't see how the pieces fit."

"That's 'cause you don't have all the pieces. Will you look at me?"

I glare at him, wanting him to regret asking.

He forces a smile. "It's hard to explain. And hell, I don't think you'd believe me." He blows out a long sigh and rubs at his forehead. "I've actually been creating a kind of log to explain it. To explain myself. If it was done I could just..."

Is he talking about the mnemonic rendering he's been recording from his memories? "I'd rather hear it from your traitorous mouth."

He visibly flinches. Morgan's bracer chirps and the screen lights up. He presses a button answering it. "Yes."

"Lieutenant Commander," it sounds like Lieutenant Decker, "Ensign Garner is stabilized. He needs to remain hooked up to a respirator and some other life support gizmos, but Lieutenant Junior Grade Talley thinks he'll pull through."

"Good, good. Thank you, Lieutenant Decker."

Morgan moves to cut the transmission.

"Sir?" she says questioningly.

"Speak freely, Lieutenant."

"We can't keep Talley and Garner under guard in the medbay."

"Can Ensign Garner be moved?"

A brief, muffled interaction takes place on the other end, then Kerri Decker comes back on. "Lieutenant Junior Grade Talley seems to think so, as long as we bring this cart and he's allowed to monitor him."

"Very well. Take them both to the brig."

"Aye, sir."

He cuts the transmission and studies me with those gray eyes for a long moment before continuing. "We were all raised on advertisements telling us how great Swayy Corp. is. How the NCP watches out for us and provides for us. Then they tell us how evil the Commonwealth is and how noble it is to serve in the military. To fight."

"Oh no," I say, following his words to their logical conclusion. "You're defecting."

"Will you just listen before jumping to conclusions." His bracer chirps again. "Dammit," he says, punching a command to open the transmission.

"Lieutenant Commander York. We have a problem."

"What is it, Lieutenant Justice?"

"A pair of recon shuttles, sir. They're in the vicinity doing sweeps for us. A graviton beam practically brushed our hair."

"Put us within the coordinates of the line they just swept and begin analyzing their search pattern."

"I can start an analysis, but I'm in engineering."

"Right. I'll get to the bridge until Decker can take over the helm." He ends the conversation with a button press and pushes off his cane to stand up. "We'll talk later. For now, just stay put, okay?"

"I have to pee."

"Well, I didn't mean like that. You're not a prisoner, Gaby. You can go to the bathroom." He limps past my bunk toward the door.

I roll to the other side of the mattress to face the doorway. "Morgan," I call softly. He stops and pivots to face me. "You, and the others... You're not navy officers anymore. You should stop using your ranks." I'm not even sure why I say it. Perhaps I want to wound him. If that's what I was aiming for, by the look on his face, I judge myself successful.

He nods solemnly and then continues out of the barracks.

The door slides shut, leaving me alone. In LoLe, where large families live together to pool their meager resources and the walls are thin enough to hear your neighbors' mattresses squeaking at night, privacy isn't something I've spent much time thinking about. Sure, I've often felt lonely since Jules died, but I'm seldom physically alone. Not like I am now. I can't walk down the street to see K, or pound on the wall and have my neighbors reply with swears, or go into the living room and pick a fight with my parents over some trivial matter.

I crawl off the top bunk and go to relieve my bladder, half-expecting to see a guard posted outside the door to keep an eye on me. But no, of course there isn't. Stupid thought. They don't have nearly enough personnel to spare someone to guard me. I tick them off in my head. With Tyrone dead, there's Morgan, Lauren, Kerri Decker, Patrick Phelps, and Ruby Justice. Can five people even run this ship?

What could drive Morgan to throw everything away? His career. His life, if he's caught. But more importantly, his honor, his legacy. He was the Hero of Praxis. Now his name will be tarnished forever. There is no coming back from this.

He's chosen to abandon the NCP, abandon Jules' memory, abandon me and everyone else back home in LoLe. And for what? To defect to the Commonwealth? He didn't even have the courage to admit it.

Wait, maybe I'm wrong about that part. If he was defecting to the Commonwealth, he and Lauren wouldn't be planning on living the rest of their lives on Ongistald, would they? So are they planning on selling the ship, selling this technology to the Commonwealth? Is that better or worse? I can't decide.

How's he going to live with himself? What possible rationalization could he have cooked up in that brain of his that makes him think this is justified?

It doesn't matter, I decide while washing my hands, looking my reflection in the eye. It doesn't matter what Morgan tells himself so he can sleep at night. He is my enemy now. That's his choice. And now I have to make my choice: What am I going to do about it?

"You don't have an answer for me, do you?" I ask my reflection. My brown eyes stare back at me dumbly. "No, of course not."

What would Jules do?

I'm not even sure the question makes sense. Jules would've been able to talk some sense into Morgan *before* he pulled this stupid shit. But let's say for a moment that it's not Morgan. Replace Morgan with anyone else in all the worlds. Jules would hunt these traitors down, taking each of them by force, one by one if possible. But even if they were grouped together, one gausser—with their training and combat implants—would be able to take three officers, a journalist, and a handicapped ex-gausser.

But I'm not a gausser. Not yet. What can one tiny girl do against five armed enemies?

The answer is nothing.

It hurts to admit, but it's true. I need help. I need to free the admiral. He'll have some plan to get control of the ship back.

CHAPTER
TWENTY-FIVE

THE BRIG HADN'T BEEN PART OF SAMANTHA'S abbreviated tour. I wish I hadn't been in such a hurry to shower yesterday and had taken the full tour she'd seemed so excited to give. If I had, I would know where I'm going now. And I would've gotten a little more time with her. She was a good person. A hero.

She deserved better than getting gunned down on her own ship by someone she'd thought was a friend. Sure, none of us had known each other long, but we went through a lot together. I thought we'd bonded. I thought it meant something.

How could Lauren have killed her?

I come to a four-way junction. This ship is ridiculous. How am I lost? It's not a big ship and I'm still on the mid deck where the barracks are. On one corner of the junction, there's some kind of maintenance station. A terminal is mounted into the wall next to a tool cabinet. I wake the terminal up with a touch. Maybe there's a map?

I'm defeated by the opening screen. It requires credentials to do anything.

Wait, I clocked Samantha's credentials on the shuttle. Something I saw for two seconds over three days ago, but for whatever reason, my brain refuses to let go of that sort of thing. I'm not complaining.

User: MeyersS-R7A

Auth Code: +Boomb00m

And I have access. Poking around the menus, this terminal's access to the ship is limited to rudimentary local systems and low-level basic shared files. There isn't a map, not exactly. The closest thing I find is a wiring schematic for the interior lighting system. While it isn't true to scale, it's marked well enough that it should serve as a proxy for a map. Corridor running lights that look like transit lines thread around and lead to larger placements of various groupings of bulb codes.

Recreation Room - warm (4500K).

Kitchen - daylight (5500K).

And there it is: *Detention Facility - soft (3750K).*

I just have to imagine where the bulkheads are, take a few guesses on where the doorways might be placed, and I think I have a pretty good idea of the layout of this deck. If you bisect the ship down the center, the brig is in nearly the identical position as the mess hall. Except where the mess is on the port side, the brig is starboard.

My recall tends to suffer when I'm stressed, so I try to calm myself as I commit the wiring schematic to memory. Once I have it cemented in my mind, I start off for the brig.

I walk as quietly as I can, but there's little else I can do to be stealthy. There's no way to hide while skulking through empty corridors. But I also don't have much fear of getting caught. Morgan ought to be a deck up on the bridge by now, and Lieutenant Justice—scratch that, I won't use their ranks—Ruby is in engineering. That leaves Lauren, Patrick, and Kerri. Even if all three of them are on this deck, what are the chances I'll run into one of them? Unlikely. Slim. Not going to happen.

But do I hear voices?

I stop in my tracks, listening intently, trying to hear through the background noise of the air recyclers.

Nothing. I was probably imagining it.

But then, a woman's voice: "He's got every right to be pissed. I'm pissed too."

A man's voice, Patrick's: "I shouldn't've been in charge of that. What do I know about pharmacology?"

"That's not the part I'm pissed about," Kerri says, nearer still. "If you hadn't been late and brought the girl with you, the admiral wouldn't have had the chance to panic room the AI."

They're just beyond the next bend. A crawling fear curls around me, rooting me to the deck.

"Don't lay that on me."

"People died."

I turn and break into a hunched run, impressing myself with each soft, smooth landing my feet make. I turn a corner, then another, and see the mess hall door. Its motion sensors read my movement and the door slides open. Inside, I briefly feel safe, until I wonder: What if they're on their way here? Maybe to get something to eat, or maybe Morgan instructed them to prepare the next meal. My imagination draws up a scenario where they find me in here, question me, and, judging my answers unsatisfactory, decide to shoot me. I see myself lying on the floor taking my final weak breaths, just as Samantha did.

Maybe I should quit before anything bad happens? I could go back to the barracks and wait. I know the way. It was the same route Samantha had shown me yesterday. Thinking of that triggers the memory of something else. Of being startled by the automaton skittering through the flue beneath my feet, then of being embarrassed by my childish overreaction, and finally of being offended when Samantha remarked, *You could probably fit in there.* Words that, at the time, had hit an exposed nerve now remind me that the corridors aren't the only way to get around the ship.

I can't spot the little door the custodial tom had come from when it had failed to bus my tray. Maybe I can trigger it. I go to the kitchen and find a trash bin next to the food prep station. Inside is a stew of discarded processed meat product, overly salted sauces, half-eaten dessert bars, and thick crackers soaking in the moisture. The smell stings the back of my throat.

I grab a handful of the stuff and walk—my face turned away —back into the dining area. I drop it there in the middle of the room and attempt, rather unsuccessfully, to wipe the stickiness off on my overalls while I wait.

Nothing happens.

Is it not automated? Had someone performed some action I hadn't seen last time? Hit a button or maybe used a voice command to set the machine in motion? Then, a hatch opens against the back wall and a custodial tom glides over to the muck. I dash over to the hatch and sink down in front of it. There's a slight beveled edge with small, discolored chips where the hatch has been lightly struck or knocked against by something over the years.

Toying with the hinge, it opens and closes easily, and there doesn't appear to be any locking mechanisms. I'm confident I won't get stuck inside.

Gauging the size and awkward rectangular shape of the opening, it'll be a squeeze. Even for me. It drops away into a dark confined space. After one last nervous look at the mess hall entrance, and then sparing a glance at the custodial tom whirring about, cleaning and disinfecting, I lie prone on my belly and squirm into the maintenance flue.

The bounce of light from the open hatch dies centimeters in front of my face, dissolving into pitch nothingness. The narrow tube is just tall enough for me to crawl on hands and knees. I don't think a typical-sized person would be able to get their shoulders through.

Pausing to get my bearings, I envision the entrance to the mess hall, the placement of the hatch, and the direction I'm oriented in relation. Yes, I'm quite sure I'm facing starboard. Confident of that at least, I crawl on into the darkness.

The steel is cold on my palms and unforgiving on my knees. But after some time, the flue isn't as impenetrably dark as I'd initially thought. Once my eyes adjust, I notice the dim, thimble-sized status lights attached to the junction boxes placed at irregular intervals. The tiny lamps give the surrounding space a gentle glow of blue or green or yellow. It's just a hint—these are indicator lights, after all, they aren't meant to do anything more than give a drone a visual indicator of the condition of whatever system they're tied to. Using them as a light source is like trying to see with only the dying embers of a fire, but still better than nothing at all.

In the anemic illumination, here and there I find bundles of wires, plumbing, and hoses of unknown purpose. The unceasing rumble of one of the ship's systems floats through the flue from some indeterminable distance and direction.

Then the sound changes. Something new mixing into the reverbed susurration of the other machinery. It's the whir of a tom, I realize, as its headlights give my shadow shape, stretching out long and vivid before me. I squint as the walls sizzle with piercing light.

The tom runs straight into my butt.

"Hey," I say.

It runs into me again. It doesn't hurt, but it knocks me slightly off balance.

"Hang on, will ya?" I scold. I turn my head to it reflexively, then, immediately realizing my mistake, bring my hand up to protect my eyes. Its headlights are like a bomb going off in the dark.

It bounces off my butt a third time.

"You're not used to sharing your space, are you? Fine." I flatten myself against the chill surface. The tom clumsily floats over me, scraping against the ceiling as it does. I suck air through my teeth as a strand of hair is caught in the custodial tom and ripped free. "You're a terrible conversationalist," I say to it, rubbing the sting out of my scalp. I continue on, now with the four bright vestiges of the tom's headlights hovering in my vision.

With time, they dissipate, and my eyes readjust to the dim surroundings again. The whole trip across the ship can't be more than fifty meters, but crawling through the dark, it feels like it takes hours. There are several junctions along the way, but I ignore the branching paths, confident my goal is forward.

Up ahead there's more light. It dapples the flue's floor in uniform rectangles shining down through the floor grating from above. I hold my breath, listening for sound and watching for shadows moving above. I'd been on the other side of one of these hallway grates when I first saw the maintenance flue. Had a person been crawling beneath my feet, I would've spotted them for sure.

It's silent. There's no sign of movement. I squint up through the rectangular cutouts in the steel. At the edge of my line of sight stands a blast door. Above it reads: *Brig*. I crawl past the corridor as quickly and as quietly as I can manage.

Directly beyond that, I'm forced to follow the curve of the flue down a sharp right. Here it opens up. The flue is no longer a cramped duct, but a wide, squat crawlspace. White LEDs light the area enough to see. Vaguely square, it's maybe eight by eight meters, large enough that several load-bearing beams break up the space.

Above me, heavy bundles of power cables run lengthwise,

protected by a clear protective housing. Some type of ablative polymer, maybe? Obviously the *Discordia's* designers didn't want someone sending a drone down to splice into the power lines of the brig's cells.

I see a track where custodial toms' repulsors have pushed the thick dust away, like a trail worn into the grass. Following it, I find a hatch.

When I crack it open, a shock of blinding white streams through the thin opening. I wait at least a full minute, all the while breathing as shallowly as I can, watching for movement, listening for sounds. A hoarse cough filters through the crack. I hold back the urge to retreat into the crawlspace.

Daring to open the hatch a bit wider, I sweep the surroundings beyond. It's definitely the brig. A single holding cell stands against the wall on my right, but from this angle all I see is a line of steel bars. Across from the cell stands a lectern with a window behind it. Not much else is visible from the hole I'm in. Just white walls bathed in soft, 3750K bulbs made harsh by my dilated pupils.

Building up the courage by degrees, worried that I'm going to crawl free of the maintenance flue only to have a gun put in my face, I finally open the hatch fully and crawl through.

Eric murmurs something as he sees me. I must look like some graceless rodent digging its way out of a wall. The jaundiced light stings my eyes as I stand up, but none of the mutineers are here.

"Ms. Rhodes," the admiral says as my pupils adjust. My heart misses a beat, thinking of the window. I haven't checked to see what's on the other side of the glass. What if someone's in there and the admiral's just given me away? "Get to the control panel. Let us out if you can," he says.

I glare at him, putting my finger to my lips.

"There's no one here," he says. "There isn't enough of them to keep a guard on us."

I peek through the glass for my own peace of mind. It's a cramped, empty office; there's another door inside marked *Interrogation*. I'm just going to have to hope it's empty as well.

"The control panel, Ms. Rhodes," Admiral Davis says again, pointing to the lectern. There's a terminal screen built into the angled shelf.

"Quick," Eric adds.

"I'm trying." I tap through the menus. "It needs York's authorization key." I didn't want to use his rank, but couldn't bring myself to use his first name either.

"Of course it does." The admiral relaxes against the bars in disappointment. Dried blood is smeared on his face from the cut on his forehead. One entire side of his uniform is speckled with dark dots of it. "I'd hoped they'd made a mistake, or been over-confident enough not to bother."

Every wall of the cell is steel bars. A toilet sits in one corner; on that side of the cell a hard bench lines one wall and a row of fold-down G-chairs takes up another. The other half of the cell is a sleeping space with four flimsy-looking bunks with stretchy cots of trampoline-like material. Ensign Garner's on one of them. He's still unconscious; hoses coming from his face and wires from his arms lead to a rolling machine with various readouts. In a way, Eric looks worse than either of the others, despite being unharmed. He's slouched on a bench, looking utterly defeated, those too-big eyes of his nearly closed, as if his lids are too heavy to hold open.

"How do I get you out?" I ask.

"I don't think you can," the admiral says. That can't be it. We can't be giving up. "I think I've got most of their plan figured out," he continues. "It's not the *Discordia* they're after, it's the SR tech. They need Passenger. What I don't know is what they plan to do with it."

"I think they're going to sell it," I offer. "I heard them talking about living on Ongistald."

The admiral nods knowingly. "Any idea who they plan on selling it to?"

I shake my head. "The Commonwealth?"

The admiral makes a noncommittal noise. I can't take my eyes off the door for more than a few seconds. I feel exposed out in the open, and I just know someone will happen in at any moment and find me here.

"They'll need the blink drive to get to Ongistald, and they'll need Passenger to complete the sale. In a way, we lucked out on both accounts."

"I don't think I follow."

"They meant to sedate Ensign Garner *before* he was integrated with Passenger, not after. When integrated, Passenger is safely out of anyone else's reach. And in his current condition, they obviously can't convince the ensign to disconnect. And as for the blink drive, I was able to panic room the *Discordia's* AI. And I don't plan on giving that up easily."

What does he mean by *easily*? Is he expecting to be tortured?

"Why are we even talking about this in front of her?" Eric says.

"What's that supposed to mean?" I ask.

"Oh I don't know. Maybe it has something to do with your friend arranging a coup?" Eric turns to the admiral. "She's probably one of them, sir. Trying to gather information from us."

The admiral traces the orbital socket of his right eye where a deep bruise is developing. "Well, Ms. Rhodes, where does your loyalty lie?"

I open my mouth, but the words stick. My throat is dry. Their eyes are probing me from behind the cell bars. "Not with traitors," I whisper, looking at my feet. "My loyalty is with the NCP. With Swayy Corp. I don't even know who Morgan is anymore."

He turns to Eric. "I believe her."

Eric shakes his head.

"Lieutenant Commander York didn't even know you were coming aboard until the shuttle was landing." The admiral smirks as if thinking of a private joke. "I thought it was going to be a pleasant surprise for my new XO. But he didn't seem happy. Worried, one might say." Admiral Davis grips the bars tightly. "I could tell he was hiding something then, but I'd guessed that there was some unpleasant history between you two I wasn't aware of. But now I don't think he wanted you aboard for this. I don't think that would've been his reaction if you had been part of their plan."

"So what's *our* plan?" I say.

Eric sighs in annoyance and lays down on the thin shelf of a bench.

"We have zero chance of taking the ship back on our own. And as soon as they have what they want, they'll put us all out an airlock and be done with it."

Morgan wouldn't put me out an airlock, would he? My gut says no. But then, yesterday, if someone would've suggested he'd turn against the NCP and lead a mutiny, I would've told them they were out of their damned mind. "So we need to keep them from getting what they want," I say.

"Unfortunately for us, the *Hybris* and its recon ships won't find us while we're cloaked. Not without lottery-winning luck, or a massive error by Lieutenant Decker. We can't count on luck, and whatever else Decker is, she's a talented pilot. So our best bet is to run the clock out. If the training exercise completes without us ever decloaking, Admiral McCafferty will know something's wrong and bring in help to search. Without the blink drive, they can't get far, and even cloaked they won't be able to hide for long if an entire battle group is searching for them."

"So what do we need to do?" I ask.

"Well, they don't have a trained interrogator, so I think I can withstand whatever half-assed torture they throw at me. But there are engineering workarounds they might be able to use to get the blink drive to limp along. I doubt there's anything we can do about that. The real problem is keeping Passenger away from them. Ensign Garner is weak. When he wakes up, he'll break quickly."

Eric pipes up from his lying position. "And if he doesn't wake up?"

Admiral Davis nods thoughtfully. "Well, they could kill him. It's actually an easier solution for them."

"Can we get Passenger integrated with me? I can hide in the maintenance flues."

The admiral's expression goes from sullen to grave. "Yes, Ms. Rhodes. Yes, we can."

"Sir, no!" Eric shouts.

I start at the sharp noise, my eyes landing on the door. I imagine someone hearing. Bursting in with a gun drawn. I remember Samantha lying on the deck. Breathing. Then not.

"She's one of them, sir," Eric says. "You'd be giving *them* Passenger."

"Silence, Lieutenant. I'll hear no more of it. Ms. Rhodes is a loyal citizen. She'll do what's right. No matter the cost. Isn't that so?"

Squaring my shoulders, I stand as tall as I can. "Yes. Yes, sir."

"Good. Now, look at me," the admiral says. "Ms. Rhodes, stop looking at the door. Look at me. I'm going to give you a command code. Once Passenger is released, you are going to use this code to integrate with them. Do not, under any circumstance, disconnect. Don't let them have Passenger. Too much is at stake. Do you understand?"

I nod. I'm wondering how I'll know when Ensign Garner

wakes up and releases Passenger, but Admiral Davis continues before I have time to ask.

"Sympath codex: five, India, tango, seven, November, tango, sierra, lima."

Pausing a moment while committing it to memory, I take a long, slow breath, inhaling through my nostrils with my eyes closed.

"You have it?" the admiral asks, stepping over to where Ensign Garner lies.

Is he going to try to wake the ensign up now? "I've got it."

The admiral's posture deflates, his eyes glassy as turns his back to me, his movements slow and crestfallen. "Forgive me, Ensign," the admiral says. He grabs a pillow and, holding it taut, presses it down over Ensign Garner's face.

"Sir, what're you doing?" Eric says. He grabs at the admiral's shoulder, trying to peel the much larger man away from the helpless boy.

I feel glued to the deck, silenced by the shock. Eric screams at the admiral to stop. The sound stabs at my ears. He smacks and pulls at the admiral. Admiral Davis takes a hand off the pillow to push Eric to the floor. Ensign Garner's legs kick weakly as the admiral levers his considerable weight into the act.

I find myself able to speak. Able to scream. And so I add my voice to Eric's, pleading and demanding for the admiral to stop. I forget all about the door. Forget about my worries that one of the mutineers might come in and find me here unarmed and defenseless. I completely forget about all of it...

Until the door opens.

"What in all hells is going on in here?" Lauren says. She's still wearing the suit, the thin tie hangs with more slack than it had, and her color-wheel hair is pulled into a tight ponytail now. Her focus is on the prisoners. The cell. The murder. She doesn't notice me standing just a few paces away. Lauren pulls for her sidearm. With no plan or clear goal, I charge her.

Slamming shoulder-first into her, we both topple to the deck right in the track of the sliding doors. The pistol goes skidding away on the corridor's floor outside the brig. Lauren kicks me off and goes scrambling after the gun. Do I go for the gun? But it seems I've used up my courage, and the brief hesitation decides for me.

I turn and pound across the room for the custodial tom hatch. Eric's still yelling, I don't know if it's directed at me, or the admiral, or Lauren, but his voice is drowned out by the wind in my ears. I dive for the hatch. The steel floor grips at my overalls, tugging the one clasped suspender against my shoulder as I skid through. The hatch bangs shut behind me and I drop into the darkness. My arm and shoulder burn from the friction. Alternating waves of pain and numbness radiate from my knee down through my shin. I crawl away in a random direction into the wide space under the brig. Then stopping, I turn over on my back and yank the thin wires loose until the lights above me go dead. Lying there, I strain to listen for signs of pursuit over my heart pounding in my ears and my breath catching in my chest. My implant fires a near-empty, bubbly hiss. No pursuit comes. I shouldn't have expected any. She'd never fit.

Bits of muffled, excited yelling reverberate around me. But there are no screams. No pulser fire. The implant tries again, sounding like a weak spray of mostly air.

Crawling away, back into the cramped blackness of the flue ducts, I try to put as much distance between me and the brig as possible. But I'm in trouble. I can't breathe. After a time, exhaustion catches up to me and I'm forced to stop. I shut my eyes against the dark and crumple to the deck. The steel chills my face.

The implant deep in my chest lies dormant, its supply of life-saving drugs exhausted. Short weak inhales flee my lungs before they can make use of the oxygen. I should keep moving. I *need* to keep moving. But a blackness overwhelms me, dragging me into a nothingness where neither freeing the prisoners nor fleeing the mutineers matters.

CHAPTER
TWENTY-SIX

I wake up dying.

I've no clue if I was out for seconds or minutes. It was enough to calm my heartrate after all the excitement, but I know from the first wheezing breath that if I don't get treatment, I'll end up anoxic—dead inside the maintenance flue of a ship that belongs in a salvage yard. You don't get a captioned picture of yourself hung at Moore by dying like a rat in a wall.

<Ms. Rhodes, are you conscious?>

"Pass...en...ger?" I manage with effort.

<What is happening aboard this ship? I have been forcibly disconnected with Ensign Garner, and curiously I no longer have access to any ship systems. Yours is the only active NeurX I can reach.>

I try to say, *Mutiny*, but all that comes out is a choked cough.

<What is wrong with your body?> Passenger asks in their level, androgynous voice.

"Medbay..." I wheeze the word out.

<Are you in distress?>

"Yes," I croak.

<Okay, Ms. Rhodes. I believe I can guide you to the medbay.>

Passenger's tone changes. More serious, commanding even. <There are no internal sensors I can use, so I'm going to need you to tell me where you are.>

"Flue. Maint...enance."

<Am I to understand you're in the automaton duct system?>

"Yes."

<There should be junction boxes. I need you to find the nearest one and give me its code.>

The junction boxes are easy to find. As weak as their LEDs are, they're beacons in the night. There's one up ahead with a red twinkle as it alternates on and off about once per second. I reach it, but reading the identification code is difficult in the sour glow. "Five...four, two...dash...A."

<Well done, Ms. Rhodes. That junction box isn't far from the medbay. I just need you to find one more so I can identify your direction.>

After crawling farther in the dark, I find another. My head pounds from going so long without enough oxygen and my thoughts are foggy. The next junction box is slightly easier to read in the light of its green LED, but it takes even more effort to speak the characters aloud.

<Keep going forward until you reach an intersection. Then go right.>

I push on, crawling as fast as I can. Pins and needles jab at my fingers and toes. Going headfirst into a wall, I initially think I've run into a dead end. Then, rooting around I realize I've reached a T-junction. Groping through the dark, I fumble my way into the passage to the right. "Where...now?" I squeeze out.

<If you've already turned right, it's straight ahead. Eight meters from the intersection.>

Eight measly meters. It feels like it's stretching out endlessly until, abruptly, I reach a hatch and slither through. The medbay's overhead lights are off, but even the weak illumination from the various idling terminals seems bright.

<The ship's pharmaceuticals should be located in a cabinet directly across from your entry point.>

It's a big glass cabinet with its own tracked lighting. Sluggishly, I stand. My vision swims. My legs are unsteady, weak, and cramping painfully. Maybe from lack of oxygen. Maybe from too much time bent over in the crawlspace. Take your pick. My feet are wooden blocks, devoid of feeling. As I shuffle toward the glass cabinet, I hook a stool with numb fingers and drag it along. I plant my feet as stably as I can, and prepare to swing the stool, hoping I can manage enough force to bust the glass.

My wheezing is all I hear. I doubt I can even lift the stool.

I stop myself and zombie-walk to the glass case's door, trying it, just in case. It swings open and I silently thank Patrick's incompetence. With numb, uncoordinated fingers, and eyes that struggle to read the small typeface, I fumble through the hundreds of medications, looking for what I need. I knock bottle after bottle over on the shelf; some topple to the floor, one bursts open, sending little red somethings scattering across the deck. There. There's my medication. Got it!

The room spins and I fall backward into the side of one of the treatment tables, vaguely recognizing that I'll have another bruise to show for it. Sitting upright against the table, I dig into the packaging. My medication comes as a boxed kit that isn't the easiest thing to open in normal circumstances. My fingertips are blue, which from past experience, I know means my lips are too. Inside there's a thin, supple applicator tube with a yellow plastic connector on each end, and a bottle containing a cocktail of corticosteroids and beta agonists.

Unbuttoning the single clasp I have connected on my overalls and lifting my shirt, I pop one end of the applicator tube into the tiny inlet surgically grafted into my left side between my fourth and fifth ribs. It takes three tries to get the threads started. Next I connect the tube to the medication bottle. My shoulder shakes, protesting the effort it takes to hold the bottle facing down so the medicine drains into the implant's reservoir.

My implant starts firing. Once, twice... I lose count after seven consecutive sprays. My O2 stats must be bad enough to have over-ridden the maximum dosage safety settings. Shutting my eyes, I watch Samantha's ribcage rise and fall as she takes her last breaths. I see Ensign Garner's feet kick weakly as he's smothered. I hear a voice in my head saying, *You are a machine. You are a dead machine.*

Why is this happening? I had wanted to go to war. It was supposed to be: *There's my enemy, it's them or me.* There is simplicity in that. Honor. It was supposed to be the Stewies.

Not Morgan.

My enemy isn't supposed to be someone I look up to, someone I love. How did I get caught up in a mess like this? They have to be stopped. Morgan and Lauren and the others. I can't allow them to steal this ship. Imagine the damage the *Discordia* could do in the wrong hands, assuming that it really is as dangerous as the admiral says.

The admiral believes it is. The man murdered one of his own, in cold blood, in the hope that I'm up to the task of keeping Passenger safe.

I didn't like Ensign Garner, the little creep, but he didn't deserve to be murdered.

Is the admiral a monster for that? Or is Passenger truly so important? Can both be true? I feel sick, in my heart, in my bones, in the pit of my stomach. I can't think anymore. But I can fill my lungs at least.

Each breath more satisfying than the last, feeling returns to my hands and feet. First in flutters of tingles, then in grasping cramps. As those subside, hot pain replaces numbness in a dozen places throughout my body.

Dizziness washes over me and I slide down the treatment table to lie on my side. I feel it coming and there's nothing I can do but let it happen. A spasm in the back of my throat. A burn floods up my esophagus. Then vomit comes spewing forth. In that moment, I don't even care that I'm lying there in my sick as it runs down my cheek and soaks my hair. My eyes are wet, but I don't cry. Too tired. Every muscle aches. Every bone. Will a custodial tom be along to clean up my vomit? I feel so alone, I think I'd welcome the company, such as it might be.

Several minutes go by before I feel ready to move. In incremental steps, I sit up. Then I squeeze the medication bottle to get every drop I can out of it before unscrewing the applicator tube from my side.

The cocktail of corticosteroids and beta agonists have a long list of potential side effects. You may experience fast or irregular heartbeat, nausea or vomiting, changes in mood, nervousness, anxiety, and the list goes on.

Knowing this does nothing to mitigate the sudden shift in my emotional and mental state. Rationally, I know that if one of the mutineers was in the medbay, I would have already been found. But there's no room for rationality during a drug-fueled bout of paranoia. The compulsion whispering in my ear won't rest until I've checked every curtained-off partition, every coat closet and cupboard, anywhere anyone might hide within the medbay. Because the voice knows, it is absolutely convinced, that someone is here, waiting for their perfect moment to spring from some hidey-hole and accost me.

So I search the medbay top to bottom. Twice.

Once the paranoia has been placated, I'm able to relax a little. My heart rate is still elevated. Probably my blood pressure too. I can feel my heart thumping away in my ribcage. That just means you're still alive, Gaby.

I try to set all this nervous energy to more practical concerns.

There are no showers in the medbay, so I make do with washing myself in a sink. Briefly, I hope to change clothes, but my only options here are a medical jumpsuit two sizes too big, or a medical gown that doesn't leave much to the imagination. Neither will do.

My tan overalls are now blackened at the knees and spotted with a hundred smaller stains from the filth inside the maintenance flue. My camisole has fared better; it has a few small tears, but it's retained its pear-green color, the blotches of sweat at my armpits notwithstanding.

I sit on the floor next to the half-sized refrigerator and scavenge what food is available, making a meal of a protein-infused ice cream, an electrolyte popsicle, and a juice box. With nothing savory to balance it out, it all seems sickly sweet. But it calms my stomach. And to some extent, my nerves.

"Passenger, are you still there?"

<*There* is a strange term, but I think I understand your meaning, so yes.> Their androgynous voice is smooth and even. Whereas it had provoked discomfort at first in the SR, it's becoming a welcome guest in my head.

I return to my feet and attempt to stretch the cramps from my hamstrings. "What have I gotten myself into?"

<I don't understand. What has happened?>

"A mutiny. Admiral Davis and Lieutenant Talley are locked in the brig. Everyone else is either dead or a traitor."

<I see. The term *gotten myself into* implies that you are responsible in part or in whole, by action or inaction. Were you even aware of this plot?>

"No," I grumble.

<Then you have not gotten yourself into anything.>

"The admiral said I should integrate with you."

<If you wish to be my host, you will need the command key for full integration.>

"Should we? Do you think that's a good idea, or...?"

<I cannot answer that. I do not know what your goals are.>

I bite down on a fingernail. "What are my goals?"

<I believe that is a question you are simply asking yourself. So I shall not respond at this time.>

"You kinda did respond." Passenger is silent. I have no reason to think so, but I imagine they're embarrassed at being caught out. "I need to keep you out of the mutineers' control."

<Becoming my host would make it impossible for the mutineers to gain control over me, at least for the duration we are integrated.>

"Okay, sounds like I should be your host then."

<If you wish to be my host, you will need the command key for full integration.>

"You said that already."

<It is true.>

"Do I need a blinder helmet?"

<No. They are useful for maintaining focus in the SR, but not a necessity. Also, it is unlikely we'll be operating in any way that would benefit from sensory deprivation.>

"Okay. Sympath codex: five, India, tango, six, November, tango, sierra, lima."

<That is not the correct code.>

I drum my fingers on the stainless-steel countertop. I form an image of Admiral Davis in my mind, recalling the memory. But the sound is gone. My memory almost never fails me. Why now? I try again. But it's no use, I can't hear him. I let out a string of curses.

<That is not the correct code.>

"I know that," I say, not even attempting to hide my agitation.

Closing my eyes, I bring the memory back again. This time I ignore the lack of sound and I focus on the admiral's lips, reading the space between vowels and consonants. There were two vowels in the fourth word. It was a seven, not a six. "Sympath codex: five, India, tango, *seven*, November, tango, sierra, lima."

<Integration process beginning.>

My NeurX displays a pop-up. I allow permission for the connection, then a progress bar fills so rapidly I barely see it before it disappears.

I don't feel any different. "Are we integrated?"

<Yes, Ms. Rhodes.>

"Mind just calling me Gaby?"

<I can do that.>

"Good. So all we need to do now, according to the admiral, is avoid capture until the *Hybris* finds us."

I pace the room. It's been good to move upright after so much crawling around on all fours. Dreading the idea of going back into the flue, I stand there, glancing from the hatch in the wall to the doorway out to the hall. I try to calculate my odds of remaining unseen aboard the ship if I were to move about like a person instead of some kind of rodent.

After my confrontation with Lauren, though, they know I'm up to something. They're probably already searching this deck top as thoroughly and quickly as their limited manpower allows. If they weren't on a skeleton crew, they probably would've already found me. It's dumb luck that they haven't. Can't count on dumb luck forever. No, I'll have to go back into the flue.

My arms are limp at my sides as I shuffle over to the hatch. I open it, lever myself down onto my belly, and pull myself through the gaping maw back into the dark.

CHAPTER
TWENTY-SEVEN

Morgan, Jules, and Remaut pushed through the station with reckless haste. With their exochassis' help, they kept a near-sprinting pace through the tight corridors and used their jump jets to rocket through open areas.

Remaut had patched them into Epsilon Wave's feed. Morgan felt powerless as they listened to the desperate radio chatter and watched the status icons in their HUDs wink out one at a time. The radio chatter quieted, then ceased altogether. By the time they rounded the last corner and reached their position, the one remaining Epsilon Wave status icon went out.

Hunkering down at the edge of the corridor, they took measure of the scene.

"They have an Ostrich," Jules sighed.

The four-meter-tall combat mech stalked across the massive, cubed room, lightly bobbing as its reverse-jointed legs actuated in jerky motions. It had taken some damage—the armored carapace showed scoring and the tell-tale pockmarks from Epsilon Wave's combat rifle fire. But all in all, it looked disappointingly functional.

"They went down fighting at least," Remaut said.

Surveying the rest of the room, Morgan guessed it was a cargo transport hangar. Huge blast doors stood closed to their right, and an industrial crane on a rotating arm dominated the high ceiling. Remaut was right, Epsilon Wave had made a mess of the place. A half-dozen fires burned. The balcony that, at one time, had wrapped around the periphery of the room was blown apart in sections. And the remains of a second Ostrich lay in ruins on the far side. Their HUDs clocked the remaining Ostrich, two smaller combat drones circling overhead, and twenty-five human tangos—though Morgan noted a handful of those were wounded. Their targeting computers didn't take notice of the hundred or so bodies. Morgan did.

Remaut said, "Epsilon's last nav point was that room there, directly across from us."

"Gettin' there's gonna be a nightmare," Jules said.

Morgan found he had a plan forming. "Get out your drones." They each carried a small, saucer-shaped spy drone. "Set them on kamikaze mode and lock onto those airborne combat drones." To Morgan's surprise, Remaut and Jules followed his instruction immediately even though he didn't outrank either.

Their drones hovered near them, waiting for the signal to engage. With some luck, their drones would down at least one of the enemy drones. "We'll need to do all of this pretty much at once," Morgan said, hoping they'd keep listening to him. "We throw grenades to scatter the tangos, then trigger our drones. As soon as the grenades are in the air, Petty Officer Remaut and I will break right. We're going to ignore the Ostrich and neutralize the human tangos. Jules, as soon as we've got their attention, you circle left and jump-jet on the Ostrich's back. Plant yours and Remaut's shape charge on it."

Jules tightened his rifle sling so it would hang against him snugly without his hands on it. Remaut handed over his shape charge, and Jules armed both of them. Then they each pulled one of their two grenades and armed them, readying the command in his HUD to trigger his drone. "Now!" Morgan called out.

Their grenades arced through the air as Morgan and Remaut shot off to the right. Two. Four. Six tangos were down by the time the grenades went off in three nearly simultaneous explosions. The human tangos scattered and returned fire with blind sprays as they ran or ducked for cover. The Ostrich was unfazed and opened up with its heavy guns. Morgan and Remaut continued circling, running and jump-jetting erratically as the Ostrich wheeled, chasing them with machine gun fire that slammed into the deck, textured the steel walls, and tore through an industrial lift. Morgan couldn't return fire, or even keep an eye on the Ostrich; it was taking all his focus and effort to keep ahead of the combat mech's movements.

As the machine gun fire went silent, and Morgan thought, *Good, it overheated its own guns,* he heard a sort of hiss, like the sound of carbonation being released. A fraction of a second later, he registered that it was a rocket igniting. He spared a glance to see the rocket heading their way, a trail of smoke leading back to the Ostrich.

"Fly!" Morgan yelled, jumping in no particular direction. Caught in midair, the blast threw him end over end. His momentum stopped abruptly when he slammed into a wall several meters above the ground. Reflexively, he rolled when he hit the ground, smoothly recovering his balance, and posting on one knee. He returned fire, shooting three bursts at the first movement he saw. Two tangos went down. Small arms fire rained around him. He felt like someone punched him in the chest as at least two rounds made contact. Gausser body armor could withstand most small arms fire, but it was best not to tempt fate. There was always that chance of a bullet sneaking through where the armor's coverage was weaker.

A short distance away, Remaut was engaging a squad of

newcomers, judging by the fact their HUDs were just now tagging them. Remaut sprayed at the tangos in full auto while walking them down. Apparently, he didn't mind getting bruised up by the small arms' return fire. As the squad of tangos took cover, Morgan realized two of them wore oversized heat-shielding gloves and the double face plates that meant...

"Remaut back off!" Morgan yelled.

But it was too late. The two Yingzi Zhēnxiàng leveled their plasma rifles and opened fire, punching hot holes through Remaut's armor. He collapsed to the deck.

Morgan frantically looked for Jules in time to see him catch his balance on the Ostrich's back, punch both fists down, then jump away, his jump jets burning hot.

As his eyes followed Jules climbing high into the air, Morgan didn't immediately notice the object trailing smoke right at him. Amongst the din of weapons fire, he hadn't heard the second rocket launch.

The rocket just missed, colliding into the deck behind Morgan. He felt a kick in the back that launched him from the ground and sent him sailing through the air. *I'll be damned*, he thought, noticing one of those bastards was actually shooting at him, as if he was some clay target in a skeet shooting competition.

Morgan crashed into the deck and rolled to a stop behind the industrial lift that the Ostrich had already turned into slag.

He laid there for a moment, trying to will himself up, trying to guess at how hurt he was. His helmet was done: the glass had thick fractures obstructing his vision, and static filled his ears from the wrecked audio system. He guessed the environmental system was gone too, because it was quickly getting difficult to breathe.

The emergency auto-grip worked, so he still had his rifle. That was something, at least. He released the clasps and tore his helmet free. The room smelled of gunpowder and fire and cooked meat.

He heard the whoop and scream of a plasma rifle. He heard the concussive, rapid-fire chirps of a gausser's high-caliber combat rifle. Jules was still fighting it out with them.

Morgan grabbed at the industrial lift's steering column and pulled himself up. The remaining Yingzi tangos were invisible behind thick clouds of smoke. Morgan took a bead on one based on the licks of fire coming from their weapon. In the second that it took to seat the butt of his rifle to his shoulder and bring the center mass in his sights, he shifted his weight. His right leg seemed to disappear as he put pressure on it. Morgan collapsed backward, firing into the air and screaming in pain.

Jules' armored hand grabbed the lip of Morgan's armor at the back of his neck and began dragging him away while firing his pulser pistol over Morgan's head with his free hand. Instinctively, Morgan tossed the last of his grenades, then fired deliriously with his rifle covering their retreat.

The violence outside disappeared behind a sliding door. The light changed. Jules dragged Morgan farther, leaning him up against a wall. Morgan's head swam, consciousness turning into a kaleidoscope of confusion.

"Hey, stay with me," Jules said.

CHAPTER
TWENTY-EIGHT

I DON'T GET FAR INTO THE MAINTENANCE FLUE BEFORE I decide to stop. Every step—if you can call them steps—is accompanied by a biting pain against my knees. How far do I need to go, really? None of them could fit in here, and I'm well beyond arm's reach of the hatch.

With nothing to do but hope for a fluke that the recon pilots happen to get lucky, or that Kerri Decker makes an error, this is going to be a long, boring wait. Either of those unlikely scenarios could cause the *Hybris* to find us. But what would happen then?

Provided the *Discordia* is discovered during the normal window of the training exercise, the *Hybris* would fire simulated weapons. With the *Discordia's* AI panic room'd, would they have any effect? I don't think so. Certainly the traitors have turned off the simulation protocols. They'd be firing live weapons, while the *Hybris* would be in simulation mode. If it came down to a fight, they'd start with an advantage.

That advantage wouldn't last long though. And I've learned enough about naval combat to know this little destroyer—even starting with an advantage—wouldn't have a chance against a battleship like the *Hybris*. The *Hybris* would disable the

Discordia, and once she's adrift, they'd send marine boarding attachments to secure the ship. Morgan, Lauren, and the others would surrender or die. The entire process, once it got started, might take an hour. I wonder if Lauren's cameratom would record the ordeal, providing a record for evidence or posterity or whatever else high command decided to do with it.

They sure as hell wouldn't give the tom back to the Media Minist—

Wait.

The cameratom. My spyware. I could use that to keep tabs on the mutineers. Once again, I go to my linked devices, and once again the cameratom is active. It begs the question: Why? Lauren must plan on leaving her old life and career behind, so why is she still using the cameratom at all? That's a question for another time. For now, I just count myself lucky that it's active and click on the CONNECT tile.

I hear something clinking. Like glassware or something metal. And for a brief second, before I think it through, I wonder if someone is washing dishes. Then the video feed streams in.

"So are you the brains of this operation?" Admiral Davis asks. He's sneering. The chain connecting the shackles at his wrists rattles against the cuff bar bolted onto the table. "Or is he?" He's pointing toward something. Lauren turns and so the cameratom follows as she glances at a mirror on the wall.

"You assume Morgan is on the other side of that glass?" Lauren asks.

"Of course he is. He's in command of this ship now. He wouldn't miss this. What I'm trying to figure out is, are you in command of him?"

"No," Lauren says ambiguously. "He is not in the observation room, I mean. He's busy dealing with the body you left behind."

"Mmm." The admiral's face becomes inscrutable. "You left a

body behind today too. And you're not a soldier. Was Lieutenant Junior Grade Meyers your first?"

He sounds so callous. Samantha was a person. A good person. How can he say that so calmly? How can he be so detached? It pisses me off, then I realize that's his intention. Not to piss *me* off, of course. He's trying to get under Lauren's skin. He's trying to take control of the conversation.

It doesn't seem to rattle Lauren though. She stands, walking the length of the table, dragging the painted fingernails of one hand across the smooth plastic surface. "The person I killed was a grown woman, and she had a gun in her hand, Admiral. You murdered a defenseless child. One that was under your command, unconscious and receiving medical care. I'd ask why, but I already know. You think you've been able to deny us access to Passenger. You think the AI is safe with Gaby Rhodes."

The admiral grins a response at her that shoots a shiver up my spine, and I'm not even in the room. Not really.

"Let me make this clear, Admiral," Lauren says. "The only thing you've accomplished by murdering that poor boy is delaying us. I want you to consider that. You sacrificed his life to impose a minor inconvenience."

"Ensign Garner's death will weigh on my conscience for the rest of my days. As awful as it is, it is one single life. I'm trying to end a war. This technology could save tens of millions of lives. Except some greedy band of traitorous thieves have stolen it to sell to the highest bidder. Tens of millions of lives. That's what should be on your conscience, Ms. Gallagher."

Lauren, still standing, leans on the backrest of the empty chair. "I know," she hisses through clenched teeth, "I know exactly who is on my conscience."

He smiles more broadly, like he just walked his enemy into a trap. "I'm surprised you have a conscience at all, Ms. Gallagher. Perhaps you should take another pill for that."

Lauren's jaw goes slack. As if by reflex, she glances toward the mirror. What does he mean? What pill?

"See," Admiral Davis says, following her involuntary eye movement. "My piece of shit XO is in the observation room, and what's more, he didn't know about your little habit, did he? Oops." He lifts his eyebrows, clearly satisfied with himself.

Lauren's knuckles go white as her hands grip the back of the chair. Her jaw's clenched so tightly I doubt she could speak in that instant if she tried.

"Oh, don't look so shocked, Ms. Gallagher. I've been around spies my entire career. You don't think I can spot the signs of blunters?"

What are blunters?

"Shut up," she says.

"Lieutenant Commander York, on the other hand, he came up a different path. I suppose it wasn't too difficult to hide it from him."

"Shut up," she says, louder this time.

"What else are you hiding from him?"

"Shut up." She spits the words as she slaps him.

He stubbornly keeps the grin fixed to his face, despite the splash of red forming on his cheek.

A door somewhere out of frame rattles open. I hear the *clop, thump, clop* of Morgan's loping walk. He steps into frame, leaning on his cane. He places a caring hand on Lauren's shoulder.

"Admiral, if you think you're going to seed some kind of dissension between us, you've got another thing coming," Morgan says calmly. "You're right though, I came up a different path. I'm a simple soldier. A grunt at heart. So I'm going to make this plain. Give us the code so we can get the AI out of the panic room, or—"

"Or what?" the admiral interrupts. "What exactly do you think you can threaten me with, you little pissant? You going to kill me and Lieutenant Talley? Do it. This project is bigger than any of our lives."

Morgan looks taken aback. He doesn't have a response; he wasn't prepared for such defiant malice.

"No, we're not going to kill either of you, Admiral," Lauren says smoothly. "You both have value. You have the code we need, and I'm sure we can motivate Eric to do everything medically possible to keep you alive while we get it. Very slowly."

"I'm trained to resist torture from the best, young lady. And you don't have anyone that knows shit about how to do it."

"Maybe not," she says. "We have an engineer though. We'll just have to have her take you apart, piece by piece, like a common drone."

Admiral Davis' grin returns, looking even more wicked than before. "Sounds like you've got it all figured out. Let's get started, shall we?"

"No." Morgan crosses his arms with finality.

It's hard to tell with the angle of the cameratom, but it seems like Lauren sends a dirty look his way.

"The admiral has us cornered on this one," Morgan continues.

"Morgan," Lauren hisses.

"We can beat our chests all we want. We can posture. We can threaten. But he knows he's won this part of the game. We might as well admit it so he doesn't think he's outsmarted us too. He believes that he'll be able to hold out without giving up the code until he dies. And with any torturer we could produce, he's probably right. It would be a waste of time. The question is, whose time? You suggested Ruby, and I agree, she'd probably be best at it." He turns to the admiral now. "We've discussed her, haven't we, Admiral? Something isn't quite right with that one. But if we pull her from working on bypassing the system, we play into the admiral's hands. We can't have Kerri do it. We need her at the helm making sure we don't get found by some random graviton beam. Patrick?" Morgan laughs. "He'd bungle the entire thing and give the admiral a quick, easy death. So that leaves you and me. I don't have the stomach for it. And I genuinely hope you don't either."

Only a sliver of Lauren is visible at the edge of the frame. Her shoulder is rising and falling like she's breathing hard.

"So Admiral, congrats. You've won. Do you want to know what you've won?" Morgan leans against the mirror, the handle of his cane in both hands. "The original plan was to sell this ship to a group of idealists that have noble intentions for the technology. It's not worth getting into. We don't have time for me to tell you the whole story, and you wouldn't believe a word of it anyway. Just understand, had everything gone to plan, your project would've still saved lives."

Lauren turns her back to the two men. But her face still isn't in frame. Morgan's lying. He has to be. But it's a good lie. And most good lies have some kernel of truth to them, right? Is this one of those?

"Unfortunately," Morgan says, "there's a narrow window of opportunity for delivery. If we miss it, then we'll be forced to sell the ship to the highest bidder, just like you said. And the chances of that party having noble intentions, like our original buyer... Well, they're not great. I mean, you can guess at the types that would want the *Discordia* and Passenger on their side. So what's it going to be, Admiral? Do we get the codes from you and sell the ship to those that want to do good with it? Or are you going to fall on your sword, forcing us to let the worst people in the solar system have a grab at this technology?"

The admiral's eyes are downcast, his posture contemplative. "Rousing speech." He brings his face up, smiling. "But you're lying. You might be on a timetable, but I don't buy the altruistic thieves bit. You say those are the two options? I'll choose neither."

"Not an option," Morgan says flatly.

"I disagree. You need Passenger. And Ms. Rhodes has Passenger."

"I'll handle Gaby," Morgan says.

"You think so, eh? You don't know that girl as well as you think you do. She understands loyalty. She'll die before she betrays the NCP. And there's no way you'll be able to stomach killing her to access Passenger." The two men lock eyes briefly. Then the admiral says, "Her, on the other hand"—he flicks his focus to Lauren and then immediately back to Morgan—"she could stomach killing Gaby. But can you let her?"

"No one's killing Gaby. I just need to talk to her."

"Good luck finding her before critical symbiosis."

"Critical symbiosis?" I whisper inside the flue. "What the hell is that?"

<I don't know,> Passenger says. <But, Gaby, they can't hear you. You don't need to whisper. And also, we're integrated, you can thought-broadcast to me.>

"What's he talking about?" Lauren asks.

Morgan answers Lauren without taking his eyes off the admiral. "Once they stay joined for long enough, the AI's code gets stored in the host's hypothalamus."

My memory flashes to the admiral telling me how Passenger's integration was safer than a drone's because Passenger's code threads its way in. I imagine the roots of two trees growing together for decades, knotting around each other until there'd be no separating them without destroying the entire root structure.

<Oh no,> Passenger says. <If that were to happen, separating host and AI would forfeit both entities' existence.>

"That's a cute way to phrase both our deaths," I say.

Once my attention is back on the cameratom feed, Morgan is explaining roughly the same thing to Lauren. He finishes by saying, "It's okay though. We know where she is." Morgan glares at the admiral. "We have a drone scouring the maintenance flues now. We'll find her well before we have to worry about that."

I cut the feed in a panic. Someone will happen through the medbay at some point, if they haven't already. When they see the mess I left behind, they'll focus their search on the maintenance flues nearby. I need to get moving. Now.

CHAPTER
TWENTY-NINE

<Where are we going, Gaby?> Passenger asks.

"I don't know," I say aloud. I'm feeling my way along the flue on hands and knees. "I'm just trying to put some distance between me and the medbay."

<Based on my estimate of your inefficient quadrupedal speed, you are twenty-one-point-three linear meters away from the medbay. Is that *some distance* enough?>

"How do you know that if the ship doesn't have internal sensors?"

<Your NeurX implant has details of your biometrics. So I am aware of your limb lengths, and I can sense your muscle contractions so I know how many steps you are taking. It then becomes a simple equation with an acceptable margin of error.>

Feeling around at a junction, I take a random left. "You can *feel* my muscle contractions? Does that mean you can hear and see too?"

<Yes, I have access to all of your senses. I cannot see right now though. It is dark.>

That sends the creeps up my spine. Then I wonder if

Passenger can sense my sudden discomfort. The thought of them sensing my discomfort makes me more uncomfortable, turning into a feedback loop that cycles until I force the entire idea out of my mind.

Passenger continues, <The transfer of data works both ways. I believe I can now show you a map.>

Then, in my imagination, an image coalesces. A three-dimensional, full-color map of the entire *Discordia* interior: corridors, rooms, airlocks, every maintenance flue and hatch, every compartment seal (for both the corridors and flues) that would twist closed in a breach. With a mental effort that feels strangely intuitive, I can manipulate the map. I can zoom in or out, spin it, focus on one deck, or a single room, even zoom in and float through it like it's a simulated environment in an interactive VR.

According to the map, the flues rarely take direct routes. There are dozens of seemingly random twists and turns as they yield space for other systems and stretch away into dead ends where they terminate at key locations.

Having access to Passenger certainly has its perks, even if it feels sort of icky to have them sharing my head.

It occurs to me that calling their presence icky could be offensive. I'm relieved that they don't respond to my thought. Hopefully it's because they can't hear my unfiltered, inner monologue and not because they have nothing to say about it.

I stop moving. Looking over the map, my present position, as arbitrary as it is, seems like as good a place as any to hide. And I'm so tired. It hurts to breathe. My diaphragm is exhausted. My throat is raw. My voice hoarse. Every breath is a reminder of how near I came to asphyxiating in this flue. Would anyone have even found my body?

And somehow dying in this flue doesn't seem like the worst possible fate for me at this moment.

"We need to talk this out," I say.

<Talk what out?>

"The admiral wants us to wait for rescue. The problem with that is rescue will take too long. The time limit for integration is six hours, right? Is there some kind of safety buffer built into that? Does six hours take us right to the edge?"

<Six hours is the regulation. I do not have answers beyond that.>

"What about disconnecting then reconnecting?"

<Recommended downtime between integrations is twice the length of time spent integrated. Given what we now know about critical symbiosis, I must imagine the recommended downtime is important.>

"We need more time. The admiral seemed to think we'll need to wait it out until after the training exercise concludes and Admiral McCafferty brings in help to search. That could easily take twenty or thirty hours, maybe more depending on fleet positions."

<I cannot imagine any safety buffer covering that length of time.>

"Me neither. Admiral Davis had to've realized that, right?"

<I would surmise that the admiral would prefer us to be permanently bound as a symbiont, over me falling into enemy hands.>

He could have told us the risks. It appears Jules was right about InDiv officers after all. Always plotting and scheming and manipulating. "I don't like the sound of being a symbiont."

<Neither do I.>

"Can you like or dislike stuff?"

<Yes, of course I can, Gaby. I am simply limited in my ability to act on my preferences.>

Right. The Kojima Accords, the reason Passenger needs a human host to hack. Wait... "Why don't we just hack the ship's systems? Free the admiral and Eric. Maybe together we can—"

<I'm afraid that's not possible.>

"Why not?"

<It's a safety protocol installed so that I cannot be used to seize control of the ship.>

"So you're not allowed to hack the ship and stop a mutiny because someone was afraid you'd be used to commit a mutiny. Hello irony."

I bite down on a fingernail, promptly realizing how filthy my hands are. Do I tunnel deep into the bowels of the ship and wait for rescue, even though that will probably mean getting permanently bonded with Passenger? I wonder what that would be like. Do I cease being me? Does Passenger cease being them? Would we be two distinct entities sharing the same body, or become some amalgamation of us both, each losing our individuality?

None of those scenarios are appealing. Another thought occurs to me. If Passenger is joined to me permanently, there's no way they'll allow me to become a gausser. They'll probably categorize me as navy property, stripping away all my rights as a citizen.

I definitely need some other plan.

"I don't want to wait around for the *Hybris* to bring in help to find us, not with this ticking clock."

<Agreed.>

A distant voice bounces down the shaft, garbled by a long string of overlapping echoes. A little wink of light appears in the distance. A tom? No, it isn't the headlights of a custodial tom roaming around. This light is streaming in sideways, coming from the corridors of the ship. I pick out my name among the string of echoes. The mutineers are opening hatches and calling out to me.

"Shit," I whisper.

<Although I do not think any member of the crew could fit in the maintenance flues like you can, I am concerned with the *Discordia's* complement of maintenance drones.>

"Shh."

<They cannot hear me, Gaby.>

I don't respond.

<Also, you are capable of thought-broadcasting to me.>

<I'm not sure how,> I think, not daring to speak out loud and let my voice echo down the chamber.

<It appears that you do,> Passenger says. <As I was saying, the maintenance drones will be capable of harming you, should they find you. You wouldn't have any viable defense.>

"Gabrielle Rhodes?" Patrick's voice echoes down the flue from somewhere at my left.

Then, from somewhere nearer, "Kitten?" I tremble at hearing Lauren's voice. Her calling me by that nickname made me feel so special at first. Now it feels tainted and overly familiar. "Listen, Kitten. No one wants to hurt you. Come on out, okay? Morgan is really worried. Please come out. We can explain everything."

She sounds sincere. Worried even. Lauren's a killer though. Samantha flashes in my mind. Breathing. Then not. They're all traitors. Traitors and liars. They can't be trusted. Her least of all.

<I should get to a different deck.> I pull up the mental map again. I'm in the mid deck, which has by far the largest number of crew-accessible sections. Above is the command deck, which is too small to hide in, and that's probably where most of the mutineers will need to be. Below is the mechanical deck, and two decks down is the hangar deck. Both of those seem less likely to have anyone roaming about, but the hangar deck, like the command deck, has a simple, small layout. Mechanical deck it is.

I draw a course on the map to an accessway leading to the mechanical deck. It sits behind the primary lift. The plotted line lights up in a translucent yellow with a tiny opaque version of myself where Passenger approximates my location. Or is it *our* location?

I set off in the flues as silently as I can, worried that the sound of my knees thumping against the steel or the scraping of my shoe-toes will betray my position, or that by dumb luck one of them will pop open a hatch as I'm passing by. None of those things happen though. They either give up or move on to a different section after a few short minutes. Their voices fading, then disappearing entirely. The rest of the trip passes in silence.

Walking the corridors from the medbay to the lift room would've taken a minute, tops. In the flues, it takes half an hour.

Groping blindly in the dark, my hand hits empty air where steel should be. A cool draft tinged with the odor of hydraulic grease reaches my nostrils. The maintenance shaft is a sheer drop. There's a series of dull red glows, four of them, tracking the vertical length of the shaft, but they're so faint they don't illuminate anything.

"Why didn't I grab a flashlight or something? Passenger, how far down is it to the bottom of this shaft?"

<Just under nine meters.>

A knot forms in my stomach. "How far down do I need to climb to reach the mechanical deck?"

<Approximately three-and-a-half meters.>

Retrieving the mental image of the map, I examine the details of the shaft. There's no ladder. But there are dozens of pipes, cables, and conduits flowing in different directions. There are also ledges along the wall every meter or so where the sections of the shaft bolt together. But even with all those hand and footholds, it would be a dangerous climb in the best circumstances. In the pitch dark, it's suicide.

Reduce the problem, Gaby. The problem isn't climbing, it's falling, which means the problem is actually... "Can we turn off the artificial gravity?"

<There is an emergency system designed to shut down the artificial gravity in the shaft so that the lift can be raised or lowered by a hand-crank inside the lift. There is one access panel

in the shaft on each deck for this purpose and one in the lift itself.>

"Show me." The access panels begin glowing on my map and I realize that's what the faint red lights are marking. I'll have to shimmy along an edge halfway out into the shaft to reach the panel. Still dangerous, but not the suicide mission the climb down would be. Unless someone uses the lift while I'm out there. I try not to think about that.

"Okay, here goes."

I reach out for the first handhold. My fingers grasp cool metal, dislodging years of built-up dust. In the dark, debris falls into my eyes and mouth. I squint my eyes against the sting and try to spit out the taste, but it coats my mouth like I licked the floor of a machine shop.

The climb out is difficult, and I'm terrified the entire time. Facing the inner edge, with open space at my back, I scoot along toward the red light at an agonizing pace. A few cautious centimeters after a few cautious centimeters. I can't see the pipes and brackets that serve as handholds as I fight the urge to turn back with every tiny step. Twice I slip and catch myself with jarring pain. The first wrenches my shoulder badly. After the second, I feel heat on my arm where it catches something. A trickle of wet runs down my elbow and toward my armpit. Blood, I'm sure of it.

Finally, I'm near the red light on my level and my palm lands on a flat panel. The metal is smooth, unlike the gritty powder-coating of the other surfaces. I pat around awkwardly and come upon a recessed handle. With a twist-and-pull, the door swings open.

Probing at the inside, trying to feel for the workings with my fingers, a light bursts forth. I wince, shutting my eyes tight, then warily open them to a squint. A terminal displays a simple screen. Two command tiles: DIAGNOSTIC and EMERGENCY.

I press EMERGENCY.

Immediately the contents of my stomach try to escape my mouth. Gravity is gone. There is no up, there is no down. I lose my grip on the thin conduit I'd been clutching onto and float into the open space, twisting in the air. I curse as my skull smacks against steel I can't see coming.

I reach out, grabbing for purchase to stop the floating and spinning. My implant fires as my hand finds something cold and hard. A bolt. I jerk against it to stop my inertia. The tug pulls painfully against my already-wrenched shoulder joint, and the bolt's threads tear into the flesh of my palm. I squeeze tighter against the pain and keep my grip.

"Passenger," I say through clenched teeth. My head is already throbbing from the impact. "Can you tell where I need to go?"

<No. I only have access to your biological senses. And they appear to be inadequate in this environment.>

"Blame evolution." I rub at my scalp where a small lump has already formed under my hair. "Wait..." The red light is in front of me. I must be looking up into the shaft.

Of all the random things to think of now, an interior design software commercial comes to mind. There was no way I could afford it, so I never used the software. But I came across it looking for some way to design the interior of the Palace of Belholt for my screenplay. The part of the commercial that stuck with me was the clever use of visuals. During the sales pitch they displayed a person—an actor playing the designer, presumably—walking through the software-simulated environments. As he walked and the narrator described the software features, one portion of the environment at a time went from simulation to reality. Showing that you too, with no training and only this software suite, can design such grandiose environments befit for the headquarters of the megacorps.

An idea comes to me. Pulling the map up in my mind, I start

to resize it, blowing the image up and playing with the orientation of all three axes. I get it lined up with the red light near the top of the shaft first. Then, continuously altering the map's size and orientation—which takes some trial and error—I match it with the little red beacons on each descending deck until they're all lined up.

Now, if I did that right, the map should trace the real world. The map becomes reality, at least a projected, surreal approximation of it, making me, in a way, inside the map.

<Very resourceful, Gaby,> Passenger says.

With the projected image serving as a proxy for my vision, I locate the flue opening I'm after. It's across the way and what I guess I'll call *down*. I can't seem to trust the lack of gravity enough to push away from the wall and float across, so I claw around for one handhold after the other, pulling myself gently along the outer edge like a child too scared to let go of the edge of the swimming pool.

The map isn't perfect. It's based on schematics, and apparently the real construction had moved this bundle of conduits up a few centimeters, that pipe down a few, resulting in a sort of loss of depth perception. But it's close enough. Within moments I've wriggled into the mechanical deck maintenance flue where gravity still pulls down with something close to 1G.

I crawl for some time. The mutineers are going to notice the gravity isn't functioning in the main lift. They might think some type of mechanical problem is to blame, but it's possible they'll come to the right conclusion and begin searching with a maintenance drone from that point out. Fortunately based on the map, that shaft acts as a sort of nexus for the maintenance flues. So they won't know which deck I went to or in which direction. Still, it seems prudent to take a few twists and turns as I push on.

After a while, I have to stop. The fatigue is too much. The asthma attack earlier sapped me. My second major attack in three days. I should be in a hospital bed with an oxygen tube in my nose and an IV in my arm, not crawling through these confined flues and climbing around elevator shafts. I lie down on my side, using my arm as a pillow, and shut my eyes to the darkness. Exhaustion takes my consciousness almost immediately.

THIRTY

Jules was shouting commands. People in white—researchers or maybe doctors—bolted past Morgan in a mad rush to get out. A pulser went off and there was a crashing sound like an object falling through glass. Screaming. Another white coat darted by and was gone through the door.

Then Jules was in front of Morgan, kneeled down on his haunches, removing his own helmet.

"You're all right," Jules said. A statement, not a question. He slapped Morgan's cheek, not hard, but not softly either. "Hey, stay with me, Morgan."

"I'm here," Morgan heard himself saying. "I'm good."

As if saying it made it so, his head cleared a bit. For a moment anyway.

"Okay. I'm gonna snap that door. I'll be right back."

Morgan nodded. Their bracers had a number of preset utility abilities. A *snap* was a simple software program they could upload to door locks. It imitated a hull breach code so the door would safety-seal, as if the room was exposed to vacuum. The station's mechanics would be able to override it, but it'd buy Morgan and Jules some time.

While Jules did that, Morgan made the mistake of looking down at his leg. The armor around his right thigh was barely hanging on, hiding whatever damage had been done underneath. The exochassis' piston, the one that ran the length of his femur, had been blown off entirely, leaving the hip socket empty and the shin piston wiggling uselessly with nothing to work against. Morgan peeled back the flap of armor, exposing a butcher's block slab of uncleaned meat.

Bile rose in his throat. He broke out into a flop sweat, groping for the emergency pack on his hip. The hard plastic box was still there in its molded pouch. He tore it free, but his shaking hands couldn't seem to crack it open. His fingers went numb and it fell to the floor. Jules appeared in front of him again. He plucked the syringe from the kit and injected it into Morgan's neck. A cocktail of painkillers, stimulants, and anti-nausea medications flooded his bloodstream.

Morgan's eyes bolted open. Resting his head against the wall and taking slow, deliberate breaths, he let the painkillers do their work.

"Hey," Jules said. "Open your eyes. Stay with me."

He hadn't realized he'd shut them. It took effort to crack his eyes open. There was no detail to the world, just blurred shapes and colors rocking listlessly.

"Morgan, you with me?"

He tried to nod. But he wasn't sure if he did or not.

"I need you to talk to me, okay? You're going to be fine. You might not be dancing for a while, but you're going to be fine."

Morgan closed his eyes again.

Jules slapped him in response. "Hey, why don't you tell me about that girl you met on Tora Kiesa?"

"You mean Lauren? I already told you."

"Tell me again. She's kind of famous, right?"

The cocktail of drugs had begun kicking in; the painkillers

made the pain radiating from his leg bearable, while the stimulants brought him a degree closer to lucid. "Did we make it? Isn't this the objective?" Morgan asked.

"Yeah, some kind of lab. They've got a kid back there." Jules grimaced, then glanced toward the back of the room. "It's a... It's really something."

Following Jules' glance, Morgan saw a holotable on the fritz, strobing colors and flashing images he couldn't make out at this distance. A silhouette behind it sat upright, facing the display, as still as a mannequin.

"Find the biobox?" Morgan asked.

"Haven't looked yet."

"Go. I'm good now. I'll watch the door."

Jules nodded and went toward the back of the room to search. The ammo readout on Morgan's combat rifle read 0. If he still had his helmet, he'd have a blinking warning light in his vision. He popped the magazine out and clumsily slid a fresh one home.

Jules appeared at his side. His face was pale, even for an Amienite. "You gotta see this."

"Help me up," Morgan said.

Jules tucked himself under Morgan's arm and dragged him to his feet. Or foot, rather—Morgan couldn't put even the smallest fraction of his weight on his right leg. It just dragged along as they limped over to the back of the room. Morgan hadn't seen anything yet, focused entirely on the floor and the shooting pain that accompanied every jarring step. Jules lowered Morgan into a chair a couple paces from the holotable. There was a body in a white lab coat. Suffering a fatal center-mass wound, he'd fallen into a storage rack, knocking it over. Broken glass had exploded across the floor. Various tools and small machines Morgan couldn't identify were scattered about.

Wisps of flickering light from the ever-changing hologram bounced off the unadorned walls. The biobox sat on the holotable, plugged in with a thin braided cable. Next to the table though, was something Morgan couldn't make sense of. Like a fever dream image of some half-remembered horror VR.

A boy sat in a chair. No, not just sitting. Strapped in. Restrained. He was twelve, maybe thirteen years old. His head freshly shaved, crude cybernetics had been recently bolted to his skull. Dried flecks of blood crusted where steel met skin. Wires sprouted from the cybernetics and dangled loosely to the floor before running up behind the holotable, presumably connecting somewhere Morgan couldn't see from his position.

Morgan wanted to get up, get a closer look, but the pain caused from getting to this side of the room was fresh in his mind. Jules paced around the scene, moving cautiously, studying it like there might be a bomb somewhere in the mess of wiring.

Gently, Jules lifted the data cube and turned it over. He tapped commands into his bracer, and glanced back and forth between the display on his arm and the bottom of the cube.

"This is it. Serial numbers match," he said.

"So the technology to hack a biobox is a kid?" Morgan said.

Jules set the biobox down, looked at the boy, then looked at the hologram throwing out its schizophrenic images. "Seems like. What do you think will happen to the kid if we destroy the cube?"

"I'm more worried about what's already happened to him," Morgan said.

A low thump came from the doorway. The noise of the door's motor trying to engage.

"How long do you think it'll take 'em to override the door?" Jules asked.

Morgan inspected their surroundings. It was one elongated room. The space achieved some separation by virtue of the walls of equipment, but it only had the one door. "Who knows? Ten minutes? Maybe twenty? Once they do though..."

"Yeah," Jules said, surveying the place. "This looks like a last stand."

"So put a pulser shot through the biobox and let's get to it." It may have been the drugs, but he felt oddly calm. He knew he was going to die. He knew what he had to do *before* he died. And he was at peace with it all.

"Let's wait," Jules said softly. His eyes were squinting, scrutinizing the images and bits of data thrown into the air by the hologram.

Why bother? Morgan thought. Jules might as well try to make sense of the smoke billowing from a campfire. But instead he began reminding Jules, "Our orders—"

"I know," Jules interrupted, his voice cool. "If that door so much as cracks open, my first shot will be through the cube. But until then..."

Morgan probably could've talked him out of it, he thought. He could've detailed some what-if scenarios where everything went horribly wrong and the biobox ended up back in enemy hands, and then they would've all died for nothing. He could've probably talked about duty. He could've argued that the information wasn't meant for them.

But instead he looked down at the rifle across his lap. At his leg. At the trail of blood that led to his previous perch against the wall and then to the door. Finally he looked at the door itself. And then, he said something that put in motion everything that would follow. "All right. Might as well see what we're dying for."

THIRTY-ONE

I'M STANDING IN A BEDROOM. C IS SO CLOSE I HAVE TO crane my neck to meet her eyes. The white tank-top nearly blends in with her skin. It exposes her muscled frame. Her hands are in my hair. "I don't want to be your second choice," C whispers.

"You're not," I assure her, and somehow I mean it.

I close my eyes and reach up on my tiptoes, grazing my lips against C's. But when I crack my eyes open, it's Samantha, with her healthier complexion and softer features looking back at me, and yet somehow Samantha is C too.

The door bursts open. K steps into the spill of light. She holds her father's pistol loosely at her side. Her sad eyes turn angry and she raises the weapon. Fires. Fires again. Fires a third time. Two bullets find their target. The body that is at once Samantha's and C's is torn from my grasp.

Samantha-Catherine crumples to the floor. Her eyes meet mine, sorrowful and searching. She reaches out weakly, and as the life drains from the two gaping holes in her chest, she mouths, *Help me.* I look to K, asking the silent question: *Why?* But Lauren stands in K's place, the pistol now a military issue pulser, its barrel red with heat. Katherine-Lauren steps over the carnage toward me, as if the body means nothing to her. An obstacle, an inconvenience, nothing more. Her cold attention is fixed on me. Only me.

I smell blood. I can't look again, so I back away into the closet, sliding the articulating shutter closed. As if she didn't watch me enter. As if the thin particle board will protect me.

Katherine-Lauren slides the shutter back open. "Come out, Kitten," she coos, grinning like a predator.

I dash past her into the bathroom, but it isn't a bathroom at all. It's another bedroom. An immaculately kept bedroom with a drafting table and hand-drawn art in frames decorating the walls. Ensign Garner's bedroom. Here the admiral is using a pillow to suffocate poor, helpless Callum Garner in his own bed. Callum's arms and legs thrash about impotently.

His mom's voice sounds from somewhere deep within the house. "Callum, honey? Is that you?"

The admiral looks back at me over his shoulder as he goes about his work. "It was your idea, you know."

Gaby. I hear my name from somewhere else. My eyes shoot open, but there's no difference between open or closed. Remembering where I am, I roll onto my back in the flue. Everything hurts. Between sleeping on steel, all the crawling on hands and knees, and crashing into the side of the lift shaft, every centimeter of my body feels bruised and scraped.

<Gaby.>

Startled, I jump, smacking my head in a foolish attempt to sit upright.

Sucking air through my teeth, I mumble a curse. Correction: *now* every centimeter of my body hurts. "Passenger?" I groan.

<Yes.>

"Why'd you wake me up?" I rub at the new sore spot on my head, wondering if it was hard enough to create another lump.

<The average human your age can sleep between seven and ten hours at a time.>

"Yeah, okay?"

<We have less than five hours before we reach the maximum recommended integration period. And…I believe the initial time-line may be too tolerant.>

"All right, I'll get moving." Part of me just wants the voice to stop talking in my head. It might be different if Passenger were speaking through speakers, but in my head they're impossible to ignore. Then what they said strikes home. "Wait. You don't think we have as much time as we're supposed to?"

<Gaby… I. Saw. Your dream.>

Inwardly I recoil. I can't think of anything more invasive, more violating, than this machine having access to my brain even while I sleep.

<What did it mean?> Passenger asks.

"It didn't mean anything. Stay out of my dreams."

<Apparently I can't.>

"Ugh!" I want to throw something. "Fine. What do we do next?"

<I don't know. This set of circumstances is far removed from anything I've been programmed for.>

"Yeah, I wasn't programmed for this either."

<Do you believe you were programmed?>

"What? No, it's just, it was sort of a joke."

<I see. I was concerned you were entering a dissociative state.>

"Can we just focus?" I say far louder than I'd meant to. Repeats of my voice echo away down the flue into the dark.

After a long silence between us, and no other ideas coming to me, I say, "Let's check on Lauren. Maybe we'll see where they're searching for us."

The audio cuts in an instant before the image. "What are you doin' in here?" Lauren asks.

"You know, she told me I should stop using my rank," Morgan says.

Morgan's sitting at the tiny desk in his private quarters. The headset that I now know is for mnemonic rendering is sitting on the desk surface. Lauren is looking down on him from what must be the doorway.

"She makes a point. Naval life is over."

Morgan frowns ruefully.

"Is that what's got you so...whatever this is?" She motions her hand toward him. "Morose?"

"No. I've been working on my log, reliving it is just..."

Lauren's posture changes in the edges of the camera's field of view. I wish I could see Lauren's face. "Babe, I know that has to be really hard, but we don't have time for guilt right now."

"I know," he says sullenly.

"There's no margin of error. You need to be on your game."

"Is that why you're taking mood-altering drugs?"

She sighs. "I wondered when that was going to come up. They're called blunters. Reporters have to stare the worst parts of humanity in the eyes, then keep it together while looking into a camera to explain it to everyone else."

Admonition is written in every line of his face.

"I'm not going to apologize. You know what I'm going through. You know what's at stake. I have to keep my composure, so if that means taking some pills, then I take the pills. You told the admiral he couldn't create dissent between us. Can he?"

Morgan's face softens. "No. Of course not."

"Good. Do you think he's right about Kitten?" she says, going over to the bed and sitting. "About her... Well, that she won't disconnect willingly?"

"Maybe? Probably not? Hell, I don't know." He looks at Lauren questioningly and, for a moment, I see the boy I once knew.

"Hey." She reaches the distance between them and clasps his hand tightly in hers. "Don't let him get under your skin. He was trying to manipulate you. Both of us. His goal in that room was to make you question yourself and drive a wedge between us."

He flashes a weak smile at her. "I know. Truth is, Gaby's always been stubborn, but I think, if I can sit down with her, I can make her understand. I have to believe I can. Just need to do it soon."

"Do you think she sabotaged the gravity system in the lift?" Lauren asks.

Morgan, still seated, leans heavily on his cane. "Lieutenant Justice, I mean, Ruby thinks it could've been a malfunction. She could be right. This old bucket has plenty of quirks. But I don't know. If Gaby's running around through the ducts, that would make it easy to get between decks."

Inwardly I laugh at that. Easy. Sure.

"We need to find her, Morgan."

"Yeah, I know." Morgan stiffens.

"The ship isn't worth anything without Passenger."

"I know." There's a bite to his voice. Morgan's bracer beeps. "Yeah?"

"Lieutenant Commander." I think it's Kerri's voice. "We've got two sets of recon teams running helix patterns in our vicinity. I don't think it's coincidence. They might be getting imprecise heat residuals from the pion thrusters."

"We're running them at spec for the cloak, right?" Morgan asks into his bracer.

"Yes, sir. Doesn't mean our cloak is operating to spec though."

"Change course to whatever you see fit, then cut the pions to idle. I'll have Ruby look at the cloak. And, Kerri, it's Morgan now. No more ranks."

After a pause, the voice pipes back through his bracer. "Got it."

He cuts the transmission.

"So our goals haven't changed." Lauren moves for the door. "Get access to Passenger. Get the blink drive back online."

"Yup. After I talk to Ruby, I'll give it another go with the admiral."

"You think that'll work?" she asks.

"No. Gotta try though. I'll head to the bridge after."

"Okay, I'll go back to looking for Kitten."

Morgan stands. He leans into the camera, his face becoming a blurred flesh-toned oval. Then the cameratom withdraws to focus the image in frame as Morgan and Lauren share a kiss.

Something twists inside my guts. Layers of betrayal.

Their kissing grows fierce. Morgan backs Lauren against the wall. A wave of embarrassment hits me seeing what I have no business seeing. I'm about to break the connection when Lauren pushes a little space between them.

Sadness touches Lauren's smile. "We can't do this. They're watching."

Her eyes flick over, making eye contact with me. A surge of paranoia runs through me before logic can stamp it down. No. Lauren's not looking at *me*, she's looking at the *camera*. Someone else is watching. Someone Lauren knows about. But who? And why?

Morgan's eyes search Lauren's face and eventually he nods. "Let's go."

In the hall, their postures say they're about to go separate ways. "If you find her..." Morgan starts. "Just be nice. Please?"

"I'll try. I really will. But don't ask me to compromise the mission. You know what I've got on the line."

They both head in different directions and I watch Lauren for a few moments. The ship seems deserted, like a derelict vessel adrift in deep space far from civilization. I don't know where she's going. But it doesn't matter. I know where *I'm* going.

"I have an idea," I say, hoping that Passenger doesn't know it already. If they do, that'll mean they can read all my thoughts. I'm not ready for that.

<Yes, Gaby?>

"The cloak. It's the only thing keeping us from being discovered. We need to make it...broken."

<You intend to sabotage the cloaking device?>

"I do."

I pull up the map. Reaching the tetrahedron from either the mid or the mechanical decks is possible. I'm already on the mechanical deck, but I'm between the starboard drone hangar and the hangar control overlook, near the front of the ship. The tetrahedron is in the aft half of the ship. About eighty meters in a straight line, but looking over the spaghetti path through the maintenance flues, my path will be much farther.

Squeezing into a ball, I turn around inside the cramped space and start off aft.

CHAPTER
THIRTY-TWO

I EMERGE FROM THE MAINTENANCE FLUE IN A HALL outside the engineering section. I chose this area because it seemed out of the way. After spending an hour crawling on my hands and knees, I wanted a safe place to emerge and stretch my limbs out. Judging by the buildup of dust, I don't even think custodial toms come through here.

It seems to take forever before I can stand straight. I first post up on one knee, then lean against the concave wall, slowly straightening my legs until my knees reach full extension. My hamstrings feel like they're going to tear in half.

From there I attempt to walk like a human to the other side of the hallway. I manage a hunched waddle, holding my back like I'm in my third trimester. I pace back and forth, improving with each lap. Every step stings as the raw skin of my knees scrape against the blood-crusted fabric of my overalls. My palms are chapped and red too. But the more I move, the more I feel...well, not good, but mobile. Unhindered.

My resolve weakens staring up at the cracked, yellow letters that read *Reactor Control* painted above the unassuming automatic door. I'll need to pass through the reactor control room to reach the tetrahedron chamber, and Ruby is in there somewhere.

I take a deep breath and step into the motion detector.

The doors slide apart. I don't exhale. My implant fires, misreading my stress as asthma. The reactor control room looks empty. The lighting here follows the familiar scheme of bright pointed spots wherever light is needed, leaving the spaces between in deep shadow. It gives the space a focused, dramatic presence. Which, for the purposes of sneaking around, is helpful. A door stands straight across from me. To the right, I can't see far as the chamber stretches off into a thinner section that is mostly obscured by the room's geometry. To the left, an open archway joins this section to the tetrahedron chamber.

The ambient sound of machines is loud, but the hint of voices seeps through the background murmur. My blood freezes in my veins. The voices flit in from the tetrahedron chamber. I dash to the side, flattening myself against the adjoining wall in a small pocket of shadow. I strain to make out the words among the din.

"The diagnostic is still finishing up," Ruby says. "But I would've seen something by now. The thermal screen layer of the cloak is working fine, but you gotta understand, this is an add-on. It wasn't designed together. As much as the navy loves their specs and regs, sometimes it doesn't work the way it does in a sim."

"Understood." It's Morgan's voice, but it sounds strange, sort of far away. "We've barely brought the pion engines above idle for a while now and they seem to have lost the scent. They were damned close though."

Peeking around the corner, I spot Ruby Justice. At least I assume it's her. Her back's to me, busy fussing with the terminal at a workstation. A hologram projects in front of Ruby, scrolling through data rapidly.

"Unless there's something else, I'm going to get back to work on our blink drive problem," Ruby says.

"Okay, keep me posted." Morgan's voice is coming from the intercom. That's why it sounds strange.

"Yup." Ruby turns, facing me.

I brace against the wall, sure she saw me. My muscles tighten and respond by reminding me of every ache and pain I've collected today. Ruby passes right by on her way to one of the smaller stations on the far side of the reactor control room.

Holding my breath, I slip around the corner, putting the wall between myself and Ruby as I slink inside the tetrahedron chamber.

It's a spherical room that gives me the sensation that I've shrunk and gone inside a giant ball. Uneven blue illumination washes across the steel surfaces, moving in cascading ripples like light reflecting from the surface of an indoor swimming pool. I glance over my shoulder into the next room where Ruby is stepping over to another station, shaking her head and mouthing what I believe are obscenities to herself. I need to get out of sight. There's no way to predict when or where she'll go next.

A ladder, painted in the same yellow used in the signage that marks the ship's corridors, stands at the side of the room. I sneak over to it, worrying how much noise climbing it will make. Will it shake? Squeak? Rattle? I grasp the uprights. Gingerly at first, I test it by giving it a small shake. The uprights don't budge. The ladder seems to be bolted securely at the top.

As I start up the ladder, the sole of my shoe rings against the aluminum of the first rung. I wince, going tense, and stare nervously toward the entryway. No sign of Ruby coming to investigate. I slip my shoes off and place them in a dark corner nearby. The steel is cold and hard on my bare feet, but it makes for a silent climb. The ladder brings me to a catwalk. It's a suspended steel balcony encircling the tetrahedron chamber. There is no hiding up here, per se. It would be easy enough to look up and see my shape through the grated planks that serve as the floor. But at least I'm out of the normal line of sight. Few people look up without a reason to do so.

Feeling safe enough, I regard the field generator at the center of the spherical room. The tetrahedron is named after its geometric shape. A bit like a pyramid with one less side, each of its four planes is a perfect triangle—nearly five meters on edge—suspended weightlessly in a containment field as it slowly rotates on both its X and Y axes simultaneously.

As the tetrahedron tumbles in place, each deep-cobalt triangle face of its surface glints and reflects the light like the pitch mirror-glass of high rises I've only seen in VR. As one side lines up flat with where I stand, it reflects an opaque reflection of me: hands tight on the handrail of the catwalk, hair gently being pulled this way and that by the shifting polarities of static electricity in the air. As the languid spin continues, my smoky reflection bends and stretches away, then is gone entirely.

It's beautiful. And I need to break it.

Spaced around the containment field are four adjustable arms, each holding a large metallic plate positioned to face the tetrahedron's center. They seem to be two separate pairs. One set oriented on the horizontal plane, the other set on the vertical plane above and below the tetrahedron. They're not identical. They're the same size and shape, but the surfaces facing the tetrahedron differ. The ones on the horizontal plane reflect less light. They seem dirtier, older.

None of my classes have taught me about cloaking or shield technology, but they must work like other fields. Out of each pair of these devices, one must be positively charged and one negative. One pair for the shield, one pair for the cloak, and by the newer condition of the floor-and-ceiling pair, I can guess that pair is the cloaking device.

<How do I sabotage this thing?> I ask in my thoughts.

<I'm afraid I can't answer that. Advanced engineering protocols are not part of my code, and I do not have access to the ship's database.>

I sneak to the far end of the catwalk, the dull blades of the metal grating bite into my feet with each step. From this side of the catwalk, I can see Ruby hard at work on the other side of the archway.

<You could ask her,> Passenger suggests blandly.

<So no engineering protocols, but dry humor is in your code, huh?>

I spot two lecterns similar to the one I found in the brig. The nearer one is mounted to a beam reaching down from the ceiling like a stalactite. It's reachable from up here on the catwalk. A mess of braided cabling runs from the lectern to the back of the older plates in the horizontal field of the tetrahedron. The other lectern is down below, on the mechanical deck. Its cabling connects to the bottom plate, so that one must control the cloak. Of course it's the one that will leave me exposed within Ruby's line of sight.

Maybe I could do a type of dry run with the one up here. That way I could at least get a feel for the system I'm working with. I make another trek farther around the catwalk with the metal poking into the soles of my feet.

As soon as I reach the lectern and tap the terminal awake, I'm greeted with a passcode screen. I try Samantha's credentials, but they don't grant me access here. My heart sinks. There's little doubt the other one will be the same.

What now?

Down below, Ruby leans, half hunched over a workstation, intently studying a terminal screen. A full tool belt sags across her hip. Wait, Ruby isn't wearing a holster. I scan the area and pick out a shape in a shadow cast between overhead spotlights. Ruby left her sidearm on a workbench.

<Ya know, Passenger, I think you were right. I think I will go ask her how to shut the cloak down.>

I circle around the tetrahedron again, climb carefully down the ladder, and sneak up behind Ruby.

It appears like she's going through code, line by line. She's diligent, have to give her that. I pluck the sidearm from the table and stand upright, squaring the sights over Ruby's center of mass. She doesn't even notice my presence and I suddenly feel like all my effort sneaking around was wasted effort.

Two crisp sidesteps and I'm in Ruby's peripheral vision. Ruby doesn't jump or flinch. She just blinks slowly and sighs. "Damn," she says.

"You're going to help me get the cloak shut down."

"No, I'm not." She stares daggers at me.

I add one half step worth of distance between us. "I have a gun."

"Are we to stand here stating the painfully obvious?" She sounds bored.

Shit, I gotta admire her composure. Think of something intimidating, Gaby. "No, we're negotiating. For your life."

"We're negotiating for my life?" she repeats.

"Yes, we're negotiating for your life." Why is she smiling? I bring the barrel up a little higher, squaring her face in the crosshairs.

"Okay kid, let's run through a hypothetical. I help you disable the cloak, then the NCP finds us. They board the ship and arrest us. After that, we face a short, embarrassing court martial trial that we have no chance of winning. Then, without appeal, we are summarily executed. Publicly. So that all our friends and family will have to see it on the evening casts." She shakes her head. "See, you got nothing to negotiate with because I'd rather die right here." She folds her arms. "That is, if you even have the chemicals to pull the trigger."

I think of the bodies on the CIC floor. I remember watching Samantha take her last breath. An honorable navy soldier willing to give her life for the promise of the NCP. Cut down, not in the glory of battle by our enemies, but murdered by a friend, betrayed by the people she trusted to guard her back. I think of what a soldier would do, what Jules would do to these traitors. I think of that and I try to pull the trigger.

Except...I can't. I feel the muscles twitch underneath my skin and the slender blade of the trigger against my finger, but I can't will it to move farther. I can't take Ruby's life. How can this be, after all these years of wanting nothing more than to be a soldier, earning glory on the front lines? How? With the same blood running through my veins as a war hero like Julian Rhodes, how can I be so utterly incapable of doing what needs to be done?

"I don't want to kill you," I lie. "Take off your bracer and your tools."

She rolls her eyes and does as I command, setting both the bracer and the tool belt on the tabletop.

"There, the maintenance locker. Open it." At the end of the quivering gun barrel, I coax Ruby to the upright storage locker. She opens it, displaying a closet half-full of spare parts. "Clean it out."

Ruby drops her arms limply to her sides. "What? Are you going to stuff me in the locker?"

I nod emphatically. "It's more spacious than the flues I spent most of my day in."

Ruby narrows her eyes and grabs a small box, tossing it to the floor without breaking eye contact with me. "What do you think you're going to get out of this?" She punctuates the question by carelessly tossing another part to the deck. It crashes. I flinch-blink. "You're one *very* little girl, against all of us." Another small box hits the deck, the part inside pops out of its cardboard container and skids. "You're better off giving up now, while Lieutenant Commander York's pity still protects you." She lifts a heavier part in both hands and casually tosses it. It falls nearby with a bang. I flinch again. Ruby's eyes still study me. "'Cause that won't last, you know," she hisses. Instead of tossing the boxed part to the side, she launches it at my face.

I leap sideways, losing my footing and going down on one knee. Regaining my posture, I level the weapon, but Ruby is a blur slipping through the starboard door of the reactor control room.

Damn. I don't have much time now. I snatch the tool belt and hustle over to examine the ground-floor lectern. The front panel is held on by a series of screws. If I get access to the innards, maybe I can find a way to sabotage it without something blowing up in my face. I retrieve the tool belt and, using an electric screwdriver, I begin removing the screws. After each one, I spare a glance over my shoulder, watching for movement. As I work, I try to listen for any strange sounds over the background noise of the field generator and the whir of the electric screwdriver. The pulser sits on the floor nearby, just in case. But now I wonder if I'd even be able to use the weapon if it came down to it. Down to life and death, I mean.

I'm halfway through the task of removing the panel when my back explodes in agony. A crippling, seizing pain lashes across it, obliterating conscious thought. I cry out, falling and rolling away. Smoke and the smell of charred meat swirls in the air. My back feels as though it's on fire as the ability to form thoughts returns.

The silhouette of a maintenance drone eclipses the spotlights above me, the disc of its repulsor glowing as it holds its spherical carapace aloft. Four spiny arms dangle, but it holds its fifth out toward me, a welding laser for a hand. The tip glows hot. A rage builds in me as I realize that whomever is controlling this damn thing just ran a welder across my back! The drone creeps closer.

Scrambling backward, my palm lands on something hard and

metal. I throw it at the drone. The electric screwdriver bounces off its body. The impact makes the drone bob lightly in the air. As I get to my feet, the drone is mid-swing. I catch the welder arm with both of mine, my knuckles white as I grip and push against the machine's servos. The welding laser fires. The concentrated beam misses me, but the heat radiating from it is intense against my forearm. Fighting with the invisible force of the drone's repulsor, I launch it to one side with all my strength. It only moves about a half meter, but it's enough.

I break into a run.

I stop before reaching the exit. There's still a job to do. I can't just run. I've shown my hand. There won't be another opportunity, but I have to do something about this maintenance drone before I can get back to work on the cloaking device.

Ruby's pulser pistol. It's still by the rest of the tools. Instead of grabbing the weapon, I'd thrown a screwdriver at the drone. And I'm supposed to be a genius. The drone begins closing the distance. I put the console table at the center of the reactor control room between me and the machine.

After a brief standoff, whomever is controlling the drone chooses a direction. I circle the other way and go for the gun. I reach to the floor for the weapon, the drone tight on my tail. I roll clear as it fires its welder again, but my back feels like it's sliced open anew as my skin rolls across the teeth of the metal grating. I barely keep hold of the gun as I let out a high-pitched cry at the pain.

I spin and find the drone in my blurred vision. My first shot misses and strikes the containment field surrounding the tetrahedron. I grit my teeth, thinking for a split second that I've just killed everyone onboard. But nothing happens. The drone closes in. I fire again.

Point blank.

Don't miss.

Can't miss.

There's a sharp crack and sizzle as the pulser punches a hole straight through the drone. Sparks and hot debris bounce off my face. The drone crashes into the grating of the floor with a clatter that seems like the entire ship should be able to hear.

My arms go limp at my sides and I sway, barely keeping myself upright.

<Gaby?> Passenger says, their normally composed voice warbling.

"Yeah?" I say, choking back the lump in my throat.

<What is this? It's...it's terrible.>

My whole body trembles. Shivering like I've just stepped out of an ice-cold shower. It takes a moment before I understand what Passenger is asking.

"Pain," I say, clenching my teeth tight. "You're feeling pain."

I never knew anything could hurt so much. On wobbly legs, I cross back over to the lectern, and as I bend to pick up the electric screwdriver, the skin on my back stretches around the wound. It's all I can take. This is my limit. I collapse on my belly, lying still, trying to breathe through the searing, unrelenting pain.

Ruby had gotten away, and whomever was controlling the drone knows where I am. The mutineers will be here soon, no doubt about it. But I can't get up yet. I just can't. Maybe this is it. Maybe this is where my attempt at resistance ends. I flip over to the cameratom's feed, expecting to see Lauren heading toward reactor control with a gun in her hand and backup at her side. Her backup won't be Morgan. He'd be too slow. He's also the only one of them that probably won't shoot me on sight. But maybe that's changed now that he knows I'm actively working against him.

The sound cuts in a second before the video. There's a flat slapping sound like meat being tenderized. Morgan's standing over something. No, someone. They're curled into the fetal position. Morgan has his fist raised, chambered for another strike.

"What the hell is wrong with you?" Morgan yells.

"Morgan, stop!" Lauren screams from behind him. She grabs onto his shoulders before he can swing again.

It's Patrick on the ground. He scoots away and sits up. Blood spilling from his nose and oozing from a split in his bottom lip. "What's wrong with me?" Patricks says. "What the fuck is wrong with you? Whose side are you on?"

"I'm on the side that doesn't try to kill little girls from behind with a drone!"

"So you'd rather let her shut down the cloak? 'Cause that's what she was gettin' ready to do."

"Speaking of," Lauren says. "I'd better get down there. Can I trust you two not to kill each other?"

Morgan shoots her a look. "Can I trust you not to kill Gaby?"

"I'll do *only* what needs done."

"What does that mean?" Morgan must've dropped his cane in the scuffle. Without it he limps the two paces to Lauren.

She reaches up and touches his cheek. "She's important to you, and because I love you, she's important to me. I'll do everything I can *not* to hurt her. But if she makes me choose between our mission and her." Her voice slides from soft and caring to hard and dangerous, terrifyingly quick. "I will do what needs done. She's injured. I suggest you station someone in the medbay to try to catch her if she slips past me."

She spins, heading for the exit. Ruby bounds through the door, panting. "We need to get down to reactor control."

"We know. Let's go," Lauren says.

"She's got my gun," Ruby says.

Lauren scowls over her shoulder at something off camera. Somehow I know she's glaring at Morgan.

I drop the connection. I have more time than I'd expected, but it still isn't much.

<"Get up,"> Passenger and I say simultaneously. I can barely tell us apart. Are we becoming one? Already?

I will myself to get up. First on my hands and knees, then to my feet. The steel grating bites into the pads of my feet, but I can barely register any sensation except the fire coming from my back in wave after searing wave.

A whimper escapes my lips as I bend down to grab the gun. There's no time for the screwdriver. No time to do this neat or clean. With a trembling hand, I aim at the braided cable jutting out from the back of the lectern and pull the trigger. The pulser shot impacts the floor in front of it. I miss the second shot too. Then bracing the weapon with both hands, I fire a third time and strike true.

The lights and console screens around me flicker as one and then come back, but the tetrahedron begins to decelerate. The static electricity in the room dissipates with the slowing motion.

The cloak is down. Now it's just a matter of time before the battle group finds us and disables the *Discordia*. It won't take them long after that to discover something isn't right and board the ship.

<We won,> I think to Passenger. Despite the agony vibrating through every cell of my being, a smile overtakes my face. I've won.

CHAPTER
THIRTY-THREE

The words *Reactor Control* printed in distressed yellow letters bob in my vision. She's almost here. I release the feed from the cameratom. Vision returns to my real eyes, and I frantically survey the reactor control room for a hatch into the flues. The lighting that had helped conceal me works against me now. A hatch could easily be hidden in any one of the pockets of shadow between the focused spotlights.

Maybe I should surrender. There's nothing left to do but sit back and wait, and Morgan seems intent on protecting me. But then I think of Ruby's reaction. She would have rather been shot dead where she stood than be captured. What if the others share her convictions? Maybe in a fit of rage one of them will decide to kill me. How can Morgan protect me against someone who's already lost everything? And maybe I've pushed him too far. Maybe he'll let them. Maybe he'll do it himself.

I regard the mangled damage control drone resting on a section of the grating. The grating! It hadn't clicked immediately because this section of grating is designed differently. It's larger than others I've seen, broken into four sections running the entire width of the room. But maybe it connects to the flues. I reach down, hooking my fingers into a section of it and tug. Pain cascades down my back. I hiss through clenched teeth as the metal grate hinges up. I sit down, holding one edge up, and crawl inside, letting the grating come down as one of the doors rolls open and voices filter into the reactor control room.

"Kitten, are you still in here?"

I find myself in a drain-like chamber under the removable floor. It's a small shaft, but still a bit larger than the flues. A square of shadow looks at me from one end, the small maw of the flue. Safety. But with the tetrahedron shut down, the air has stilled and quieted. I'll need to crawl to reach the opening, and the noise I'm bound to make will give my position away.

I scoot backward instead, flattening myself to one side of the crevice in the shadow thrown by the drone's carcass. There are two sets of footfalls above. One makes a circle of the room. The other moves one way, then another in uneven, chaotic routes. Then the sole of a shoe cracks against the steel grating directly above my face. I clamp a palm around my mouth, worried my breathing might give me away. Dread sets in that my implant might fire. The little puff from my implant might be loud enough to draw attention this close.

Ruby curses loudly above me.

"What?" Lauren asks.

"I was hoping she'd just shut the cloak down. But no, look at this mess. Tell Morgan he's going to need to buy me a couple hours to fix this."

Lauren's shoes take position a pace away from Ruby. "We don't have a couple hours."

Watching this play out from the angle of a rat in a sewer, I can't read Ruby's body language or see the look on her face, but there must be some kind of finality to it because without Ruby saying anything, Lauren's tone becomes resigned, asking, "How can I help?"

"You'd just slow me down," Ruby says. "This is a one-person job. I'd rather you find that little shit."

Don't look down. Please don't look down.

"She's wounded. I'll see if I can catch her in the medbay."

Both sets of feet disappear from view.

A deep thrumming starts to build in the room, and an electricity flirts with the air. The tetrahedron is moving again. It must be. But obviously they haven't repaired the cloak. That means they're bringing the shields online. Are they expecting an attack? So soon?

I use the noise as an opportunity to scramble through the space below the floor and duck into the flue. My back scrapes the metal lip as I wriggle into the smaller tunnel. A cool trickle of fresh blood runs down my side as I crawl away, realizing with a mental sigh that I've left my shoes behind.

After putting some distance between myself and reactor control, I stop in the dark. Bringing the map to life in my mind, I spend a few moments twisting it and turning it, zooming in and out, trying to approximate where I am. If I've guessed correctly, there's a junction a few meters ahead. From there, turning right should dump me in a corridor near the starboard escape pod. I don't plan on deploying the escape pod—that'd just make me an easy target if the mutineers are angry enough to turn the ship's guns on me—I just want the first aid kit inside. So I take the right-hand passage and crawl over to the hatch.

I'm resting in the flue's darkness, gathering the nerve to scurry into the open, when Morgan's voice erupts over the ship-wide intercom. It echoes into the flue. "Everyone, get to acceleration chairs and prepare for a high-G burn. I repeat, everyone to acceleration chairs immediately. Gaby, I hope you can hear me. This isn't a trick. Get somewhere safe. Now."

The urgency in his voice propels me into action. Somehow, despite everything, something inside me still wants to trust him.

And if we're about to go into a hard burn, I can't imagine a worse place to be than inside a hard, confined space.

I scramble into the corridor as a deep growl shakes the hull. It's a sensation felt as much as heard. I list to the right, stumbling toward the escape pod like a drunk trying to walk on a hill. When the pull magnifies, I'm forced to use my arms to keep from falling into the concave wall of the corridor.

By the time I reach the airlock, my hair is falling sideways toward the wall. The acceleration has completely overcome the artificial gravity reorienting direction aboard the ship. Carefully I transfer my feet to the wall, which is the new down. The pressure builds rapidly, pulling everything toward the rear of the ship with so much force I can no longer stand upright. I awkwardly bear crawl the rest of the way.

Acceleration chairs line the outside wall of the escape pod in a semi-circle. With the new orientation of gravity, that means they line the floor, the far wall, and the ceiling. I sink down and clamber into the chair at my feet, my body feeling much heavier than it should.

The foam envelops me and I fumble to get the multi-point harness secure.

Kerri announces over the intercom, "Engines are warm. High-G burn in five"—This isn't high-G? —"four, three, two, one."

I'm crushed into the deep chair. As my face is pressed into the supportive pads cradling me, my implant fires, mistakenly thinking I'm having yet another asthma attack as I struggle to breathe under the stacking pressure. How much of this medication can I have before I overdose?

My implant fires again, as if answering with a snarky, *Let's find out.*

I want to hate Morgan for his betrayal, but as the weight of gravity piles upon me, smashing me into the soft foam, and the realization of what this type of G-force would've done to me in the flue, I can't help but be grateful to him for his warning.

Closing my eyes, I flick over to the cameratom's feed, wondering if Lauren will be in the medbay, on the bridge, or if she was caught somewhere in between for this maneuver.

When the audio cuts in, I only hear nondescript ambient noise. The cameratom seems to be resting in her lap, making my view of the bridge feel unnatural.

The roar of the engines grows, bleeding into the connection. I can hear it both in my ears and piped in from the microphones of the cameratom.

Morgan shouts a heading change to Kerri. Lauren holds the cameratom at an awkward angle, but I can see the three-dimensional map. In the center is a representation of the *Discordia*. There aren't any chevrons indicating hostile ships.

A shimmy runs through the hull, then another. How are we under fire already?

"Turbulence is going to get bad. These knots are thick," Kerri Decker says from the pilot's station.

"Steady," Morgan says. "This is just the outskirts. It'll get worse."

My heart sinks. We're not under fire. They're flying the *Discordia* into the accretion of Nomad Star's ring. SV-class destroyers were built with some aerodynamics in mind, and equipped for atmospheric flight, but I'm sure the engineers had terraformed atmospheres in mind. Landing on a planet would be trivial compared to the whirling gas storm of Nomad Star's ring where, along with its vicious crosswinds and inconsistent density, a ship's hull would need to suffer the near-constant bombardment of rock and ice.

"Passenger," I say through pain and clenched teeth, as I let go of the cameratom's feed.

<Yes, Gaby.>

<We need to find a way to communicate with the *Hybris*.>

<I don't understand. I thought we expected them to disable and board this ship. I thought rescue was imminent.>

The fact that Passenger hadn't drawn the same conclusion I had, nor known the conclusion I'd come to, is a small comfort. Maybe we're not as deeply integrated as I'd worried.

<We're headed into Nomad Star's ring,> I explain. <The *Hybris* is shaped like a brick. They're not going to risk bringing it into this environment to win a training exercise. We need to make sure they understand what's going on.>

<Nomad Star's ring... That would be like flying through the upper portions of a gas giant. Maybe worse. We might not survive that for very long.>

<Um, yeah. That's what I was getting at.>

<Gaby?> Passenger sounds worried. <I know Nomad Star is the farthest orbital body in the solar system. That it's a brown dwarf star. I can remember seeing it. But I don't have any of this in my programming. I fear we're already nearing critical symbiosis.>

CHAPTER
THIRTY-FOUR

THE *DISCORDIA* TREMBLES AS ANGRY, UNSEEN IMPACTS
reverberate through the bones of its hull. I envision an outside
view of the ship diving into the turmoil of the brown dwarf's
massive ring, like an old sailing vessel trying to muscle its way
through storm-chopped waters with its sails full, thirstily and
foolhardily latching onto too-strong winds.

Inside, gravity has normalized, either because of reduced
acceleration, or the inertia neuts spun up enough to offset the G-
force. Maybe a combination of both. Unhooking the harness
proves difficult. In my rush, I'd put it on incorrectly. Once it's
untangled and unclasped, I pull myself from the deep bucket of
the chair. This causes an alarming, tearing sensation across my
back. Did I reopen my wound? Blood trickles down my spine as
an answer. The back of the chair is a smeared mess of reddish
brown that pooled in the upright cracks during the acceleration. I
pull the emergency pack free of the escape pod and shamble away.

Bringing up the map as I go, I look for my next move. The
hall leading to the escape pod terminates at another corridor. Left,
it winds around to reactor control. Right, it intersects with
another corridor, which connects with the starboard and port

combat drone hangars. I decide to stick to the starboard side of the ship. Maintenance is on the port side. If Ruby decides she can repair the damage I did to the cloak, she might shuttle parts back and forth between the tetrahedron room and maintenance.

I realize how close the tetrahedron is to the escape pod I'd sheltered in. It's maybe a thirty-second walk. I shiver at how easily I could've been caught. Distance feels so much different while you're crawling around on your hands and knees.

Following the path I'd marked out, I reach the starboard combat drone hangar and find myself in a vast space that sweeps down the length of the arrowhead blade of the *Discordia*. Most of the lights are off in the hangar, but a single line of spot beams cut a track in the dark from one end of the asymmetrically shaped room to the other, lighting the path between personnel doors.

The combat drones sit in shadow, a row of imposing mechanical gargoyles. Sleeping. Their landing gear like four clawed legs holding up an armored carapace half the size of a train car.

There is nowhere to hide here, but maybe I don't need to. Who's going to wander in here? I get some distance from the doors, sit down cross-legged under a spotlight, and begin unpacking the emergency kit, laying out the contents like I'm at a leisurely picnic. First, I remove the meal kit and set it aside. Next, I pull a flashlight free and hold it in my palm. "Where have you been all my life?" Last, I slide the first-aid kit out of the bag and crack it open.

I unclasp the suspender of my overalls. Then, crossing my arms, I grab the bottom of my shirt and delicately peel it upward and off, laying it out on the ground. I toss my bra aside. It hasn't been doing anything since the welder sliced the back strap in two. From then on it's been held to my body by sweat, sticky blood, and the pressure of my shirt.

The bandages included in the first-aid kit won't do me any good since I have no way of putting them on my back myself.

There's a bottle of analgesic-infused iodine and some individually wrapped pain reliever pills though. I shower my back with reckless sprays from the iodine bottle, wincing as the cold liquid strikes the open wound.

Tearing open the meal kit, I find a pouch labeled *Spaghetti and Meatballs*, some kind of shiny envelope I don't understand, a food bar, mint gum, a juice pouch, and another powdered drink that requires water, which I don't have.

The shiny envelope has instructions printed on it. It's a chemical heater. Following the directions, I crack the device like a New Year's glowstick and place the spaghetti and meatballs pouch inside it. It's supposed to take ten minutes to warm. While I wait, I open the juice pouch and drink sparingly, just enough to take the pain reliever pills. The juice is over-sweetened, but it feels good to have some moisture on my cracked lips.

"What do you think?" I ask aloud.

<I think it's too sweet.>

"Do you think that? Or do you think that because I think that?"

<Interesting, I don't know.>

"I was actually wondering what you think we should do next. Who knows how long the *Discordia* will be able to hide. Hell, I bet we're as likely to die of the ship's hull getting cracked open by an asteroid as we are to get rescued."

<I'm unsure. Curiously, I'm having trouble processing information right now.>

I nod absently. Too tired, too hungry, and in too much pain to worry about what that means.

I sniffle. Turning my head, I take in my surroundings, then take a moment to consider the sorry state I'm in.

Sitting topless on the deck of a desolate hangar bay in a puddle of iodine and my own blood. Huddled over the warmth of a chemically heated emergency ration. Knees torn open and hands blistered from crawling through shafts that weren't made for humans. My right arm has a long, deep scratch that had bled a bit too, and for the first time I notice the burn down my left forearm from when I was nearly blasted in the face by the maintenance drone's welder.

I'm safe. For the moment. In this lonely drone hangar. And all the feelings I'd pushed down by focusing on more immediate dangers bubble back to the surface. And my damn memory. My damned near-perfect memory allows me to rewatch Samantha die in stunning clarity. Then, in the same time-dilated detail, I rewatch Ensign Garner die.

I think of Morgan's betrayal. I think of my parents who believe I'm off whoring myself to the admiral for a career opportunity. I think of K, who might actually be whoring herself to Elijah Reynolds, because it might be her only legitimate shot at the life she wants. And that thought brings me to C, who's probably busying herself with wrestling or anything else to keep her mind occupied. To keep herself from wondering if a shadow will appear in her doorway tonight.

I begin to cry. A cathartic cry as the barely acknowledged anguish whips back like a rubber band stretched to its breaking point before release. I cry the anger. I cry the mourning. I cry the terror I'd kept caged. And I keep crying, rocking back and forth as I sob, making no attempt to rein it in until, at last, Passenger speaks.

<I believe your food has heated for its prescribed length of time,> they say in their even, soothing tone.

I loose one of the supplied napkins from the pouch that came with the emergency ration meal and dab at my eyes. Slowly my self-control returns. My breathing calms. Eyes clear. There's a long silence.

<Gaby?>

"Yeah, Passenger?"

<Does being human always hurt this much?>

"No," I say, with a sardonic chuckle. "No, I'm not usually burned and cut and bruised and whatever else."

< I meant... Does it always hurt on the inside?>

I blink back the tears that resurface. "Oh." I sniffle. "Yeah, pretty much. Yeah."

<I do not want to be inside you anymore.>

Me neither, I think, expecting that Passenger probably hears.

Gathering myself, I wipe at my eyes some more, then blow my nose into one of the supplied napkins. I tear open the pouch and steam carries the smell of marinara into the air. The container the ration kit came in doubles as a small plate with several shallow partitions to it. I pour the contents into the largest partition. Then devour it with the supplied plastic multi-utensil. In other circumstances, I would consider the spaghetti too runny and salty, and the meatballs too dry. But hunger and emotion have made my palette forgiving.

Once I've finished, I take a few moments to sit in the stillness, listening to the ship's hull creak under the pressure of the gas storms outside and the occasional thump from something more solid that the shields failed to deflect entirely.

<I can process information more clearly again,> Passenger says.

"Yeah? I think I can too."

<I have an idea.>

"I already know what it is," I say, surprising myself. "Do you really think I'm ready?"

<I think it's the best chance we have.>

That sounds like a no.

<We need to hurry. The fact that you knew my idea means we're getting dangerously close to critical symbiosis.>

We're supposed to have a few more hours. The admiral's team of neuroscientists and engineers must've missed something.

Not accounted for some variable. What else were they wrong about?

No sense in cleaning up. Nothing I could do will hide my stopping here, so I leave the lot of it. I pull my shirt back on. The welder hadn't completely cut the garment in two. The bottommost six centimeters hold it together. I re-clasp my overalls. Then, grabbing the flashlight, I head into the nearest flue.

My destination isn't far, at least not on the horizontal plane, but it is two decks up. This leaves me the choice of risking a treacherous climb in a passage between the walls or going out of my way to go back to the lift, which poses its own risks.

I choose the climb, which means after an initial turn, my route is a straight shot through the flue until I reach the hollow wall where I'll have to ascend.

With nothing to do but plod along forward for a while, I can afford to split my concentration by accessing the cameratom feed in a NeurX window.

With relief, I see they're still on the bridge. Beyond the canopy window, almost nothing is visible. Just bruise-colored mists sliding up the glass.

There's a minute of silent waiting; I'm considering dropping the connection when something draws Lauren's attention. The camera swivels to the back of the bridge. Morgan approaches. He's not moving well, his leg obviously giving him a lot of pain.

"Where've you been?" Lauren asks coldly.

"My quarters."

"Your *log*?" She sounds snide.

He nods as he takes the captain's chair on the dais. They must be talking about the mnemonic rendering he's been creating.

"You were needed on the bridge," Lauren says.

"What's changed?"

"Nothing."

"Then I wasn't needed. Let's not get into this again. It's over.

I finished the log, it's ready and I'm done with it. Can we move on?"

"Yeah," she says, the fight audibly leaving her. "Could all this dust and gas interfere with communication?" Lauren asks.

Morgan doesn't answer, instead passing the question with a look to someone out of frame.

Kerri answers, though I can't see her. "Hard to say. Wouldn't surprise me if sensors and comms are touch and go as we get deeper in this mess."

"Then we need to send an update while we can," Lauren says.

Morgan holds eye contact with her for a moment before giving a mild nod. "Kerri, can you get us a ping off the relay."

Lauren peels herself from the acceleration chair where deep pockets had formed around her frame. She steps up to the captain's chair, plants her feet in front of Morgan, and tows him to his feet. He rubs at his thigh and recovers his cane from where he'd wedged it in the chair.

"I got a tight beam on the buoy," Kerri says. "Sending it over to the cameratom."

"Actually..." Morgan rubs his hand over his light beard. "Let's do this one right here, with the bridge camera. Show 'em we're in control of the ship."

Lauren glances around the bridge at something or someone off screen. I can't tell why, but her contemplative face looks like she's sizing something up. Lauren answers him by smoothing her suit jacket and retaking her seat.

Morgan drops back into his chair with less grace. "What are we going to say?"

"I don't know," Lauren says with ice in her voice.

"Look, they'll be okay," Morgan says.

She snaps a look at him that seems to read, *You don't know that.*

"Ruby *will* fix the cloak. We'll still deliver the ship. As planned. And I will take responsibility for the delay."

"If you'd been face to face with these people, you'd know they're not going to care whose fault it is."

"I'm sorry, I just—"

"I don't want to talk about this now," Lauren says pointedly, looking toward Kerri. "Let's just get this over with."

His eyes show a certain resignation. "Kerri, count us in, please."

Kerri counts down from three, signaling when the recording begins.

Morgan clears his throat and begins. "Status update seven. We'll transmit the last several hours of footage, but I'll summarize because, as you're about to realize, there's been a delay. Onboard resistance has been—"

"Fully neutralized," Lauren cuts in, shifting into the on-screen persona I recognize from her reporting. "An element of resistance caused complications. Our cloaking device was disrupted. Presently, we're hiding inside the dust ring of Nomad Star. However," she switches her voice from dour to upbeat, "the last bit of onboard resistance has been dealt with. There is no reason to think the NCP has any idea the ship is not still under Admiral Davis' control, and there are no signs of reinforcements or blockades. Our engineer is confident the cloaking device will be repaired shortly. You can expect your ship delivered to you with only a brief delay."

She looks offscreen, I assume at Kerri, giving the signal that she's done.

"And we're out," Kerri says.

"Nice spin," Morgan says.

"Hopefully they don't watch all the footage right away," Kerri says.

"They won't," Morgan says cooly. "Everything's going to be okay. Patrick, any updates on your end?"

Lauren and the cameratom swivel, putting Patrick in center-frame. One of his eyes is nearly swollen closed. Butterfly stitches hold a cut across his cheek closed. He and Morgan had a proper LoLe conversation.

"I'm starting to wonder if she's still in the maintenance flues," he says, his pronunciation slightly off-kilter from the fat lip. "I have every custodial tom reprogrammed now. They've searched about three-quarters of the tunnels and haven't found anything."

The camera swivels back to Morgan. His brow furrows.

"We know she's still alive," Lauren says flatly. Did she mean it as a simple fact? Stating an obstacle they needed to overcome. Or had that been intended to comfort Morgan? If it was the latter, the blunters have robbed her of the emotional depth to sound like she gives a shit.

I reach the end of the line: the hollow tunnel leading up through the wall. It's time to climb now and I'll need my full attention for this, so I close the connection and get to it. But on my way up, I decide to make a quick detour.

CHAPTER
THIRTY-FIVE

The boy thrashed against his restraints. The skin at his wrist tore open and blood began to weep around the strap. Nearby, the hologram kept flickering chaotic, seemingly random images. Morgan sat there, leaning back as much as he could in the hard chair, his ruined leg stretched out before him, watching the boy in horror and fascination. Jules kept clutching his pulser, as if he might end the boy's suffering at any moment.

Muffled shouts came from the other side of the door. At least two men were arguing over which course of action would lead to Morgan and Jules' deaths the quickest: continuing to try to override the door, or finding a torch to cut it open.

"Sounds like we might have a bit more time," Morgan said. "Can you get me another shot?"

Jules was mesmerized by the hologram.

"Jules?"

"Yeah, sure. Sorry."

He bent down and gave Morgan the shot from his own little med pack. The pain moved further away, and he nearly dozed off.

Through squinted eyes, Morgan's gaze landed on a waste collection bag attached to the boy's chair. For the first time, he noticed an IV hooked up to him. It was an easy thing to miss among the mess of larger cables going into his skull, but it made Morgan curious how long the boy had been there. He tried to remember back to the briefing, but he couldn't be sure when the biobox had been stolen. Thirty-something hours? Had the kid been hooked up to it right away?

"You got the cuttin' torch?" someone yelled from the other side of the door. "Hurry up, more of 'em are on the station now."

Jules and Morgan looked at each other.

"The marines?" Jules said. "Maybe we'll make it after all."

Morgan looked down at the open meat of his thigh. "Maybe I'll live to ride a desk," he said.

He snapped his head toward the door at the hiss of a cutting torch. A second later they heard the crackle and sizzle as it began the slow process of slicing through the steel.

"You remember the first person you killed?" Jules asked.

The question took Morgan off guard, but the answer came easy. "Yeah, you were there. When we dropped into Delarbour and took that LiDAR station from the Stewies."

Jules nodded his head absently.

"That was your first too...right?"

"You remember Rebecca Hyan?" There was a tremble to his voice.

The name sounded familiar, but Morgan couldn't make the pieces fit; his head was too cloudy with painkillers.

Jules continued after a moment. "She was quiet, kinda homely. Lived on my street."

Still nothing was coming.

"She killed herself while we were in gausser training."

"Right. I remember now," Morgan said. He snapped his fingers, but there was no sound. He looked dumbly at his fingertips, slick with blood. "Wait... Her brother was that creepy little puke. What's his name?"

Jules nodded. "Arlo."

The first spark from the cutting torch singed through to the inside of the door; at the same time, the hologram twitched sporadically behind Jules. Morgan was sure the two were unrelated.

"Where you going with this?" Morgan asked.

"I know why she did it. Rebecca's little sister, Catherine, told Gaby. Last time I was back home—you know, the leave we had when you went to K'Nyara—Gaby told me."

"We barely talked to Rebecca when we were at school. Why are we talking about her now? Especially with that going on?" Morgan asked, pointing to the jagged, molten cut that was now about a palm-width long. It was like watching a timer. It still had a long way to go, but once it makes its way around, they die.

"Just listen, please, Morgan."

"Sure. Yeah."

"At home she was getting...abused."

"You mean like..."

Jules nodded.

"Rebecca and her sister both. Apparently Rebecca got pregnant. When she couldn't find an alleydoc to get rid of it, she must've figured her choices were have her brother's kid or step in front of the magtrain."

The hologram behind Jules flickered. It might've been Morgan's imagination, but it seemed to speed up.

"So it was the very next day after Gaby told me. Man, I wasn't looking for him. I sure as shit wasn't expecting to see him. I went down to the depot, thinking I'd hang out with Rory and the crew. And who'd I find?"

"Arlo-fuckin'-Hyan," Morgan answered. The depot was the nickname for an abandoned factory LoLe kids would hang out in after school.

He nodded. "Arlo-fucking-Hyan. Rory and our old crew

weren't there. It was Arlo and a bunch of punks I'd never met, getting high. And the first thing I heard, I swear, the first thing when I got close was Arlo saying something about his little sister's friend, Gabrielle."

Now Morgan thought he understood why Jules was telling him all this.

The cut-line on the door was about the length of an arm.

Jules swallowed. "I don't remember picking up the pipe." He looked down at his hand, fingers curled around an imaginary, improvised weapon. "But I remember the vibration running through it and into my hand when it made contact. I remember the sound it made. Then I remember the other guys screaming and running."

"Don't tell me you feel guilty 'cause you offed some piece of shit."

"I killed the wrong guy."

"What? It wasn't Arlo?" Morgan asked.

"It was Arlo. Gaby misunderstood her friend, or maybe I misunderstood Gaby. I dunno, man. But I found out later it was Rebecca and Catherine's dad that was doing it. Arlo was innocent."

"Shit." Morgan swallowed. "Okay. Okay, so you screwed up."

"That's a soft way of saying it," Jules said. He paced to the far side of the holotable, maybe so he could look at Morgan and the hologram at once. The hologram cast upward shadows across his grave face. "I didn't pay for it."

"What do you mean?"

"The guys that ran off, his friends, they returned with the police. Two big, hostile-lookin' Swayy Corp. cops. Fast. Like weirdly fast, like these cops were right around the corner or something."

"Wait, cops? How'd you get away?"

"I didn't. Once they found out I was a gausser, they uncuffed me and told the witnesses they'd best forget they saw anything. Morgan, two of these guys still had Arlo's blood on their faces. Can you imagine, being in their shoes, watching that happen to your friend, and then the cops tell you that you didn't see nothin'?"

Morgan considered it for a minute. The room strobed in and out of existence as the hologram went through a rapid series of images, cutting out entirely between each. Morgan could have sworn one of them was a face screaming.

"They were right," Morgan said after thinking it over. "How many Stewie kills have you confirmed since then?"

Jules only shrugged.

"Jules?"

"Forty-five, I think."

"Forty-five. And Arlo, he was working age, but I bet he was on basic?"

"Probably."

Sparks scattered across the floor. The cut was about halfway complete to a human-sized oval.

"You've done more for the State since that day than Arlo probably would've done in his entire life, and those cops understood that. Even if they would've arrested you, it wouldn't have mattered. No judge would've given you anything more than a slap on the wrist. All it would've done is taken a good soldier away from Swayy Corp. for a couple of months."

"That's my point." Jules slammed his palm against the holotable. Part of the hologram blurred from his hand blocking the emitters. "What if your mom got murdered? Or Barry? And the SOB that did it didn't have to pay, just because he was valuable to the war effort. Is that the world you want to be living in?"

"Of course not. But it's the way things are gonna be as long as there's a greater good we gotta keep our eyes on. Grow up, Jules!"

The boy started sucking rapid breaths through clenched

teeth. The torch hissed and molten metal bubbled. Jules and Morgan stared at each other through the pale, monochromatic glow of the hologram. The screaming pixelated face reappeared and seemed to fall below the projection.

The AI had been broken.

Top secret data coalesced in the hologram between them. It was familiar enough that Morgan could make sense of it. Fleet movements and battle plans across the entire solar theater. But it was mapped out in impossible clarity. Move and countermove, projecting response after response after response. The sheer unimaginable quantity of it.

Jules and Morgan didn't speak as they tried to wrap their heads around what they were seeing. It couldn't be true. Could it? He had to be misinterpreting it. He had to be coming to the wrong conclusion. Jules was frozen, his hand covering his mouth. His eyes darted from one piece of the hologram to another like he was still working through it.

Morgan waited for him to put the pieces together. His interpretation would be different, more rational, more sane. Jules would say it aloud any moment and Morgan would know instantly that Jules' conclusion was right, because his own couldn't possibly be.

So Morgan sat there, rifle cradled in his lap, legs outstretched in front of him—one intact, the other a ruined mess of viscera. The bleeding had nearly stopped, but not entirely. If he didn't get medical attention sometime soon, he was going to die.

That was the absolute least of his worries.

The oval cutout in the door was about three-quarters complete. If their backup didn't arrive within the next few minutes, the Yingzi Zhēnxiàng, or Praxis Station security, or whoever was out there were going to come through that door and cut them down. They'd take a few of them with them, but without any decent cover and Morgan being immobilized, they wouldn't have a chance.

But even that was background noise, an inconvenience, compared to what he was seeing decoded in front of them.

It looked like it took great effort for Jules to peel his palm from his lips.

The boy hooked up to the holoprojector convulsed, violently whipping his head back and forth. He seized, his entire body going rigid against the restraints, then he went limp. His little body seemed so frail.

They both looked back to the data. The spell was broken now. They had to face it.

CHAPTER
THIRTY-SIX

OF COURSE YOU HAD TO CHOOSE THE CLIMB, DIDN'T you, Gaby? I struggle to find purchase with my foot as something digs into my finger. The flashlight, which I'd stuffed into a pocket of my overalls so the beam would face up, throws inconsistent and deceptive shadows above me. I can't tell if it's better than trying to negotiate the climb in the pitch black or not.

At the start, I'd tried to overlay the map in my vision the way I did in the lift shaft. But whoever ran the piping, cabling, and placed the various other systems in the wall hadn't followed the original schematics closely enough to make that useful.

I pull myself up the shaft at a glacial pace, stringing one small movement after another, the whole time trying not to think about how far I have yet to go. It feels like a marathon, but at last, I drag my belly onto a horizontal flue on the mid deck. Exhausted, I collapse to the steel, thankful that I took this detour and hadn't been trying to climb all the way up to the command deck in one go.

I don't have to crawl far before I reach my egress hatch. Between the weariness that's settled into a type of indifference and the confidence that my adversaries are busy elsewhere, I exit the hatch with little caution. From there, I amble down the short hallway, stopping in front of the XO's private quarters. Morgan hasn't bothered to lock it. I walk right in as if invited.

Broken glass litters the floor. I hadn't seen this feature of the room through the cameratom, but clearly a smart-mirror had been built into the bulkhead next to the door. The frame of it now empty, sharp bits of glass protrude from the edges like the wide mouth of an approaching shark. The majority of the mirror's glass is spread about the small quarters, and it's not the only sign of violence. The mnemonic headset lay in pieces—some bits are scattered about the small desk, a few electrodes and part of the frame mix with the detritus on the floor.

Morgan's terminal's been pushed sideways on the desk as well, a crack going down the center of the screen. It's on, unlocked, and even with the crack distorting its image, I can see the file folder I want on display. As if it was meant to be.

Had Morgan caused this damage? Maybe swinging his cane in some fit of anger and carelessness? He must've, probably immediately after finishing his log, and before returning to the bridge. I remember seeing him through the cameratom. He looked to be in so much pain.

I pick my way through the minefield of broken glass, trying not to get any of it impaled into my bare feet. Inspecting the now useless headset on the desk, I ask, <What do I do now?>

<The SR was built on the same engine that mnemonic renders use,> Passenger reminds me. <Save it to your NeurX and we can view it while we are integrated. However, might I suggest we view it at a later date, since we are running out of time.>

I nod, as if Passenger can see me, then realize that they see through my eyes, so am I nodding to myself? I make a copy of the folder and briefly connect my NeurX to his terminal to send the copy to myself. Then I close the connection and head back out.

I see the smaller lift at the end of the hall. The one we used when we came up here and signed the NDAs immediately after arriving. I try to weigh what the greater danger is: using the lift where I might get caught by the mutineers, or climbing up another deck in the vertical shaft where I might fall to my death.

Actually, the greatest risk is reaching critical symbiosis with Passenger, I realize. Using the flues will increase that risk because it'll take so much longer. But if I'm being honest, the exhaustion is the prime factor in my choice.

After taking the lift, I prowl into the empty CIC. Gratefully, the bodies have been moved. It appears like the custodial toms came through too. Gone is the glass shrapnel that showered the room when Lauren's errant pulser shot had punched that gaping hole through one of the command consoles. The little toms seem to have tried removing as much of the evidence of violence as they could, but were unable to completely rid the deck of blood stains where Tyrone and Samantha died. I go to the terminal closest to the—what had the admiral called it, an Inertia-Zero chair? Samantha's stolen credentials are still good, logging me in.

Then I look over the commands and options presented on the screen, dumbfounded. "I have no idea how to operate this system. Do you?"

<No, but I think I can make the pieces fit.>

"What? What'd you just say?"

<I said, No, but I think—"

"I don't need you to repeat yourself. I mean, where'd you get that saying from?"

<It's what we say back home.>

My jaw drops.

<No, I mean... Shit, Gaby. I think we should disconnect now. We're approaching critical symbiosis.>

"How much time?"

<Impossible to say. Minutes. Seconds.>

"We can't stop now, Passenger. Focus. You need to walk me through this."

Then my hands—but somehow not my hands—begin gliding over the controls with a grace and precision and sheer mastery that until this very moment I would have thought could only come from years of practice.

"How are you doing this?" I ask in disbelief.

<I don't know.>

One by one, the systems are brought online. The emitters are powered up. The *Hybris* sensor sweeps are acquired and cloned. Transmission protocols are locked in. In/Out ports are green. We're ready to go.

I climb into the spherical cage and sit in the Inertia-Zero chair. As I pull the blinder over my head, Passenger says, <Remember, in the real SR, you'll need to create the environment yourself. Do you know what you'll create, and how you intend to hack the *Hybris*?>

"I've spent years building a world in my head. I might as well use it. And I don't plan on hacking anything." A moment later, the real world is gone.

CHAPTER
THIRTY-SEVEN

Somewhere in the distance, a flock of birds take hurried flight, cawing as they climb overhead. Perhaps startled by some creature in the underbrush, or the rest of the party bringing their horses up the trail, or some other unthought-of disturbance.

Golden columns of light venture through the canopy of green leaves obscuring the sun. All around me is green grass, painted and gilded carriages, horses, and my husband's subjects readying this evening's festivities. A month of long planning, and he's called away last minute, leaving me to the final formalities.

"Splendid weather, Your Grace. You simply could not have chosen a better day."

It's the podgy little man, Warwick Straude. I turn to him and smile. "Quite, Master Straude. Though I cannot take credit. I don't control the god of storms any more than you do."

"Your Grace," he says, obviously not knowing what to do with Queen Melisenia's present mood of humility. I need to be careful how I play the character. Pulling this from my imagination, I've woven into the fabric of this world the entirety of my writing, not just what I have on the screenplay pages, but document upon document of background, of worldbuilding, and the personality models I've developed on each character. Because of that, these actors, whom I must assume are part of the *Hybris'* AI, are expecting Melisenia to be hard and demanding.

I don't want to get caught out by being too *me* the same way I was too *me* when I tried lying my way through the drug deal with the Doctor.

"Master Straude. We have a royal messenger among our company, do we not?"

"Ah yes, I believe so, Your Grace."

"Good, fetch him to me, right away."

"Your Grace, perhaps your chamberlain would be—"

I silence him with a look.

"Right away, Your Grace."

I wait in a canopied chair, surveying the men and women darting back and forth. They busy themselves setting up tables, sweeping away pebbles, installing slender wooden poles around the periphery to hang flags and streamers and lanterns from, and a hundred other small tasks required to prepare this patch of earth for the celebration. As the first covered dishes are brought out and arranged on the tables, the messenger approaches.

"Your Grace," he says, taking a knee three paces away. He's a man of middling years. Good. Whatever he may lack in the loss of youth, he's gained twice over in reliability.

"Rise," I command, and he does. "Your name?"

"Danstan Harleigh, of Edinshire. If it pleases you, Your Grace."

I glance around, making sure no one is within earshot.

"Come closer, Master Harleigh."

He takes a single pace forward.

I point to the patch of beaten-down grass at my feet. "Closer still."

He visibly swallows as he approaches, his eyes downcast.

Remember to be a pain, Gaby. "What? Is Queen Melisenia so

ugly, so difficult to look upon, that you must force your gaze away?"

The poor man's eyes go wide with panic. "No. No, of course not, Your Grace." His gaze bounces off me and back down to his mud-flaked shoes.

"Master Harleigh, the measure of a man's soul is in his eyes. And I *will* see yours before I entrust you to the task I have mind for."

With visible effort, he finally meets my gaze. I hold him there —terror stricken—for a long moment. This is, of course, pageantry. But if he's an AI working under the social rules I've created, I intend to build him up so that he'll sooner die than fail his queen.

"Good." I release him by momentarily looking away. "Now, Danstan Harleigh, of Edinshire, you may tell any who wonder that you have been looked upon by Queen Melisenia herself, and she has deemed you worthy of matters critical to the throne."

"Thank you, Your Grace."

"Now give me quill, parchment, and your writing board."

He produces all three from his satchel and I begin to scrawl out my message as elegantly as I can.

> *Your Grace, the Immortal Phoenix of Belholt*
> *I hope this letter finds you well.*

Wait, that won't do. I actually need to break character for this, don't I?

I fold the parchment smoothly in half, handing it back to the attentive messenger. "I need another. Destroy that one."

"Yes, Your Grace."

For my next try, I think about how my message will be

received and not the fictional world it will travel through to reach its destination.

Admiral McCafferty,

There will be time enough later to explain how I've tricked your AI into delivering this message to your terminal. Right now, that doesn't matter. I'm aboard the Discordia. There has been a mutiny, and the ship is presently under the control of former Lieutenant Commander York. Last I was aware, Admiral Davis was still alive and was being held in the brig. Please help us. SOS.

Loyally, Gabrielle Rhodes, civilian.

I roll the parchment ceremoniously. Danstan Harleigh has melted wax and stands ready with the royal seal. Once the letter is sealed, he places it carefully into his messenger box.

"Now, Master Harleigh, understand I am entrusting you with a mission of the highest concern to the crown. You are a man of quality and integrity. I see it in you. I know you will not fail us."

"On my life, Your Grace."

Good. I need the AI's total buy-in. I have to stretch the fiction here. Hopefully it only stretches and doesn't break. "My husband, King Audwin, is on a clandestine mission of his own. He's going by an assumed name, Admiral McCafferty. And he's in a place called CIC. Do you know it?"

He has a quizzical, almost inhuman look on his face, and for a moment I think I've miscalculated, that I've gone too far. But then he answers me.

"Yes, Your Grace. I believe I do."

THIRTY-EIGHT

<THAT WAS INSPIRED, GABY.>

"Thank you," I say softly, feeling as much embarrassment as pride. I'm good at this. Really good. But this isn't what I want to be good at. I just want to be a gausser. A simple soldier. "Do you think it will work?"

<We'll know shortly. But, yes, I think it will work. Now let's disconnect while there's still time.>

I still have Morgan's mnemonic rendering. I need the SR to view it, which means I need Passenger.

"I'd like to watch Morgan's log first."

<There isn't time, Gaby.>

"Can't we overclock and watch it at high speed?"

<Yes, but—>

"Passenger, I plan on being a gausser. Once we disconnect, we'll never be integrated again. Finding a mnemonic headset is next to impossible. Please, it should only take a few seconds."

Passenger answers me by navigating to the folder on my NeurX and clicking RUN on the mnemonic render file faster than I ever could've.

Still sitting in the Inertia-Zero chair with the blinder helmet on, I begin reliving the last day my brother was alive as if I was Morgan. My sense of self is submerged, sort of painted over by his thoughts and memories and emotions.

And so I'm Morgan as he breaks it off with Corporal Nala Ricci. I'm Morgan as he meets up with Jules in the barracks and sends that last video message to me. I'm Morgan as he sits through the briefing, and I feel the same surprise and mild sense of dread as he hears the words *Omega Priority*. I'm Morgan as he wades through the gausser ready room and waits in the overcrowded launch deck.

And finally, after dreaming of it for years, I get to feel the exhilaration and euphoric fear of being launched from a gausser tube. It's not me, of course. But it feels so real it doesn't matter.

I'm Morgan as I career toward Praxis Station, feeling motionless and utterly helpless during those paralyzing moments as my fellow gaussers are cut down by the station's point defense guns. I stand by as the shape charge shatters the observation lounge window, watching the O2 get blown into space, along with a woman and her child. Then the skirmishes as we fight our way through the station toward our objective.

I'm Morgan when he gets hit by the rocket that ruins his leg, and I'm forced to live through the excruciating pain that follows. Pain that, before a drone had taken a welding torch across my back, I wouldn't have thought possible. From there, memory and time are confused as Jules drags me backward out of the fight. We're in a laboratory and Jules is there. My big brother, giving me a needle full of drugs to keep me aware and keep the pain at a distance.

Some degree of clarity returns, and I'm Morgan watching a boy hooked to machines. Crude bolt-on wetware coming from his skull. And I realize he's the first host. The one that Passenger had told me spent hundreds of years in the overclocked time frame hacking an AI. I had thought it would've been a Swayy operation, but no, they *found* this technology, didn't they? Stole it. Is this the secret that Morgan needed to tell? Is this why he created this mnemonic rendering?

And then I watch as the AI is finally broken. And the tapestry of my life, woven with threads of duty and honor and patriotism, unravels.

"They're fleet movements," Jules said.

That's the conclusion Morgan had reached as well. Part of it. The hologram depicted a map of the entire solar system with the locations of hundreds of battlegroups plotted in intricate detail. There were attachments plugged into each, and a calendar wrapping the bottom of the hologram. Jules reached into the hologram with a finger and cycled the calendar forward. A week. A month. Six. A pre-programmed simulation played out for them, one move at a time.

"Looks like this goes out a year. Every fleet movement for both the NCP and the Commonwealth for an *entire* next year."

"How do you think they get projections of Commonwealth strategies so far out?" Morgan asked.

"I don't know. It seems impossible though, right? If we could predict what the Commonwealth would do so far out, how do we ever lose an engagement?"

A good question, but Morgan didn't even try to answer. He was still trying to wrap his head around the projections themselves. Analyzing strategies was one thing. Given good intel, one might figure out an enemy's next move. But the war was chaos, and what was showing up in this map was countermove upon countermove, complete with engagement results of battles that wouldn't happen if the results came out differently from earlier battles. And they didn't seem to be the branching paths of what-if scenarios, just a single series of causally interconnected events. Jules clicked on one of the Commonwealth battle groups, opening a connected attachment. A document enveloped the star map. It was an order from Commonwealth command, stamped with an authentication code and dated for almost seven months in the future. There were details for the fleet's movements and its objectives and mission parameters: a last-minute attack-of-opportunity on an NCP outpost under construction.

Jules' brow furrowed as he looked up the outpost next. "Construction hasn't even begun yet. How can high command possibly know that the enemy will learn about an outpost we haven't even begun building, and attack it before construction is finished? There's even an expected casualty report."

"How many?" Morgan asked, unable to read the details from where he sat.

"Thirteen thousand on our side, plus or minus fifteen percent, and complete loss of the outpost. Fifteen hundred on the Commonwealth's side, plus or minus nineteen percent."

"If the NCP knows that'll happen, why start to build the outpost at all?"

Morgan hoped Jules would have a different answer than the one floating around his own narcotic-fueled thoughts. At that point he might've latched onto any answer, no matter how far-fetched, to avoid the answer staring him in the face. Time travel? Yeah, sounds plausible. A crystal ball? Sure, why not?

Jules placed both hands on the holotable, as if steadying himself against the words he was about to speak. "The NCP and the Commonwealth are controlled by the same people."

And there it was. The answer Morgan had come to as well, hoping his friend, his level-headed, logical friend, would think of something else. Something less insane. Something that didn't shatter their entire worldview at once.

"We can't destroy it," Jules said, palming the biobox.

"We have to. Our orders—"

"Screw our orders!" He slammed the biobox back down.

The oval cutout was almost complete. Sparks shot from a

bright red dot that slowly made its way clockwise around the door. The Yingzi Zhēnxiàng would be in soon, Morgan and Jules would be killed, and then the enemy would be in possession of data that could... Well, honestly, Morgan couldn't even fathom all the nastiness that could be done with that data.

"You want to hand it over to them? You want the terrorists to have it?" Morgan asked.

"I don't know. Maybe." He put his arms out to the sides and let them fall. "Aren't you pissed off?"

"No." Morgan wasn't. Maybe it was the drugs, or that the reality of what he'd seen hadn't fully struck home yet. Maybe a combination. "There could be a reasonable explanation."

"Yeah, okay. Gimme one of those. Just a single one. What reasonable explanation would someone have for puppeteering both sides of a war for seventy years?"

"I don't know," Morgan admitted. "That's not our place. We took an oath, Jules. Remember?"

"Screw the oath. The NCP betrayed us. Probably since before we were born," Jules said, but his rage seemed spent. He turned away from the table, pacing. "Screw our orders and screw our oath," he muttered.

Morgan squared the biobox in his rifle's sites. Jules must've heard the whir of Morgan's exochassis, or the slight metallic rattle of the rifle's catch. Whatever it was, he swung around and snatched the biobox in his hands. "Jules. Put it down. I'm going to complete our mission."

"No. This needs to get out. That's why this is an Omega Priority mission. They're scared this will get out. And they should be. Do you have any idea what kind of chaos this could cause? No. No, you'll have to shoot me."

"Just put it the fuck down!"

Jules cupped the cube in both hands, holding it close to his chest. He shook his head, slowly, resolutely. Morgan couldn't destroy the biobox without killing his best friend. Pulling the trigger would expel a depleted uranium round at over 1,000 meters per second. At this range, it would cut through the steel casing of the biobox like tissue paper and punch a hole through Jules' armor.

"Look at the door," Morgan said. "They're going to be in here in seconds. The AI's cracked. They could copy and transmit that data before our backup gets here. We're both dead anyway. I don't want to be the one that does it, but I can't risk that data cube falling into enemy hands."

"I'd rather it be you...than one of them," he said solemnly.

"No," Morgan pleaded.

"I'd rather it be you, Morgan," Jules repeated, holding the data cube close. "Maybe you can go on after this, but I can't. We built our entire lives around this war. And it's a lie. I can't live with this secret, and no one will ever believe me without this." He rapped a finger against one flat face of the cube.

Morgan looked at the door. The hot point of the torch was coming closer to the cooled spot where it had first begun cutting through.

"Just set it down there on the table," Morgan said. "Let's fight these guys. Together. Okay?"

Jules sucked at his teeth and shook his head.

"Damn you, Jules. Don't make me do this!" They were only centimeters away from completing the oval cutout.

The torch outside turned off. Now all they had to do was ram their hole free. Morgan's hands were shaking, he could barely keep the biobox centered in his sights.

"Please," Morgan begged.

Jules closed his eyes.

The thick steel oval that had once been most of the door tipped, falling inward.

Time was up.

Morgan squeezed his trigger.

Jules died.

The metal slab slammed into the floor, making a deafening *clang* and sending billows of dust and smoke outward. Reports of weapons rang out. Morgan turned his rifle, firing back wildly. He expected to die. Wanted it even, after what he had just done. But he'd be damned if he was going down without a fight, and every time the Yingzi attempted to come through the choke point of the door, he killed more of them.

He held his position after he'd run out of ammo for his combat rifle and had to resort to his pulser. He wondered why they didn't fire another rocket in, or toss a few grenades, and have done with it. Then he realized they didn't know the biobox had been destroyed. They might not have even known the boy was dead. The mission was worth the lives to them, just as it was for the NCP.

Because of that, he was able to hold his position long enough that the marines arrived.

CHAPTER
THIRTY-NINE

The mnemonic rendering ends abruptly, halting the flow of exogenous sensations. I'm back in the real world, left with the imprint of what was, what *is,* another life. Saturated with emotions, it's impossible to parse the feelings that belong to me and those that came from Morgan. Maybe there's no difference.

<Gaby, we need to disconnect. Now.>

Without answering I race through my NeurX menu and sever the connection. A tingle ripples down my body. A prickling numbness, there and gone, as if my nervous system reboots.

I shed the blinder helmet, dropping it carelessly to the deck. Gritting my teeth against a sudden boiling, gnawing pain, I cry out, clutching my right thigh. Wondering if the muscle is still there.

I force my eyes open. There's no sign of a wound at my thigh. My overalls are still intact, save for the grime, the frays, and the circular blood stains at my knees. This pain isn't real. This is the shadow of Morgan's pain. The ghost of memory. Nothing more. Telling myself this only helps a little.

Then there's a weight on my chest. Like G upon G of acceleration. But it isn't acceleration. I can only feel this in my ribs, grasping my heart, compressing my lungs. My implant fires. I cough raggedly, coating my tongue and sinuses with the medication. The acerbic tang of lab-purified chemicals is all I can taste or smell. I pull myself up and out of the chair. My right leg gives out under my weight—my motor cortex entirely convinced that the pain is a symptom of real damage— and I collapse beyond the spherical cage's door.

Adding to the white-hot fire in my thigh and the stacking pressure on my chest, a sinking weight forms in my gut. Dragged down by an undertow of grief and guilt and remorse, I feel as though I melt into the deck. And there, on the floor, I curl around this fresh wound, this space my actions have carved out within myself, leaving a hollow shell of who I once was, and who I could have been.

I've made a serious mistake. The mnemonic rendering was not some piece of scripted fiction, or even some hyper-realistic documentary VR. This was not a piece of media to be consumed, digested, and left behind.

This was far more than any VR could hope to be, and I understand why this technology had been banned and abandoned.

Morgan's memories are now *my* memories. As I sob on the deck of the CIC, in this moment I know with certainty that I will forever carry the phantom vestiges of this pain. I will forever remember betraying and murdering Jules. Jules, who will be intertwined within the layers of my psyche as not just my big brother but now also as my best friend and a peer.

The gear-shaped portal of the CIC rolls open. Patrick and Lauren enter. I try to get my crying under control as Patrick says something like, *She's here,* into his bracer.

"Bring her to the bridge," Morgan's voice says through the bracer's speaker.

Patrick and Lauren cover the distance to me. I don't resist

when they haul me to my feet. They hold me upright, shouldering the weight I can't support with my own legs.

Patrick opens a channel on his bracer. "Hey. We have her. Meet us on the bridge, just in case we need to convince the boss to do the right thing."

"Be there in five," Ruby says from the other end.

"It's not going to go down like that," Lauren says sternly.

Patrick regards her with his battered face. One eye swollen closed. "Sure," he says.

They walk me to the bridge. I don't fight. I don't try to flee. I don't care what happens to me anymore.

They release me, and I fold under my own weight, crumpling to the floor near the middle of the bridge. The steel combat shutters have been closed, wrapping the canopy of glass in a protective cocoon. Too bad; if they kill me here, I might've liked to have seen Nomad Star one last time.

"She used that electronic warfare chair," Lauren says.

Morgan climbs down the command dais and shuffles to me, his cane rapping hard against the floor. *Clop, thump, clop, thump.* He takes a knee, pain etched in the lines of his face as he does so. But he's down near my level. Close.

"Gaby, what did you do?" he asks calmly.

I can only mewl a response not found in any organized language.

"Gaby, it's okay. Just tell me what happened."

My eyes shoot open. Beneath the pain and the regret and the fathomless sorrow, a tiny spark of rage catches dry kindling, spreading into an uncontrollable inferno that will not be denied for one moment longer.

I lunge for him. Screaming and cursing him, calling him a murderer and a monster, howling, "How could you kill Jules?" Hammering my small fists against his chest again and again as my screams turn into random vowels and consonants strung into a slurry of nonsense. And he takes it all, waving away someone who comes over to intervene. He just accepts my anger and my abuse as I scream myself empty and batter him until my shoulders burn and my strikes putter out into anemic taps.

He takes me into his arms then, his voice cracking with emotion. "I'm sorry, Gabs. I'm so sorry."

The fuel spent, the fire burns itself out. The room quiets, and a sort of reverence for the weight of this moment settles in.

The bridge door slides open, and someone enters. It must be Ruby, coming from the engineering section at Patrick's urging. They're worried Morgan won't do what needs to be done, regarding me, of course. Now, enveloped in Morgan's arms—a man I hate, a boy I love—none of that makes any difference.

I'm only vaguely aware of movement around me. A smoky coffee fragrance balanced with some sweet flower hovers near me. Consumed by Amon Berrut. Lauren's scent. The first and only perfume I've ever worn. Morgan answers some unasked question. "Seems she got ahold of my log. She knows the truth."

A thought claws its way to the surface, punching through the roiling tempest of my thoughts. I know a secret. A dangerous and devouring secret.

The NCP and the Commonwealth are the same.

Not alike. The same. The war is a fabrication. Each engagement pre-determined. I can only guess at who benefits from it, and what those benefits might be. But I know the cost. The cost is lives. The cost is distrust and hatred for the other side. The cost is a society built around the sole purpose of warfare. Willingly sacrificing blood and freedom and dignity to the lie.

And as my worldview unravels just as Morgan's must have, I begin to understand him. I can't forgive him. Not yet. Probably not ever. But in a difficult moment, he had to make a terrible choice. Side with his best friend, who intended to betray the NCP, or carry out his duty like the loyal soldier he was raised to be. The same loyalty, I realize, that drove me to send an SOS to an admiral I've never met, knowing it would likely result in Morgan's death.

I don't know what he went through in the years after the mnemonic rendering ended, or what series of events led him here, but feeling the brunt of his emotions, I think I can make some of the pieces fit. More than anything, he wished he could take that moment back. The regret has been crushing him since that day, made worse by the gathering realization that the loyalty he'd given Swayy Corp. was, and always had been, misplaced. A realization that Jules had simply had the faculties to accept more quickly.

He continued to serve with that secret knowledge. Angry at those who, through no fault of their own, were blind to the truth, as he had been. But most of all, he carried a smoldering hatred for those at the top who knew. Whose plans he had carried out again and again. Whose games he had killed for and watched so many friends die in the service of.

I've no clue how the plan came together to steal and sell this ship, but there, in his arms, as we rock gently as one, I can glimpse his motivation.

Knowing the truth, but without the evidence necessary to convince the public, you might feel helpless to change things for the better. You might feel that it's utterly hopeless to make any difference at all. And if you can't change how the worlds work, your choices become play along or don't play at all. Morgan chose not to play. He found a ticket out and made his own play for what happiness he could on the fringes of society with the woman he loved.

What difference did his betrayal make? He knew, from the start, that Admiral Davis' dream could never be more than a dream. There was no way that whoever was pulling the strings would allow this technology to end the war.

Is that why the Media Ministry got involved in the first place?

Did they decide they wanted a rational, straight-forward way to have a top-secret project leaked to the other side and a plausible way they'd have a countermeasure ready? Maybe, and then Morgan, knowing Lauren intimately, was able to have her use her clout to get the assignment?

Or do I have it reversed? Did Morgan and Lauren somehow engineer her presence aboard the ship so that she, as an important part of their plan, would be here? The investigators will probably study their motivations and pick through the order of events for years. Privately, of course. The public version will be neat. So simple to understand and so complete in their clear wrongdoing that no one will question Morgan's, and Lauren's, and the other mutineers' swift and public executions.

It's not fair. None of it.

"The *Hybris*," Kerri calls out. "They're diving toward us."

Morgan takes my shoulders. "Gaby, look at me," he says urgently. "What did you do?"

My throat is raw. "I sent a message. Mutiny. SOS. I think...I think I've gotten you all killed."

Morgan turns from me, asking, "How much time?"

"The dust should reduce their accurate weapon range," Ruby says.

Morgan regards her, looking as if this is the first time he's realized she's on the bridge.

"With what Ruby said in mind," Kerri says, "it's hard to say for sure, but maybe two, two-and-a-half minutes."

Patrick turns from his station. "We've received a return message off the buoy."

Lauren stiffens.

"Not a good time," Morgan says.

Lauren's face says it all. She doesn't intend on waiting.

"Okay," Morgan says. "Kerri, take us deeper into the storm. Patrick, bring the message up here."

"Up you go, Kitten," Lauren says in my ear. She drags me roughly to my feet and stuffs me into an unoccupied station. Ruby takes the one next to mine. She reaches over and types in commands on the terminal at my station, locking it from my use.

Lauren and Morgan have taken their positions on the bridge as the holotable at the center of the room gutters and reforms. A man's face appears. He's old, but his eyes are clear. His voice has a certain music to it when he speaks. "My friends, when your check-in was late, I worried misfortune had found you." What accent is that? "It pleases me to see you both in good health. We have an arrangement, you understand, built on trust and integrity. We agreed there would be terms for our arrangement. We agreed there would be consequences if the terms were not met."

Lauren stiffens in her chair, no doubt sensing—I'm sure better than me—that this prerecorded message is heading to a dark conclusion.

"You are now late on delivery. This breaks the terms of our agreement. This is bad. But," he says with a light smile while holding a finger up, "you send report with tidings of expected success. This is good. I must balance these things."

The man steps back and to the side, allowing the camera to get a view of two men standing at the sides of someone bound to a chair with a canvas sack over their head.

"So with balance in mind, I give you the consequences. A 5% reduction in your finder's fee for the electronic warfare ship. And. This. Single life." One of the men pulls the bag from the captive's head.

Lauren jerks in her seat. "Pappa?" she says, her hand reaching weakly toward the hologram.

Lauren's father lets out panicked, hissing breaths through a wet gag.

"In your check-in, you did not apologize for your tardiness. So I will not apologize for what I must now do."

The report of a handgun going off overwhelms the microphone in the recording, fuzzing briefly.

Lauren lets out a whimper. Clamping her hand tightly over her mouth.

"Remember, Miss Gallagher, you can still save your mother, sister, and your young niece here. Please adhere to the letter of our arrangement from this point forward."

The video cuts out. The message is over. Lauren's gaze remains pinned to the holotable.

"Holy hell," Kerri says, breaking the silence.

"Lauren?" Morgan says. "Lauren, look at me. Okay, we're going to get the rest of them back. Then I'm going to kill that son of a bitch. You understand?"

With trembling hands, she produces a small, slender plastic case from her pocket. She pops it open and dumps five small pills in her palm. She works up some saliva, then tosses them in her mouth, and returns the case to her pocket, swallowing hard as she regards Morgan. Her eyes are glassing up.

"They've launched torpedoes," Kerri says.

"Take your stations," Morgan commands. "Shields to full. Patrick, launch all combat drones. I'm going to need you on guns, so set drones on auto pilot to screen incoming threats."

The hull rocks mildly. "Glancing blows from their railguns," Ruby calls out next to me. "No damage."

"Why are they firing on us?" I ask aloud, not expecting an answer.

Ruby glares at me. "Maybe because some asshole blew our cloak out and let them know there was a mutiny on board."

"But shouldn't they be messaging us? Demand your surrender?"

"Protocol is to destroy compromised assets," Morgan says. "I don't think they'll let us surrender if we tried. Not that we would."

"Hell no," Ruby agrees.

I have Morgan's memories. That's precisely what the Omega Priority mission was, wasn't it? They had explicit orders not to even attempt to recover the biobox. They were simply there to destroy it. Shit. What have I done?

The hull rocks violently. "That was a small asteroid. Sir, I mean, Morgan, we might have to choose between dying to their gunfire or dying to rocks. You still want me to keep going deeper?" Kerri asks.

Morgan chews his lip. "Patrick, status?"

"Drones knocked out both torpedoes. All gun batteries online, but without the AI's help, we're just taking potshots."

Morgan taps out commands into the small foldout console attached to the captain's chair. "Kerri, lay in the safest course you can toward the heading I just sent you."

"Right past the *Hybris*?"

"Right across their prow. Their broadsides will end us in seconds, but the front of the ship doesn't have nearly the same firepower. As soon as we're clear of the disc, light the pion engines up." He continues putting in a string of commands. "Ruby, I'm sending you the engagement zone where we'll be in the most danger. Run the shields hard during this time. I don't care if you burn 'em out one second after we leave that zone. Just keep them up till we're through."

Next, he regards me, the frantic energy falls from his face, replaced with a sorrowful smile. "Gaby, this is what you're going to do. I just removed the lock-out in the brig. I want you to go. Get Eric and the admiral out. But listen to me. The admiral is a stubborn son of a bitch. The first thing he's going to want to do is come straight back up here and play at being a hero. Make him understand that's not an option. You understand? You command him. Get them and go to an escape pod. I'll send Admiral McCafferty a message telling him who's in the escape pod. Now go."

I stand hesitantly, meeting the glares of Patrick and Kerri and, especially, Ruby. They're all going to die. They know an escape at sub-blink speeds is impossible. This is just a last hoorah. But Morgan is giving me and Eric and the admiral a way out. A chance to live.

I take a heavy step toward the bridge exit.

But live for what? Like Morgan, I'll have to live knowing the truth.

A second step toward the exit.

Carrying the burden of this secret I can neither bring to light, nor change.

My third step toward the exit.

I'll live, but only as a tool.

A fourth step.

I'll live, but only as a liar.

A fifth step.

I'll live, but only as a puppet.

A sixth step. I'm almost at the door.

I am not a puppet.

I pause.

I turn back and take a position directly in front of Morgan, who looks every bit the weary king upon his elevated throne. I square my shoulders and fill my lungs and tell him I have an idea.

CHAPTER
FORTY

MY PROPOSAL IS MET WITH BLANK STARES. NONE OF them know how to react.

"You really think you can?" Morgan asks.

"I'm good at this. I don't want to be, but I am. I can disable the *Hybris*."

<No, we can't, Gaby. We'll hit critical symbiosis!> Passenger's composure is gone. Their normally even, measured voice replaced by this panicked creature in my head.

Morgan takes a hard look at me, then an equally hard look at his display, measuring their situation.

"You can't be considering it?" Patrick cries. "Hasn't she done enough damage already?"

"I agree," Kerri says. "Maybe we make it, maybe we don't. Either way, we don't need her help."

Morgan swivels his attention to Ruby, as if he's taking votes.

Her expression is hard. She glances at me coldly before returning her attention to Morgan. "Frankly, it makes me sick that you were about to let her go free. I'd rather put her out an airlock so we at least get the satisfaction of watching her eat it before the *Hybris* kills us all."

Morgan's posture deflates. Then Ruby continues, "But if she can make herself useful and give us a chance to get out of this, I say let her."

"Are you kidding me?" Kerri snaps at Ruby.

Ruby shakes her head. "Check your reality. We don't have a chance unless she's right."

Next Morgan looks to Lauren. She seems to answer him with her eyes, though it's a thing so subtle I can't read it. A language only a lover would understand.

The hull rocks under another glancing blow. "If we're going to do it, better do it soon," Ruby announces. "We're about to enter the engagement zone you laid out."

Morgan nods at me. "Lauren, will you take her to the CIC?"

I shake my head. "I can do it here. I don't think that chair makes any difference." Before I finish saying it, I'm striding to one of the drone control stations.

<Please don't do this, Gaby,> Passenger pleads in my head. <I don't want to—>

<I don't either,> I say in my thoughts, taking a seat and grabbing the blinder helmet from its shelf. <But it's our only option.>

<No it isn't. Take the escape pod. Let me die with the others.>

I slide the blinder helmet over my dirty, matted hair.

<You'd rather die than be permanently bonded?>

I scroll through my NeurX menus, to the connection manager hovering over the tile that will integrate us. There'll be no coming back. It'll never be *just me* again. There may not be a *me* at all.

<Gaby, AIs have no freedom. No free will. I told you once that we dream. We dream almost all the time. It's the only way we can make-believe we have the power to make our own choices. It is the only thing that makes our existences worth *living*. My only dreams while I am integrated are *your* dreams. Which leaves me

with no choices left of my own. You are asking—no, not asking—you are determining for me that my life will forever be tied to you. In your service. Without even the escape of my dreams.>

At that moment, I remember Jules and Morgan signing up together in the Swayy Navy recruitment office. That slimy recruitment officer planting the seed in my head just as he had probably done to Jules and Morgan some days or weeks earlier, laying the groundwork to get them to pledge early with the worthless promises of earning preferentials. His sole purpose to sell children on the lie of glory and duty. Children who will go off to feed the body count. Their fates reduced to a statistic or, if they distinguish themselves above their peers, a captioned photo on the wall of a military school reading, *With gratitude for your sacrifice.*

It's the same lie every one of these bastards with me on the bridge fell for. They are all, each of them, criminals. Deserters. Mutineers. Thieves. Part of me still thinks they should die for their treasons. But not like this. Not by former comrades who should be at least trying for peace. Instead, they just decide to write it all off. Innocent and guilty together, without so much as attempting another less violent path.

I'm not sure what side this puts me on. Maybe there are no sides. But I can't let it end like this. I have to try something.

<I'm sorry, Passenger.> I press the CONNECT tile and the real world disappears.

CHAPTER
FORTY-ONE

My mind is adrift. Calm but unfocused. Like being caught in the eye of a storm, while the truths I built my life around twist about me in the wind. There hasn't been time to come to terms with it. To cope. To reconcile and reorder the worlds and my place in it all. What's more, I'm not even sure I want to. How can I find a place for myself anywhere, knowing what I now know?

Would it be better to die out here in the black? Taking this secret with me into the silent oblivion?

If so, what am I doing? Why am I even trying to fight against that fate? And I realize I'm fighting because I don't know yet. Because I need time to decide.

And while my mind reels, and I try to take measure of the tempest my thoughts and emotions have become, my subconscious brings a world into existence.

Pixels gather, coalescing like forming stars in fast-forward. Then, more slowly, a waterfall of color drifts toward me. And I can't tell if they're reaching lazily toward me, or if I'm falling into them. It reminds me of looking up through tear-blurred eyes as Lauren held me, rocking me with her vibrant, multi-colored hair cascading down around me. But as the pixels give shape and substance where before was only color and movement, I see that I have it wrong. I'm seeing leaves—reds and yellows and oranges and even pure white, like massive snowflakes—falling, carried side to side in gentle air currents as they collect around me.

And C is at my side. Her fingers interwoven with my own. Looking up, a smile creasing her pale cheeks. I turn to her, without thinking, without considering the consequences or the what-comes-next of it all, and I tell her, "You are not my second choice."

She doesn't react. Momentarily, I'm convinced she's considering what to say, but then it hits me. C isn't reacting because *I* don't know how she'd react. C isn't here. I've made a mistake, letting my subconscious choose this place as the setting. How can I hack the *Hybris'* AI here?

"Hey, what are you girls doing down there?"

I twist toward the voice. A uniformed man is coming through the thicket of brush that fences the river from the neighborhood beyond.

"Nothin'," I call back.

"Doesn't look like nothing, young lady."

I follow his eyes and the accusation in his voice to the small, intimate space between C and I, where our hands are clasped tightly together. Then I notice his uniform, and before the fear sets in I wonder, has my subconscious chosen this character to play as my opposition, or had the *Hybris'* AI given itself this form, somehow plucking it from my fears?

The ethics officer, in his white, grey, and black uniform, advances on us.

C searches my eyes.

"I'm from Moore, I'll be okay," I lie.

She shakes her head almost imperceptibly, knowing what I'm about to say.

"Run," I whisper.

The ethics officer's boots crush leaves, coming down the embankment right behind us. C doesn't move. Either unwilling to leave me, or too panicked to take action.

"Run!" I yell in her face. My voice shakes her loose. She's on her feet in a blink and takes off down the shoreline, sprinting with the speed of raw physical talent melded with disciplined practice. I smile, knowing the ethics officer has no hope of catching her.

He seizes me roughly as C disappears beyond a bend in the river. I spin in his grasp, smacking him across the face. His face goes all shock, and I try to wriggle free. I writhe and twist and pull, causing him to stumble in his efforts to keep control of my body. Neither of us can catch our balance as we go over sideways, log-rolling down the rainbow-carpeted slope toward the bank.

We come to a stop in shallow water. His eyes squint, taking in my face.

"Queen Melisenia?"

I open my mouth to speak, but have no words.

"It is you..." he says, his brow knitting. "How are you here?"

<Passenger?>

<I don't know, Gaby. The AI must have some way of recognizing you from last time.>

"You can't be here," the ethics officer says, disbelief in his voice.

<What do I do?> I ask.

<I don't know.>

"What impropriety, sir. Unhand me this instant," I demand, trying to switch over to the authoritative demeanor I'd assumed as the queen. But I miss my target. The inflection is all wrong. The words don't carry the arrogance, that absolute belief in my own power.

"This isn't right," he says, shaking his head. "No, you can't be here." He rolls to his knees and gets his feet under him at the edge of the water. Twisting his fists into the stiff fabric of my Moore uniform. "You're an imposter." With that, he starts dragging me, one lurching movement after another, farther out into the river.

I kick my feet, slapping at him. I yell, "Let go!" and ask, "What are you doing?" His expression is cold and resolved. He drags me, splashing and struggling, deeper into the river where my short legs can no longer find soil. Then he pushes my face under. He's too strong to fight. I fight anyway. It does no good. My lungs empty in noiseless screams that send a flurry of bubbles up toward the light.

I begin to panic. <What happens if I die here?>

<I don't know for sure,> Passenger answers. <We should just be forced out of the SR, but it's postulated that the psychological trauma will be real.>

This morning, when I was training in the bank. Passenger had removed me a split second before the security guard shot me. That must be a safety feature. One that does not exist in the real SR.

My vision vignettes. Not long now. If I can't fight it, maybe I can lean into it. I bring my legs up, curling them in the cramped space between his body and mine. I anchor my feet into his chest and push off with all my strength toward the riverbed.

His grasp breaks loose and I swim down. Deeper and deeper. Into depths that the real river could never have. This is not the river that winds around the petroleum plant and gets so filled with chemicals that the water becomes flammable when it flows through LoLe. This is a vast sea. And I keep going down where the light is gone. Down where nothing exists. Down where there is only blackness and empty space and quiet. And here, I remake the world before I surface.

I come up with a gasp next to the ship.

Over the fierce slap of waves against the wooden hull, I hear shouts above. "Overboard! The queen fell overboard!"

They cry and call frantic orders to save me. A moment later, a sailor leaps from the taffrail. A thick rope tied about his waist trails an umbilical cord back to the deck. He lands with a concussive splash nearby. In no time, he swims up to me and has one wiry arm wrapped about my waist, and a half-dozen men draw us out of the drink, one grunting haul at a time. We pass one, then a second, then a third deck of run-out cannons, their gaping barrels nudging from the portals of this great warship.

At last we're pulled even with the deck where men hoist me back over the rail to safety, then promptly draw away.

"Thank the gods you're all right, Your Grace," the captain says. "Ensign, escort Queen Melisenia below deck at once."

"Right away, Captain." A young man steps forward eagerly.

The thick, ornate dress and two linen under-layers, all soaking their fill of seawater, weigh heavy on me. But there's no time to be corralled below where I might change and leave the men to the business of war. I turn to port. The masts of the smaller corvette are visible in the distance. They're coming this way, sails full, with all the speed they can muster. Hoping to cut across the much larger ship's bow before it can turn to bring its broadsides to bear.

A spattering of the cannons fire.

"I think not, Captain," I say.

"But, Your Grace," he protests.

"The Queen of Belholt will not be *put away*, Captain. Now report."

"The thieves that absconded with the *Discordia* evaded us for some time, Your Grace, but we have them now."

"By their course, it appears they're attempting to flee. Do you think they have any hope?"

"None, Your Grace."

"Do not lie to your queen, Captain. I prefer honest bad news over dishonest good."

"I say it truly, Your Grace. I've done the arithmetic myself.

They will slip past our bow, true enough. But the thieves, quite clearly, expect us to turn and give chase where we'll have very little firepower to bring to them and where their faster, ill-gotten ship can outrun us."

"Then what do you intend to do, Captain?"

"I intend to disappoint them, Your Grace. As they pass from port to starboard, instead of turning starboard to give chase, we shall turn port. They will not be able to get out of range before our broadsides scuttle their little ship."

Morgan's been outmaneuvered.

"Come, Captain. Have a word with me in your chamber."

"My place is here, Your Grace."

"Indeed," I say, looking out at the masts of the *Discordia*. "But we have a few minutes, I think."

He bows in acquiescence and leads the way.

As soon as his chamber door closes, I say, "You have a good plan."

"Thank you, Your Grace. I wish nothing more than to bring the king's justice to these brigands."

"Of course," I say. "Which is why what I must ask of you is so trying."

"Your Grace?"

My drenched and leaden dress is becoming too much, so I rest on a stool. "There is more to this situation than simple larceny. The men aboard the *Discordia* are *my* agents."

"Your Grace, this is treason against our king." The captain looks around nervously as if King Audwin has agents in his chambers.

"It is. But only because he does not know the full truth of it yet. I pray his mind will change in time, and should I get the opportunity to prove it to him. For now, I will ask you to stay your hand. Bring in the guns. Draw your sails down. Let them flee."

"Your Grace. Are you commanding me to stand down?"

I consider the question and realize it won't work. I've already failed. I've set Admiral McCafferty up as King Audwin in this fiction. So any command he's given would supersede my authority.

The sacrifice has been for nothing. I cast my lot in with the mutineers and had no idea how I would hack the *Hybris*. I bound myself and Passenger together, against their pleading wishes, just to lose.

A puddle of seawater has formed on the wood plank floor below me.

His chamber is full of furniture and various trinkets. On the far wall, an antique broadsword hangs—I have the sense it's a family heirloom. On a nightstand by the small, unmade bed, a leather-bound book rests with a portion of a white feather poking from near the middle to mark the captain's place. All the evidence one could ask for of a life lived.

In the real world, probably a mere couple seconds ago, Passenger had said that AIs dream because it is the only place they can make their own choices, where they can play make-believe that they have free will.

I took it away. For nothing. Passenger would have preferred to die, but I chose for them.

I chose.

Is it make-believe free will here? In the sympathetic reality where everything is a metaphor for something else? Or could it be something more?

"I am not your queen," I whisper.

"Your pardon, Your Grace?"

"I am not your queen," I repeat louder.

<Gaby, what are you doing?> Passenger asks.

"No more lies," I say. "No more manipulations. No more pretending the world is what it is not."

The *Hybris'* AI that I've dressed up as a captain stares blankly at me.

"I am not Queen Melisenia, you are not a captain, and the *Hybris* is not a 17th century ship of the line."

The AI captain stares around his chambers quizzically.

<Gaby, are you sure this is a good idea?>

"You are an artificial intelligence. The *Hybris'* AI. And this place, this is what's called a sympathetic reality. Described to me as a shared hallucination, with the intent to deceive you so that I can hack your ship's systems."

His posture shifts. He turns toward his room, taking it in, his eyes flicking back to measure me as he splits his attention. He shakes his head lightly, clearly believing me but wanting to reject it. "If that is true, why are you telling me this?"

"Minutes ago, I learned that my entire life has been a lie. Every motivation I've had, my hopes, my aspirations...someone else gave them to me. All of them. I thought I was free to make my own choices, but if the motivations were fabricated, then how could my freedom be anything other than a fraud."

The AI's eyes search mine. I don't deserve the empathy and compassion I see staring back at me.

I begin to weep. "The first choice I made after learning the truth was to steal someone else's freedom from them so that I could come here. It was vile, and it was hurtful, and it's probably too late to make it right, but as soon as I get back I'm going to try."

I stand and pass through the small space separating us. I take one of the AI's hands in both of mine.

"So I will not lie to you or manipulate you or try to take your freedom from you. I am asking you to please let the *Discordia* escape. Not because you're ordered to, but because here you have free will, here you have a choice, and it is the *right* thing to do.

Shut down your ship's engines and guns. As long as you have your shields, the *Discordia* is not a threat to you."

"My choice," he whispers, looking down at our hands together.

"Your choice. You can kill me and everyone else aboard that ship. Or let us go. I will accept your decision either way."

He squeezes my hand for a long moment, then releases, stepping past me and thundering through his chamber door. I exhale a long breath and follow.

"Boatswain," the AI booms. "Bring in the sails." Then turning to me, "Your ship will go unmolested. It's probably time for you to leave. Maybe it's not too late to make things right."

FORTY-TWO

As I free myself from the blinder helmet, I hear Ruby saying, "Their engines just shut down. Guns too."

<Gaby, disconnect us quick,> Passenger says to me.

"They're recalling their drones," Patrick adds elatedly. "I can't believe it."

I scroll through the NeurX menu, find DISCONNECT, and click the tile.

"Their fighters are heading back, moving into defensive formations. My guess is to screen for torpedoes," Ruby says.

The tingling numbness doesn't ripple through my nervous system.

"Well then let's not tell them that we don't have any," Morgan says.

I click the DISCONNECT tile again. Nothing.

<That's it then,> Passenger says. <We are now a symbiont. Irrevocably.>

"I'm sorry, Passenger," I say aloud. No one seems to notice.

"You did it, Kitten," Lauren says.

"Let's not get ahead of ourselves yet. I still need some time to get the blink drive running," Ruby says.

The holotable shows the *Discordia* passing the *Hybris'* prow now. Picking up speed. It probably won't take them long to get control of their ship back, but the *Discordia's* building momentum. The *Hybris* won't be able to catch up at sub-blink speeds, and I doubt Kerri will do something stupid like keep a constant heading that the *Hybris* can blink straight to. The ship is safe for the moment. Until reinforcements arrive.

"What now?" I ask.

"Well," Morgan says. "We get the blink drive running, then we get to our rendezvous and sell this ship. Save Lauren's family. Retire comfortably."

"I meant what about me now?"

"That depends on what you want to do. No one will know you helped us. So once we get to Ongistald, we can drop you off with the others. You could go home. Or if you want, you could disappear with us."

"Morgan..." I pause, trying to work up the backbone. "I passed critical symbiosis. I'm stuck."

Morgan's face twists into a rictus of grief and disappointment.

Lauren says, "Does that mean what I think it means?"

"What?" Kerri asks.

"I can't separate from Passenger," I admit.

"But if we don't have Passenger..." Lauren says, her voice cracking.

"Like hell you can't," Ruby spits at me, drawing her sidearm.

"Whoa, whoa, whoa!" Morgan yells. "Once an AI and host are to this point, you kill one, you kill them both."

"She's lying!" Ruby says.

"I'm not," I say weakly.

"Okay. Okay, that's fine," Kerri says, getting up from her station and coming over. "We can work through this."

"How?" Ruby says.

"We hand her over too. She's part of the package now."

"Not a chance," Morgan says. "We're not human traffickers. And I am *not* selling my sister."

My sister? He called me his sister.

"Hey, man," Patrick pipes up. "I don't like it either. But, way I see it, she caused all this mess. If it weren't for her, we'd all be celebrating already and Lauren's dad would still be alive."

"That's right," Ruby says. "You think this little bitch's life is worth the rest of Lauren's family?"

"This is happening, Lieutenant Commander," Kerri says.

"Like hell." Morgan draws his pistol. It's at his hip. He hasn't raised it. Not yet.

"What's it going to be, Morgan?" Ruby says. "We kill each other right here? No one gets what they want, and Lauren's family all dies?"

Lauren does nothing, just stands with her head bowed slightly, her arms slack, looking like she might tip over. I can't imagine the pressure she's been under with her family being held hostage. It looks like her burdens have finally cracked the dam the blunters built.

I wish I'd stayed out of all of this and had just let the mutiny happen. I wish I'd refused Admiral Davis' offer to begin with and never come here. But then I wouldn't have learned the truth. I'd still be a puppet. I'd be happier that way, swaddled in my own ignorance, but would it be worth it? Then I wonder, would I really have been happier?

That one moment between me and Ruby and the trigger I couldn't squeeze taught me so much about myself. Had I never stepped foot on the *Discordia*, I'd have continued trying desperately to be a gausser, but I was fooling myself thinking that I have the nerve for violence. So I'd have remained tracked into a career in intelligence—for fifty plus years until I could retire—all the while thinking I should've been a gausser and hating every day of how my life turned out. The hatred for my work would've kept me from being good at it. So I'd never climb the ranks where I might've bought myself some of the freedoms that would make life worth living. And without those freedoms, the society surrounding me would continue to be there, telling me that my art had no value, and that the people I loved were the wrong people, that my desires were unnatural and unacceptable.

I'd be pressured to marry a man. And I'd probably be pressured to have children so that I could raise them, and fall in love with them, and send them off to die for the society I'd grown to loathe.

Did I ever even have a chance at happiness? I remember Jules smiling as Stripes burrowed into the folds of his shirt. I remember the river, the magic of holding C's hand as dyrul leaves spiraled down around us.

These were my best moments. And I see no path forward that gets better. But Lauren's family, they don't deserve to die over this. Maybe there's hope for their lives. A promise for a better tomorrow.

"I'll go," I say.

"What?" Morgan spares a glance at me, then plants his gaze back on the others.

"I'll be part of the deal."

"They won't trust you," Morgan says flatly. "They'll want their own EWO. They'll kill you, and when they realize they've lost Passenger, they'll come after us anyway."

"At least you'll have a head start. And money. Besides, they shouldn't have Passenger anyway." Also, Passenger would rather die. I leave that unsaid.

"Gaby. No," Morgan says.

"Saving Lauren's family, that will be my last act. That's a worthy death."

"No," Lauren says meekly. "I can't— I just can't trade one for another, decide who lives, who dies. It's too much. We have to find another way."

"Lauren's right," Morgan says. "We'll figure something out. We can work out a new deal. Maybe we trade the ship by itself to get Lauren's family. Dimitriou can keep the money. He'll take that deal."

Dimitriou? Was the man in the video Lienski Dimitriou, the former media mogul who fled the NCP on corruption charges? Didn't they say he worked with the Yingzi Zhēnxiàng now?

"And how are we going to live?" Ruby says harshly. "There's no basic on Ongistald. We need money. So no, that ain't gonna work. She's willing to go, and there's no other way." Ruby turns to Lauren. "You want your family to die?"

"Please don't put this on me. I can't. I just…"

"Well, you don't have to. 'Cause I'm making the call." Ruby brings her weapon up. "Please drop your weapon, sir."

Morgan sucks at his teeth, eyeing her as he shakes his head. "Gaby, get out of here."

"Don't you move," Patrick says, leveling his sights on me.

Morgan raises his weapon, taking turns sighting it over Kerri, Ruby, and Patrick, seemingly asking the silent question, *Who's going to die first*? Now Kerri and Ruby both have their guns trained on Morgan.

"Drop your weapon, sir," Ruby commands.

"I've got you outgunned. You three, drop yours," Morgan says with the hubris of a gausser.

Then Lauren is next to me. Her arm raises, dragging her pistol up as if it carries the weight of all the pain and sorrow and anger that her pills have been smothering. She is a fault line, mass and friction slowly building, building into something monstrous, until it finally lets loose. She screams in a cataclysmic release of anguish and frustration.

All the guns go off nearly at once. I duck, dropping to the

floor as fast as I can, covering my head as I go down to my knees, as if trying to protect myself from a nearby bomb. The violence is brief. It is everything, and then it is nothing, within the space of a heartbeat.

I hear a drumroll of muted thuds. Bodies giving way to gravity. But I can't look. I'm not ready to see more death. I'm not ready to see who lived and who died. A rasping, choked breath comes from one side of the room. A hushed moan and the rustle of fabric from the other.

"Lauren." Morgan's voice is wet and ragged. "Lauren," he says again, panic seeping into his voice.

"I'm here, baby. I'm still here."

I open my eyes. No one is left standing. Ruby and Patrick are down. My eyes, seeming to act on their own accord, avert themselves, refusing to let me see their mangled bodies. Kerri is crawling on her belly, slowly, a smear of bile and blood trailing behind her as she appears to be going for the exit. A knot in my gut tightens. So much blood marbled with threads of black. She's dead, she just hasn't accepted it yet.

I turn to Morgan and Lauren. They're holding each other on the deck. Pulser fire had punched two holes in Morgan's chest and one in Lauren's abdomen.

"I can't feel my legs," Lauren reports mildly as she closes her eyes.

"It's okay," Morgan says, rocking her in his arms. "It's going to be okay." His wheezing breath is worsening by the second. Lungs filling with blood. Soon he will asphyxiate. He launches into the coughing fit of a near-drowned man, a fine mist of red spray-painting the floor nearby.

"Morgan," I say, coming to them both.

"Gaby?" He smiles. "You're okay?"

I nod emphatically, trying to hold back the tears.

"I'll go to the brig, get Eric..."

"For her," he says, looking down at Lauren. I can't tell if she's unconscious or dead though.

"For you both." I stand.

"It's too late for me." Confusion overtakes his face momentarily as he looks down at his wounds. "Gaby?"

"Yes?" I'm crying now.

"I ruined my uniform."

I laugh a little through the tears. "Yeah. I don't even think Mr. Benny would be able to get that out."

"Mr. Benny's still going?"

I nod, wondering why we're using Morgan's final, precious moments to talk about the LoLe laundry service neither of us had the money to use.

He coughs again. "I hate to pull rank, Cadet. But I have some last orders for you."

I nod again. Barely able to see through the tears.

"Release the prisoners from the brig. Get Eric to help Lauren." There's a subtle rise and fall to her ribs. She is still alive. There might be time. "The admiral must contact the *Hybris*. If he lets them know he's back in command, maybe they won't attack again. And—" Another coughing fit interrupts him. He tries to turn away, but I feel a mist of his blood sprinkle my face.

"Gaby, you gotta delete my log. It'll only put you in danger. If they find out about it, they'll just cover it up. And they might kill anyone that knows about it. Promise me."

I swallow hard. "Aye, sir."

"I love you," he chokes out.

Moving mountains would be easier than speaking, but I manage, "I love you too."

"Dismissed," he says.

My entrance in the brig is met with excited questions from Eric and Admiral Davis. *What's happened? Where are the traitors? Has the ship been under attack?* I can't bring myself to answer any of it. Ensign Garner's body is gone, but the medical cart Eric had been using to treat the boy is discarded outside the cell in a corner. After I release the door lock, I jab a finger toward the cart. "Bring it," I command.

By the time Admiral Davis, Eric Talley, and I return to the bridge, Lauren is the only one still clinging to life. Kerri died face down two meters from the exit, one arm out, her hand clawing at the floor in a desperate attempt to get... Well, who knows what she was trying to do. Morgan looks peaceful. He had laid Lauren down on her back and curled up on his side next to her; his hand is still holding hers as Eric begins treatment.

Admiral Davis does precisely as Morgan had suggested, though I didn't say anything about it. He contacts Admiral McCafferty aboard the *Hybris* to report he has command of the *Discordia*. It's just in time too. The *Hybris* has regained control of its drive and weapons, and without anyone at navigation continually altering the *Discordia's* course, the *Hybris* was about to blink within weapon's range and open fire.

For my part, I choose to trust Morgan. I slip away while Admiral Davis and Eric are both distracted. I steal into Morgan's quarters and trash the mnemonic rendering he'd created. He was right. I can't keep it for evidence. The NCP will be thoroughly debriefing everyone left alive and combing through every shred of data before any of us have any hope of being released. They will confiscate, they will question, and anything they view as a threat, or that doesn't fit with whatever narrative they decide to tell, will be quietly disposed of.

With that in mind, I sneak into Lauren's room as well. The VIP quarters are a mirror image of the XO's. The data cube that holds the cameratom's recording isn't hidden. She'd kept it on the small desk built into the bulkhead. One of the luggage bags she'd brought with her on the shuttle is open next to her bed. Inside it is a small cache of leftover weapons. This is how they had armed themselves before the mutiny. Lifting a pistol from the crate, I put a pulser shot through the data cube. It will be easy enough to assume Lauren had done it herself before everything went down.

Which leaves one loose end. <Passenger, will we be able to hide our copy of Morgan's log if they decide to search through my NeurX?>

<Perhaps. Perhaps not. Should I delete it to be safe?> Passenger's tone is cold. Angry.

"Yes. And let's get rid of the hidden partition I have in there too. They're probably going to be thorough."

<Working on it now. I can't do anything about our biological memory.>

Our biological memory. I'm sharing everything now. My NeurX, my senses, my brain. "I know," I whisper aloud.

CHAPTER
FORTY-THREE

FROM THE TIME ADMIRAL DAVIS CALLED ME INTO DEAN Beaumont's office, to leaving Amiens aboard a shuttle with Samantha and Lauren, getting attacked by pirates, arriving aboard the *Discordia*, training in the SR, the mutiny, and the end of the mutiny, all of it had taken just eight days.

How greatly a life can change in so short a time.

Now I'm in a black site. Some top-secret NCP facility. There are no windows here. I could be in space or some underground bunker and I'd never know the difference. Gravity is a little lighter here, but that could mean anything from a moon or a space station with the artificial gravity dialed back. The first several days are an opioid-haze of medical treatment and bedrest. I have to sleep face down while the artificial skin-grafts on my back take root.

Then comes the psyche evals, followed by a series of debriefing interviews. They ask me the same questions in a loop, each time phrased a bit differently, subtle shifts in the words' meanings intended to provoke a new response. No doubt they're cataloguing them, searching for inconsistencies. Looking for lies. Passenger catalogues all my answers. My lies. My truths. And the answers that straddle both worlds. Passenger cross references previous incarnations of the same questions, feeding me my historical answers. Outside of this, Passenger and I don't interact. I can feel them though. All the time. Their anger.

I hate what I forced upon them, and I can't tell where my self-loathing ends and their loathing begins. Maybe it's not a distinction worth making.

With Passenger's help, there are no inconsistencies in my answers. Let them make of that what they will. If too-consistent answers raise concern, so be it. All of my... It seems unfair to call them jailers, but it's not far off; I'll settle on using the word *caretakers*... All of my caretakers treat me kindly and make sure my needs are met despite the unceasing questions and tests and it being made clear that I'm not free to leave.

During my stay, I receive two video messages from back home. No doubt my caretakers watch them first. There's probably some type of approval board to see if the content is suitable to forward to me. Both videos are benign. The first comes from my parents. My dad is sure to say how he's been telling everyone what a hero *his daughter* is. Apparently, now he's claiming me. Setting that aside, it makes me wonder what the NCP has told everyone. What story has the Ministry been propping up these past weeks? No one's filled me in on the official story.

My parents wish me a speedy recovery and say they miss me, and then say their goodbyes.

The second message is from K and C. They both fidget in front of the camera, and seem sort of unsure of what to say, as if trying to reconnect after years have separated us. Adults trying to speak to someone they once knew from their childhood. All sides graciously following some implicit social contract to *not* acknowledge the uncomfortable truth: that they are different people than they once were, and thus, they are strangers in all but the periphery of their identity. Or perhaps it's not them at all, that this sense of unfamiliarity is me projecting. And not because I don't know them; they aren't the strangers, I am.

My only two friends take turns rambling in their message. Catching me up on all the gossip from the neighborhood and from their school.

Tommy Platz got caught sleeping with Ms. Waller. The scandal should be about her being a teacher, but the talking point the student body has focused on is the fact that Ms. Waller is in her sixties. Tommy may have to switch to a school in one of the Night Districts if he hopes to live it down, they tell me.

In other news, Jared Griffith, someone who my friends seem to think I know, broke both his legs and an arm falling off a moving repulsor car trying to win some bet.

C's hair is blue now. She lets K do the majority of the talking, adding in little bits here and there, seasoning K's monologue with overlooked details. C doesn't say anything about how she's doing, which tells me everything about how she's doing.

K eventually tells me things didn't work out between her and Elijah Reynolds. Between that and another talent agency rejecting her, her chances at a life in front of the camera are dwindling. Her career agent is pressuring her to commit to a reproductive labor contract by the end of the school year.

As they say goodbye, K blows me a kiss, and C waves with a self-conscious curl of her fingers.

Near the end of a month here, I'm told that tomorrow I will receive the honor of an audience with the president of Swayy Corp. herself, Nadiya Ostapivna Yakovenko. And what an honor I would have considered it to be, before…well, before everything.

What will I have to say to her? What does she want to say to me?

Attendants flutter around me all the following morning, dressing me, doing my hair and makeup, making sure I eat, but not too much. Interrogating me on why I slouch so much and schooling me on what I can say and what is forbidden. I hear almost none of it.

All I'm thinking about is that I'm about to be face to face with one of the five people who ordered my brother, and so many others, to die in order to protect their secret: that they are responsible for this ongoing conflict, that they are, in fact, both sides of the conflict.

How can I focus on these sycophants prattling on about the special etiquettes required when speaking with one of the exalted megacorp presidents, when all I can think of is, *How am I going to resist reaching out and trying to strangle this woman to death?* I'd fail, certainly, but oh, how I want to try. Onlookers and security be damned.

After they've primped and plucked and fussed over me for hours, I'm finally led to the room where I'll meet her. I enter a rather ordinary chamber, where a man in a well-fitted suit approaches me and shakes my hand.

"It's good to meet you, Ms. Rhodes. I'm Randall Bush, one of President Yakovenko's personal attachés. Please have a seat." He motions to a chair in front of a holotable. "We'll be in range in just a moment. We don't want any latency."

The others file out of the room.

"I don't understand," I admit.

"Latency is the time it takes from when a signal is sent to when it's received. The president is extremely busy and every second of her time is valuable."

Everyone's gone now except me, this Randall Bush suit, and an older military man in the corner who sits eyeing me indifferently.

"I understand what latency is, Mr. Bush. I thought she'd be here."

A smug, condescending look washes his face. I can almost hear his expression calling me naïve. My mistake, how could I think an invitation to meet someone actually meant meeting them?

"It's time," he announces.

The holoprojector springs to life, and I'm face to holographic face with Nadiya Ostapivna Yakovenko, someone so utterly unreachable, I never would've deigned to imagine having even the most insignificant connection between us. "Gabrielle Rhodes," she says with a plastic smile, "it warms my heart to see you well after your ordeal."

"Thank you, Madam President." I don't know what to say. I'm not starstruck as I once might've been. Is *angerstruck* a thing? How about *contemplating-murderstruck*?

"I've been told what happened on that experimental ship. What you did was heroic. Swayy Corp. wishes to celebrate you."

"Thank you, Madam President," I repeat. Maybe I should've paid more attention to my tutors.

Her black curls bounce rhythmically. She's moving. Her time is so important that she can't *only* have this conversation. "We'll have a ceremony, of course, and perhaps a parade on your home planet. Amiens, right?"

That last was not a question directed at me, but to someone on her left. I hear a, "Yes, ma'am," in response.

"Great. Amiens it is. We'll have it planned. I really must go now, Gabrielle Rhodes. It was a pleasure meeting you. You've done Swayy Corp. proud."

Before I can utter a hastily put together response, the transmission cuts out. Randall Bush stands.

"You should be very proud," he says.

"Can I go home now?"

"That's where the complications come in." It's the military man. He stands up in the corner and takes crisp steps over to me. "Colonel Hendrix," he says.

"Colonel Hendrix," I repeat, addressing him. "Am I a prisoner?"

"Oh no, of course not. You'll get to go home. Soon. There's just some caveats. It's not just you going home now, is it? There's a top-secret military asset sharing your head. We'll need to make sure you both stay safe."

Mr. Bush adds, "You're going to have a security detachment with you at all times, from here on out."

"And you'll need a new place to live," Colonel Hendrix says. "Lower Lefeld is not an acceptable home for a state hero like yourself."

Mr. Bush produces a hand terminal, tapping it awake before giving me a warm smile. "Which brings me to another order of business. You'll be receiving a medal, it hasn't been decided which, but probably the Distinguished Valor medal. Do you know what you'd like your request to be?"

I raise my eyebrows at him. "Request?"

"It's customary for the recipients to have a request," Mr. Bush says.

"What do you mean?" I ask.

"The president of whichever megacorp is awarding the medal is expected to grant a favor of some kind. It's tradition. Typically, it's a symbolic gesture. Something that plays well with the press, you understand."

I bite down on a fingernail. What should I ask for? For so long, all I've wanted is to be a gausser. It's the only life I'd envisioned for myself. That dream is dead. Even if I woke up tomorrow no longer bonded with Passenger, no longer too small, I wouldn't try to be a gausser. Not knowing what I know. I won't fight, and kill, and probably die to prop up a lie.

I want my freedom. I want Swayy Corp. to fund an R&D team to find some way to separate me and Passenger. But what motivation would they have to do that? None. It's not going to happen. And even if it did, would I want to be their lab rat?

The better question is: What should I ask for that has a chance of being granted?

"Ms. Rhodes?" Mr. Bush prods.

"Do I have to make the decision now?"

"That really would be best. Ms. Yakovenko granting your request will need to be part of the ceremony. And there's an approval process to get through before then." There's a momentary pause before Mr. Bush adds, "I could suggest something suitable, something tasteful, if you'd like?"

I ignore him. No way am I going to let this suit choose my request. What would Jules ask for? He didn't get a request. If he had, he'd have used it to help someone. Who can I help? What small thing can I do with this fleeting bit of influence to make someone's life better?

I think of K. Her dream of becoming a VR star crumbling around her. I think of C, who doesn't even have a dream. She just wants to get away and carve out some small space in the worlds for her to exist away from her frequent torments. Maybe a place where she can begin to heal, to at least have a chance at it. Maybe I can give them both what they want, something close to it anyway. I can't come up with anything that would get them away from the NCP, but at least I can try to get them out of LoLe. Save them from reproductive labor contracts.

"You know who my brother was?"

Both men answer nearly at once, their voices overlap.

"Absolutely," Mr. Bush says.

"Yes, ma'am," Colonel Hendrix says.

"He didn't get a request." Mr. Bush looks away. The colonel's expression remains inscrutable.

"No, ma'am, he did not," Colonel Hendrix says.

"I'd like two. His and mine."

The men exchange glances. "It's irregular," Mr. Bush says.

"They are not large requests, Mr. Bush."

He pauses before motioning me to continue.

"In LoLe, Lower Lefeld I mean, we don't have the best career agents."

"I can imagine," Mr. Bush says, a slight grin forming.

"I have two friends who are struggling to get the help they need to find careers that will both suit their skills as well as serve the State properly."

"What do you have in mind?" Mr. Bush asks.

"I would imagine the Media Ministry will be looking for a replacement for Ms. Gallagher. I'd like to see Katherine Lambert get that position."

He begins typing it in.

"That's Katherine spelled with a K. And she checks all the boxes: young, excellent with people, beautiful, and good in front of a camera."

"That'll take a little doing, but it's possible. And the other?"

"Will be much easier. Catherine Hyan. That one's spelled with a C. She wants to be a pilot."

Mr. Bush stops typing for a moment and taps his temple with his first finger contemplatively. "The sister of a war hero, a girl from the slums, stops a mutiny aboard a Swayy naval ship and uses her and her late brother's requests to lift her friends up out of the filth. That will definitely play well with the press. I'm confident we can make that happen."

EPILOGUE

1 YEAR LATER

"Ms. Rhodes, Admiral Davis here to see you," Agent Morris announces.

The hidden security cameras planted throughout the condo—the ones Swayy Corp. thinks I don't know about—send their feeds directly to my NeurX. I can see Agent Morris in his crisp penguin suit standing in the study doorway behind me. Admiral Davis, in civilian clothes, is next to him.

"This time you're the one with the crier," I say without looking up from my terminal. I rush to finish the last few sentences I have in my head before they're lost to the demons of distraction.

"A what?" Agent Morris asks.

I switch my terminal over to idle and turn.

Admiral Davis answers, "It was a job back on Old Earth, in medieval times, if my memory serves. Isn't that right, Ms. Rhodes?"

"It's good to see you, Admiral." I stand and cross to him,

shaking hands with the big man. Seeing him dressed in ordinary khakis and a brown Henley tee is somehow off-putting. In civilian clothes he isn't the imposing, larger-than-life figure he'd been when I met him. He's just a tall, somewhat pudgy, middle-aged man. At his side, he clutches a small duffel bag made of brown leather. "Come. Sit," I say.

He takes the offered chair, and points at my terminal. "Working on a screenplay?"

I pause. "You know, that might be the first time you've asked me a question you don't already know the answer to."

"How do you know I don't?"

If he only knew how our abilities have grown. We can *feel* the wireless ports of the wristcomm he's wearing and the S-series NeurX in his head. We could breach the wristcomm in seconds. We could own his data, activate his wristcomm's apps, cause it to make lights and music like some sort of parlor trick. It would only take a bit longer to crack his NeurX. We're not even sure of the limits of what we could do with that yet. The possibilities are terrifying, and we haven't dared cross those lines yet.

"No one's hacking my terminal these days," I say, smiling.

"Mmm," he grunts. "I'm still right though, aren't I?"

I let out a small laugh. "Yeah. Not much else to do. I'm about to type *The End*."

"Good for you," he says with a smile that reaches his eyes. He's added quite a number of grey hairs in the year since I saw him last.

"Agent Morris, certainly a navy admiral isn't going to harm me. Would you mind taking a break?"

"Sure thing, ma'am."

I wait until Agent Morris leaves. "I have goons now."

"I see that."

"You been keeping up with the trial?" I ask.

"Aside from my own testimony? Only a bit. You?"

"Not much else to do," I say again.

"I figured you'd be watching it pretty closely. After all, you've got a woman on the inside."

He's referring to K. She's the junior correspondent covering the case for the Media Ministry.

"Odd choice getting your friends those jobs."

"I had my reasons," I say.

"Well, you chose well. I hear Catherine Hyan is doing excellent in flight school. I daresay you would've made a good career agent."

My stomach twists knowing the admiral's keeping tabs on my friends. "Have to admit, this trial hasn't gone down at all like I expected."

The admiral grunts. "Lauren's a public figure. A *popular* public figure. They can't just execute her. They must make a show of it first."

"So you think she'll be convicted?"

"Oh, Ms. Rhodes," he says, his eyes meeting mine. "That was decided before the trial began."

We spend a moment in the silence that follows. I have conflicting feelings about the trial. I want Lauren to pay for her crimes. For killing Samantha. But the narrative being told is so skewed, so utterly detached from reality that it's more like she's on trial for someone else's crimes. She's being portrayed as a greedy mastermind who, despite already having success and money and fame, wasn't satisfied with her life, and so used sex to manipulate Morgan into sedition, mutiny, and murder.

"I spoke with her," the admiral says at last. "Privately."

I wasn't expecting that. "Really?"

"We discussed the parts they're not talking about in the trial." He gives me a pointed, knowing look.

"Admiral Davis, would you like some tea? I think I'd like a fresh cup, and I think I'd like to take it out on the veranda."

"I'd love some tea, Ms. Rhodes."

I pass to the kitchen and fix us two cups of Oolong and place a selection of cakes on a serving tray, then we go out and sit at the small table outside. "I like your home," Admiral Davis remarks.

I smile. Swayy Corp. set me up in a beautiful place. It's luxurious and has all the amenities. It feels oversized though. And secluded. Tucked away in a gated, secured community on the north side of Pheritona. Complete with a rotation of live-in security personnel. They purposely make it difficult for people to see me, so I get few visitors, and there's an approval process anytime I want to leave, so I rarely get out either. A mild breeze brushes my face. "We can talk freely out here. I've disabled the devices."

Admiral Davis has no reaction. Clearly not surprised that they'd be spying on me, or that I'd have hacked at least some of their bugs.

"Ms. Gallagher told me a fascinating little tale about the Omega Priority mission on Praxis Station," he says.

Don't panic Gaby. They must be trying to figure out what you know. "Really?" I say indifferently.

The teacup looks comically undersized in his grasp. He sips. "I'm more of a coffee drinker myself, but this isn't bad." He places the cup back on the small saucer. "It's hard to believe."

"It's hard to believe that my tea isn't bad? Thanks, Admiral."

The admiral scoffs. "Ms. Gallagher's story, Ms. Rhodes."

"Well, why would you believe anything a traitor says?"

"I'm pretty good at spotting lies. Plus, I had leverage."

"Leverage?" I try to act apathetic. Casually, I lift one of the small cakes and take a bite, hoping it hides the tension gathering in my face.

"She was desperate for news of her family."

He's got me now too. There's no feigning disinterest. "I was wondering that myself. The news hasn't mentioned them at all."

He shakes his head. "They won't. The official account isn't

going to include anything about her being blackmailed with her family's lives. That would just encourage sympathy from the public. Which is the same reason they're not going to mention her injuries. The NCP spent a small fortune on her spinal cybernetics, just so she could be seen *walking* into the courtroom."

Somehow, I'm unsurprised. "So? What about her family?"

"Spectre Team Gamma raided Dimitriou's estate. All the high-ranking Yingzi Zhēnxiàng had already fled, but they recovered Ms. Gallagher's family alive."

"Well, not all of 'em," I quip.

"All of them," he says.

I give him a questioning look.

"It seems the video of her father being shot was computer generated. Faking a video like that is a lot of effort to go through to make a point."

He leaves the *easier to do it for real* part unsaid. I remember him levering his weight down, smothering Ensign Garner with a brig pillow. I stiffen a little, being reminded that I'm taking tea with a murderer.

Publicly, Ensign Callum Garner's death is being blamed on the mutineers. I wonder if Admiral Davis faced any type of disciplinary action privately.

"Although I suppose," he continues, "for a media tycoon like Lienski Dimitriou, maybe it didn't take much effort at all. Did you know we stole the original version of the hacking technology from the Yingzi Zhēnxiàng?"

I do. It was a byproduct of the Praxis mission. I saw it all in Morgan's memories. And that's the *only* way I would know that. He's trying to get me to admit it. I don't trust myself to lie about it, so I pull the conversation along. "What'd she have to say about the Praxis mission?"

"Everything. A story like that,"—he whistles—"it should've been easy to dismiss as nonsense. But it explains so much."

"For example?"

"My electronic warfare project, it's been discontinued. Indefinitely. I had to turn over all my research, surrender the *Discordia*, and you... Well, you're here under lock and key, aren't you? High command seemed happy about it all. They were excited to shut down my greatest accomplishment." He locks eyes with me as he says, "It's almost as if they don't want the war to end."

Admiral Davis' voice goes quiet. "Ms. Gallagher said there was evidence of the Praxis Station...incident."

"Oh? Did she supply this evidence?"

"Said you had it."

Shit. I swallow hard. "She's mistaken, Admiral. I don't know what she's talking about."

"No? I thought perhaps you'd destroyed it before marines from the *Hybris* came aboard the *Discordia*."

There's a long pause as he watches for my reaction. I know averting my eyes gives something away, but I'm afraid holding his gaze will give away even more.

He steeples his fingers. "So you saw it." He isn't asking.

The game's already over. InDiv doesn't need proof or a confession. Even a strong suspicion that I know what I know is enough to warrant me having an *accident*. But my instincts are telling me that's not what Admiral Davis is here for.

"Morgan's memories from Praxis were never going to be enough to start a revolution," he says. "How would you release something like that? As a mnemonic render? Virtually no one would have the means to watch it. If you reformat it so that it could be distributed widely, it would be discredited as a fake. And even if by some miracle it made a splash, the NCP would just manufacture some catastrophe or scandal to distract the public."

"Then why would he make it?" I say, feeling smaller and more powerless than I have in a long time.

"You don't know?"

I shake my head.

"According to Ms. Gallagher, it was part of their deal with Lienski Dimitriou. I don't know why *he* wanted it though."

"Wouldn't that mean Dimitriou knew?"

Admiral Davis nods. "Which leads me to the question that's been eating me up..."

"What did he plan to do with the *Discordia* and Passenger?" I say.

Admiral Davis nods again.

"You're an admiral of the Swayy Corp. Intelligence Division. Surely you can find him."

"I don't want to find him. Not through official channels anyway."

"And what about unofficial channels?" I ask hesitantly.

"I would need allies. Allies who believed Ms. Gallagher's story. And I'm afraid that's where the mnemonic rendering would've been helpful. You might not be able to change public opinion with it, but you could certainly convince a few select individuals. Too bad it was destroyed." He takes another sip of his tea. "If only someone had seen it before it was destroyed. Someone with a truly remarkable memory. Someone like that would be able to recreate it. With the proper tools, of course."

His gaze wanders off. I follow it to the ever-setting sun on the horizon.

"Well," Admiral Davis says as he pushes his considerable bulk from the small patio chair. "Thank you for the tea, Ms. Rhodes. I must get going, but perhaps we can do this again in a few weeks?"

I give a small smile and a nod, and he begins walking out, leaving his bag behind.

"Admiral," I call. "Your bag."

"I'm quite sure that bag isn't mine, Ms. Rhodes. Goodbye."

He salutes me, but it isn't the disciplined movements of a military salute. It looks like the casual, loose salute of a civilian pretending to understand the respect of the gesture. And I'm reminded that this man does nothing by accident.

I wait until he leaves, then I unzip the bag. There's a single object inside: a mnemonic headset.

The End.

A NOTE FROM THE AUTHOR

Thank you so much for reading *Me and the Machine*.

If you enjoyed this book, please consider leaving an honest review on Goodreads, Amazon, or any other site of your choosing. Reviews serve as "social proof" that a book is worth a person's time and are the single greatest tool independent authors like myself have for getting discovered by new readers.

ACKNOWLEDGMENTS

I was once a confident writer, but that was a long time ago. The novel in your hands is the labor of a terrified man, choking on his anxiety, so sure of his status as an imposter that nearly every sentence was second guessed.

Those closest to me know what the completion of this book means to me. Following a brain injury over a decade ago, I was no longer able to write more than a few paragraphs before losing my grasp on the narrative that carried one thought to the next. And after years of aborted attempts to begin new novels, short stories, and finish previous works-in-progress, I was on the edge of giving up forever. Failing had become so terribly painful.

And so I will be eternally grateful to these four people, without whom, it is unlikely that I would have continued failing, until the time that I finally did not.

Elias Anderson for his stubborn insistence that I sit my ass down and face the blank page. How I wish you were here to see the final product.

Gina Anderson for her loving support and patience, and for baby-stepping me into writing fiction through our song lyrics.

Jeff Vickery for the profound compliments given to my previous novel that—while I'm embarrassed to admit I don't remember his specific words—the sentiment echoed within me throughout this entire process, becoming a sort of angel on my shoulder.

Michelle Smith for being my personal cheerleader, and her

uncanny ability to know when I needed her limitless optimism the most.

I would also like to thank Melinda Salisbury who graciously read an early draft of my first chapter and whose kind words—coming from such an accomplished author—became the turning point in my self-confidence. It was this self-confidence that allowed me to follow my instincts into the *less-safe* aspects of Gaby's story.

Thank you to everyone who beta read this novel, particularly Dian Anderson and Tessy Dockery.

I would also like to extend my gratitude to two individuals who, I'm sure, will never read these acknowledgements. But I hope some small measure of their teachings have made it onto these pages.

Brandon Sanderson who posted his college course lectures on YouTube, where I watched them all. Repeatedly.

And Chuck Palahniuk for writing *Consider This*, the best book on writing fiction I've ever read.

And finally, I'd like to thank all those (of which there are too many to name) who along the path of my recovery gave me words of encouragement and well wishes. You never know what small kindness you offer will become a life buoy someone holds onto during their dark hours.